NADINE
DORRIES

The Ballymara Road

HEAD
of ZEUS

Head of Zeus Ltd
Clerkenwell House
45–47 Clerkenwell Green
London EC1R 0HT

WWW.HEADOFZEUS.COM

For Clifford

1959–1991

It's a long way to Tipperary...

Chapter One

IT WAS EARLY on Christmas morning at St Vincent's convent in Galway.

'Frank, wake up, did ye hear that?' Maggie O'Brien prodded her sleeping husband in the back, in an attempt to wake him. 'Frank, 'tis someone knocking on the lodge gate. Wake up now.'

Frank O'Brien was not in bed with his wife. Deep in the heart of a dream, he had just won first prize for his best onions at the Castlefeale show. All around him, people clapped and cheered as he stood at the front of the produce tent, holding high a bunch of onions so big, brown and sweetly perfect that it aroused naked envy in the eyes of the assembled gardeners and farmers.

'Frank, will ye fecking wake up, 'tis the gate. Who can it be, knocking at this ungodly hour? 'Tis the middle of the night.'

Frank woke with a start, as his ethereal body entered its earthly form with an unpleasant jolt. Startled, he begrudgingly opened one eye and viewed the world of the living. His first-prize elation faded within seconds. Blinking in the darkness, he rolled over to face his wife, but she had already leapt out of bed and nimbly hopped onto the wooden bench under the high, arched, mullioned window that looked down onto the main gate.

As the bench rocked back and forth, precariously and noisily, on the uneven stone floor, Maggie reached up to draw the heavy curtains and, in doing so, exposed her plump and naked backside beneath her old and tattered nightdress.

This is no ordinary morning, thought Frank. It feels special.

'Ah, 'tis Christmas,' he said, smiling as he focused his gaze on his wife's round buttocks.

Maggie was blissfully unaware of her husband's burgeoning arousal as she attempted to peer out, carefully peeling the curtains back from the thick layer of ice that coated the inside of the window.

'Merciful God, it has snowed heavily overnight. I don't know how that car has made it here. Maybe it has trouble, that's why they is knocking,' Maggie hissed as she rubbed her eyes, blinded by the car's headlights reflected in the window.

''Tis odd, indeed, to be knocking on a convent gate at this time,' said Frank, swinging his legs out of bed to place his feet on the cold stone floor.

All thoughts of an early romp between the sheets with his Maggie disappeared as she finally managed to draw the curtains, leaving behind thin threads of fabric stuck fast to the ice.

Frank squinted as the car headlights flooded the small lodge with their brilliance. 'Fecking hell, I can't see a thing, 'tis so bright,' he said furiously.

Frank and Maggie worked as the gardener and cook at St

Vincent's convent, on the outskirts of Galway. It had been in existence for just a few years, having been hurriedly established by local Catholic dignitaries and busybodies to meet what they believed were declining moral standards amongst the local female population. It was five miles away from the more established Abbey, which was run by the same order of nuns and so full to the rafters with sin that it couldn't possibly take any more.

The convent chiefly comprised the large main house and an adjoining chapel, connected by a long passageway. A mother and baby home occupied the top floor and the girls – mothers and penitents alike – slept in the attics. Closest to the elements, they froze in winter and boiled in summer. A chapel house in the grounds was home to a retreat, used mainly by visitors from Dublin. An orphanage lay on the outskirts of the convent, almost entirely concealed from sight by an overgrown hedge of juniper trees.

Maggie and Frank, who also doubled up as gatekeepers, lived in the tiny lodge at the entrance to the grounds, which was as near to the main house as any man was allowed after dark, unless he was a priest. Frank maintained the grounds and grew enough produce to ensure that the convent remained amply supplied. Maggie ran the kitchens with the help of the orphans, who, as she constantly grumbled, were used as nothing more than slaves by the sisters, even though they were paid for by the state.

Maggie and Frank had grave misgivings about both the mother and baby home and the orphanage, but they were wise enough to keep their own counsel and, with it, the roof over their heads.

'Jesus, Mary and Joseph, it is not yet five o'clock in the mornin',' said Frank, as he pulled on a donkey jacket over his nightshirt. Then, placing his cap on his head, he stepped out through the front door into the snow, making for the pedestrian gate set into the green iron railings attached to the lodge.

'Have ye trouble?' he asked, shining his torch into the face of the tall man outside the gate.

Frank felt as though ice-cold water drizzled down his spine as the man's eyes met his. He wore a trilby hat, not usually seen in the country and certainly never before on any visitor to the convent. It was pulled down low, obscuring his face, and his overcoat was buttoned up to the neck, with a scarf wrapped around his mouth.

'No, no trouble. I think I am expected,' the man replied through the scarf in a muffled English accent.

'Not here,' said Frank. 'I have no message to expect ye and I'm the gatekeeper. Is it the Abbey ye want? If so, 'tis a further five miles towards Galway. Ye do know it's Christmas morning, don't ye? We aren't expecting anyone at the retreat today.'

As soon as Frank had spoken, he heard Sister Theresa's voice behind him.

'I will deal with this, thank you, Frank.'

'Reverend Mother, what are ye doing out in the snow at this time in the mornin'?'

Frank was incredulous. Life at the convent followed a very strict routine. No one ever caught sight of Sister Theresa before she began prayers at five-thirty and never, since the day Frank arrived, had she walked down to the gatehouse to meet a visitor. Not in fine weather, and very definitely not in the snow, at four in the morning.

'That will be all, thank you, Frank,' Sister Theresa replied curtly. 'You can step back indoors now. I will deal with this.'

Frank turned to look at the stranger once more. He didn't like him. He said later to Maggie, 'He was shifty-looking, all right, and something about him made my skin crawl.'

'Well, who will lock the gate then, Reverend Mother? Sure, I can't leave it wide open.'

Frank was not as keen to move indoors as Sister Theresa would have liked. He did not like disruption any more than she did.

'Wait then, Frank, and lock the gate when we have finished.' Sister Theresa, distracted, had already begun talking to the man directly. 'It's impossible. You can't drive the car up,' she said. 'She will have to walk. There is no guarantee you would make it, either there or back again. The slope leading to the house is very steep.'

The man appeared relieved. 'I would rather just hand her over here, if it is all the same to you,' he replied. 'The bishop said he didn't want her to be seen, so I hope everything is as discreet here as it should be.'

Frank noted the sideways glance the man threw in his direction.

'There is only one return ferry to Liverpool today and I need to be on it.'

Frank watched as the man opened the back door of the car; to his amazement, a young woman stepped out. She was very well dressed, wearing a smart hat, and although the man had clearly woken her from sleep, she appeared quite content.

11

She also recognized Sister Theresa. 'Hello, Reverend Mother,' she said enthusiastically. 'Are they here?'

'Hello, Daisy,' said Sister Theresa, who, it appeared to Frank, was less than pleased.

The man lifted a small suitcase from the boot of the car and placed it on the frozen ground, next to the girl, saying, 'I will be off now.'

And Frank, with his mouth half open in shock, watched as he jumped into his car and drove away. Sister Theresa turned on her heel and marched up the driveway, with the young and tired woman following along behind.

'Well now, it never broke anyone's mouth to say a kind word and yet no one out there had one, not even for the young woman, although she looked as though she could do with one and as likely give one back, it being Christmas morning an' all.'

Frank made this speech at the back door as he removed his coat and cap, shaking snowflakes onto the floor, before he hung them both up to dry.

He gratefully took a mug of tea out of Maggie's waiting hand. Much to Frank's disappointment, she was now dressed in a long, black quilted dressing gown, decorated in bright red roses as large as dinner plates. Her hair was wrapped in a turban-style headscarf and her eyes twinkled, alight with curiosity concerning their early visitor.

'Was she a postulant, maybe?' she asked eagerly. 'Although, sure, 'tis an odd time to be arriving, on a Christmas morning.'

'I have no notion, Maggie, but no postulant arrives wearing a hat as nice as that one. We know from your sister's girl that anything half decent they leave behind for the family to wear. What use is a fancy hat to a postulant? I know this much, the Reverend Mother recognized her and called her Daisy.'

'Well, I know of no Daisy who has visited here before,' said Maggie thoughtfully.

'Me neither, but then they keep so much secret up at the house, what would we know anyway? They told me the nuns was digging that land for medicinal herbs and yet there's not a sign of anything green put into the ground, but they keep on digging.'

They both stood and looked at each other.

'Is it blasphemous to say what I think is happening?' whispered Maggie.

'Aye, I think it probably is,' Frank replied. 'When I asked the priest what they had been digging for, he near exploded in front of me eyes and ripped the tongue right out of me head, so he did.'

Maggie and Frank both made the sign of the cross and blessed themselves.

'Well, I'm sure the nuns and the priest know what they are doing and, sure, 'tis none of our business. We're here to grow food, cook it and answer the gate. We should remember that.'

Frank sipped his tea. He hadn't told Maggie that he had seen babies and children being carried out from the orphanage and laid in the earth. No coffins, no prayers, no headstones. Just two stone-faced nuns with a couple of shovels.

The nuns had used older girls in the orphanage to help dig the huge burial plot, for those unfortunate enough to succumb to any one of the diseases that stalked the cold, damp building, to claim the malnourished and broken in soul.

Frank couldn't tell Maggie about that. It would be the end. Every day she threatened to leave, but where would they go?

'No point in getting back to bed now, is there, Maggie. The cold has woken me for good.'

'Please yerself. There's another hour waiting for me under that eiderdown and I'm not wasting it.'

Maggie slipped under the covers, still wearing her dressing gown, and soon filled the room with her snores, seconds after switching off the lamp.

Frank smiled at his wife. He couldn't have slept even if he had wanted to. He had never slept well since the eviction. Reaching up to the mantelpiece, he took down his dudeen and, pushing in a new plug of baccy, he slowly lit up, drawing the air in through the long clay stem.

A proud and hard-working tenant farmer, Frank had made his farm so productive over a period of twenty years that it became highly attractive to potential buyers. Never one to miss an opportunity to line his pockets with gold, his landlord had sold the fields right out from under them at auction, giving Frank and Maggie twenty-four hours to pack up and leave. It was a shock so huge that neither of them had fully recovered even to this day.

By a fortuitous coincidence, just as Frank and Maggie were made homeless, the sisters arrived and took up residence in what would become St Vincent's.

Their arrival had been announced at mass at their local church, the day before Frank and Maggie were evicted from their home. It had been a Sunday just like any other, when they had lit the fire, milked the cows, had rashers and tatties for breakfast and walked to mass.

Frank could remember every single second of that last Sunday on the farm and he frequently replayed each one in his mind as he went about his work.

The landlord had not even had the courtesy to inform them he was putting the farm and their home up for auction. Their only clue came in the form of a tall man in a scruffy suit, who had arrived unannounced and began strutting around the farm on the Friday afternoon.

'Landlord sent me,' was all he said to Frank as he left his car parked across the gate and then strode out along the bottom field, peering into the ditches.

Frank had worried all weekend.

'If there was anything to worry about, the landlord's agent would have told us,' Maggie had protested. 'Stop fretting, ye panic when there's nothin' to panic about.'

Yet all the time she had felt so sick with anxiety herself that she was unable to eat or sleep. A cold hand of fear had rested on her shoulder and there it had remained ever since.

The priest in the local church had been overly excited about the nuns arriving and the establishment of St Vincent's. Nuns spoilt priests and that was a fact.

'The sisters are here to protect your loose morals. The bishop has recognized that I, being the only man of Christ's teaching in the area, am indeed struggling,' he had announced in a scathing tone.

'Who is he talking about, Frank?' Maggie had whispered.

'I've no idea, Maggie, but they say 'tis free love all over the world, especially in Liverpool. They have the Beatles and everything. Maybe they's worried we will be next, all lovin' each other.'

Maggie knew it wasn't funny and she tried hard not to laugh. One of the daughters on the adjoining farm had become pregnant without any notion of free love and she had been sent away to the Abbey. It had been a shock to Maggie, who had thought the girl a beauty, both in looks and in nature, and Maggie failed to understand how she had become pregnant at all.

''Tis beyond me. She has never set foot away from her own farm and family. How in God's name could she be pregnant?'

Four years later, the girl had still not returned, and she wasn't the only one.

The sisters had moved into an old manor house that had been deserted by an English lord following the potato famine and had been purchased, via the Vatican, at a knock-down price. It didn't take long for the nuns to realize that their order had bitten off far more than they could chew.

The gardens and land had not been tended in many years and were as wild as any jungle. With men and young boys from the village leaving for Liverpool to join their friends in building homes and laying roads on the mainland, labour at home was scarce.

As soon as the priest heard what had happened to Frank and Maggie, he had taken them straight to St Vincent's. The newly established sisters needed considerable assistance with the overgrown and rundown manor, and the priest became a hero in their eyes for finding it in the shape of the rotund, married, middle-aged Frank.

Frank had not been truly happy since the day they had arrived. Although he loved working in the large gardens, there were strange goings-on up at the convent that made him feel very unsettled.

'I would love to know that the potatoes and vegetables I grow find their way onto the plates of the children in the orphanage,' he said to Maggie, 'but how can they? Them kids look half starved. The skin is hanging off their bones.'

Maggie was equally perturbed.

'I cook only for the nuns and the retreat. The orphanage has its own kitchen. I don't know what the orphans eat. Almost nothing is delivered up there. I have no idea where our slops go. They don't go to the pig man, but they disappear from the bucket, sure enough. I hope to God the orphans aren't fed that. It would taste too disgusting for anyone to eat. Surely not, Frank?'

Frank shook his head. The truth was, neither of them knew and they dared not ask.

Frank and Maggie knew very little of the convent's business. Their hours were strict and their routine rigid. They simply provided and cooked the food. That was their role, nothing more nor less, other than manning the gates.

Frank pulled on his pipe and inhaled deeply. Something in the eyes of the man who had dropped the woman off that morning had made Frank feel uneasy.

When Maggie rose an hour later, Frank was still on the settle, nursing his empty mug in one hand and his extinguished pipe in the other.

'Are you still sat there? That mug won't fill itself by you looking at it now. Why don't ye put the kettle back on. And as the ground is frozen today, ye can help me in the kitchen this morning.'

Frank didn't reply, still deep in thought, holding in his mind the image of the young woman, Daisy. There was something about her that perturbed him, a sweet, trusting innocence. He trusted no one.

Yesterday he had picked the vegetables for the Christmas lunch. They lay in flat wooden trugs on the stone floor of the kitchen cold store, waiting for Maggie to prepare and cook them.

'Frank, what is up with ye, cloth ears? Will ye help me or not?'

'Aye, Maggie, of course I will, love.'

Frank leant forward and placed his elbows on his knees. Maggie knelt down in front of him to stoke up the lodge fire.

'Ye know summat, Maggie,' he said to her back, pushing baccy into his pipe with his thumb. 'I know this sounds fanciful, and I know ye is going to say I is mad an' all, but even though 'tis Christmas morning, I think today I met evil for the first time in me life. It was dressed up as a man in a hat, but 'twas the divil himself, all right, and of that I am sure.'

'Well, if ye did, that doesn't bode well,' said Maggie.

Her husband wasn't fanciful by nature. She sat back on her heels.

'There was a time when we woke on our farm on Christmas morning to the sound of a baby singing,' she said as she looked wistfully into the fire. There were many things Maggie had yet to recover from and, Frank knew, the death of their child would always be one of them. Their only son, lost to diphtheria, had been born on a damp night, on a straw-filled mattress at the farm in front of a roaring fire. They had been two, alone. He had arrived in a hurry and then in the wonder of a moment, they became three, complete.

She dealt with life by keeping busy, but he was aware that memories pained her every day.

For a moment, they sat in companionable silence. Frank knew that, like himself, Maggie had returned in her mind to the last Christmas morning they had spent with the only child they had been blessed with.

Frank put his hand on his wife's shoulder. His clumsy gesture, well meant, was intended to ease her pain. She patted the top of his hand with her own.

'I have to leave for the house. God knows how many busy-bodies they have coming for lunch today. Councillors, doctors, priests, the bishop, his bishop friend from Dublin. There's been so much fuss, I wouldn't be surprised if the Pope himself pops in for a cuppa.'

As Maggie entered the convent kitchens, she flicked on the light and almost immediately jumped with shock at the sight of the young woman sitting at the end of the long wooden table.

'Well, hello,' said Maggie. 'I near jumped out of my fecking skin then. Who might you be?'

The girl, her face streaked with tears, looked tired.

'My name's Joan,' she said softly. 'Reverend Mother says I have to work down here with Maggie. Is that you?'

'It is me, and there is no other, so ye are in the right place,' said Maggie. 'Have ye had any tea?'

The girl shook her head.

'Did ye get any sleep?'

The girl shook her head again.

'Have ye been sat there since ye arrived, in the dark?'

The girl nodded. 'The Reverend Mother took my clothes and then gave me these.' She looked down at the regulation serge-blue calico worn by all the girls and orphans.

'Well, that's the first thing we have to do: get a cuppa tea and some breakfast inside ye. And when we have done that, ye can start telling me how ye ended up here at four o'clock on Christmas morning. I also know yer name's not Joan, 'tis Daisy.'

Daisy looked afraid. She had been told her new name was Joan and to forget that she had ever been called Daisy. She knew how strong the wrath of the nuns in Ireland could be if you disobeyed an order.

'Don't worry,' said Maggie. 'I know the name of everyone here is altered from the moment they arrive. I've yet to work out why in God's name that happens. 'Tis a mystery to me. Are ye pregnant?'

Daisy looked stunned. 'No, I'm not.'

'Well, ye aren't on a fecking retreat. Are ye an orphan then?'

'I had thought I was. When I was a child I lived in an orphanage in Dublin, with Sister Theresa, because they thought I was simple, but then I went to Liverpool to work as a housekeeper. A few weeks ago, my brother and his family made contact. He wanted me back with himself and his wife and children. They was so upset. He knew nothing about me or that I had been given away to the nuns when I was a baby. Miss Devlin, the teacher at the school in Liverpool, told me that my mam and da had even paid for me every year to be looked after – that was how I came to be in service.

'I was supposed to be with my brother now, at Christmas. We were all so excited in Liverpool; Miss Devlin bought me a hat and they gave it to me at the school nativity play. My brother was due to meet me at the ferry, but then it was such a surprise to see the policeman on the ferry. I don't think anyone can have known he was there or they would have said and he brought me here. Now they have told me I have to stay and work in the kitchens. I thought my brother would be here, waiting for me. That was what the policeman told me.'

'Whoa, whoa, steady on. Ye lost me back at the orphanage in Dublin,' Maggie said as she tipped up a bucket of coal into the oven burner. 'Tell ye what, Daisy, we have a Christmas dinner to cook for every sod and his wife today, so why don't ye help me do that for now? But there is going to be lots of time for us to talk so don't cry any more tears. Me and my Frank, we get upset when we see people cry, now. Ye saw my Frank when ye arrived and he is worried about ye. Don't tell the Reverend Mother we have spoken, but me and Frank, we will help ye to get things sorted.'

Daisy smiled for the first time since saying goodbye to Miss Devlin in Liverpool before she boarded the ferry.

They were interrupted by the sound of footsteps as the nuns who helped prepare breakfast ran down the worn stone steps towards the warmth of the kitchen.

'Shh, now. I will call ye Joan, in the kitchen, but to me an' my Frank, ye will be Daisy.'

That night, sitting on the settle in front of the fire, each with a mug of poteen, holding hands, even after all their years together, Maggie and Frank discussed Daisy.

'There's something not right there, Frank. The bishop from Dublin came down to have a word with her and she burst into tears right then and there in the kitchen, in front of everyone.'

'What are ye thinking of doing, Maggie?' He knew Maggie had a way of getting to the bottom of every situation.

Frank leant forward to poke the fire, sending a fresh shower of sparks up the chimney and out onto the hearth. Maggie instinctively drew her feet in closer.

'I don't know yet, but she shouldn't be here and if it is my job to find out where she should be, then so be it. Maybe we were sent here for a reason. Maybe God put us through what he did, when they took our farm away, because he could make use of us here to help others.'

'Well, we have nowhere else to live. If we cross the nuns, no other convent or church anywhere would help us, so for God's sake be careful.'

'Aye, I will, but that poor lass is sleeping on a mattress in a store in the kitchen. For some reason, Sister Theresa doesn't want her mixing with either the other girls or the nuns. It doesn't smell right, Frank. I will bring her down here tomorrow night. She can sleep in front of our fire and, that way, I can find out more.'

Frank stood and filled Maggie's mug. He loved her best when she was plotting. When her interest was keen. The sparks from the fire reflected in her eyes as he lifted her to her feet with a smile. Then he led her to the bed, to finish that which, given half a chance, he would have begun, at five o'clock that morning.

Chapter Two

'Do you want to know a secret?' Little Paddy whispered to his best friend Harry four days later, as they sat on the small squat lump of red sandstone known as the hopping stone, positioned on the edge of the green.

Snow had fallen heavily in Liverpool, on and off since before Christmas. Crystal-white pillows nestled on the lids of metal bins and windowsills while the cobbles lay buried under a glistening, dimpled blanket. Soot-stained bricks and chimneys that spewed acrid smoke had, for a short time only, taken on an aura of purity and cleanliness.

The boys were shivering on the cold, late December evening. Harry drew his thin coat tightly around him in a feeble attempt to shield himself from the brutal wind blowing up from the River Mersey.

Little Paddy didn't own a coat. He shivered the hardest and the loudest. Harry had loaned him the overly long scarf, which Nana Kathleen in number forty-two had lovingly knitted him for Christmas, although now Harry wished he could have taken the scarf back from Little Paddy and wrapped it around his own exposed neck.

It was the school Christmas holidays and, although it was

much warmer indoors, neither boy wanted to be inside a cramped two-up, two-down that was jam-packed full of siblings, babies and steaming nappies, drying on a washing pulley suspended from the kitchen ceiling.

Harry, the more sensible and sensitive of the two, shuffled on the cold stone, trying to secure a more comfortable position. Its carved surface was undulating, as though to actively discourage anyone from loitering around for long.

Harry ignored Paddy's question and began to speak, more in an effort to distract his mind from the biting cold than from having anything interesting to say.

'You know that if you're running from the bizzies and you jumped onto this stone, the police couldn't arrest ye until ye fell off? Did ye know that?'

Harry was right. The stone was no man's land, a stubby oasis of temporary refuge on the four streets where petty pilfering was essential, in order to survive.

'Yeah, me da told me. The O'Prey boys were always jumping on and off it before they went down. It never saved them,' said Little Paddy, feeling very clever indeed to have been able to impart this information to Harry, who was the cleverest boy in the class. Little Paddy jumped up and stood on top of the stone.

'But I suppose it's hard to balance, when yer hands are full of a tray of barm cakes you've just robbed out of the back of the bread van.' Little Paddy hopped from foot to foot, as though testing how difficult it would be to balance on the stone.

Harry smiled as he remembered the O'Prey boys, the over-indulged sons of Annie, who lived across the road. They had been a great double act. What couldn't be sourced from the docks when it was needed, the O'Preys would acquire. From a pair of communion shoes, to a wedding dress or even a wheelchair, for a small fee the boys could be depended upon to provide anything within reason, or even without, for anyone on the four streets. They thieved to order and were paying the price at Her Majesty's pleasure.

'D'you wanna know my secret, or not?' Little Paddy was becoming disappointed with Harry's apparent lack of interest.

'Paddy, ye always have a secret. Does gossip just fall out of the sky and land in your kitchen?' Harry replied, exasperated but interested, despite his determination not to be.

Harry was still in shock at having discovered Little Paddy had known all along that big Sean, who was married to Brigid, and Alice, who was married to Jerry, had been blatantly carrying on right under everyone's noses. To add insult to injury, his mammy, Peggy, had even seen them running away together the night before Christmas Eve, when everyone else had been watching the school nativity play. Gossip about the runaway lovers raged through the four streets, and everyone buzzed to distraction, all over Christmas.

Harry's mammy, Maura, had been mad about Peggy's role in this and had given out something wicked to Harry's saintly da, Tommy.

'Gossip carts itself to that woman's door, so it does, because it knows it will get a good hearing and then a good spreading after.'

Tommy had looked across the table at Harry and winked whilst Maura ranted. It was taking her some time to adjust to the fact that Peggy had known – long before even Maura herself or Jerry's mother Kathleen – about the devastation

26

that had torn apart the lives of Maura's closest friends. This was a thing of shame. Both Maura and Kathleen would have difficulty holding their heads up amongst their neighbours for some time to come. Their credibility as the wisest, holiest women on the four streets had been shot to bits. And who would now visit Kathleen to have their tea leaves read, when she couldn't even foretell the catastrophe that was occurring under her very nose, in her own home?

Maura was not happy.

'To think, the shame for Kathleen, with Alice married to her own son and living under the same roof, and neither she nor Jerry had a clue. Can ye imagine the lies, and the stealth? God, what a wicked woman that Alice surely was. The cut of her. Didn't I say so all along? Was I not the one who was never happy with such a union? Didn't I say this would happen, eh? Eh?'

Maura banged her rolling pin on the wooden table and then waved it at Tommy. Flour flew from the end, dusting Maura and transforming her raven hair in metal curlers into an even, rolling, snowcapped range.

Tommy didn't dare say that, since the day both of them had been witnesses at Alice and Jerry's wedding, Maura had never even intimated that Alice would have an affair with Sean, the husband of another of Maura's closest friends on the street, and then have the audacity to run away to America with him. When Maura was in this mood, there was only one thing to say and do.

'Aye, Maura, ye did sure enough,' he said, nodding sagely.

'Did Jer never so much as say anything to give yer a clue as to what was going on? Did he not? He must have said something, Tommy. How could yer miss summat like that? Was Sean not acting different, like? Holy Mother, Sean was one of yer mates and he has run off with yer best mate's wife. Ye work with them both all day, every day, and yer never knew a thing. Jaysus, Tommy, ye are a useless lump sometimes.'

Tommy, the meekest of men, forgot his own rules of engagement and took mild exception to this latest criticism.

'Me? For feck's sake, Maura, Kathleen runs an industry reading the bleeding tea leaves every Friday and she read fecking Alice's every week. If she couldn't see it coming, how did ye expect me to? On the docks we don't talk about such things as women. We talk about the horses and football, so don't blame me.'

'Bleedin' football and horses, when there is really important stuff going on under yer very nose. Ye amaze me, Tommy Doherty, ye really do, so.'

Maura undid her apron, throwing it onto the table. Then she flounced out of the back door, crossing the road to Jerry's house to speak to Kathleen. There, once again she would offer solace and comfort, in the midst of the shameful tragedy that had befallen both of their houses.

'Put the boxty in the oven,' she had thrown over her shoulder as she left. 'Do ye think ye can manage that? Have ye brain enough, eh, Tommy?'

Maura hadn't waited for a reply. As the back door slammed, Tommy turned to Harry, who throughout his exchange with Maura had been watching his da intently.

Watching and learning.

'Always agree with women, Harry, 'tis the only way to a quiet life.'

28

And with that, relieved that Maura had left to vent her irritation elsewhere, Tommy extracted a pencil stub from behind his ear and continued to mark out his horses in the *Daily Post* for the two-thirty at Aintree.

'Put the boxty in the oven, lad,' he said as he shifted his cap back into place. 'I'm fancying "Living Doll", a nice little three-year-old filly at seven to one. What do you think, Harry?'

Slamming the oven door shut, Harry rushed to sit next to Tommy to continue his education in how to be a man, whilst his twin brother, Declan, ran round the green, kicking a ball and pretending to be Roger Hunt.

Scamp, Little Paddy's scruffy, grey-haired mongrel, ran across the green towards the boys and flopped down into the snow at their feet, grinning proudly. From his jaws hung the carcass of a steaming-hot chicken, one leg hung by a sinew, dripping hot chicken juices onto Harry's shoe.

'Fecking hell, where has he nicked that from?' said Little Paddy as both boys stared at the dog, their own mouths watering.

In truth, Little Paddy was acting. On the four streets, no one locked their doors. The always hungry and artful Scamp had returned home, on more than one occasion, carrying a joint of hot meat. Just last week, Peggy had snatched a shoulder of lamb from his jaws, rinsed it under the tap and then thrown it in to the pot with their own meagre meal, a blind stew, which until that moment had comprised of potatoes and vegetables. Once the stolen shoulder of lamb was in the pot, all evidence of Scamp's kill was concealed and they were safe from any neighbor who chose to burst through the back door yelling, 'Have you seen me joint?' Which was exactly what did happen only moments later.

'That'll do nicely and, ye lot, keep yer gobs shut,' Peggy had said to her wide-eyed children, once the kitchen had returned to normal, as she dried her hands on her apron, which had been in desperate need of a wash for almost a month.

The boys only occasionally saw a roast chicken on Sunday and not always then, either. Quite often a Sunday roast would be without meat of any description. Instead it would consist of two types of potatoes, roast and mash, with mashed swede and carrots, topped with a great deal of fatty gravy. This was made with dripping and surplus meat fat left from previous meals that had been saved in an enamel bowl. Amazingly, here was Scamp, with half a steaming chicken in his mouth. As good a piece of meat as either had ever eaten on Christmas Day.

Both boys were by now salivating as they wondered who on earth on the four streets could afford to cook a chicken on a Tuesday.

'Maybe we should run home, before whoever it does belong to runs down the street, looking for it. I'll get the belt from me da, without wanting another from somebody else an' all,' said Little Paddy as he looked up and down the street nervously. But there was no sign of anyone.

Harry felt sorry for Little Paddy. Tommy had never so much as raised his voice to any of his children. They often heard Big Paddy next door laying into his kids and Harry knew it pained Tommy. But there were rules of survival on the four streets and one was that when it came to matters of children being disciplined, you didn't interfere.

One evening, Little Paddy's cries were so loud that Harry had begged his da to save his friend.

'Da can't, Harry,' Maura had said, pulling him to her and giving him an almighty hug, while she shielded his ears with her hands. 'We can't interfere. It's the law.'

Little Paddy, made nervous by the arrival of Scamp and the stolen chicken, was now becoming impatient with Harry. 'Do you want to know a secret or not?' he demanded, hands on his hips.

Harry's stomach was rumbling at the sight and smell of the chicken and his attention had wandered from Little Paddy's secret. Always mild-mannered, unusually for him, he was not in the best of moods today. He didn't really want to know. He was more interested in reading than in gossip. School didn't begin for another week and he had read every book he had been allowed to bring home for the holidays. Without another world to disappear into, he felt adrift.

Tommy had promised that tomorrow he would take him into town on the bus, to the second-hand bookshop on Bold Street, to see whether there was anything suitable for him. The new library, being built alongside a new children's nursery on the bombed-out wasteland, was only halfway through construction. Harry was possibly the only child on the four streets to have lost sleep with excitement at the thought of having an endless supply of books at hand and no longer having to beg them from the sisters, or explain why he wanted something other than the bible or a prayer book.

'Make sure you choose the biggest book they have, if they are all the same price. It will last longer,' Maura had said when Tommy had made the suggestion early that morning.

Maura had never read a book in her life.

Neither Harry nor Tommy commented, but Harry saw the little smile reach the corner of his da's mouth as, once again, he gave Harry that wink. The wink that told Harry: they were united, father and son. A team. Together.

Paddy had persuaded Harry to watch him playing footie on the green with his brothers and the rest of the local boys. Harry's asthma meant that he couldn't join in, but he enjoyed watching. Harry looked up at Little Paddy and nodded.

'Go on then. You look as though you will explode if I don't listen to whatever gossip it is ye have now. Although God knows, Paddy, it always gets you into trouble with ye da and I have no notion how it is ye get to know all these things.

Little Paddy needed no further encouragement. He was now unstoppable. He jumped from foot to foot on top of the stone and spoke at double his natural speed.

'There's a new priest arriving at the Priory. His name is Father Anthony and he has said that he is going to get to the bottom of who killed Father James, so help him, God.'

Little Paddy roared the 'so help him, God' bit, and raised his fist to the sky and dropped his voice an octave to mimic an older man.

Little Paddy continued, 'Mammy went to the Angelus mass last night at St Oswald's and she heard it herself from Annie O'Prey. Sister Evangelista has asked Annie to give the Priory a good dusting before they arrive and to be the new cleaner, now that Daisy has gone. She's to help the new father's sister, Harriet, who is coming to look after him and protect him from murderers. Annie is taking over from Daisy, so she is, and she's right pleased about it, too. And there's more. They think Daisy has gone missing, so she has, and never got off the boat in Dublin, or met her brother.'

Harry was now impressed. This was serious news, but he also knew his mother's chagrin at Peggy's having heard first would know no end, especially as it concerned the arrival of the new priest.

His mother was always the first with gossip from the church, her being so holy. Before the murder of Father James, followed by Kitty leaving so suddenly to visit Ireland on her far-too-long-for-Harry's-liking holiday, his mammy had never missed the Angelus. With her being the most religious mother in the street, she would surely have had that gossip first.

Twilight was falling. Both boys lapsed into silence as they looked across the misty graveyard towards the Priory. Harry felt an icy shiver run down his back as the lights in an upstairs window flicked on and then off again, as the night closed in.

Downstairs, in the Priory basement kitchen, Annie O'Prey was almost on the edge of hysteria. Sister Evangelista was trying her best to calm her down.

'Jaysus, it was there, so it was, on the kitchen table. I went upstairs for no longer than five minutes to light the fire in the study. I came back down and the chicken was gone. What am I to do if I have no food ready for the new father and his sister? What kind of welcome to the streets would that be, now?'

Sister Evangelista was relieved that a new priest was arriving and that his spinster sister was accompanying him to act as his housekeeper. They had left Dublin that morning and were expecting to be welcomed with a quiet supper at the Priory, with a full meal at the convent with the sisters the following night.

Sister Evangelista had been glued to the phone since Christmas Eve. As yet, she had told only the few nuns she could trust that the previous housekeeper, Daisy, had failed to meet her family at the port in Dublin. Daisy's brother and his wife were convinced that Daisy had never boarded the boat at Liverpool. But Sister Evangelista knew better. Miss Devlin, a teacher at the school as well as a good friend to the convent and to Daisy, had put her on the boat herself. She had even asked two elderly ladies to look after her, until they berthed in Dublin, so they knew she had caught the ferry. Neither of them had a good Christmas, worrying about Daisy's whereabouts.

What was more, the bishop had been less than sympathetic. He had even shouted at Sister Evangelista down the phone and since then she had refused to talk to him again.

'Take a hold of yourself, Sister, you are like a hysterical farm girl from the country,' he had said. 'Take charge of your senses and stop yerself from turning everything into a crisis, when none exists, will ye? I am fair exhausted with the carryings-on at St Mary's. Father Anthony and his sister will arrive shortly, so just leave it all to him. And remember, ye tell him nothing of what ye found in the Priory, before Father James was murdered by whoever it was who savaged the poor man, do ye hear me?'

She had heard him all right. Having discovered in the Priory, following his death, the father's dirty secret and a heap of filthy photographs of young children, she wasn't so sure she would describe him as a poor man any longer. She had also heard the bishop singing a different tune altogether regarding the arrival of Father Anthony, who had been sent directly to Liverpool from Rome via Dublin.

The Pope was none too keen on his priests being murdered and their private parts dismembered. So the Vatican had taken Father James's replacement out of the hands of the bishop, who had been incensed from the minute he was told the news.

'Apparently, Father Anthony has been at the Vatican for a number of years and is very well known and trusted. Seems to me the Pope knows exactly what he's doing and, regardless of what the bishop says, I am mightily grateful for the Vatican's intervention,' Sister Evangelista had told Miss Devlin, the teacher at the school.

Sister Evangelista had been made very angry by the bishop's tone. There had been two murders, not one: Father James and their neighbour, Molly Barrett, who had been found in her own outhouse with her head caved in. Sister Evangelista had had to beg the bishop to visit Liverpool and take some responsibility, but had been bitterly disappointed. He had been no help at all, leaving Sister Evangelista to deal with the police single-handed. It was not until she found the disgusting photographs in Father James's desk that the bishop had bothered to visit the Priory. As she had confided to Miss Devlin, this was all very strange behaviour indeed.

'Sure, he was never away from the Priory when the father was alive. Now that he is dead and we need the bishop's assistance, I'm having to beg. That is a sad situation altogether.'

Miss Devlin had agreed, but the bishop had been put there for one purpose only, to be obeyed, and neither of them felt inclined to challenge his authority.

Sister Evangelista once again felt a familiar sense of helplessness and isolation. Father James's housekeeper, Daisy, was missing and the bishop just couldn't care a jot. And after all the trouble she had taken to follow his precise instructions for Daisy's safe journey to Dublin.

So much had happened in the aftermath of the two murders that Sister Evangelista had found herself struggling yet again. When she heard that Father Anthony and his sister Harriet would be arriving to lead the church, she had dropped to her knees in relief to give thanks to God.

Another welcome pair of shoulders to carry the burden of upholding the authority of the Church in the parish of a murdered priest.

The devil had brazenly strutted down their streets and Sister Evangelista was convinced that she was possibly the only person in the whole world who knew why.

Maura let herself in through Nana Kathleen's back door, to find Nellie washing the dishes, Kathleen rolling out her boxty on the kitchen table and Joseph snoozing in his pushchair.

Maura smiled at Nellie, the child whose birth had taken the life of Bernadette, Nellie's mother and Maura's best friend, and who was up to her elbows in soapsuds.

'You all right then, Nellie?' Maura asked.

'That poor Nellie,' Maura had said to Tommy in bed only the night before. 'First her mammy dies and then her stepmother runs away with the father of one of her best friends, leaving the little lad behind for her and Nana Kathleen to look after. What child deserves that, eh, Tommy? What next? Nothing, God willing, because that child can't take much more. She has lost enough.'

Tommy pulled Maura to him. 'No one was closer to our Kitty than Nellie, that's for sure. She will be missing Kitty badly, so she will. Ye can't worry about everyone, Maura. Once our Kitty is home and Nellie has her friend once more, they will both be back to normal.'

Within seconds Tommy had fallen into a deep sleep, but Maura lay awake into the small hours, worrying about everyone and everything but most of all about Kitty, whose secret baby was to be delivered at the Abbey mother-and-baby home in Galway. Almost no one, other than those closest to her, knew.

No one on the four streets, not even nosy Peggy next door, had suspected what had really happened to Kitty, or why.

'I'm grand, thank you, Auntie Maura,' Nellie had replied without her usual bright smile. 'Would you like a cuppa tea?'

'Aye, put the kettle on, Nellie,' said Kathleen as she slapped the big round potato-bread onto a tray and slid it into the range oven at the side of the fire. Every woman on the four streets baked in the morning, using the roaring heat of the first fire of the day, before they began to simmer the stock.

'Any news?' Maura asked Nana Kathleen as she pulled a chair out from under the table.

Kathleen knew exactly what she was talking about. Both women had been waiting for some kind of fallout since the night Jerry's wife had left him for his workmate and neighbour, Sean. But Jerry had barely reacted at all. The emotional tempest anticipated by the women had never arrived.

'No, not a dickie bird. I have to say this about our Jer, I've never seen a man recover from a broken heart as fast as he has, so I haven't. Seven days they have been gone and this morning, he didn't even mention her. Nothing like when Bernadette died and he was beyond any consolation that I, or anyone else, could give him.'

'What about little Joseph?' Maura whispered, so as not to wake him.

'Well now, that's different altogether. He's asleep now because he's been awake all night. The poor child has no idea what is going on. When he is in my arms, he pulls me to the kitchen window and I know he is looking down the backyard for his mammy. Maura, what can I do? I cannot even say her name, so I can't, or I will risk setting him off. Thanks be to God for our Nellie. She can really distract him now, much better than me, can't you, Nellie?'

Nellie looked across at them from the range and nodded. Maura noted that she looked sad-eyed, as though carrying the weight of the world on her shoulders.

'And what about poor Brigid?' said Maura.

Maura was referring to Sean's wife: the wronged woman, deserted without the slightest inkling that anything had been amiss and left with a house full of little red-haired daughters to keep and care for. A woman who was both extremely house-proud and very much in love with her husband and her perfect family. Perfect, that is, until the moment on the night before Christmas Eve when she had opened a note she found propped on the mantelshelf, informing her that Sean, the husband she had devoted her life to, had run away to America with Alice, the wife of her friend Jerry.

That was the moment when everything had altered. When her love had turned to hate. In one tick of the clock, her life had gone from light to dark. All she believed was true in their world had washed away before her, in a river of tears.

'We should call in and see her this morning,' said Kathleen. 'The poor woman is distraught.'

Nellie was pouring boiling water into the tin teapot when she saw Bill from the pub burst through the gate, run down the yard and in through the back door.

'Maura,' he panted. 'Maura, ye have to get to the pub now, yer relative from home, Rosie, she will be calling back in thirty minutes. She says to tell ye she is phoning from Mrs Doyle's in Bangornevin. She needs to speak to ye as well, Kathleen. She said I have to take ye both together 'cause she won't have the chance to call back again, she needs to speak to ye both and that I had to make sure of that.'

With that, Bill ran back down the yard to the pub where the draymen were in the middle of a delivery. But that mattered not a jot. News from home was the most important kind and not to be kept waiting.

Kathleen, Maura and Nellie looked at each other, but no one spoke until Nellie whispered into the silence, 'Can Kitty have had the baby?'

She put down the kettle and moved closer to the others. They were in their own home and no one could possibly overhear them, but they were the only females in Liverpool who knew why Kitty was in Ireland. She had slipped across the water, in the dead of night, with Kathleen and Nellie for company.

The baby growing in her belly had been put there by Father James, and Tommy had ensured he paid for it. A priest's murder, dismembered of his langer, coinciding with a child's pregnancy would surely have guaranteed that Tommy would have been hanged once the police realized he had been defending his daughter's honour. The connection was too obvious.

Kitty had awaited the birth in Galway, hiding in a convent and working in a laundry. Waiting out her pregnancy and delivery.

Sister Evangelista and Kitty's school friends believed that Kitty was visiting Maura's sister who was poorly and needed help, but on the four streets only three women – Maura, who was Kitty's mother, and her closest friends, Kathleen and her granddaughter, Nellie – knew the truth. Or so they had thought.

'She's not due for three more weeks, but it is possible,' said Maura.

'If it's Rosie wants to speak to ye, then that baby has been born and if Rosie is at Mrs Doyle's, it's her way of letting us know Kitty is at Maeve's farmhouse and safe,' said Kathleen.

Maura was already standing at the back door, holding it open and waiting impatiently whilst Kathleen tied her headscarf and fastened her coat, ready to run to the pub and reach the phone to hear news of her daughter. She had counted the days, one by one, since Kitty had been dropped off at the Abbey. Thoughts of her daughter were the first to enter her mind as she woke in the morning and the last as she closed her damp eyes at night. The pain of missing Kitty was almost more than she had been able to bear.

But Maura knew that the existence of Kitty's baby would have provided the police with a motive and a direct line to the murdered priest.

The only way Maura had been able to maintain any degree of normality, after she returned with Kathleen from Ireland, was to believe that Kitty was happy and being well looked after. That she would have made friends with the other girls, and that the nuns would not have made her work too long, or too hard, in the laundry as her pregnancy progressed. These thoughts had sustained her throughout the months of missing her daughter.

'As God is true, I have been counting the days to this news, Kathleen,' Maura said as they ran down the entry together.

'I know, Maura. Jeez, can we stop a minute. I'm pulling for tugs here.'

Maura stood and waited for the older woman to catch her breath. Kathleen, red in the face and panting, reached into her pocket for her cigarettes. 'It helps me breathing,' she said to Maura, offering her the packet to take one.

The phone rang just as they pushed through the wooden doors and Bill smiled as he waved them over.

'Aye, they are both coming through the door right away. Ye can speak now ...'

His words trailed off, as Maura grabbed the phone from his hand.

'Rosie, have ye any news?' Maura hissed, her heart beating wildly.

Rosie was a relative by marriage and a midwife. She had been due to deliver Kitty's baby at the convent, in the middle of January.

'Is she at Maeve and Liam's? Shall we come to fetch her?'

There was silence at the end of the telephone.

Kathleen didn't want Bill to hear the conversation between Maura and Rosie. There had been too many people interested in one another's business since the murder of the priest, and then there had been poor Molly Barrett, bludgeoned to death in her own outhouse. That one had stumped even Kathleen.

She knew who had murdered the priest all right but Molly Barrett, that was a mystery, which had perturbed them all.

'It's freezing out there, Bill,' said Kathleen. 'Any chance of a couple of ports before we run back? Not often we get news from home in a phone call.'

'It's more often than not a birth and sometimes a death, Kathleen. Has your Liam got Maeve with a babby on the way, then?' said Bill, grinning as he took a bottle out from underneath the bar and began pouring the ruby-red liquid into two glasses.

Kathleen grinned back uneasily and, taking the glass of port, used all her willpower not to down it in one.

'Ye have been through a bit of bad luck, with Alice and all that business there over Christmas,' said Bill to Kathleen, leaning on the bar.

'Rosie, can ye hear me?' said Maura, her voice louder this time.

'Aye, Maura,' came the reply down the crackling line. 'I have just asked Mrs Doyle if I could speak in private and had to wait while she moved into the back of the post office.'

Maura could visualize the hovering Mrs Doyle, who looked as much like a crone as anyone who hadn't met her could possibly imagine and a crone with more than her fair share of rotting teeth.

Rosie's voice crackled down the line again.

'Kitty has had the baby, Maura, but I'm afraid I was not in attendance. The snow brought the Abbey telephone lines down and they couldn't get through to me, until yesterday morning.'

'Oh, Holy Mother of God, is she all right?'

Maura's eyes filled with tears. The longing to be at her daughter's side clutched at her heart, robbing her of breath and dragging her down, till she was bent double over the counter with her free hand involuntarily clutching her abdomen.

'The baby was born on Christmas morning. It was a boy and his adoption to an American couple was arranged even before he had filled his first nappy, so it was. I got her to Maeve's as quickly as God allowed me. I have news, Maura ...'

The line crackled and hissed as Rosie's voice faded.

'Rosie, Rosie, are ye there?'

The line was totally dead. The crackling had stopped.

Maura cared nothing now of what Bill could hear. Rosie had just said that Kitty had had the baby and then – nothing.

'Rosie!' she yelled down the line.

'Is everything all right, Maura?' asked Kathleen, concerned.

'I don't know. She said she had news and then she disappeared.'

With her hand outstretched and shaking, Maura handed the receiver to Kathleen.

'Hello, hello, *hello*!' Kathleen said loudly, and then she heard Rosie' s return.

'Kathleen, thank God you are there.'

Chapter Three

IT WAS TWO days after Christmas. Within a second of her opening her Dublin office door with her Yale key, the black Bakelite phone on Rosie O'Grady's desk rang. It was as though it had been patiently waiting for the first familiar sound of her return following the long Christmas break.

'Oh, Holy Father, would you believe it,' Rosie muttered to herself. 'I'm not even through the door yet and it's started already.'

The previous evening Rosie had doubted that she would even make it into work after a sudden and very heavy Christmas snowfall, which had covered Ireland from coast to coast. The roads in Roscommon, where Rosie lived, had been impassable in places, but she was relieved to see that, in Dublin at least, some effort had been made to clear the main roads.

Rosie had not missed a day of work in her entire life and there was no way she would allow the weather to defeat her now, despite the ploughed walls of snow on the roadside standing as high as six feet in places. As the head midwife at Dublin's maternity hospital, senior midwife tutor and the chair of the Eire midwifery council, Rosie took her responsibilities, as well as her reputation for high standards and reliability, very seriously indeed.

The midwifery block was reached via four red sandstone steps that led up to an imposing, semicircular entrance hall, complete with parquet floor, whose windows overlooked the car park. The administration office doors flanked a wooden arch beyond which lay the wards and the main hospital. Rosie occupied the most impressive office, in accordance with her status, for she also had responsibility for the training school from which she proudly turned out twenty well-trained midwives each year. The majority of Dublin's babies were delivered at home, but a growing number of women were choosing to give birth in hospital, especially those who were likely to have complications.

'Morning, Mrs O'Grady.'

As Rosie passed through the revolving glass doors into the hospital foyer, Tom, the head hospital porter, greeted her from behind his high, glossy, dark-wood desk, tipping the brim of his cap as a mark of respect. She stamped the snow from her boots on a large coconut-hair mat before stepping onto the freshly polished wooden floor.

The hospital caretaker had taken advantage of the Christmas lull to buff every floor in the hospital. Rosie stood for a moment as she removed her headscarf and shook the last of the snowflakes onto the mat, inhaling deeply the familiar smell of fresh lavender floor wax. It had a calming effect on her.

'I said if anyone makes it in today, it would be you, with you having travelled the furthest an' all. On ward three, there's a midwife not turned in for her shift yet and she only lives across the river. You have put her to shame, so you have, struggling all the way in from Roscommon.'

'Well, it wasn't easy, Tom,' Rosie replied as she searched in her handbag for her office keys. 'It took the help of a tractor and a very good husband to see me onto the Dublin road, or I would indeed still be stuck in Roscommon. We had all our animals down on the lower fields to make it easier over Christmas, so it hasn't been too bad for us. I could at least commandeer the tractor without too much guilt, now. But that didn't stop yer man grumbling, and, sure, being as he's a farmer, he doesn't usually need much of an excuse, now, does he?'

Tom laughed out loud, feeling sorry for any man who tried to cross Matron O'Grady.

'Aye, well, you have still made it in and that is to your credit. We can complain all we like but to wake up on Christmas morning to a white Ireland, that was a miracle, was it not?'

Rosie smiled at Tom. It had been very special indeed. The fields and the church had looked magnificent. Even the old prison walls became magical and romantic.

'Aye, Tom, it was a miracle. Deep snow on Christmas Day, who would have thought it?'

'Shall I ring the kitchen, shall I? And ask Besmina to bring up your tea?'

'Oh God, wouldn't that just be grand. I'm parched,' Rosie replied. 'You can always rely on Besmina.'

'You can, that. She will always be grateful to you for the job you gave her. You have a loyal employee for life there, Matron, and that's for sure.'

Rosie's husband had done everything possible that morning, to try to persuade her not to travel to Dublin.

'Are ye mad?' he had said when she had asked him to tow her car out onto the main Dublin road, using his farm tractor. 'Phone lines are down all over the place. No one is driving anywhere. I will be halfway to Dublin by the time I find a decent stretch of road to leave you on, and then how in God's name would I know ye had made it in? And tonight, how will ye travel back if it freezes over? It's a Hillman Hunter ye drive, not a bloody tank.'

'Aye, I know that,' Rosie had replied. 'Calm down for goodness' sake. I don't expect you to take me all the way to Dublin. Just leave me on the first clear stretch and I will manage the rest of the way.'

It didn't matter how much he remonstrated with her, no one could alter Rosie's mind about anything when it was made up. Once she had set herself on a course of action, she was unstoppable.

'Jeez, the mule is less stubborn,' her husband had grumbled as he set about moving the tractor out of the barn.

As she opened the office door to the ringing telephone, Rosie hastily dropped her bag onto the floor and pulled off her leather driving gloves with her teeth. She noted that at least the hospital phones were working. Having removed the second glove, she just had time to lift the receiver to her ear before the caller hung up.

'Good morning, Rosie O'Grady, matron midwife,' she trilled down the line, cheered after her long and cold journey by the knowledge that tea was on its way to her office to warm her.

She secretly hoped that the office kitchen maid, Besmina, would pop a slice of thick, white, hot buttered toast onto the tray, as she often did. It had been over three hours since Rosie had left home to set off for the hospital and the loud rumblings from her stomach were letting her know as much.

The crackling phone line was poor, which wasn't surprising, given the weather, but Rosie could just make out the voice on the other end as that of the Reverend Mother at the Abbey convent and laundry out in the windy west, near Galway.

She had been dreading this call.

Her heart dropped into her boots. There was only one reason why the Reverend Mother would be telephoning her now. Rosie was very careful to keep her distance from any of the laundries or the mother and baby homes run by the sisters. Their very existence made her uncomfortable.

For many years the Irish government had made use of the laundries to imprison women and hide them away. Rosie knew that girls were sent to the abbeys and convents by the authorities, for the most spurious of reasons, and would remain incarcerated there for their entire lives. Many were not, nor had ever been, pregnant. Some were sent for being nothing more than a pretty orphan, assigned to the Abbey for her own protection, away from the lure of temptation and sinful ways.

These girls, known as penitents, were transferred to the Abbey straight from the industrial schools, run by the nuns and brothers. Many were country girls from the village farms, victims of incest and rape, or just a girl carried away at a dance, or a fair. Those who found themselves pregnant outside of wedlock would be deposited abruptly at the Abbey's doors by their parents or by the local priest. In their imprisonment, some went mad from grief and despair.

Many in Rosie's circle knew about the laundries. An industry run by nuns who made vast profits enslaving women deemed to be sinful. The sisters and the government, worked as a team.

This had made Rosie cross herself in shame when she last walked through the Abbey doors. If the penitents were lucky, after three long years of unpaid work in the laundry they might manage to buy back their freedom, provided that their families could supply the necessary one hundred and fifty pounds. However, before they left they would also be required to agree to give up their babies and to allow the Abbey to sell them on to American families.

For the country girls, there was no way to bypass their years of slave labour. There wasn't a farm girl from one end of County Mayo to the other who would ever see that kind of money in her entire lifetime.

For young Kitty Doherty from Liverpool, Rosie's involvement with Sister Assumpta and the Abbey had been necessary.

A necessary evil.

Kitty was neither a penitent nor a country girl but, for her own sake as much as anyone else's, for a short while she had needed to become one.

Rosie had agreed to personally deliver the baby at the Abbey when Kitty's time was due, but, based on Rosie's examination a few months earlier, she had thought that wouldn't be until the middle of January at the very earliest.

Rosie was one of very few people who knew that Kitty's secret arrival in Ireland was in some way connected to the murder of the priest. The news of the murder had been all over the Dublin newspapers for almost a week.

Since it seemed like half the men of County Mayo had travelled to Liverpool, to work on the roads, at the docks or building new houses, anything that happened in Liverpool was news in Ireland too.

Rosie didn't want to know the details of why or how Kitty had become pregnant.. Sure, hadn't she seen enough girls in Ireland in the same position. The priest in Liverpool was not unique. She was delivering Kitty's baby under a cloak of secrecy, at the request of her sister-in-law, Julia, who lived in Bangornevin in County Mayo. Refusal was not an option. A girl was in trouble. It was the job of the women to find a solution to her problem. Kitty Doherty's name had been changed to Cissy so that no one would ever know she had been at the Abbey. It had been drilled into Rosie that no one must know where the girl was, who she was, or that she had given birth. Once she had done so, she would need to return to Liverpool as soon as possible.

Rosie was well aware, without having to be told, that the part she had played – in helping to hide the child at the Abbey to have her baby – had saved Kitty's father, Tommy, a good man, from the gallows.

The justice of the four streets was brutally simple.

An eye for an eye. A life for a life stolen.

The family had altered Kitty's name to Cissy, to hide her

true identity from the nuns, and Cissy her name would remain. Unlike the other girls in the Abbey, who had their name removed on the day they arrived.

No one was allowed to use her real name whilst resident at the Abbey. Hair was cut short, personal possessions removed and girls were not allowed to speak of their past. In fact, they were not allowed to speak.

Kitty's case was slightly different. She was to be resident at the Abbey for just a few months, rather than years. Kitty had not been dropped at the door. Nor was she a penitent.

Kitty wasn't even an Irish resident and had been registered under a false name from the very beginning.

'Shall I put the tray on the table, Mrs O'Grady?' Besmina whispered to Rosie.

For a second, Rosie almost lost her concentration and focus on what the Reverend Mother was saying, as her stomach responded to the smell of the hot tea and buttered toast. She winked at Besmina who began to pour her tea from the aluminium teapot. The porter had slipped into the room with his arms full of logs and set about lighting the fire, hoping to warm the cold office, which had been empty for almost a week.

The voice at the other end of the line was as cold as the room.

'The child was delivered in the early hours of Christmas morning.'

There was no compassion in the words of the Reverend Mother.

Rosie felt a sudden chill, which had nothing to do with the temperature of her office.

The Abbey's delivery practices were barbaric. Pain was regarded as an atonement for sin. Stitching was not allowed. The perineal tears were looked on as a continuing physical reminder of the need to seek forgiveness.

'Where is she now?' Rosie had already forgotten about the tea and toast. She knew all was not as it should be.

Besmina, the kitchen maid, arrived at the hospital only a few months previously. It hadn't taken long for the staff, over tea and brack, to discover that Besmina had detailed knowledge of the Abbey, where Kitty had been left to deliver her baby in secret. The moment Rosie discovered that Besmina was familiar with the Abbey, she pressed her for information.

It had been a difficult task. At first she was very nervous but, gradually, she had opened up to Rosie. The staff had no idea why Rosie was so interested and she wanted to keep it that way.

She wasn't the only one keeping secrets. There was much Besmina hadn't told Rosie, or anyone else. She would never confess that she had been an unmarried mother herself or to having birthed her child at the Abbey to save her mother and grandmother from the shame. Or that she had escaped with the help of a child from Liverpool by the name of Nellie.

'Thank you, God, for sending Nellie to me,' was the opening line of Besmina's first and last prayer of every day.

Besmina had informed Rosie that, behind the Abbey, in the middle of a copse of trees, were graves, dozens of them, belonging to girls as young as thirteen. And babies. Lots of babies.

For this reason Rosie had been very glad that Kitty's family, related to her own, had asked her to deliver the baby herself.

Rosie knew that Kitty came from a loving and caring family. God alone knew how that priest had been able to do what he did.

The Reverend Mother had ignored both Rosie's question and the tone of her voice.

'I have given orders for her to be left in the labour room until you arrive. I do not want her working in the laundry any longer. A baby conceived in sin, but born in the Abbey on Christmas morning, is not viewed as helpful, Mrs O'Grady. I don't need to explain to you how unsettled this birth has made everyone. I would like her to be removed as soon as is possible.'

'Right, how is she?' Rosie asked. 'Was the delivery straight-forward and is she recovering well?'

'You will be able to answer those questions when you collect her, which I hope will be today. Her baby was a boy. I had him removed to the nursery, immediately following his birth, and I am delighted to say that his new parents are making haste trav-elling from America to view him. They will take him back as soon as possible once a passport can be issued.'

'View him? Well, goodness me, what an odd expression. That is very quick altogether, is it not?'

Rosie was no stranger to efficiency, but the Reverend Mother appeared to have moved with unseemly haste to have the baby adopted.

'It is our normal practice to keep the children until they are three. Adoption takes such a time to arrange in America. A letter can take as long as six weeks. When a new baby is available, we have the very best Catholic families on standby who will drop everything once they receive a telegram from us. I hope there will be no complaint? The girl has already signed a contract, stating that she relinquishes all rights to the baby and that she will never attempt to make contact with the child or his family, at any time in the future. What time can we expect you?' Her tone brightened as she added, 'Sister Celia would love to bake you a cake.'

In her state of trauma following the delivery, Kitty had signed the contract using her real name. The Reverend Mother, in her haste to have the contract signed, had not noticed Kitty's error.

Rosie was speechless. The journey to Dublin from Roscommon had been an ordeal. Now she would have to drive across country to Galway and then take the girl on to Ballymara.

'I hope to arrive at the Abbey at around two o'clock, all being well, so long as I am able to drive down all the roads, please God. Thank Sister Celia, I am very much looking forward to her wonderful cake.'

Rosie frowned as she replaced the receiver. She felt intensely uncomfortable but she knew that she must make her way to Kitty, as fast as she possibly could.

Rosie whispered a prayer, 'At least the girl is alive, thanks be to God,' and blessed herself. She quickly telephoned Mrs Doyle at the post office in Bangornevin and asked her to send someone across the road to fetch her sister-in-law, Julia, to the phone.

Whilst she waited for Julia to call back, she just had time to drink her tea and eat her toast before making another call to her husband, who was less than pleased by her news.

'Rosie, if the baby has been born, why can ye not wait for the weather to clear? I've been looking at the sky and, sure, 'tis as heavy as a sinner's heart. There will be snow tonight again, I am certain of it.'

'I will be fine. You know me, always the lucky one. Stop fussing now and get back to work. There won't be much light today.'

'Aye, right, well there is no use me arguing now. I will make sure Julia knows to put the watch on from Castlefeale and have them ring me, as ye pass through. Drive with care, Rosie.'

As Rosie finished her last phone call, she once again reminded herself how blessed she had been to marry a man like JT. Never once had she known him to lose his temper, which could not be said for some of the men of rural Ireland. On countless farms, husbands and fathers ruled by the fist.

She set off into the snow once again, this time with her Gladstone bag full of dressings, sutures and useful things she might need for Kitty, as well as a little extra knowledge, which she had artfully gleaned from Besmina as she cleared away the tea tray.

When Rosie turned in through the Abbey gates at three o'clock, the light was already fading fast. At the best of times she thought the Abbey looked like the coldest and most miserable of institutions, but today in the frozen mist it appeared even more forbidding than usual as it loomed up, like a white effigy, against the dull grey sky.

To the right of the main building was a long glass corridor, which led to the laundry; on the opposite side lay the chapel and convent. Rosie knew the girls' dormitories were up in the roof.

She wiped the misty windscreen with her leather glove. From the window on the top floor shone the single, dim yellow light of the labour room, which was where Kitty would be lying, probably alone.

'Merciful God, the poor child,' she said out loud as she pulled up in front of the convent.

As Rosie turned off the engine, she saw a huddled procession of girls shuffling in a straight line down the steps, from the Abbey nursery to the laundry. Rosie wondered if this was the end of the one hour per day they were allowed to spend with their babies and children, and were being herded back to commence another five hours of hard work. Two girls looked directly at Rosie and then began talking to each other. One smiled at her nervously, as though trying to attract her attention, before being sharply prodded in the back by the nun walking alongside.

Rosie had been told by Besmina that whenever a child was adopted, the mother was made to carry it down the long corridor to the door at the far end. There, she would have to hand the baby over to the person who would oversee the handover to the new parents, at Shannon airport.

''Tis the walk of shame,' Besmina had said, 'and the nuns, they all line up in a row on either side, praying for forgiveness, which, if you ask me, never seems to come. If the mother breaks down, or becomes upset, Jesus, she is punished so bad.'

'How, Besmina, how?'

Rosie had asked this question before but it was not until today that Besmina had answered her, with uncharacteristic bitterness.

'They are taken into the Reverend Mother's office, where they have their heads shaved and painted with gentian violet. Then they are beaten with a cane, tied to a chair and left in a room, alone, for hours. The nuns can be witches, so they can.'

Rosie assumed purple gentian violet would be a physical warning to the other girls, should they dare to shed tears as they handed over their babies.

Besmina, who was a good girl, had told Rosie very little but what she did say had shocked her. Rosie was a good Catholic, but sometimes even she worried at the corruption of her religion, and wondered how there could be a justification for such places as the Abbey.

The Reverend Mother stood waiting, framed in the doorway, a vision in black. By the time Rosie had reached the top of the steps, a flustered, white-veiled novice was also hovering behind her, twittering.

'At long last. I thought you would never arrive,' Sister Assumpta exclaimed impatiently, as though Rosie had travelled from the local village on a dry and pleasant day. 'I have tea ready for you in my office.'

At last, an acknowledgment of the dreadful conditions I have driven in, thought Rosie.

'We saw the lights of your car and had it made immediately. Sister Virginia, show Mrs O'Grady to the bathroom and wait to bring her back. Then you can have your tea and cake, midwife, and Sister Virginia will escort you to the labour room, to collect the girl. Sister Celia has made you the most fabulous sandwich cake and covered the top in melted chocolate. Can you imagine that?'

Rosie followed the novice down the highly polished corridor laid with a green Persian carpet, and lined with heavy, dark wood furniture, with ruby brocade curtains hanging at the windows. Against the wall stood an overpowering statue of St Anthony that had obviously been recently carved. She wondered exactly how much money the nuns were bringing in on an annual basis from their laundry work and baby selling, in order to fill the Abbey with such finery.

The ceremonial tea and cake in the Reverend Mother's room were consumed in minutes. Rosie was keen to see Kitty as quickly as possible, so she stood and picked up her heavy bag. She had to admit, to herself, it was the best slice of chocolate cake she had ever eaten. An unexpected sweetness.

'Er, before you take the girl, I am afraid we have a small problem.' Sister Assumpta's voice, behind her, had now dropped an octave to sound almost menacing.

As Rosie turned back to face her, Sister Assumpta averted her gaze and shuffled pieces of paper across her desk.

'And that would be what, Reverend Mother?' enquired Rosie.

The atmosphere in the room had taken a decidedly frosty turn.

'Do you have the money with you? There is a further eighty pounds outstanding, before the girl can leave.'

Rosie felt her blood boil. She had had a very long day and the last thing on her mind when she had received the Reverend Mother's call was driving to Bangornevin to collect what amounted to bail money. There had been only one idea in her head as she had replaced the receiver and that was to make haste to Kitty's bedside as soon as God and the weather would allow.

Rosie looked the Reverend Mother straight in the eye and spoke with more authority than she actually felt, especially as a painting of the Holy Mother seemed to be staring down at her with a touch of disappointment in the eyes that she had not noticed until now.

'No, I do not, as it happens, because you have given me no time to organize the payment. You appeared very keen indeed to have Kitty removed from the Abbey when you called me this morning, and so I am afraid you will have to wait until I can send someone over. You will have to take my word, unless you would like to hold me for a ransom?'

Both women laughed. A dry slightly shrill laugh, although not one even remotely funny word had been spoken.

Turning on her heel, Rosie crossed the acreage of plush carpet to the office door and almost had to edge the novice aside, to place her hand on the brass doorknob.

'I know my own way, thank you very much,' Rosie hissed as she opened the door with a flourish, almost flattening the simpering novice.

She could feel Sister Assumpta's eyes burning into her back as she made her way down the corridor to the main staircase. Rosie, who held a powerful position and moved in elevated medical and religious circles, knew that, in a direct challenge of authority, Sister Assumpta would not want to cross her. Rosie felt sure that the Reverend Mother would avoid at all costs any situation that encouraged more questions about the running of the mother and baby business.

Rosie's heart began to beat slightly faster, as she waited

for a voice to ring out behind her and order her to stop. There was nothing but silence. She let out a deep breath. She had won.

Not for the first time, she detected something malevolent and sinister, cowering in dark corners. Now, it followed her, down the long corridor. Rosie gave an involuntary shiver as she approached the stairs, feeling the hairs on the back of her neck stand up and goose pimples break out on her arms.

'Don't be ridiculous,' she whispered to herself as she hurried up the stairs. 'They can't hold us prisoner.'

Rosie opened the door to the labour room, and was immediately assailed by the smell of stale blood.

'Holy Mary,' she gasped, covering her mouth against the stench.

Across the other side of the room, Kitty lay on her back on the hard delivery bed, looking small and frail. One arm flopped down over the side, almost reaching the floor, like the broken wing of a bird. It was quickly apparent to Rosie that Kitty was in a great deal of pain.

As Kitty's head turned towards Rosie, instant tears of relief ran down her cheeks. She reached out and grabbed Rosie's hand.

'Oh God, it hurts so much,' she cried. 'I feel so sick, the pain is so bad.'

Rosie dropped her bag on the floor and dragged over to the bed a white enamel trolley that stood against the wall. Hurriedly she retrieved equipment and dressings from her bag, placing them on the top of the trolley.

'What hurts, Kitty, where? Is it down below?' Rosie said as she prepared her trolley.

Kitty nodded and put both hands on her abdomen. 'God, it is so bad, and here,' she cried, placing a hand on her chest. Rosie could see that someone had attempted to bind Kitty's breasts, one of the other girls, she supposed, but had not made a very good job of it.

'I need to examine you, Kitty, but when I am done sorting you out, I am putting you in the car and taking you home. Your time here is over.'

Rosie had thought she would drive Kitty straight to Ballymara, to Maeve Deane and her husband Liam, Kathleen's middle son and Jerry's younger brother.

Kitty sobbed loudly, almost screaming and thanking God that she was no longer alone. It was difficult to distinguish her cries of pain from those of relief. Before Kitty had entered the Abbey, she had spent time at Maeve's farmhouse, becoming very close to her and Liam. Now, as Rosie looked down at her chalk-white face, she wasn't so sure Kitty was well enough to travel even that far.

Kitty's cries were heart-wrenching, rising in a crescendo and bringing Rosie, an experienced midwife to the verge of tears herself.

'It hurts, the pain, oh God, the pain,' Kitty yelled again.

Rosie began to palpate Kitty's abdomen and did not like what she felt. It was rigid and hard, resistant to her touch. She pressed her fingers flat against Kitty's uterus and as she did so, Kitty let out a terrifying scream. It was as much as Rosie needed to know. She lifted up Kitty's knees to examine her, but it took every ounce of her willpower not to allow the disgust to register on her face.

In her twenty-five years as a midwife, she had never seen

lacerations so bad. What was worse, they looked seriously infected. However, Rosie knew that the external appearance of an infection was only part of the story. She quickly took Kitty's temperature. It was 104. Rosie was very used to dealing with girls from the tenements, who arrived at the hospital in a similar state, but in Dublin she worked in a controlled environment, with professional colleagues, doctors and midwives. She had never seen a girl in such a post-delivery state, even one who had been brought into the hospital from the country.

'Mother of God, who has been looking after you?' she asked as her own eyes now began to fill with tears. Wasn't this girl going through enough, after all that had happened to her?

'Aideen and Agnes,' Kitty sobbed, holding tightly onto Rosie's hand, as though terrified to let go, lest Rosie disappeared.

And then, as if by magic, as if summoned by angels, the two girls who had delivered Kitty's baby, and done their best to help her, slipped in quietly through the door. Rosie recognized them as the girls she had seen trying to attract her attention when she arrived.

'Thank God you are here,' said Aideen to Rosie, without the ceremony of introduction. 'I'm Aideen, I delivered baby John. The fucking midwife went away on Christmas Eve and she hasn't returned yet. She said Kitty was nothing to do with her and she wasn't coming back just to see to her. There's no baby anywhere near due for another month so we haven't had sight nor sound of her since.'

Rosie was no stranger to bad language. She had heard some of the finest ladies in Dublin use exactly the same words, and worse, when in the middle of a contraction.

'Aideen, can you help me,' she said, with an edge of desperation to her voice. 'Kitty is in a very bad way and I must stitch her before I can move her. Can you fetch me a bowl of hot soapy water from the sink, please?'

Agnes looked alarmed. 'It's not allowed,' she hissed, almost in a whisper. 'The Reverend Mother will go crazy mad, so she will, if you stitch her. She says the rips are put there by God to teach us what we have done wrong and no woman should try to rectify God's own handiwork.'

Rosie felt as if it was now her turn to swear. However, with a great deal of effort, she retained her cool, taking the Spencer Wells forceps and catgut out of the autoclaved pack she had brought from the hospital.

'She is held together by blood clots, Agnes. I cannot move her in this state. Here, can you help and get this tablet down her, and maybe some water to follow? I'm going to give her an injection, to help with the pain, but it may make her feel sick and we can do without that, on a car journey.'

Rosie could tell Agnes was the more nervous and gentle of the two. Life had been harder on Aideen, that much was obvious.

Rosie quickly drew up a vial of pethidine and within seconds had injected a large dose into Kitty's thigh. Rosie noted that Kitty was in so much pain she didn't even flinch.

'We aren't allowed to have painkillers either,' whispered Agnes, who was now in awe of this strong and defiant midwife.

'This is not God's doing, Agnes, but it is the work of the devil himself to leave a poor girl in this state. I will be no part of that,' Rosie replied.

Pouring her antiseptic wash into the bowl of warm water, which Aideen had set on the trolley, she began to swab Kitty.

It took her almost an hour to rectify the damage. Kitty had torn down into her perineum and backwards deeply into her rectum. She bled profusely, as Rosie worked to ease away the huge clots and crusts of blood, which were by now over two days old. As they reliquefied, they filled the room with a sickening metallic smell. At times, both Aideen and Agnes looked pale and nauseous but, dutifully, they held Kitty's hands and remained upright.

While Rosie worked, the girls whispered soft soothing sounds. Aideen had placed a folded rag between Kitty's teeth, just as she did when she was in labour, in fear of her moans attracting the nuns. Like dancing moths drawn to a flame, the sisters always fluttered to the sound of pain.

As Rosie worked, Agnes prayed over Kitty, who had become quiet and drowsy. The pethidine was working at last. She had injected Kitty with one of only four doses of the emergency drug she had popped into her bag as she left the hospital. As the full effect of analgesia worked its magic, Rosie wondered, would Kitty feel safe enough to let go? To relax and sleep?

'Will you girls land yourselves in trouble for being here?' Rosie asked, gently stroking Kitty's hair away from her damp and clammy brow.

Aideen replied with a hint of fear, 'If we wasn't with you, midwife, we would be fucking whipped for coming here, and kept without food for days, but the witches daren't do that because we are with you. They are scared of you, I know that because I heard one of the postulants say so, I did.'

'Yes, but I will be gone soon,' said Rosie, her voice loaded with concern. And then she had an idea. 'I will tell them, when I leave, that I am returning with the money and that when I bring it I have promised to look in on you both, to let you know how, er, Cissy is doing. That should buy you some safety.'

For a split second, Rosie had almost forgotten Kitty's secret name.

Aideen and Agnes looked at each other and smiled. Then, together, they both reached down the front of their calico skirts into their knickers and handed Rosie two warm letters.

'Would you post these for us, please, midwife?' whispered Aideen. By far, the bolder of the two, she had made the decision that Rosie could be trusted. 'You know, we aren't allowed any post in or out and have no contact with the outside world. I need to know, is me mammy coming with the money to get me out of this hell-hole soon, or do I have to escape?'

'Escape?' said Rosie. 'That sounds so desperate.'

'It is fucking desperate. Poor Agnes, she was sent straight here from an orphanage, because the fucking authorities didn't know what else to do with her. That's not fucking right.'

Rosie nodded. She still wasn't shocked. She had once overheard a politician's wife say the word 'fucking' more than three times in thirty seconds when she gave birth, more noisily than at any time before or since.

As Rosie bandaged Kitty's breasts, Agnes gently mopped Kitty's face and washed her hands with a fresh bowl of warm water, drawn from the long shallow sink. Apart from the bed and the trolley, it was the only piece of furniture in the room.

Rosie packed her bag and stowed away the letters. Then

she scribbled down her home address and the number of the hospital office on a piece of paper and handed it to Aideen.

'Here,' she whispered. 'Keep this somewhere safe and away from prying eyes. If it reaches the point where you have to escape, contact me and I will help.'

Aideen grabbed hold of Rosie's hand. 'Thank you,' she said, displaying the first sign of gentleness, and her eyes filled with tears.

Rosie watched as Aideen ripped away the surplus paper, leaving only the area on which Rosie had written, and then rolled it between her finger and thumb, over and over, until it was a tight cylinder. She tucked the almost needle-thin paper roll through the stiches in the hem of her baggy calico knickers.

Aideen grinned to Agnes. 'The bitches won't find it there, will they?' The light of hope sprang gleefully into both girls' eyes. 'We do all the laundry, so they will never find it.'

Rosie felt overwhelmed with tenderness towards both girls. Aideen might be a farm girl with little education, rough around the edges, but she had heart and humanity enough to risk angering Sister Assumpta by caring for Kitty, as best she knew how.

'If it comes to that and you do escape,' Rosie's whisper was barely audible so the girls leant in close to catch her words, 'make sure you leave my address behind, for anyone else who may need it. I have a good kitchen maid at my hospital, Besmina. She has told me a great deal about what goes on here and I want to help, if I can.'

'Besmina!' Both Aideen and Agnes looked at one another in shocked surprise.

'That's right. I think she worked in the kitchens here, before her grandmother brought her to me to give her work at the hospital. When I was a district midwife, I delivered Besmina at her grandmother's house in Dublin.'

Aideen smiled, knowingly.

'Yes, that's right, miss. She worked in the kitchens,' said Aideen slowly.

The three women now began to help Kitty to her feet. Dehydrated and with a dangerously high temperature, she was mumbling incoherently as though delirious. Rosie knew Kitty could have a febrile fit at any moment. God only knew how she would cope with that, here in this godforsaken place.

Rosie was eager to get Kitty to hospital. Out in the country, in the rural farms and on the bogs, she had seen girls develop serious infections after giving birth. By the time Rosie reached them, peritonitis had often fatally set in. She would do everything in her power to ensure that did not happen to this child.

Moving as softly as they could, Aideen and Agnes helped Kitty down the stairs. When they reached the bottom step, Agnes suddenly froze.

A ghostlike shadow upon the wall announced that the imposing form of Sister Assumpta was gliding silently towards them, the Persian silk runner absorbing the sound of her inescapable approach.

They were trapped. Motionless, they stood as if turned to stone whilst her shadow turned the corner and enveloped them.

Her mouth dry with fear and her knees turning to jelly,

Agnes clung onto Kitty's arm, holding her upright in the process.

She had felt bold, sneaking away to see the midwife, passing on the details of the birth and helping the poor girl. They had guessed by her accent, she must have come from Liverpool and that for some reason she had told no one her story. They had all guessed that Kitty held a secret.

'God knows, don't we all have our own,' Aideen had said to Agnes.

But now, with the wrath of Sister Assumpta bearing down upon them, their boldness fled.

Jeez, we are mad, thought Aideen. What had seemed like a brave idea only an hour ago now appeared reckless and foolish. They had broken every rule in the Abbey, including having spoken to Rosie and each other. Agnes felt as though she would wet herself in fear at the consequences.

Sister Assumpta stood before them, not speaking a word, staring first at Rosie and then at both girls.

'And what, may I ask, are you both doing in the main house at this time of day? Why are you not in the laundry?'

Rigid with terror, neither girl could utter a word of response. Aideen tried, but her tongue stuck to the roof of her mouth in dread.

'*Speak!*' Even the mice shook at the sound of Sister Assumpta's anger.

Neither girl could have responded even if her life had depended upon it. Agnes began to shake.

'Sister Celia!'

Sister Assumpta's voice boomed out again, although her lips appeared not to move, nor her glare to leave the girls.

However, she needn't have wasted her breath because Sister Celia almost immediately waddled into view, carrying the leather holdall Kitty had brought with her on the day she had arrived. It contained her own clothes, which had not been seen in months.

'Take these girls into my room immediately and search them, please, Sister.'

With no grace and even less kindness, Sister Celia dropped Kitty's holdall on the floor. Grabbing Aideen and Agnes each by the arm, she marched them both away down the corridor. As Kitty began to slip to the floor, unsupported, Rosie had to move swiftly, placing her arm under her shoulders and round her back.

Sister Assumpta said to Rosie, 'I told them on the day they brought this – this girl,' she almost spat out the words; she had wanted to use a very different term but she had eighty pounds owing to her, and was not going to put the payment in jeopardy, 'that many of the girls here are penitents, placed here into my care by the government. I have a job to do here, midwife, and, as I told you, I would prefer you not to speak to the girls for any reason at all.'

Rosie was not easily intimidated, and she had no intention of apologizing, but right now she just wanted to be out of the Abbey and on the road to Dublin. Stooping to pick up the holdall she shuffled Kitty towards the door.

Sensing the sister's hot breath on her neck, Rosie gave way to rising panic. When she finally managed to open the door, she took a deep breath of the chilled, rejuvenating air. She was nearly there.

'Thank you, Reverend Mother. The girls have been very

helpful. I am sure I will have messages of thanks to deliver to them, from the family, when I return with the payment. I hope to see them again.'

As she walked out, she knew that Sister Assumpta still stood in the doorway, rooted to the spot, observing her every step.

And she also knew that she would not be allowed to see Aideen and Agnes ever again.

With an effort, she laid Kitty down on the back seat of her Hillman Hunter. As she closed the car door on her and placed her holdall into the boot, she heard the sound of stifled cries. Rosie felt sick at the thought of the girls being beaten, only a few yards away, but right now she had a sick girl only forty-eight hours post-partum with a temperature of 104, lying on the back seat of her car. She prayed that her contact details were not found in the hem of Aideen's calico knickers, and quickly checked that the letters were safely in her handbag before placing it on the passenger seat beside her.

The sky was darkening rapidly as Rosie left the Abbey. When she pulled away, she was aware that her retreating car lights were being followed: from behind the twitching, heavy curtains by disapproving nuns' eyes downstairs, and by grateful waves from unknown girls through the cold, uncurtained windows of the top floor and the laundry.

As she looked across the vast lawn towards the trees, in the bright moonlight she noticed a gravestone. Rosie shuddered. Each one of those girls in the graveyard would have died terrified, screaming in agony, feeling unloved and alone. Rosie crossed herself as she pulled out of the gate and sped, as fast as the icy road would allow her, on to Dublin.

In less than ten minutes, she realized she would never make it. An abandoned bus completely blocked the road. Rosie left her car and shouted up into the driver's cab, but there was no one inside. The door was locked and footsteps leading away, lightly covered by fresh snowfall, told her that the driver and passengers had long since left.

Kitty slept fitfully on the back seat with Rosie's spare sheepskin jacket laid over her and an Aran picnic blanket rolled up under her head for a pillow. There had been no tea or cake for Kitty. Rosie knew she was weak and in danger. The Kitty she had known before the delivery had been a bright girl. Now she was without the energy even to cry. The only words she had spoken, as the car had pulled away from the Abbey, were, 'Rosie, fetch the baby, fetch John,' before sleep possessed her.

Rosie made a decision there and then. She would drive as quickly as possible – in the opposite direction, to Maeve and Liam's farmhouse on the Ballymara Road.

She would pass the doctor's house on the way and would collect some antibiotics and ask him to put up a drip that Rosie could look after whilst she nursed Kitty at Maeve's. The doctor would trust her. She could provide him with an entirely false name for Kitty and, if he pushed, she would make him aware that no further information would be forthcoming. Not even a doctor would push for information regarding a young girl, with no baby to show for her pains.

The drive to Bangornevin was tortuous. With the coming of night, the temperature had plummeted and what had earlier been the soft snow, during the day, had frozen into solid ice along the narrow country lanes. The road, which was not easy to drive on at the best of times, now felt to Rosie as unyielding as iron.

She knew the route well, but the fog and mist that had rolled down and onto the fields confused her. Every few yards or so, a cow in search of warmth loomed up from the mist in the dim yellow headlights as a ghostly spectre, causing Rosie to yelp with fright.

The moon was full, and the sky ahead appeared to go on forever, an inky-black carpet of glittering stars, interspersed with heavy clouds full of snow. Rosie gave thanks, more than once, for the ethereal, sparkling light, which reflected from the ice, transforming the road into a frosted satin ribbon, winding its way along the riverbank, leading them on.

The moon kept with her all the way, refected in the fast-flowing river beside her, watching and guiding her. Even in her gloves, Rosie's hands were near frozen and the heater struggled to make any difference whatsoever to the temperature inside the car.

On a number of bends, Rosie missed the road entirely when the car jolted frighteningly against the roadside scrub and stones. At one point, she had to get out of the car and push the tyres out of a shallow dip. By the time she was back in the driver's seat, wet and chilled to the bone, she had to scrape the ice from the inside of the windscreen before she could safely continue on her journey.

They had not passed a single car along the way. She felt gripped with terror when she realized that if anything did happen to the car, both she and Kitty would surely freeze to death before they were discovered. She was glad that Kitty was sleeping and unaware of their danger.

Rosie had no idea that since her baby boy had been born and taken away from her on Christmas morning, Kitty had lain awake, day and night, yearning for Rosie to arrive. She had barely moved her gaze from the window, watching for the car headlights. Kitty was now in the deepest sleep. With her pain controlled by the pethedine, her body had surrendered.

Although she was cold, Rosie was sweating with fear and praying out loud.

'Thank you, Lord, for bringing me here. Now, could you just take me a little further, please God.'

Rosie prayed to every saint a day was named after, to every angel whose name she could remember and to the Holy Mother. She barely stopped to draw breath as she did so. She knew that if she stopped to think about their predicament, she might lose her resolve. Rosie was tough, having seen and dealt with most things. Now, however, she was alone. Her ability to reach help was at the mercy of the elements and she had never before felt so out of control, or been so afraid.

Irish winters were harsh and the locals in Bangornevin still spoke sadly of the two brothers who had been discovered in their farmhouse, snowed in and frozen to death, in 1947, as though it had happened only yesterday.

Rosie reached over to the back seat to place her hand on Kitty's forehead. The girl appeared to be more unconscious than asleep. Despite the cold, Rosie knew, with heightened concern, that Kitty was burning up.

'Oh, God in heaven, no. Please, not peritonitis, Lord, please, no,' Rosie whispered to the heavens, putting her foot down and trying in vain to drive faster and more safely.

'God in heaven, help us,' she whispered, crossing herself,

as she followed the river round to Castlefeale. Tears of fear filled her eyes, as she began to shiver violently with the cold.

Rosie thought about her husband and their animals on the farm. Maybe he had been right. Maybe she should have listened to him. 'That would be a first if ever there was one, eh, Kitty,' she said aloud and laughed nervously. What she wouldn't give now to have her husband here, giving out to her for not listening to him.

'Ye always think ye knows best, Rosie, but ye don't, not always!' How many times had he said that to her and she had scoffed in his face, right back at him.

Talking out loud to Kitty, albeit it with a trembling voice, helped to calm her fear and made her feel less alone.

'What I wouldn't give right now for you, Kitty, to sit up on the back seat and tell me you are feeling much better. God in heaven, I would gladly give away everything I owned, if that would happen just now.'

But there was no response to her frantic gabbling. Not a sound.

She leant over the steering wheel to scrape away the ice, yet again, from the inside of her windscreen. She could see her breath before her, forming into soft grey clouds. She blew hard on the glass, hoping it would make some difference.

Never in her life had she known a night as cold as this. Never.

As she rounded the bend into Castlefeale, turning away from the river, Rosie's heart sank further. They had lost the moon.

'Well, there goes the moon, so we are on our own now, Kitty. At least it kept us from driving straight into the river, thanks be to God.'

She was talking faster as her fear mounted.

The road became dark as the mountains rose up on either side, casting their shadows, obscuring the torch of the moon that had illuminated their route, but then suddenly, as though in answer to her prayers, it slipped out from between the two mountains and illuminated the way ahead.

'Oh, thank you, Lord,' Rosie now sobbed in relief as once again she scraped furiously at the windscreen.

After what seemed like hours, they passed through Bellgarett and Rosie gave a huge sigh of relief. They were heading towards civilization, such as it was in this part of the world. As she drove past the post office she noticed that they had been spotted. Her husband would now be telephoned and told she had passed safely through. She wound down the window and waved feebly before quickly drawing her arm back inside.

'We've been clocked, Kitty,' she said. 'They will be ringing on ahead now so that they will be watching out for us in Bangornevin. By the time we arrive in Ballymara, they will be waiting for us with a smashing dinner. Won't that be grand?'

As she reached the doctor's house she pulled up sharply in front of the gates but her heart sank. The building was in darkness and the gates were firmly locked. Shaking her head, she quickly slipped back behind the wheel and carried on towards Bangornevin, heading through to Ballymara.

Rosie wondered what reason Maeve and Julia would have given to Mrs Doyle, the nosiest postmistress in all of Ireland, for this visit on the coldest night of the year. She told herself that no one would notice Kitty, lying on the back seat. They would think something was up at the farmhouse for Rosie to be so mad as to drive on a night like this.

'A good meal in your insides is what we need next, eh, Kitty. Sure, we must be the only people in all of Ireland not indoors.'

Rosie could not hear a sound from the back seat. Not even the faintest breathing.

But her fear began to subside as she felt the watching eyes of the home villages, following them on their way. At last, they were safe. No harm would come to them now. The hardest part of Rosie's journey was yet to come: the mile and a half down the bumpy terrain of the Ballymara Road. Although she was used to being in charge during difficult, even life-threatening situations, she felt a huge relief to see Maeve and her sister-in-law Julia running out to meet them when she finally drew up outside the farmhouse.

Through the doorway, a warm light radiated onto the road. She could see the welcoming flames of the peat fire licking up the chimney; she could smell the freshly baked bread wafting towards her. Rosie felt as though she had driven into heaven.

The skies were darker over Ballymara and as Rosie opened the back door of the Hillman Hunter, the flakes began to fall thick and heavy.

'God in heaven,' said Maeve as she saw Kitty asleep on the back seat. 'Julia, get Liam out here now.'

Within seconds, Liam was at her side and between them they slipped Kitty out through the car door. Liam carried her into their kitchen and laid her down on the padded settle in front of the fire.

'She hardly looks like the same girl we dropped off at the Abbey,' he said, with more than a hint of anger in his voice.

'She looks desperate, Rosie,' said Maeve.

'Well now, I'll not hide the truth from you in your own home. It is desperate,' said Rosie. 'I think she may be developing an infection. I called into the doctor's house when I passed through Bangornevin, but there were no lights on.'

'They have gone back to her mother's house in Liverpool for Christmas,' said Maeve. 'They won't be back until after the new year. And even if they were there, no one can know about this. What in God's name do we do?'

'Well, right now I want to give her a proper clean-up and check the stitches I rushed to put in at the Abbey. Have you any chicken stock to get down her, Maeve? It's the next best thing to penicillin. The Abbey girls told me the poor kid has lived off next to nothing for months. It's a wonder she had the strength to give birth to her baby at all. We need to pray hard, ladies. This child is as sick as sick can be. Frankly, if she was on one of my wards I wouldn't give much for her chances, never mind out here in the country without a doctor or a hospital for miles.'

Julia crossed herself. 'I need to drive to the post office and telephone Kathleen in Liverpool so that she can break the news to Maura and Tommy.'

'No,' Rosie said sharply. 'There is nothing they can do. They couldn't even travel here in this weather. Let's leave it for a day. I need a chance to nurse her back to health, if I can.'

'Well, ye don't need to do that alone, Rosie. Mrs McGuffey has the cure for this. Liam, Liam!' Julia shouted, rushing through the kitchen to the back porch, where she knew Liam would be. 'Can ye get the van out and get to the McGuffeys' in Gisala?'

'Aye, I can do me best,' said Liam.

Within minutes, they saw the van lights disappearing slowly along Rosie's fresh tracks in the snow, up the Ballymara Road.

Maeve, who was forty and childless, was filled with sadness at Kitty's return to the farmhouse, alone, without her baby. Maeve would have loved to have adopted Kitty's child, but Liam wouldn't hear of it.

'We still have time for our own yet,' he had whispered to her in the dark when they were lying in bed. Maeve had used every trick in the book known to woman. If she couldn't persuade Liam to let them adopt the baby, when he had a belly full of Guinness in the moments just after sex and before sleep, she knew she never would.

Julia came in to set down a bowl of hot water and a pile of clean, warm towels.

Rosie said, 'God, it is better facilities here than it is in the Abbey, I can tell ye, Maeve.'

Kitty would need to be washed down. Both Maeve and Julia had noticed a smell of stale blood as she entered the warm farmhouse.

'What was the baby?' Maeve whispered to Rosie as she ladled soup out of the pot into mugs. Maeve was sensitive to the fact that even though Kitty was half unconscious, she might be able to hear.

'The girls from the Abbey told me it was a boy. I spoke to the one who was there, Aideen, her name was. She said it was an awful time, but, she swore, God held her hands as she delivered him. She told me he was beautiful, with dark hair and bright blue eyes. Kitty named him John, although, God knows, his adoptive parents will already have altered that.'

Maeve handed Rosie the mug of soup. 'Did she have any time with him?'

'Not long. She was forbidden from leaving the labour room. Apparently the nuns were all of a dither that a beautiful baby boy had been born at the Abbey on Christmas morning, it being a full moon and all. One of the sisters said she had seen an angel rise over the Abbey, when the boy was being born and it sent them all quite senseless. The Reverend Mother had the boy taken straight to the nursery and out of sight at first light, so Kitty had only a couple of hours with him. The girls said she didn't put him down from the moment he was born at about four o'clock until the Reverend Mother had him taken away.

'She was distraught, the girls said. She has been asking for him constantly since he was taken. God knows, the girls who helped were relieved to see me. The chatty one, Aideen, thought Kitty was killing herself with the grief and looking at her now, she may have been right. Her chances of making it to this time tomorrow aren't great, I can tell you.'

'Aye, but ye didn't know about Mrs McGuffey, Rosie,' said Maeve. 'We don't lose many women around here, once they have been given a few doses of Mrs McGuffey's home brew.'

'For goodness' sake, Maeve, I'm a trained midwife and I'm struggling. How can Mrs McGuffey know what to bloody do?'

Rosie was never one to let her professional demeanour slip. A look of surprise crossed her face as she realized she had sworn for the first time in her life. Despite the seriousness of the situation, she found herself laughing. She was only too well aware that in every country home there existed a potion for every ailment known to man.

'I'm sorry, Maeve, it's just that out here in the country, between you, every house has it covered from impotency to impetigo. God alone knows what the doctor does.'

As Rosie and Annie began tenderly to undress Kitty, Rosie didn't notice a tear slide down Maeve's cheek.

The perfect loving wife, the kindest friend and neighbour, Maeve now felt desperately sad. She had never asked her husband, Liam, for anything. She had never needed to but, now, although Liam was a good and loving husband, for the first time in her marriage she felt angry.

In the only thing she really needed from Liam to ease her deep sadness and make her happy, he had refused her. She could have brought up Kitty's baby as her own. They would have found a way and then Kitty could have been an auntie to the baby. Sure, how many families did they all know of in Ireland and Liverpool where that happened? There was a family on every street. It was the widely accepted thing to do. Why couldn't Liam do it too?

'I couldn't love another man's child, Maeve, so I couldn't,' he had pleaded. 'If it isn't ours, how can it be our baby?'

'Because people can and do,' Maeve had replied. 'Ye love that mangy dog that goes everywhere with ye as if it were ye son. Am I wrong? Am I?'

Liam had stormed out of the room. He did indeed love his dog and Maeve's question was a fair one, but he just couldn't answer it.

'Maeve, is that you?'

Kitty had woken as Rosie and Julia began to wash her down, making soothing noises as they did so. Maeve already had nightclothes warming for Kitty by the fire. She had hung them there as soon as she heard Kitty was coming.

Rosie was removing Kitty's blood-soaked knickers and they were both trying to sit her on the chamber pot, which Liam had tactfully placed on the floor before he left for Gisala. Maeve held both Kitty's hands to steady her as she wobbled to one side. Kitty looked as though she would break if she fell off the pot.

'Aye, Kitty. You are back in Ballymara and we are going to look after you here. You will be right soon enough and back in Liverpool before you know it.'

Kitty wasn't listening to what Maeve said. She stared straight into her eyes.

'I have to find him. I have to find my baby.'

Rosie said, 'Kitty, we need you to concentrate on getting yourself better. We will talk about the baby later. Let's just think about you. Here, swallow this.' Maeve held up to her lips a mug of oversweet tea with aspirin dissolved and concealed in the thick, brown liquid.

While Maeve held Kitty upright on the pot, Rosie poured the jug of soapy water over her wounds to clean her stitches. Then, placing a towel under and across her, they lifted her onto the huge padded settle and laid her down on a feather eiderdown covered with towels.

Rosie whispered to Maeve, 'I have to return tomorrow with the rest of the money. Can you believe it? The sisters are charging us to half kill the child. The money from the Americans to buy the baby isn't enough.'

'That cannot be right,' Maeve replied.

'It isn't,' said Rosie. 'I've already made enquiries but you know the Church, all powerful, more powerful than the government, even. It is all a cosy agreement if you ask me. Everyone knows what is happening but it is all kept secret. They have no such institutions for the boys, mind.'

Rosie felt Kitty's pulse; it was weak and thready. Her skin was sallow and hot, her abdomen was distended and hard, and a foul-smelling pus oozed from her perineum. Rosie crossed herself. The pus was as nothing, compared to what might be developing internally.

Rosie sat down on the end of the settle with a sigh.

'Go to bed, Maeve,' she said. 'I will sit with her for the night. She is in my charge. I will need your help in the morning, but for now, you grab what's left of your sleep.'

'I will not,' said Maeve. 'We will have a drink and a ciggie here and wait and see what Liam fetches back from Gisala.'

Maeve moved over to the press and poured two large glasses of whiskey. She winked at Rosie and said, 'Get this down ye. It's amazing how much better ye will feel after and, if ye don't, I'll fetch the bottle.'

Maeve took her rosaries out of her apron pocket, kissed them and wrapped them around Kitty's unresisting little fingers.

It seemed as though they had been sitting for only an hour or so when they heard the sound of the van return. Julia bustled into the room with Liam.

'Well, that was difficult, I can tell ye. Maeve, I had to say it was for ye sister. Thank God she had that little girl last week and ye must remember to tell her what I said. 'Tis a tangled web we are weaving here all right.'

'Well, everyone this side of Bellgarett knows Rosie is here,' said Maeve, 'so it fits.'

Rosie wasn't listening; she was busy removing the straw stopper from the green bottle that Liam had handed her.

'Jesus, what is in this? It smells like pee,' she said, pulling her nose away sharply.

Julia shrugged. 'Aye, well, likely it has a bit in there, but it's mainly plants and things, usually. Do ye have anything better?'

'It won't be human pee,' said Maeve helpfully. 'Most likely from their goat and, anyway, it'll be whatever is mixed with it that does all the good. Stop yer complaining now and get it down her.'

'That goat wins the show at Castlefeale every year, so it does,' said Julia. 'There's so many put out around here by it, I'm surprised someone hasn't slit its throat. It's well known the McGuffeys make a fortune, so they do, from the magic of its medicine.'

Lifting Kitty's head, they managed to pour half of the bottle down her, followed by some soup, painstakingly fed to her by Julia, one teaspoon at a time.

Julia and Maeve retired to bed, more comforted to have seen Kitty settled.

'Everything you will need is in the press,' Maeve whispered, giving Rosie a hug. 'She looks so much better already. The McGuffeys' medicine has done the trick.'

Before Rosie could respond, Maeve left the room, knowing she would be required in the morning to help with the more practical things like stacking the fire, preparing food and persuading Rosie to catch some sleep.

Rosie wrung out a cloth in the fresh warm water Julia had left by her side and began wiping down Kitty's arms with long strokes, in an attempt to bring her blood to the surface and cool her down. Rosie was desperate to take on the high temperature and conquer it. She was experienced enough to know Kitty was on the way down, not the way up.

It would be a long night.

Rosie woke to the sound of a loud knock at the front door.

It was light, the cock was crowing furiously, and through the window she could see that although the sky was loaded with snow, for now at least, it appeared to have ceased falling.

'Morning, Aengus,' she whispered, as she recognized one of the young McMahons from the farm next door standing on the step.

'Morning, Rosie. John asked me to knock and check everything was good, what with your car arriving so late and with the lights having been on all night.'

'I'm fine, Aengus, tell John thank you, would you, but we are all good in here.'

Rosie saw Aengus gazing through the doorway towards the settle, where Kitty was sleeping. He looked straight at Rosie and, in that unguarded moment, his eyes asked multiple questions.

'Ye may be fine, but, sure, the car is not.' The words Aengus spoke did not reflect his thoughts in any way. Rosie saw that her car was half buried by snow.

'Don't worry, it will be gone soon. Tell Liam I will clear it now,' Aengus said, then lifted his cap and turned to walk back towards the McMahon farm at the end of the Ballymara Road.

Rosie moved back inside and found Maeve in the kitchen.

'Sure, I expected that,' she said, nodding towards the door. 'I'm surprised there was no one knocking on last night. If I had seen a car arrive at the McMahons' I would have been out there like a shot to see if all was well.'

Rosie smiled. The farmers in Roscommon liked to think they were a little more sophisticated than those in Mayo, but really it was just the same.

'Aye, I suppose a car is a rare sight on the Ballymara Road,' she said.

'Everyone in the village will know within hours that Kitty is back with us,' said Maeve. 'There will be plenty knocking on soon enough, people wondering why we have a visitor. How is she? Is her temperature down? We need to move her into the bedroom to keep her from prying eyes.' Maeve was talking as fast as her brain was working.

'She has stopped burning and fretting, and seems to be sleeping more peacefully now.

'But if people know it is Kitty, it will be obvious she has been in Ireland all along, else how would she have made it here last night in this weather? I will say she has been helping me out in Dublin, training for something or other, on a secretarial course maybe, and staying with family for Christmas, and that she has taken ill on her way to visit us. Will that do now?'

'It is as good as anything, aye, and no one will be checking up on you, will they, you being so grand and important an' all.' Maeve winked at Rosie as, between them, both women lifted Kitty from the settle and carried her into the bedroom where Maeve had lit a fire.

'Well, the sisters can whistle for their money because I will be driving nowhere today. Good job I rang home before I left for the Abbey to let them know what I was doing or my poor husband would have a search party out on the road by now.'

As Rosie pulled up the covers, Kitty opened her eyes and, for a moment, looked confused as she took in her surroundings.

'Have ye got the baby, Maeve?' she whispered.

Maeve threw Rosie a troubled look. 'I'm off to get ye some tea, miss,' she said, squeezed Kitty's hand and left the room.

Rosie sat on the edge of Kitty's bed. 'Well, ye gave us all quite a scare,' she said, picking up Kitty's thin, trembling hand.

Kitty looked at the face of the speaker, staring her in the eye. She knew this woman, she was sure, but she just couldn't remember.

'Do ye have the baby?' she asked again.

'No, Kitty, I don't. The baby has been adopted by an American family. You signed an agreement, do ye remember?'

Kitty turned her head towards the window and saw Aengus, clearing the snow from Rosie's car.

'Aengus,' she whispered. She remembered him. Maybe he would know where her baby was.

Kitty's room became a hive of activity: Maeve fed her, Rosie washed her, and Julia acted as handmaiden, changing her bottom sheet, bringing fresh water and putting her in a clean, warm nightdress. They all made soothing noises, stroked her hair and threw each other worried glances.

'A few more days and ye will be up and about,' said Maeve.

'We will have you as right as rain in no time at all,' said Rosie.

'With Maeve's cooking, ye will be giving us a dance in a week,' said Julia.

They were almost talking to themselves because Kitty wasn't there. They could see the thoughts flitting across her brain, the questions and the confusion, as she looked at them, unknowing, through narrowed eyes, her brow furrowed. And then she spoke.

'Where's my baby? Do ye have my baby?' Once she found those words, she said them again and again.

No one spoke. There was no answer.

'I think Jacko the mule must know ye are here, Kitty, he hasn't stopped braying. He's hanging around the back, waiting for ye, I reckon,' said Maeve, remembering how much Kitty had loved riding on Jacko.

But Kitty made no sign of recognition. She closed her eyes and laid her head back on the pillow, once more overcome by exhaustion. She tried to lift her hand to tap on the window to attract Aengus's attention.

'Aengus,' she whispered.

Instinctively, he stopped shovelling snow and looked towards her. He could not see Kitty through the net curtains, but he rightly guessed she was there, on the other side. In a wild gesture of hope, he smiled and lifted his hand. He was rewarded when, after just a second, he saw her own hand press the curtain flat against the glass, before it slipped down and the curtain gently swung back into place.

The three women retreated and left Kitty to sleep.

Kitty turned her head from the window and watched the bedroom door close, gently.

'Sleep is mother nature's healer,' said Maeve.

Julia placed the bacon rashers on the griddle and began preparing them all some much needed breakfast.

'I'm worried about her delirium,' said Rosie. 'Her temperature is down but I still must find some antibiotics, somewhere, this morning. Whatever was in that potion has worked a miracle, so it has. It's more her state of mind that concerns me now. She doesn't seem to understand what is going on.'

'She understands she has had a baby,' said Julia. 'Looks to me like she's on the edge of madness. I saw it once with a woman, after a stillborn. Hanged herself in the barn, she did.'

'Jeez, Julia, shush,' said Maeve. 'The girl has had a loss and been very ill. She will be well soon enough. I'd say a week from now, she will be a different girl altogether. She's young, she will bounce back in no time. Liam is ready to run ye to the doctor in Castlefeale, for whatever it is ye want, Rosie, but eat first. It could take a while on these roads.'

From the familiar bed she had slept in while on holiday at the farmhouse, Kitty could hear the muffled voices in the kitchen, just as she had heard them, only months earlier, when they had decided what to do in order to contain her secret. Nellie had been with her then, in the bed on the opposite side of the room.

'Nellie,' she whispered. Was that Nellie sitting on the bed? It was; there was no mistaking Nellie's red hair. 'Nellie,' she whispered again as she reached out her hand, but Nellie had gone.

She was alone again, or so she thought, but not for long.

Turning slowly onto her side with her face towards the window, she saw Aengus digging the snow away from Rosie's car. Kitty remembered their meeting at the harvest, their flirting and her happiness. Her eyes filled with tears. She had thought she would never see him again but she had remembered his name.

'Aengus,' she whispered. 'Aengus.'

She raised her hand again and her heart filled with joy at the sight of his smiling face.

He will know, he will tell me, he will know where my baby is, she thought. But as she saw him walk away, back to the McMahon farm, Kitty felt anxious.

'Don't go,' she croaked through her dry lips. 'Aengus.'

But he had gone. The sound of his feet crunching through the snow faded as the distance grew between them.

Kitty decided to follow him and tried to put her feet on the floor. Maybe he had left to fetch her baby, to bring him to her. That must be it. She would go with him, she must.

'Aengus,' she rasped again, setting her feet on the rag rug at the side of the bed. She felt dizzy and it was difficult to move, but then they came. They filled the room and they knew where her baby was.

There was her mammy, Maura, and her da, Tommy, and Nellie and Aengus were with them, and they were leading her away from the bed and outside to her baby. They knew where he was and she laughed. They were taking her to her beautiful baby boy, to her little prince, her baby John.

They held her hand, helped her across the bedroom floor and swept her down the corridor towards the dairy door. As it opened, the dazzling white glare from the first rays of sunlight reflecting up from the snow almost blinded her and the blast of icy air took her breath clean away, but they were leading her, urging her on. She laid her bare foot on the glistening snow and laughed but, as she looked down, a look of puzzlement crossed her face as drops of blood were falling at her feet, piercing the snow as they dripped. Deep, hot, penetrating red against the icy brilliant white.

Someone held out a hand. It was no longer Maura supporting her, but a man she didn't know, and she smiled at him as the others circled round her, calling her name.

'Mammy,' she whispered, looking for Maura. 'Mammy, I have to find my baby.' She held her face up to the watery sunlight reflected in the glistening snow, so pure and white and cold.

'Do ye know where my baby is?' she asked the man as he took her hands and led her into the deep snow towards the river's edge. And there, he pushed her down into the cold rushing water, and held her still. The last thing Kitty saw was a lady with long red hair and a beautiful smile, who looked just like Nellie, holding out her arms.

'Did ye know Kitty was back?' Aengus asked his aunt and uncle as they sat down to bacon and tatties from the range, before they began their day's work.

'No, I did not. Well, I never, I had no notion,' said his aunt.

'Well then, we will be seeing a lot more of ye around here

seeing as ye have such a soft spot for the girl,' said his uncle, laughing.

'I think she may be poorly now,' said Aengus. 'She was asleep on the settle and, later, I saw her wave from the bedroom.'

''Tis unusual for anyone to be ill when it snows,' said his aunt. 'The snow freezes all the sickness solid, so it does, inside and out. There is no cure for any ailment as good as the snow.'

Later that morning, when Aengus was leading the cows back out and taking feed to the pigs, he looked down from the top of the hill. Below him he could see Liam and Rosie, Julia and Maeve, running along the bank of the Moorhaun River, at the point where it passed from their own land onto the McMahons' farm. He saw his uncle run out of the barn and he heard Maeve scream.

And then he saw Kitty in her blue floral nightdress, floating on the fast river, and Maeve and Liam, running to catch her.

He looked to the top of the Ballymara Road, at the point where the road, the river and the village met and, for a brief moment, his eye was caught by a very large black car, gliding out of the churchyard and turning right, across the top of the Ballymara Road, away from Bangornevin and on towards Galway, the heavy wheels cutting through the snow with ease.

'Who the feck?' he whispered under his breath. As he was on his way down the hill, he wondered who was the red-haired woman, kneeling at the side of the riverbank next to Kitty.

Before he reached the bottom of the hill, she was gone and now, all he could see through his tears was Liam, staggering across the white, river-worn pebbles, carrying Kitty, dripping wet and limbs hanging lifelessly, like a broken rag doll.

Chapter Four

WHEN HE LEARNT that he was to be sent to Liverpool to assume responsibility for the parish of St Mary's, Anthony Lamb had insisted that his sister, Harriet, accompany him. He knew he would need all the help he could find, in a parish where the priest and a respected parishioner had been murdered within weeks of each other.

His wish had been granted. En route he had broken his journey in Dublin to collect Harriet, as well as to help her shut up the house, which had been their childhood home and where Harriet, the remaining spinster of the family, had been living alone.

Although she was only thirty-five years old, Anthony was aware she had sacrificed much of her own life, caring for both their elderly parents until their deaths, and he felt an overpowering obligation to protect her.

'Isn't life funny, Anthony? If Mammy and Daddy were still alive, I would still be in Black Rock, helping to run the house. Daddy just wouldn't countenance giving up the surgery to retire. God knows, he loved all his patients.'

Her parents' deaths had not been a great shock, to Harriet or to any of her eight siblings. Both had lived to a ripe old age and her father had still practised as a family doctor almost up to the day he died aged eighty-five.

Harriet, having been the youngest of nine, appeared to have missed out, as each of her brothers and sisters had carved out their paths in countries and towns too far away from Dublin to be any help when it was needed. Surprisingly, when trouble arose at home, in the places where her sisters lived the postal service often seemed to be struggling to survive. The postmen were always on strike in Watford, Luton, London, Chicago and New York, all at the same time, or so it had seemed.

Harriet occasionally resented them all, every last one of them, apart from her beloved Anthony, and then felt tormented with guilt. Her life had been given over to caring for her parents and she had longed to break free. To move away from Dublin and experience some excitement of her own, if only for a short while.

'It is not so much funny, as the way God planned it, Harriet,' Anthony said gently, smiling at his sister. He sensed she was a Catholic out of duty, not commitment. Harriet smiled back. Her lack of true belief was the guilty secret she would always carry.

Pressing her face up against the cab window as they headed up towards the four streets, she changed the subject. 'Gosh, Anthony, would you look at those shops.'

Anthony had asked the cab driver to take them on a short tour around the city of Liverpool before they arrived at the Priory. It had given him huge pleasure to see the look on Harriet's face as they drove past Lewis's and down Church Street.

'The housekeeper's name is Annie O'Prey. I have already written to her,' Harriet said as she settled back again on the cab seat. 'She said she would have a hot supper ready for us when we arrive and that Sister Evangelista would be waiting for us. Then tomorrow, it's down to work. Sister Evangelista did say we would be rather thrown in at the deep end.'

Father Anthony sighed. He had hoped to begin his time on the four streets on a more positive note, but he was at a loss to find a positive in a double murder. The world was changing fast and holding a community together in England was difficult at the best of times.

As they drew nearer, Harriet became entranced by the docks. When the klaxon sounded, the cranes, which loomed like spectres, ceased to swing and men began to appear at the top of the steps, hurrying home. Each one looked directly at the cab and lifted a hand in greeting as they looked to see who was entering their domain. Harriet felt slightly self-conscious, but Anthony smiled and waved from the window with a smile for each work-weary face they passed. A car on the four streets was an event, unless it was a police car.

As they pulled into the Priory drive, Harriet's heart sank. It wasn't because of the rows of back-to-back houses, the towering, smoking chimneys and the all-too-apparent poverty of the neighbourhood; none of that bothered Harriet in the slightest. Anthony had prepared her well and she knew what to expect. What troubled her was the eerie Victorian tombstones peering at them over the Priory wall out of the darkening mist, and the knowledge that Father James had met his ghastly end just yards from the Priory front door, where the cab now paused. She looked over the graves, down towards the river, and cold shivers ran down her spine.

The Priory door flew open. Sister Evangelista, who filled the brightly lit doorway with Annie O'Prey hovering behind her, sang out in greeting, 'Ah, thanks be to God, ye have arrived at last. Come away in, now.'

After an exchange of introductions and greetings, there was a bustle in the driveway while they tripped over one another, each trying to ease the other's burden and carry the largest number of bags indoors.

The cab had long since disappeared.

'I'll be going now, queen, if that's all right,' the cab driver had said to Harriet, taking the money from her gloved hand. 'It's a bit creepy round here, like, since the murders and I'm a bit of a wimp. I'm not one of youse Catholics.'

Father Anthony, who had carried a trunk indoors, could be heard struggling up the stairs to a concert of instructions from Sister Evangelista and Annie O'Prey. Harriet stood with the remaining bags, waiting for him to return and take her own trunk, which was too heavy for her to lift.

She looked up at the red-brick building covered in lichen and ivy, at the tall sash windows on the top floor and the even taller chimneys. She counted eight, soot-blackened doubles and she couldn't even see over the other side of the roof. She had yet to set a foot indoors, but her heart was already yearning for their white-rendered, sea-facing, welcoming home close to Dublin.

Harriet shivered. The snow-covered ground had frozen. She could feel the mist penetrating her woollen coat as it drifted over the gravestones and onto the Priory lawn, lying at her feet and rolling out a carpet of welcome, all the way to the front door.

Father Anthony's voice boomed out into the damp air.

'I'm sorry, Sister, I think that maybe 'tis a painting now on the floor as I cannot see round this corner on the stairs.'

Harriet smiled. Anthony had never been very practical, always bookish.

'Whaaa!'

Harriet screamed sharply as, apparently from nowhere, a frozen little hand grabbed her cuff. It was the iciness of the fingers that shocked her as much as the unexpected company.

'Sorry, miss, sorry, shh, please don't scream, me da will kill me if I make a nuisance of meself.'

Little Paddy was standing next to Harriet with Scamp at his side.

'Oh, my Lord, you scared me half witless,' said Harriet.

Laughing out loud at the sight before her, her laughter vanished when she saw how cold the poor boy looked. Into the light stepped another young boy, who was better dressed.

The one who had seized her cuff spoke first.

'We came to say hello, miss. Are you moving in today? My mam says you have come from Dublin to live here and you must be relieved to be safe at last. Is that true?'

Harriet instantly warmed to him. How many youngsters would go out of their way to say hello? she thought to herself. Most children were shy, especially boys.

Little Paddy continued, 'Are ye going to stay for long? They sent a priest already to replace Father James, but he spent just the one night in the Priory. He said the place needed to be burnt down and that it was unholy. Me mammy said he was really just scared.'

Harriet was thoughtful. It occurred to her that the dog looked better fed than Little Paddy, not realizing that her own chicken supper was already in the dog's stomach.

Harriet could hear the clumping of Anthony's feet on the hallway stairs.

'Well, I will be too exhausted to travel back tomorrow, so I will be here for at least two nights, that's for sure, and if I know my brother he won't be leaving until there have been definite improvements.'

'Goodness me, who have you there?' asked Anthony as he stepped out onto the driveway.

Sister Evangelista bustled to his side. 'Heavens above,' she exclaimed. 'You will get yourself frozen standing out here and what are you two doing here?'

Harriet wanted to hear more from the boys, to include them in the conversation, but was amazed to discover that they had vanished. Where they and Scamp had stood only seconds before was now empty space and it was as if they had never been.

Less than an hour later, they were all gathered round the fire in the study, chatting to Sister Evangelista after enjoying Annie O'Prey's shepherd's pie and sponge cake. Harriet sat back in her chair, fighting to keep her eyelids open, and smiled sleepily as the conversation buzzed around her.

'That was a lovely supper, Mrs O'Prey,' Harriet had said. 'I have never had cake as good as that anywhere before in my life.'

Annie O'Prey beamed from ear to ear. She liked Harriet instantly.

When Harriet smiled, Annie knew at once that the four streets were going to be lucky with her. She could feel it in her bones and see it in Harriet's eyes.

As the new father and his sister ate upstairs, Annie cleared away the pans in the basement kitchen, while chatting to her dead friend, Molly, whose bloodstained reflection gazed back at her through the kitchen window from the deep, dark night.

'Well, Molly, I can see as clear as the nose on your face they are just grand. The father and his sister, they is just what we need around here now. Yer man, the father, he is nothing like Father James, nicer altogether, if ye ask me, and his sister, well, she knows a good cake when she tastes it. I could always bake a better sponge than you, Molly, and that's a fact.' Annie turned the tap on full and filled the bowl with fresh water.

'But, you know, there are enough families on the docks could do with a bit of her kindness, that's for sure. I'll just finish this pan, Molly, and I'll make us a cuppa.'

Molly had been Annie's closest friend in life. Annie hadn't told anyone, but she knew that, even in death, nothing had altered.

Upstairs, Sister Evangelista spoke in hushed tones as she related the events that had rocked the congregation and the community to its core. While Annie conversed with Molly in the kitchen, in the study Sister Evangelista recounted the details of Molly's violent death.

Suddenly there was a loud knock on the door. They heard

the quiet voice of Annie O'Prey and the louder one of another woman, full of anxiety.

'I had better see who that is, Father,' said Sister Evangelista.

The study door burst open. Harriet was lost for words as Annie O'Prey appeared before her, in an obvious state of distress. For the second time that night, Harriet came face to face with Little Paddy, now standing at his mother's side. Both were in tears as, for the first time in her life, Peggy struggled to speak.

Maura knew she was in hell.

Leaning against the bar of the Anchor, she held the phone out to Kathleen and watched the smile on the other woman's face slowly fade as, on the other end of the line, Rosie told Kathleen the news.

Kitty was dead.

'Kitty is dead, Maura. Kitty is dead.'

With no preamble, Kathleen had said it, just like that. And in just the three seconds it took her to tell Maura that her beautiful, precious and beloved daughter had gone, before Maura's very eyes Kathleen was transformed from the upright, proud and bonny almost sixty-year-old she was to a woman who looked nearer eighty.

Maura heard the screams. She thought they came from Kathleen but then realized they were her own.

'Carol, get out here and help me quickly,' Bill called to his wife and, together, they put their arms round Maura and led her to a chair.

'Sorry for your troubles. Sorry for your troubles. Sorry for your troubles,' Carol and Bill repeated, over and over.

Kathleen pushed a glass of port into Maura's hand, but it was too late. Maura stumbled and as she hit the sawdust-covered floorboards she kept on going, plummeting all the way down, deep into her own living hell.

Tommy carefully guided a pallet of jute across Huskisson dock and took the ropes, whilst Jerry lit up a quick fag. The light was fading and they were minutes from the klaxon ushering them home.

'Oi, Stanley Matthews, get yer corner quick,' shouted Tommy to Jerry as the pallet swung round.

Jerry ducked and then, with the grace of a leopard, sprang back up to take his rope and helped to ease the pallet down. Holding his thumb up to the crane driver and moving his head from side to side, he frantically blinked away the smoke from the smouldering ciggie that dangled from his bottom lip. There was no man alive who could light up as fast as a docker.

'What's Bill's lad doing, Tommy?' asked Jerry. Throwing Tommy his tobacco tin for him to make a quick roll-up, Jerry unhooked the ropes and the pallet rested safely on the cobbles.

'What d'you mean?' asked Tommy. With a quizzical frown, he let the rope and hook swing back to the crane, then followed Jerry's gaze.

They could see Billy speaking to a policeman in the hut positioned halfway down the dockers' steps. The officer waved Billy on as he raised his helmet and rubbed his brow, scanning the dockside.

''Tis bad news,' said Jerry.

He watched as little Billy clambered over a wall of stacked jute and ran up to men who were working. He was pulling on their jackets and seemed to be asking questions. He was shouting, agitated.

'Aye, 'tis that to be sure. I've never seen that kid run before. I wonder what it can be,' said Tommy thoughtfully.

He took a long drag on his ciggie and lifted his cap to wipe the sweat from his head with his sleeve and, as he did so, he noticed a gang of men point towards them both. Tommy instantly knew not only that little Billy was running towards him, but that he carried the worst news.

Tommy, overcome with a desire to turn and run himself, knew that he would never forget these last seconds as little Billy covered the ground across the dock. He sensed that nothing would ever be the same again.

'Stop him, would ye, Jer,' said Tommy, a note of desperation in his voice.

With a furrowed brow, Jerry turned to Tommy, but it was too late. Little Billy was within hearing distance and he was shouting as loud as he possibly could. 'Tommy, Tommy, ye have to come to the pub, me da says to tell ye 'tis bad news. Maura needs ye, Tommy, 'tis Kitty, your Kitty, she's dead.'

'Tommy is on his way. Tommy is on his way. Tommy is on his way.'

Since there were no words of comfort that had any meaning or could even begin to make sense, Kathleen and Bill continued to reassure Maura with the promise of Tommy's imminent arrival, in an attempt to penetrate her despair. As though Tommy's presence would alter anything.

Tommy was the last person Maura wanted to see. If Maura had known that there was a choice – either your husband hangs or your daughter lives – Tommy would have hanged.

In the blackest days following the news of Kitty's death, Maura could not look at Tommy without wishing he was dead. She hated him. He had killed the priest and, for that, they had paid the unthinkable price.

Tommy couldn't help Maura. As far as he was concerned, the root of all the evil in their lives was Maura's vanity and her desperation to be better than everyone else they knew.

'Why else would she be so pally with the priest?' he said to Kathleen as she tried to comfort him through his anger. 'I always knew what her game was: she wanted one of our lads in the seminary, to be a priest.

''Twas not good enough, now, that a fucking priest was helping himself to our daughter in me own house. She wanted to send more of our kids their way. All Maura has ever prayed for was a son for a priest and a daughter for a nun.'

Kathleen made soothing noises, but even she was shaken by the rift between Tommy and Maura at a time when they needed each other the most.

Day after day the house filled with people calling to pay their respects.

Maura sat and stared.

Tommy was not allowed time off from the docks, for which Maura was glad.

Night after night, Kathleen tried to help.

'Away to bed, Maura, 'tis late. The kids are all sleeping now, and so must ye.'

Maura did not sleep in a bed for weeks on end. She could not engage in any activity that resembled normality.

Switching off the lights and preparing for bed, slipping in between the sheets: that was normal. Normal was what other people did. People untouched by evil.

Maura spent her nights sitting in the chair next to the range, staring at the fire. In those hours when she was alone, she relived her days with Kitty. The first time she had set eyes on her first-born's face. Kitty's first day at school, her funny sayings, the way her hair smelt when she slipped her arms around her mother's neck for her night-time kiss. Night after night, in the hours before dawn when sleep finally claimed her, Maura dipped in and out of Kitty's fifteen years, comforting herself with recent memories as well as old ones, which she forced out of the darkest corner of her mind. As Maura succumbed to sleep, her last vision was that of Kitty, standing before her in front of the range where she used to dress on winter mornings: dripping wet, cold and crying for her mammy.

Exhausted, Tommy slept on top of the covers, fully clothed. Each time he closed his eyes, he prayed into the darkness, 'Please don't let me wake.'

He regarded his children as a curse and he hated them. They were compelling him to carry on, to provide food for the table and a roof over their heads.

They did that to him, just because they were there. It was the obligation to feed his children which drove him from his bed and down to the docks. Every morning he had to wake and know his Kitty was gone. Without Maura, who was mad somewhere within a living hell, he had to cope alone. He hated his family for forcing him to survive. He hated everyone, even the neighbours who left meals warming on the range for him, because their children were still alive.

Day after day could pass without either Maura or Tommy speaking a single word, either to each other or barely to anyone else. Once Kathleen had been able to persuade Maura to sleep in her own bed, for weeks Maura was hardly able to get up again or put her feet on the floor to face the day. Many mornings, she didn't even try.

She lay in her bed, facing the wall, untouched and unaffected by the needs of her family. She was deaf to the cries of her baby, impervious to the sound of Tommy's voice, oblivious to her own basic need for food or drink.

Those were the days when neighbours let themselves into the house, unasked or uninvited, and did whatever had to be done. They had their own code. If Peggy didn't hear the familiar early-morning noises coming from Maura's kitchen, she knocked on the walls with the mop handle, the jungle drums of the four streets, to inform the others that, today, they were needed. That today was not good. And, without fuss or drama, the women of the four streets took over the running of Maura's house.

They did her washing, mopped her floor and left stews on the range. They baked her bread and cleaned her windows, letting her know they were there. Life still went on and, if she wanted, she could absent herself from it for a while but they would not allow her to leave altogether. She had children to care for. She could heal, in her own time, but she would not be permitted to wither.

With the support of old friends such as Kathleen and Jerry, and new friends like Harriet and Father Anthony, Maura and Tommy slowly surfaced from the deepest well of their own black thoughts. Their daily existence now became one of oppressive, scarcely bearable greyness. And still they did not speak.

It was Harry who eventually broke the spell of their despair.

'Mam, Mammy, Da.'

In the small hours, Angela had turned on the landing light and stood framed in the doorway of Maura and Tommy's bedroom.

Maura didn't reply.

'Mammy, 'tis Harry. His asthma has been really bad since yesterday and now he can't breathe.'

Maura sat bolt upright in bed and strained her ears. She could hear the familiar whistle coming from the boys' room, Harry's distinctive and unique breathing: short in, long out. But it was too short in and too long out.

Maura had been so wrapped up in her own misery that she had been oblivious to the fact that Harry was ill.

She shook Tommy awake and, for the first time in six weeks, they spoke as though there had never been a period of silence between them.

'Tommy, 'tis Harry, quick. It's his asthma, something is wrong.'

The thaw came as they sat outside the children's ward at Alder Hey Hospital, just as the first dawn light was breaking.

Tommy realized his anger had dissipated, to be replaced

by concern for Harry. As he carried the two cups of tea the nurse had brought him, his love for his wife flooded back at the sight of her perched on the edge of the wooden bench, looking frail and exhausted, a shadow of the strong woman she had once been.

Maura placed the cup and saucer on the bench next to her. Tommy slipped his arm round her shoulder and pulled her into him. She cried and, for the first time in his adult life, Tommy cried too.

'God, I've missed you,' he whispered into her hair.

'I've missed you too,' she whispered back. 'Please God, let Harry be all right. Tommy, I could not imagine ...'

Her voice trailed off as a doctor came out through the swing doors from the wards and made his way towards them. They could tell, just by looking at him, that he was Irish. It wasn't just his red hair, it was his facial features too. He appeared familiar. At his approach Tommy squinted, trying to place him.

The doctor was smiling.

'Harry is going to be fine, so he is,' he said.

Maura's hand flew to her mouth as she let out a sob stemmed in relief.

'We have been using a new trial drug, Salbutamol. I wish we'd had it all the years your little lad has been poorly.

'A year ago, things could have been very different indeed, given the state of his asthma when he was admitted. He has responded better than we could have hoped for. What's more, you can use it at home. It will make a huge difference to how we manage his asthma in the future. Harry is one of the lucky ones. This drug isn't available everywhere yet.

'I would just say, though, Mr and Mrs Doherty, it isn't good to leave him so long when he has breathing difficulties. It makes life very problematic for us when we can't find a vein that we can insert a needle into, to treat him with the drugs we now have that we know will work. When asthma is as bad as Harry's was, the peripheral veins shut down and, even with the best drugs in the world, if we can't get the drugs into him, treatment becomes impossible.'

The doctor placed his hand over Maura's and gave it a squeeze.

'I know you have had a lot on yer plate, but this little lad needs his mammy and daddy to look out for him. In the meantime, we are going to keep him here for a few days to make sure he is absolutely right before he returns home.'

By now Maura was beyond speech. When he spoke, Tommy's throat was thick with unshed tears.

'How do ye know, doctor,' he asked softly, 'that we have a lot on our plate?'

Neither he nor Maura had said Kitty's name out loud since the day of her funeral.

'My brother is the doctor in Bangornevin and he told me about the accident. Harry asked for his sister Kitty and then became distressed, for a short while. When he said a few things I put two and two together. I hope ye don't mind my mentioning it. He is fine now that he is breathing much more easily.'

'No, we don't mind,' croaked Tommy.

Just at that moment both he and Maura turned as they heard the footsteps of Peggy and Little Paddy, their ever faithful friends and neighbours, heading down the hospital corridor towards them.

The arrival of Father Anthony and Harriet had transformed everything, despite the fact that his first mass had been for little Kitty. It could barely be heard above the sobs of every resident of the four streets. They crammed into the pews and the aisles, with many gathered outside the church. They stood, a sombre gathering, not a dry eye amongst them.

Howard – the detective and now the new fiancé of Miss Alison Devlin, teacher at the four streets convent school – had been the first person at the Dohertys' house, following a phone call from the County Mayo state solicitor after Kitty's drowning. It had been his responsibility to take a witness statement from them on behalf of the police in County Mayo.

Howard met Peggy on the way out of Maura and Tommy's back door.

'What the fecking hell do you want?' Peggy asked, dispensing with even the most basic pleasantry.

Peggy had hardly slept the previous night. How could she? The most unimaginable thing that could happen to any mother had befallen the house next door. Howard, afraid that she might thump him, noticed that her right fist was clenched, ready. It was not unheard of for neighbours like Peggy to risk a prison sentence, in loyal defence of their friends. Howard, having served his probation on the beat in Liverpool and now having been elevated to the CID, knew that such communities took loyalty to an impressive but all too often self-destructive level.

'Ye had better not be sniffing round here, to take Tommy Doherty to the station on one of yer trumped-up charges, 'cause if ye do, ye have me to answer to. The man is beside himself with grief. Have ye no fecking respect?'

'I do, Peggy,' Howard replied, softly and meekly. 'I am here to offer my respects and to have a form signed, so that Kitty can be brought back to Liverpool to be buried. I am not here to arrest Tommy. The investigation into the priest's murder is over and we all know Tommy had nothing to do with it.'

'Aye, well, just ye fecking remember that,' Peggy had said grudgingly, 'and, if ye want anything else, come to one of us, don't go barging in there. We will be looking after them, for as long as it takes. Maura is on the floor with grief and Tommy with her. We will make them right again, but we can't do it with the likes of ye sniffing around here, causing worry, so we can't.'

And with that, in her damp, rancid slippers she had shuffled across the cobbles, out of the back gate and into her own home next door.

As he opened the back door to Maura and Tommy's, Howard was greeted by Sheila, who was stirring a huge pan of broth on the stove, and Jerry, who was squatting in front of the fire, carefully stoking the coke. He had been more welcoming altogether.

'Hello, Howard,' Jerry whispered. 'Everyone is lying down with their own thoughts. Can I help?'

As Howard had looked at Jerry, he had been consumed with guilt that he and Simon had ever suspected Jerry of being involved in the priest's murder. Here he was, rushing straight to his neighbour's side in a time of crisis. Howard knew that his own Alison had baked a plate of biscuits and dropped them over earlier. Howard was in awe of how much people cared for everyone else here. How could he and Simon have ever thought the murderer had been so close to home?

The tragedy that had greeted her on her arrival at the four streets enabled Harriet to play her part. She spent a great deal of time with Nellie, as a result of Nana Kathleen voicing her need for help.

'I am at the end of me wits, with nowhere to go, what with Nellie and Maura and Tommy. Everyone is in shock, but I have never known our chatterbox to be so quiet. She's scaring me, so she is, and I have to admit, I'm at a loss what to do.'

Harriet had left the Priory at that moment and accompanied Kathleen home. Whilst Kathleen organized others to help care for the Dohertys, Harriet spent hour after hour sitting with Nellie, holding her hand and slowly trying to coax her to speak.

Nellie barely uttered a word for almost a month and, when she did, it was as an accompaniment to a flood of wretched tears.

'I have never heard nor witnessed such sad tears, Anthony. They sounded as though they were pouring straight from her heart,' Harriet had confided in her brother over supper that evening.

'Maybe that is it now. Maybe she will begin to accept what has happened and improve,' Anthony had replied.

He himself was weary from struggling with Maura and Tommy. He felt that, along with losing their daughter, they were losing their faith, somehow blaming the Church. It was as though they didn't altogether trust him.

'How did she drown, Anthony, do we know? It seems so

tragic. One of the women told me that her cousin lives in Bangornevin and that the water where Kitty was found was less than a couple of feet deep. Can that be so?'

'Well, sure enough, if it had happened in England, it would be suspicious, certainly, but it wasn't even in Bangornevin, Harriet. It was on a remote farm just outside, in a place called Ballymara, with no one and nothing around for miles. She must have slipped and knocked her head on a rock. 'Tis a stony river and a famous one for the salmon, so I'm told.'

Jerry and Kathleen would be forever grateful to Harriet.

They were well aware that it was only because of the time that she had spent sitting at Nellie's bedside, soothing, reading and even singing to her, that Nellie had surfaced from her own deep grief.

On one of the rare nights when Kathleen had allowed herself to break down, she had cried to Jerry, 'If wasn't for Harriet, I think we would have lost our Nellie with the grief as well as Kitty. I have never known the like, a child not wanting to eat or speak. I was out of me depth, Jerry, we both were.'

It was only when Nellie had recovered that Kathleen allowed herself to grieve. Once she knew everyone else was out of the woods, in the privacy of her own home, beside her own fireside, when Jerry and Nellie were asleep, she allowed her tears to flow.

Little Paddy and Scamp did all they could. Paddy would step silently into the Dohertys' kitchen each morning, whilst Scamp waited patiently by the back door, to ask both sets of twins the same question every time.

'You all right, lads? D'you wanna game?'

Each time they said yes and the boys slipped out, to escape the gloom within. Too guilty to leave the house on their own, they jumped at the chance when Little Paddy called and offered.

For Harry, his asthma made running difficult and football impossible. Often he didn't play but just sat on the stone at the edge of the green, watching them all and waiting. He sometimes cried as he sat there, for his Kitty. Although by day, the mood of the house had improved, by night, everyone cried their own tears, under the cover of darkness.

Chapter Five

THE WINTER HAD passed and it was the first sunny day of the year when Daisy walked up to the large greenhouse with her basket and an order from Maggie for Frank.

'Morning, Joan,' shouted Frank, giving Daisy a wink.

'That girl tells me she is simple,' Maggie had said to Frank on Daisy's second day. 'She is not simple. Daisy has just never had anyone talking to her for any length of time and she's been frightened out of her wits by the priest she worked for. She speaks funny, mind, but 'tis her tongue not being exercised enough, nothing else. I tell you, one week of working with me in that kitchen and she will be talking as well as I do. No one will be calling her simple then.'

'What's she doing here? Have you found out why she arrived in the early hours on Christmas morning?' Frank enquired.

'I'm trying, Frank, but it's hard. I can't help the others if I am caught out so I have to be careful. Here, one of the girls sneaked me a letter. Can ye take it to the post office?'

Frank nodded and put the letter into his large coat pocket. Being caught would mean him and Maggie being turfed out on their ears. They were too old for that to happen a second time, but it never stopped him helping the girls when he could.

Maggie and Frank grinned at each other.

'Come here,' said Frank and, removing the short distance between himself and Maggie, he threw his arms round her.

Maggie was uncomfortable with affection of any description, preferring to display a tough and practical exterior. A front belied by her acts of kindness and the degree of danger she frequently placed herself and Frank in, by helping the girls in the mother and baby home.

'Ger off, you fat lump,' she exclaimed as she pushed Frank away, but he took no offence.

Frank knew his wife's capacity to love. He had seen her face as she held their baby. That was when Maggie had been soft, on the days she had walked out to the fields, carrying his lunch in one hand and holding their son on her hip with the other. That Maggie had never pushed him away. That Maggie had laughed when he threw his arms round his wife and baby son. If he closed his eyes for long enough, he could see her back as they walked away from him in the sunlight, his child, resting on his mother's shoulder, smiling at his da and his small hand waving goodbye.

'Maggie has sent me for greens, Frank,' said Daisy.

'Has she, now? Well, let's grab some of these, then, shall we?'

Daisy followed Frank, whom she liked and trusted, into the greenhouse.

It had taken Daisy her customary while, but she had

eventually opened up to Maggie and Frank. Each day, Maggie extracted a little bit more of Daisy's extraordinary history.

'How is it up at the kitchen today then? Is Maggie's temper holding up?' Frank said.

Daisy laughed. 'Yes, it is. She gave one of the novices a right scolding. I thought the girl was about to faint with indignation, but Maggie doesn't care.'

'Aye, that's because she knows they would fall apart if she left. They don't want to be on the wrong side of Maggie or they would all starve, so they would, but I wouldn't dare push it, mind. Me and my Maggie, we don't have too many choices now. Are ye coming down to us for supper?'

'I am, Frank. I have something to ask you and Maggie this evening but I would like to ask you together, if that's all right with you?'

'Of course it is, Daisy,' said Frank.

'Shh,' she said as she looked around. 'You know the trouble we get into for using our real names.'

Daisy wasn't really angry with Frank, and, with a smile, she picked up the wicker basket and headed off back to the kitchen.

That night, as Daisy sat in Maggie and Frank's kitchen, she told them her tale in detail.

She left nothing out. She spoke about her abuse at the hands of the priest and the bishop. It had been the very same bishop who had appeared in Maggie's kitchen and had spoken to her on Christmas night.

'He told me that I was here for my protection. That I should never tell anyone anything at all about my life in Liverpool.

He said that there were some very bad people around and I could suffer the same end as my friend, Molly Barrett, who was murdered in her own outhouse. He really scared me when he said that. Molly was the only person who knew I had seen the murder. I know that on the night she was killed, she had told the policeman about it that very same day. It was the same policeman as brought me here to the convent.'

Maggie and Frank both made a sharp intake of breath. They interrupted only to whisper the words, 'Yeah, yeah, go on now,' as encouragement for her to continue.

She told them about Miss Devlin, and how Daisy's family in Dublin had made contact, wanting her home for Christmas. She told them about Sister Evangelista and the school and all the residents on the four streets. As Maggie poured mug after mug of tea, worried that Daisy might stop, she told them about Maura and Tommy Doherty, and about little Kitty, who, she was sure, the priest had made pregnant, which was why he had been murdered by Kitty's da, Tommy.

And the last thing of all that she told them was about the goings-on at the Priory. How strange men came with pictures of children and how she and Sister Evangelista had found hundreds of black-and-white pictures in the dead priest's desk drawer.

'All the children in the four streets are poor and the priest is very powerful. If I or anyone else told what happened to us, no one would believe us.'

'Aye, well, 'tis no different in Ireland,' said Maggie. 'Make such an accusation in any of the villages around here and in no time at all ye would find yerself living as a penitent in a place like this, that's for sure.'

'It is all so wrong,' said Frank, 'and I don't mind saying that I don't understand all that much of it, but I do know this: you have to go back to Liverpool, Daisy, and see justice done. You have to take all of this to the Gardai.'

'How can I?' asked Daisy. 'The bishop knows what I have seen at the Priory and what he has done to me himself. That is why he has me prisoner here. I am trapped.'

'He was terrified of you telling your brother anything, Daisy. That's why you were as good as kidnapped by that policeman, who is obviously in cahoots now with the bishop, wouldn't ye say so, Frank?' said Maggie.

She had no trouble at all in picking up the various threads of life in a city she had never visited and, having never left the countryside, could barely imagine.

'You were sent here to be hidden and to be hushed up,' said Maggie. 'Do ye have the address of your family in Dublin?'

'No, I don't. Miss Devlin arranged everything. They would have been waiting for me at the port, but the policeman took me off the ferry. We passed through what looked like a kitchen and I saw him hand a man who worked in there a ten-shilling note and then we came out of a door and down a ramp different from the one I saw everyone else leaving by. I never even saw my family. They must be worried about me and Miss Devlin will have been out of her mind.'

'Why did ye not say something to someone as he was leading ye off the boat?' asked Frank.

'I was scared and at first I thought he was taking me to my brother's house. I had no idea.'

'Don't ask such stupid questions, Frank,' Maggie remonstrated with him. 'Do ye remember what she was like when she first arrived here? As nervous as a kitten she was. Look at her now, talks fifty to the dozen, she does. 'Tis me that can't get a word in edgeways these days. All this girl needed was for her mouth and brain to be worked a bit.

'Simple, my arse. I'll give ye this, Daisy, the butcher would find ye an easy one to cheat. Yer counting is not strong and yer trust in others is blind, but ye can hold yer own in any conversation and I'll take the credit for that. Frank, pop a drop of poteen in these mugs. Enough of the tea now, we need to think of a plan. Daisy, ye is welcome on that mattress, but ye can't sleep there forever, or in that storeroom the nuns have put you in. They keep plenty prisoner up in that place, but they can't keep ye. We have to find a way to get ye back to Liverpool. I'll tell ye this, it'll be a long time before Sister Theresa notices, so little attention do they pay ye.'

Frank and Maggie's chance to smuggle Daisy away arrived more quickly than any of them had expected. Sister Theresa had taken the decision to compete with the Abbey and convert the old stables into a laundry.

She was swayed by the opulence of the Abbey, which she and her nuns had cause to visit from time to time, and by the luxury of Sister Assumpta's office. She took little convincing that a laundry was what they were missing.

The carpets and silver picture frames ate at her heart each time she visited. Her envy was not unnoticed by Sister Assumpta.

'Did you see the way they were looking at my ornaments?' she asked Sister Celia, following Sister Theresa's latest visit to the Abbey with Sister Virginia in tow to spy.

'Were they?' asked Sister Celia.

'Were they? Of course they were. Are your eyes afflicted all of a sudden? Rome has given them next to nothing. They have a lot of catching up to do. It'll be a few years before they can afford a Persian runner or a set of French doors in the study.'

Sister Theresa, unhappy with running the most recent and the poorest convent in the area, had very different ideas. Rome had indeed been mean.

'There is machinery now that can turn those girls into a far more productive operation altogether,' she had said to Sister Virginia on their return journey from the Abbey. 'We have enough money saved to install washers and dryers. That means the girls we take on can turn round twice as much as the Abbey, at the very least, I would say. The hospital may decide to transfer its custom to us on this side of Galway.'

'Won't the girls become soft altogether if we use machines?' sniffed Sister Virginia, who was driving the new Mini the nuns had purchased from Donegal only the week before.

'No, not at all. They will still have to do all the work, the lifting, the sorting and the ironing. The machines mean that we won't lose a day's drying when it's wet and we can put more dirty laundry through and faster too. The longer we keep that bit of information from Sister Assumpta, the better. They have used their own money to buy fancy ornaments and carpets. We will use ours to buy washing machines and, once we do, we will be secure forever. It's all about making sure there are enough funds to keep the convent running, come what may, Sister Virginia. I think Sister Assumpta forgot that, somewhere along the way back there.'

*

Within a month, Frank had opened the gates to the delivery of industrial-sized washing machines and dryers.

A week later, he welcomed the fitters who would convert the barn into a laundry. Although Irish by birth, they were based in Liverpool, travelling back to Liverpool every Friday night and returning on Monday morning. It occurred to Frank that this arrangement could be quite handy. He made a point of chatting to them as they unloaded their vans. It took him only a couple of days to strike up a friendship with the works foreman, Jack, who knew the location of Daisy's former home, the four streets.

Thursday was Frank's regular night for a jar at the local pub, a habit of which Sister Theresa was blissfully unaware. When he found out that the workmen were boarding there, Frank arranged to meet Jack in the bar after work. A week after they had first arrived, Frank strolled down to the pub to meet Jack. He needed to take a measure of the man's trustworthiness.

As he walked into the bar, Frank greeted the foreman, who was more than pleased to have someone fund his night of Guinness.

It took six pints before Jack agreed to smuggle Daisy out of the convent. It took a further two to convince him to deliver her personally to the police station and to stay with her until he could be sure she was safe. Daisy had provided Frank with enough details for him to work out the address of the Priory and of Nelson Street.

The decision was taken not to smuggle Daisy out until the day the job finished and the workmen were leaving for the last time. That way, it would look as though one of the workmen was to blame. Frank and Maggie would be free from suspicion.

As the day approached, they became more and more twitchy and Frank worried that Jack would change his mind.

'Jesus, we have helped many in the mother and baby home to hear word from a relative or snuck out a letter. I've even smuggled food into the dormitory for the girls, all of which would see me strung up, but I've never done anything as bold as this,' said Maggie to Frank.

The thought of what they were about to do almost made Maggie shake with fear, but she would not let this deter her.

The night before they were due to put their plan into action, there was a gentle ring on the gate bell.

'Jesus, who can that be?' Maggie almost jumped out of her skin.

Frank had already opened the door from which he could see the gate.

''Tis the foreman, Jack.'

A minute later, Jack was standing in front of the fire with a mug of Frank's poteen in his hand. He looked on edge.

'I'm not sure we should be doing this, Frank,' he said. 'If we are caught, the Reverend Mother may stop our money and, sure, 'tis serious money. I have wages to meet for the week's work on Friday night. I cannot risk the men not taking their pay packets back to their own families.'

Maggie began to speak, but Frank held up his hand and stopped her. Instead, Maggie placed her arm round Daisy's shoulders. She looked crestfallen.

'I understand that now, Jack, sure I do, but how about this? We carry on with the plan and, if we are caught, Maggie and I will own up. We will say that it was us that smuggled Daisy into the back of yer van and ye had no idea whatsoever what was happening.'

Maggie and Daisy both gasped. Maggie was more aware of the consequences.

They would be turfed out of their home there and then. No amount of Maggie's prowess in the kitchen would save their necks from that. Within an hour, Frank and Maggie, together with what belongings they had, would be on the wrong side of the convent gate.

'Well, I'm sorry to say as I know the risk to you now, but that would put a different complexion on things. As long as I could have your word, Frank?'

'As true as God, ye have my word,' said Frank, holding out his hand to shake Jack's.

'Did I do the right thing, Maggie, love?' Frank whispered to Maggie later that night as they lay in bed while Daisy slept on the lodge floor in front of the fire.

'Ye did what yer heart told ye to do, Frank, and that can never be wrong. I'm sure someone or something was guiding yer words as there was no time to think.'

'There will be plenty of time to think tomorrow, if we are caught,' whispered Frank.

Maggie stroked Frank's arm and silently said her own prayer that they could safely survive the next twenty-four hours.

They had helped lots of the girls, but none had presented as great a risk as this.

The following morning, the tension they all felt was palpable.

'What clothes will I wear, Maggie?' said Daisy, who had worn nothing other than her calico since the day she had arrived.

The girls weren't allowed bras and Maggie always thought there was something particularly degrading in the way the nuns dressed them.

'Leave that to me,' said Maggie. 'I know where the linen room is and where the clothes the girls turn up in when they first arrive are stored. I will fetch them later, after breakfast. If I don't find yours, I'll find something better than that outfit ye is wearing now.'

Daisy smiled. The thought of not having to wear the disgusting uniform filled her with pleasure.

'Could ye look for my hat, Maggie? I don't really care about the clothes, but I would really like my new hat back.'

The hat was the only present Daisy had received in her entire life. It had happened on such a special night. She grinned stupidly to herself when she thought of that moment, seeing the mothers and children in the school hall, clapping as Miss Devlin had placed the hat on her head.

The final day of the fitting out of the laundry was one of celebration.

The bishop had arrived and was to bless the brand-new facility with a mass.

From nowhere and with no warning to Frank and Maggie, there had been a fresh intake of girls, with bleakness and sadness in their eyes. At the same time that the laundry was fitted, an attic had been converted into a dormitory.

When Frank saw the Reverend Mother inspecting the gardens, he had the audacity to ask her where the girls had come from.

'Frank.' Sister Theresa talked down to him, her expression disdainful. 'We are here, at the behest of the Irish authorities and the Vatican, to become the guardians of local morals. Where girls do not behave as they should, they are sent to me by the local priest, or the council, and they will live here. They are not girls who abide by the word of the Lord our God, Frank, they are penitents. Sent here to work, in order to seek salvation and to atone for their sinful lives. These girls will work in the new, mechanized, very latest, up-to-the-minute laundry. There is no other like it in all of Ireland, and with the sheets each girl washes, she will be filled with the knowledge that she is rinsing away the stains of sin from her life.'

'Aye, Sister,' said Frank, looking as though he fully understood and agreed with everything she said.

He had once asked one of the girls what had brought her to the convent's door. She told him she had been sent from the convent orphanage in Dublin, where she had been left by her mother when she was barely twelve, to prevent her father from coveting her. The lust she had incited in her father had made her a sinner in the eyes of her mother.

'There is nothing to choose now between ourselves and the Abbey,' said Sister Theresa to Frank, changing the subject. 'In fact, there will be many institutions preferring to use our services. We have dryers. They don't have those in the Abbey now, do they? Our laundry will be far more productive.'

'Yes, Reverend Mother,' Frank replied, 'superior altogether, I would say.'

He had no idea what they did and didn't have in the Abbey, and he cared even less.

The workmen were invited to the mass to bless the sinks and the dryers. Jack, the foreman, said they had better stay, even though the men were kicking off, all hoping to be back in Liverpool for a Friday night in the pubs, which they now saw slipping away.

Jack had also agreed to keep his promise to stop at the lodge to collect Daisy. He would hover on the outer side of the gate while Frank and Maggie bundled her into the back of his van.

When the time came, Daisy stood inside the lodge door with Frank and Maggie.

It had been difficult for Maggie to run back to the lodge, which was half a mile from the convent, since Sister Theresa had wanted to put on a special tea, to bless the laundry.

Local dignitaries had been invited, and the Reverend Mother and the nuns from the Abbey had been invited too, to admire the new equipment.

It was now their turn to be envious.

Frank watched from inside the lodge as the workmen's vans made their way down the drive.

He saw the brake lights of the first van as it slowed down to pass through the wrought-iron gate.

'Jesus, Holy Mother, where the feck is Jack?'

Frank opened the front door to look the other way down the drive. He saw Jack's van turn out of the parking area at the front of the convent at the same time as Sister Assumpta and Sister Celia slipped into their own car to return to the Abbey.

'I cannot wait to be out of here,' said Sister Assumpta to Sister Celia as she placed her key in the ignition. 'I think the bishop needs to provide a few more lessons in the scriptures down here. Are they not aware that greed is a sin? I have no idea why the Holy Father thought there was a need for another convent around here. God knows, 'tis we who take in sin in abundance and who work wonders, converting these girls into something far more holy altogether.

"'Tis we who suffer and now the Holy Father rewards Sister Theresa with the laundry equipment. They have the home and the orphanage and the retreat. Do they not have enough?'

Whilst Sister Assumpta ranted, Sister Celia listened. And then she ranted some more.

'Why is that van stopping at the gate? And that's another thing: this convent employs staff. We do all our own work ourselves. We have never employed gardeners or cooks or kitchen maids. Seems to me as though they are all a little too high and mighty around here, so they are.'

Their car pulled up behind the van, which had stopped at the gate.

The van driver put his arm out of the window and waved Sister Celia to overtake him.

'Sorry, Sister,' he shouted out of the window as she drove past. 'Something wrong with the engine now, sorry, Sister.'

Sister Celia raised her hand in acknowledgment and slowly moved round the stationary van.

She turned down the road and, as she did so, in her rear-view mirror she noticed a woman leave the lodge house and then quickly step back inside.

But Sister Celia's thoughts were elsewhere.

'Do you know,' she said to Sister Assumpta, 'I would love the recipe for those coconut golf balls. Now, where in Galway would sell desiccated coconut? Would we have the time to call in?'

Daisy was halfway out of the lodge doorway when Maggie pulled her back inside.

'Not yet,' she hissed. 'They slowed right down, once they were on the road, and all nuns have eyes in the back of their heads. I don't trust them not to see.'

Daisy threw her arms round Maggie, her eyes full of tears.

'Maggie, will I ever see you and Frank again? I can't bear it if I don't.'

'Aye, Daisy, ye will. I don't know where or when but I do know this, things are changing. I can feel it. This business of locking away for their entire lives girls who have done no wrong, it cannot carry on. The world is moving on and Ireland will be called to account for its sins one day. The biggest of them all will be this, as God is my judge. I know I'm right. God willing, we will meet again, soon enough.'

Daisy sobbed, scared. Caught up in the excitement of the adventure, she had been anticipating this moment with impatience. Now that it was here, she was loath to leave the safety, the company and the comfort provided by Maggie and Frank.

Frank was on the drive, talking though the open window to Jack.

'I've cleared a space, in amongst the tools in the back, Frank, and put some rags on the floor. 'Twas a bit dirty, like, but is all right now,' said Jack.

'Bless you,' Frank replied. 'There will be a place in heaven waiting for you, Jack.'

'Aye, well, I hope so.' Jack laughed. 'That was a close call,' he said, nodding towards the nuns' car.

'Don't leave her until ye knows the police are listening to her, will ye now, and would ye drop me a line to let me know all was well? There's a good man.'

'I will write ye a line on Sunday after mass and before the pub, and post it on the Monday. But, ye and yer missus, have no fear now, I will do all ye have asked.'

Frank looked round to see where Maggie and Daisy were. Looking up at the house, he caught sight of the bishop opening the door of his own car.

'Maggie,' he hissed. 'Get a move on.'

In a second, Daisy was by his side, pulling at his sleeve. .

'Go on now, in the back,' he croaked. 'Maggie, sort her.'

Frank pushed Daisy gently towards Maggie as she began to break down. He bent again to Jack's window.

'Don't let her come back. She will be upset but, sure, she will come to her senses quick enough. And don't stop for the bishop. He will be on yer tail now all the way to Dublin, unless ye can shake him off.'

Frank and Jack heard Maggie slam the rear doors of the van.

Frank looked up and she winked. He banged the palm of his hand twice on the van roof and, within seconds, the van, with Daisy safely stowed in the back, moved away down the road.

Ten seconds later, they raised their hand in farewell to the speeding bishop.

Frank put his arm round Maggie's shoulders and, for the first time in twenty-four hours, they both heaved a sigh of relief.

Frank noticed the tears in Maggie's eyes. 'Come on now, away inside.'

'Do you know, Frank, I reckon we could do that again one day if we needed to. We should try and help these girls more.'

'Let's hope so, love,' said Frank. 'Let's hope so.'

Chapter Six

SEAN SHUFFLED FORWARD on the back seat of Henry's newly imported red Bentley so as to narrow the distance between himself and his sister, Mary. She had shrunk so far down into the passenger seat, it was as though Sean and Henry were the only two people travelling in the car. Sean linked his fingers tightly together, his knuckles shining white through his now all-American tan, while his thumbs rolled over and over. The Bentley was an unusual sight on the streets of Chicago. Henry could have had any American-made car he chose, but that was too easy and did not confer the one-upmanship over the British which he subconsciously sought.

Sean had no idea what to do or say and so, his voice laden with concern, he said the obvious. Being a father himself, he could sympathize to some extent with the pain felt now by his sister and her husband.

He gently laid a hand on Mary's shoulder and said, 'Come on now, Mary, don't cry.'

'I'm not, Sean, I'm not crying. I'm fine, really I am,' his sister responded brightly, as she lied through her hankie. 'I'm just being silly, aren't I, Henry?' She looked sideways to her husband for support as she laid her hand on top of Sean's with a reassuring pat.

Henry didn't reply. His eyes were fixed straight on the road ahead, his facial muscles unyielding and set. The only visible movement was a vein in the side of his broad red neck, beating wildly. Henry never lied.

Sean looked directly into the rear-view mirror. For a fleeting second, his eyes met with Henry's, who quickly averted his gaze, but it was too late. Sean had noticed. The usual, ever-present twinkle of mischief and happiness in Henry's bright blue eyes had been replaced with a deep, desperate sadness, and Sean had seen it.

Sean leaned back and stared out of the side window. Once again, his hands in his lap, he continued rolling his thumbs. It was a habit he had acquired during his boxing days in Liverpool whilst he sat in the back of the arena, waiting to dive through the ropes and into the ring. It had helped him when he was anxious and his nerves had got the better of him, listening to the roar of the crowd, counting down, chanting, yelling for the blood of the poor bloke in the ring. He would rock gently, back and forth. Over and over his thumbs had rolled.

And now here he was, in the back of his brother-in-law's car, having offered to accompany Henry and his sister to the doctor's office to provide some family support. Here he was in a situation so grave that he had no idea what to say or do. Everyone had known that something was wrong with Mary and Henry's little boy.

Alice, who called herself Sean's wife, even though they weren't married, had mentioned it to him many times.

'There is something wrong with that little Dillon,' she said. 'Look at his face, he's as white as a sheet and he hardly wants his bottle. Mary keeps making excuses, but I've seen enough babies born on the four streets to know something is wrong. He's too slow to put on weight.'

Alice had left her own son, Joseph, behind in Liverpool. She hadn't seen him since the day she and Sean had set sail from Liverpool, to join Mary in America.

Sean had ten daughters by his real and only wife, Brigid, a strict Catholic who would see hell freeze over before she granted Sean a divorce. He had neither seen nor heard from his daughters since the day he had left England, and likely never would until they were adults and could meet him on their own terms, free from their mother's bitter anger.

The concern over his nephew had made him think more about his daughters and the pain in his gut was like nothing he had experienced in the boxing ring. It gnawed at his insides at times, making it impossible for him to eat.

Only yesterday, he had confided in his mother.

'I can't eat that, Mammy,' he had said, when she had placed his breakfast in front of him. They were the only two people in Mary's kitchen, which was as big as the school hall on the four streets, where Sean's daughters sat for assembly each morning.

Mrs McGuire leaned across the dining bar.

'That pain ye feel, the pain in yer gut, that's putting ye off breakfast for the first time in yer entire life, it's called guilt, so it is. Guilt and grief. I suppose I should be glad because, to me, 'tis a sign that at least I reared ye to have a conscience.'

*

Sean had worried that it must be hard for Alice, having left her own son, to live in a house with a baby boy, especially one as angelic as Dillon, Mary and Henry's little son.

Dillon was everything his parents had prayed for throughout the long barren years. Not a day went by when his parents had missed the four o'clock Angelus mass. Wherever they were, at the end of Henry's working day, they gave thanks to the Lord for the miracle that was Dillon.

Mary's happiness was infectious. She was often to be seen dancing around, holding her son.

'I prayed for a little lad and the angels sent me you,' she would sing as she swung him round and round. He spent his life being kissed and cuddled, and only because Mrs McGuire intervened did he now sleep in his own room, instead of tucked into his mother's arms.

The all-Irish team, of Henry and his two brothers, ran a large and successful construction company. They had finally persuaded Sean to take up his rightful place as a member of the family firm, making all four of them wealthy.

Sean had taken the plunge only six months ago. The delay had been a matter of frustration to everyone, Sean having been held back by his wife Brigid, who had no intention of emigrating to America. Always pregnant with another child, she had clung to Liverpool, using guilt and family to hold Sean back for too long. But then Sean had fallen in love with Jerry's wife, Alice, and she, just like Sean, wanted to seize with both hands every opportunity their new country had to offer.

Proud and strong, Henry had arrived in Chicago with his beautiful wife Mary fifteen years earlier. The only luggage he had brought with him that was of any use was his canvas bag of tools and the telephone number of someone in the city who was 'taking on' men. Today, Henry employed the sons and grandsons of the man who had given him his first day's work in the land of the free.

The strength of the Moynihan business was that it was built on the labour of people from back home in Ireland. Henry was a generous employer and looked after his workforce. Henry's two brothers regarded everyone who worked for them as extended family, and those who had been with Henry since the early days repaid his kindness with toil and respect.

Sean was about to be made a partner in the business. He found it hard to wind his head round that one, but Alice managed to do it for him. Henry had deposited fifty thousand US dollars in a bank account, as Sean's first down payment, telling him to find a plot of land where they could build a house of their own.

'Ye can't be living with me and Mary forever,' Henry had said. 'It takes a while, but ye and Alice, ye know what's what now. And I'll tell ye this, divorce, 'tis not the big deal over here that it is back home. Time you got that sorted and ye and Alice began having children of yer own. We each need a little lad to leave this business to.'

Alice had recoiled in horror. As soon as she and Sean were alone, she tackled him.

'Sean, we have enough children between us. Henry doesn't expect us to have any more, does he?'

'Well, sure he does and I don't think it's such a bad idea. Brigid could produce only girls. Ye already have a little lad so we know ye can do it. 'Twould be grand to be able to hand on what Henry has built up, and which I will be a part of, to an heir one day.'

'Hand it over to your daughters,' Alice had said with genuine amazement. Sean had thought she was joking.

'A lad would have to be born into a business like this, Alice, to understand how it works. You aren't born knowing how to price up the cost of building a shopping mall. It takes experience.'

'Really?' Alice had retorted. 'Well, seems to me that counts you out then, as the only experience you have is unloading hulls and beating the brains out of men.'

Sean had stared at her in a state of confusion. He and Brigid had never argued, not once in all the years they had been married. With Alice, arguments were coming thick and fast and Sean had no idea what to do.

Moynihan's was a name to be seen all across Chicago. It hung on banners at every new roadside and from every bridge, parking lot or school where construction was taking place.

Mary and Henry lived in a large house, drove fancy cars and could have most things money would buy, but in the years before Dillon had arrived, Mary complained loudly and often.

'This money, the house, everything, it all tastes like a brack loaf I forgot to put the sugar in, with no little ones to share it with.'

They had desperately wanted children, especially a son, to make all the hard work and sacrifice worth it. Now that the prayed-for son had arrived, Henry dreamed about eventually handing over his business, and Mary researched the education they would provide him with. They would give everything they had, heart, soul and dollars, into helping their boy achieve whatever he wanted. In turn he would give to them all the kudos and respectability money could not buy. He would have a university education and letters after his name. Dillon would make the sacrifice of leaving Ireland for America worthwhile. Their own flesh and blood could live the American dream.

It made no difference to Mary and Henry that Dillon was adopted. From the moment they heard that the baby boy they had both dreamt of each and every night was available for just three thousand dollars, they slept hardly a wink until he was safely in Mary's arms.

'Tell me if I become too besotted with our little boy and neglect you, Henry,' Mary had said, when they finally took to their bed.

And she meant it, although both of them knew that becoming besotted was unavoidable, given the gorgeous bundle of joy, which had become their very own. And he had been born an Irish Catholic too.

What was not to love?

'She has that baby on a pedestal and he's only been home for five minutes,' Henry had soon complained to his brother, Eddie, although both knew Henry was only joking. 'She leaps out of bed for his feed at two o'clock in the morning and everyone has told her not to. She's a rich woman now and living in a wealthy country. We have maids coming out of our ears, she could have as many nurses as she wants, but no, they can wash and iron my clothes, so they can, but they can't touch our little lad.'

'All women are the same with their first,' Eddie had replied. 'It'll wear off in a few weeks and, sure, definitely by the second, I would say so.'

Henry had roared with laughter. They had waited fifteen years for Dillon. By the time the second child came along, he would be old enough to be a grandfather.

Henry hadn't realized quite how upside down his world would become in the space of a week. To cap it all, he heard the Moynihan business had been awarded a contract worth millions of dollars.

'Merciful God,' he had said to Mary, 'someone is looking down on us all right. We have enough money to do anything we want and a baby on the way, Mary. How much better can life be, eh?'

'I want my mother to live with us, Henry,' Mary had replied.

Even Henry couldn't have predicted that so much good could turn so sour so fast. Henry felt his elation deflate faster than a pierced balloon.

'I want to share our first boy with her. Every woman needs her mother by her side, with a new baby. After all, she's had plenty of her own and helped Brigid raise all of hers in Liverpool.'

Henry didn't argue. He and his Mary were so blessed and happy, nothing could cloud their horizon for long, not even Mrs McGuire arriving to live with them in Chicago.

'When ye speak to yer mammy, tell her to bring Sean out here. Now that I have that contract, Jesus, we need family, people we can trust, more than ever before. Will ye do that, Mary?'

Neither Mary nor Henry were prepared for Mrs McGuire's telephone call with news from Liverpool.

It would appear there was something that could cloud any horizon, if only for a little while.

When Sean and Alice had run away, they had decided to do so by boat, rather than by aeroplane, both realizing the furore they left behind would need time to settle down before they faced Mary and Sean. They also wanted to have days and nights alone together, something they had never known, to spend time getting to know each other better and to become a real couple, before they landed and began their new life.

They had no idea whether anyone would even meet them when they disembarked, whether Mary would ever forgive Sean for committing such a despicable sin. Walking out on his children and his wife for another woman and a fresh start was a scandal few families could tolerate. Mary and Henry might decide they would not associate with nor acknowledge Sean and Alice. The thought haunted Sean during every day of the crossing.

As they stood on deck while the boat sailed into New York, watching the bands playing and the streamers flying, the first person Sean laid eyes on at the customs hall was his sister Mary with Dillon in her arms. Standing beside them were Henry and their mother, Mrs McGuire.

'My sister has a baby?' said Sean.

'Oh no, your mother has arrived here before us,' said Alice, with more than a hint of despair in her voice. 'She must have flown.'

This was the last thing Alice would have wished for and Mrs McGuire was the very last person she would have wanted to greet her in New York.

Sean was equally amazed. As they slowly walked towards his waiting family, his mother chose to dispense with welcoming pleasantries.

'Well, ye is a dark horse all right, Alice, I will give ye that. Never a clue did I have and that's for sure.'

'Mammy,' said Sean, pleading.

'Never you Mammy me, Sean. Ye could have handled things better than ye did. Whilst ye have been cruising, leading the life of Riley, I had to help Brigid and the girls. I was there when she opened yer cowardly letter. Can ye imagine what that was like for me? It was the worst night of me life and I hadn't even a notion of what ye were up to. Ye lied to me and yer kids and everyone else, running off in the night like a pair of thieves, leaving yer children to face the worst Christmas of their lives. The shame was awful, awful, it was. Can ye imagine what Brigid, yer poor wife, went through? And without so much as a word of warning, not a fecking notion did I have.'

Mrs McGuire lifted her handbag and smacked a stunned Sean, straight across the side of his face, and then, just for good measure, smacked him again across the other side.

'An' that one was from Brigid,' she yelled before she stormed away.

Sean stood with his head down, as an equally stunned and shaking Alice linked her arm through his.

'We are here now, Mrs McGuire.' Alice sounded bolder than she felt, as she spoke to the retreating back of Sean's mother. 'And even if Mary and Henry don't want us, this is where Sean and I are making our life.'

Mrs McGuire turned round and Alice looked directly at her. She challenged the older woman using only her eyes as weapons. They were as cold as steel and just as hard.

Mrs McGuire was not so easily beaten. Retracing her steps, she marched back to Alice.

'Well, be that as it may, Alice, it is just as well, for there will be no welcome anywhere for either of ye two in Liverpool. Big as ye are, Sean, Brigid's brothers would kill ye, if they so much as had a sniff of where it is ye are at. There will be no welcome in Ireland for ye, Sean. Ye have both burnt yer boats and that's for sure. Ye have no option but to settle here, Alice. Ye are here and here forever, I would say, so here's praying to God ye like it because ye have nowhere else to go. And, thanks to the sneaky, lying behaviour of ye both, and the shame ye have put me through, neither have I. I can't even hold me own head up in Liverpool now without the gossip following me wherever I go.'

Her voice trembled on the last words. Mrs McGuire loved her granddaughters. She loved her family. Nothing meant more to her than her pride. What Sean had done had put her at the centre of one of the biggest scandals to ever hit the four streets and would be a subject for discussion every time the women piled into Maura Doherty's kitchen.

Mary decided it was time to break the tension.

'You are welcome to live with us and become part of the business, Sean. Sure, the house is big enough. We have twelve bedrooms and will struggle to find you. We need you, so we do, sure, we always have. God knows what has taken you so long. But, Alice, in America you must be Mrs McGuire. I don't want anyone thinking you are both living in sin. I'll not have that shame laid at my door. And as Brigid will never in a million years grant you a divorce, Sean, you have no option, so you don't. Living your life as a lie, 'tis all you have left.'

Nothing else was said as the sombre party made its way towards Mary and Henry's car where a driver was waiting.

For almost six months Mrs McGuire did not speak another word to Alice. All conversation was channelled directly through her daughter or Sean himself. According to Mrs McGuire, it was entirely Alice's fault that Sean had left his family. Her son had never, and could never, do any wrong, as she explained to her daughter.

'Brigid was only waiting for the littlest one to grow up and that is a fact. She was most enthusiastic about bringing them all to America, Mary, that's no word of a lie. That Alice must be a wicked one altogether. I swear to God, no one other than Peggy and Paddy's lad had a notion of what was going on and he knew only because he caught them almost at it and now, sure, I imagine everyone in Liverpool knows every detail. Alice turned his head, she did. She must have bought a mighty potion from somewhere because it just isn't like our Sean, he would never do such a thing as abandon his own family. She cast a spell, I would say. Ye have invited a witch to live under yer own roof, Mary.'

'Aye, well, Mammy, what is done is done. Sean is not a mean man. Now that he is here and part of the business, Brigid and the children, they will want for nothing.'

Mrs Mcguire took comfort from this knowledge. She knew that, back in Liverpool, new possessions would ensure that Brigid rose above the shame. She could do this easily with a new twin tub, an Electrolux hoover and a nice, vinyl, three-piece suite with cushions upholstered in autumnal colours. No one else on the four streets had anything as grand.

Mrs McGuire had made it her business to ensure the money was sent to Brigid to compensate for the behaviour of her wayward son. There would be no secondhand communion shoes for any of the McGuire girls on Nelson Street. They might not have a daddy at home, but, God knew, they would wear the prettiest veils.

The passage to America had been fun for Alice and Sean. The bars, the dancing, the food. Their first night in the cabin had been one of hedonistic indulgence as they made love half a dozen times. Not until they were standing on the deck to watch the famous Liverpool portside buildings, the Three Graces, disappear into the distance, had either spoken of the families they had left behind.

Alice had loved every minute of the crossing, but if she were truthful she had to acknowledge that, as the days wore on, the fierce desire, which had drawn her and Sean together, alongside the intense longing to reach America, no longer existed. The first signs began to appear when they struggled to make normal conversation. Their lovemaking, which at first had been fuelled by greed and passion, quickly waned.

Despite the long journey to Chicago, Sean set to work with Henry six days a week as soon as they arrived. With only Sundays free, Alice was traumatized to discover that the family attended mass, twice, together, every Sunday.

Mrs Mcguire had left Alice in no doubt as to what was expected of her.

'Tell Alice, Sean, she walks with us to mass. All part of the lie ye have to both live out whilst ye pretend to be man and wife. And may God forgive ye, because I never will.'

'I don't want to attend mass, Sean,' Alice had remonstrated. 'I've never even been inside my own church in England, never mind yours.'

'Ye have to, Alice.' Sean was incensed by what Brigid and her stubbornness had denied him all these years. He was now in love with Chicago and all that it had to offer. Anger flooded him when he thought of the years he had wasted in Liverpool, scraping by. There was no place in his life for another stubborn woman. He would have none of it.

The guilt he carried around with him each day had hardened him. Alice could see that the Sean she had known in Liverpool was a very different man from the one he had become in Chicago. She was horrified too at the prospect of spending two hours of her precious Sundays in a church thick with incense.

'Kathleen and Jerry never took me to mass once during the years I was in Liverpool and under their roof, so why would I want to start now?'

'What happened in Liverpool doesn't count any longer. If it did, I would be sitting in church with my daughters. We worship together, Alice, and that is all there is to it.'

*

'Henry and I flew to England to rescue Mammy from the chaos you left behind, Sean,' Mary had whispered to him when they had a moment alone one morning over breakfast. 'We stopped until Brigid's family stepped into the breach. It was a bad business all right and not something I would want to have to do again.'

Sean felt ashamed for what he had put his children through, but nothing could stem the tide of anger he now felt towards Brigid. He would not allow this opportunity to be wasted. His share of the business would be bequeathed to his girls but, in the meantime, Alice must play her part. He would need a son to carry on the business so that it could continue.

Mrs Mcguire's dockside words had chilled Alice, but Henry's, about her having another child, had chilled her more. Sean's having a son had not been part of the deal.

'I have a son that I have left in Liverpool. Why would I want another?' she had said to Sean.

'Because of this is our new life, Alice. Do you want it to be just the two of us, growing old together? Don't you want us to be able to share our life out here with a family? Even I hadn't realized how well the business is doing. Mary had understated that in her letters all right.'

Alice didn't reply. If Sean thought he was going to make her pregnant, he could think again. What she couldn't tell Sean was that she missed Joseph. So much so that she had trouble sleeping. Deep in her heart, she missed Jerry too, as well as the four streets. She missed the life she had lived before and knowing that it had gone forever made the pain worse. While Sean worked hard all day long, Alice moped around the house or called for the driver, if the car was free, to take her to the mall.

Mary often invited Alice to her coffee mornings and fundraisers for the church, but they left Alice cold. She had never been one for small talk, and it hadn't come more easily just because she was on a different continent.

Alice had been made responsible for their banking and had been charged with sorting out the new house, with Mary's help, tasks which occupied only the smallest part of her day. But the complaints from Alice faded into the distance following a discovery that altered the course of all of their lives.

'Henry, the baby hasn't woken for his feed,' said Mary, switching on the bedside light. 'It's been a struggle all week to make him take anything. I'm worried.'

Henry sat up in bed and switched on his own light.

Dillon had never taken a whole feed since the day he arrived, always just two ounces at a time, at regular intervals.

'The doctor said not to worry. As long as he was taking something every few hours, he was fine.'

'I know, Henry, but add it up: he had only eight ounces all day yesterday and that is the equivalent of one feed, for a baby his size.'

Mary fastened her dressing gown and made her way to the adjoining bedroom.

But as she opened the door, there was silence. No gurgling, or shuffling of bed sheets, no thumb sucking, no warm breath or blinking eyelids. Nothing.

The light from the main bedroom cast a faint glow over the cot. As Mary approached, she knew something was dreadfully wrong.

'Henry,' she said in a tight voice.

'What is it?' he replied.

'Henry,' Mary said again.

Alarmed, Henry sat up as Mary came towards him, holding the baby. Dillon was flaccid in her arms, his little head lolling in her hand and his legs swinging loose.

'Dillon, darling,' whispered Mary. The baby opened his eyes and looked at her, but there was no light of recognition.

Henry noticed his pale leg, which had fallen free from his nightgown.

'What's that, Mary?' he asked, pushing back the child's white flannelette nightshirt.

An enormous black bruise covered the back of Dillon's calf.

'I don't know, but phone the doctor quick,' Mary whispered, with tears pouring down her cheeks as their son, once again, closed his eyes.

A week later, Sean was trying his best to pay back Mary and Henry's kindness by travelling with them to meet with the doctor. Today they would know the results of the many tests Dillon been subjected to. Sean felt totally helpless.

'Let's stop and get us the biggest rack of smoked ribs when we are all done at the hospital, shall we, Sean?' Henry had said earlier that morning.

They were all three assembled in the hallway, ready to leave for the doctor's.

'And, Mary, you won't have any problem with that now, will you? Not today, Mary. None of your lectures now, d'you hear me? Today we celebrate, because the doctor is going to tell us our little lad will be fine.'

Mary avoided responding by fixing her hat in the mirror.

'Ouch,' she said as she sucked her thumb, after a prick from the hatpin. 'Let's not fly in God's face, shall we? We don't try God and you should know that.'

She dipped her fingers into the stoup on the hall table, full of holy water that had been shipped over especially from the Vatican, blessed herself and pushed forward her husband and brother so that they could do exactly the same.

'What's up with ye both?' she admonished them. 'Are ye both so full of your own arrogance you have no time to bless yourselves today of all days, so help me, God?'

Mrs McGuire was in the kitchen with Dillon, rocking him back and forth on her knee. She had been trying for over an hour to coax him to take his bottle. Worry lines were etched on her face. The situation with Sean had taken its toll, and now this.

'Will you be all right, Mammy?' said Mary, fussing around.

Mrs McGuire waved her daughter away. 'Will I be all right? I'm not Mrs Clampett. I can manage very well, thank ye. Just because ye live in a big house doesn't mean anything to do with rearing a child has altered. Now go, and come back with good news that this little fella is going to be fine.'

Sean noticed how anxious his sister looked. Mary hadn't laughed for a week. Not since their last appointment at the doctor's office, when the doctor had told them that they would need to travel straight from there to the hospital where a Dr Sanjay would remain behind, waiting for them.

'For goodness' sake. Right now? What for? You're joking, right?' Mary's voice was tight. She had spent every moment since she found Dillon making herself believe that the doctor would put everything right. She had done a good job.

The doctor wasn't joking. Far from it. Dr Sanjay, a specialist, was indeed waiting at the hospital, examining a set of X-rays of their little boy.

At that moment, Henry saw his wife's spirit die. She had turned to him and tried to smile, to let him know that she would make this better, but her smile had died too.

'Don't worry, Henry love,' she had said, Mary the fixer. Mary, the mother. Mary, who made everything right.

She grabbed Henry's hand and pulled him closer to her, protecting him from the news that she herself failed to comprehend. 'It's nothing serious,' she said, with no conviction whatsoever.

But Henry had seen hope decay, right there and then.

The smile on her face. The dream in her eyes. Dead.

Their little boy had a form of leukaemia, but one that could be cured relatively easily. The chances were high that the bone marrow of a family member would be a successful match.

'In my years of practice I have never known a family match to fail,' Dr Sanjay had said.

It was all very simple. They had to place everyone on the federal donor bank today and then return to the clinic on Monday. They would have to log in their social security numbers and blood type, and once they had done that, the doctor could start work.

'The sooner we find a donor, the less the disruption to your little man's life,' Dr Sanjay had said. 'Dillon is still a baby and this will be nothing more than a correctional process. We just need to give him another blood transfusion in the next few days in order to turn his cheeks pink again. We have all the cards in our hands. I wish every child's case was as straight-forward as yours.'

Sean liked Dr Sanjay. He was calm, matter-of-fact. He had said that the little lad had an excellent chance of a complete recovery. They were the best odds.

Dr Sanjay had answered all Mary's questions honestly. Now they had to return home to Mrs McGuire and Dillon. Sean knew that Alice would be back from the hairdresser's and would be helping Mrs McGuire. The frost between the two women had almost completely thawed in their concern over the baby.

Sean knew Alice missed Joseph. It was something none of them ever mentioned.

'That is the strange thing about America,' Sean had said to Henry. 'It is as though your life before you reached these shores had never happened. When you are an Irish immi-grant in a country as proud as the USA, the only thing that matters is today and tomorrow; the past is forgotten.'

Sean was right. It was all about now. You were reborn as an American citizen and you began anew.

This filled Sean with hope. Their life would begin in earnest with a son of his own, a little Sean McGuire, and Alice would have to agree.

'Are you OK, Mary?' Sean now enquired again, this time with more confidence. 'Are you not happy with what the doctor said?'

Henry answered, 'Mary is fine, Sean. She just needs a little time to get used to things, that's all. Isn't it, love?'

Sean almost smiled. He loved the way Henry's accent was an absolute mix of American and Irish when he was calm and collected, and yet it was full-on, one hundred per cent Irish, when he was mad or worried, which wasn't very often. He was obviously worried right now.

'I'm sorry, Sean, Henry, I'm sorry.' Mary turned in the passenger seat and stretched out to take hold of Sean's hand. Her mascara had carved tiny black tracks through her powdery cheeks and the whites of her eyes were bloodshot.

'It won't be a problem, Mary, so don't cry. You just have to do as the doctor said.'

Sean didn't know what he had said wrong but, whatever it was, he had really upset Mary. She began to sob openly. Sean looked to Henry, seeking reassurance, wanting him to say something to halt Mary's distress, but tears were sliding down Henry's cheeks. What the hell was going on?

Henry put his foot on the brake and as they slowed down Sean looked out of the window. They were turning into the parking lot for the new mall that was still only half built. Parked outside, he spotted green construction vehicles with the family name, Moynihan.

'I will be five minutes,' Henry said. 'Look after Mary, Sean. I will stay home with you today, love.'

Mary grabbed her husband's hand as he moved to slide out of the car seat. He hesitated a moment with his hand on the door handle and whispered, 'Just hold it together, love, until we get into the house, OK?'

Sean shifted forward and patted Mary's hand. It didn't matter how much he scrabbled around for something useful or comforting to say, he found nothing. So he decided the best thing to do was to say nothing and just let Mary know he was there for her.

Henry, who had been gone for less than five minutes, ran back to the car.

Sean had never seen a man cry before, but now, unashamedly, with no attempt to wipe away his tears or to halt their flow, Henry wept freely.

'Tell me, Mary, what is it, what is wrong?' Sean's voice trembled slightly. He was not sure he really wanted to know the answer. They were almost home, only minutes away from being able to walk in through their own front door and break down in private. Sean thought, with a huge sense of relief, thank God, Mammy is there. She will know what to do.

Amazingly, Mary appeared to be pulling herself together just as Henry was falling apart. She turned from the front seat to face Sean full on. Picking up his hand, she began to speak.

'Sean, things are not as you think. We have only six months. Six months to find a match for Dillon.'

Mary looked directly at Henry to reassure herself before she spoke. They were words that could not be taken back once said. He raised no objection.

'We never discussed our baby boy with you because so much was happening when you arrived – the upset with Mammy, the new contract to build the flyover. It was all going on and, anyway, you never asked and why would you?

'Little Dillon, he came from a convent in Ireland, near Galway. We don't know who it was who gave birth to him and gave him up for adoption. We don't know who his family is or where we can trace them to find a bone marrow match. We flew straight from here to collect him, it was all so quick, and stopped over in Liverpool on the way back. He flew on a temporary passport. They had it all arranged before we even arrived.'

'Six months.'

Mary repeated those awful words as though they were a death sentence. The car journey had eaten up almost an hour of those six months since the doctor had first given them the news.

As they pulled into the drive, Sean saw Mrs McGuire, who been waiting patiently, struggle to open the heavy oak front door. She was more used to a cottage in the village on the outskirts of Galway, where they had all been born, or the Nelson Street two-up, two-down. Little Dillon was in her arms, looking pale and wan, but he still managed a smile for his parents' return.

Sean was struggling to take in everything Mary had said.

Only his thumbs moved, over and over.

As they stepped inside, Mrs McGuire and Alice stood in the hallway, anxiety binding them together in a flimsy companionship born from a joint concern for Dillon's health.

Mary, as ever pragmatic and fighting for the life of her little boy, knew without any discussion what she needed to do.

'Mammy, Alice, I have to travel to Galway with Dillon. Will ye both come with me?'

The three women hugged briefly and silently. They would do whatever it took, no matter how inconvenient or difficult.

The scent from Mary's jacket made Alice feel nauseous. She slowly breathed out a deep sigh of relief. Galway. It was much closer to Joseph, to Liverpool, to Jerry, and to everyone and everything she knew, than Chicago.

For the first time in her life, Alice uttered a silent prayer of thanks and made a decision to withdraw the full fifty thousand dollars in their joint bank account on the day she left.

Chapter Seven

'YOU LOOK LIKE a nervous wreck,' said Simon to Howard, as they stood inside St Mary's church, waiting for Howard's bride to arrive. 'Stop pacing up and down like a demented dog. You are making me on edge and I'm only the best man.'

Howard took out yet another Embassy cigarette from his packet and handed one to Simon.

'Here, have one, go on. Me hands are shaking, I've got to have another to calm my nerves,' he whispered.

Standing on the groom's side at the front of the ornate church, now filling with incense, Howard's nervousness was as much to do with the formality of the church ceremony, as the fact that he was about to leave behind his carefree bachelor life and marry a woman who knew how to organize a list to within an inch of her life.

Howard had completed his conversion to the Catholic faith upon the absolute insistence of his bride, Miss Alison Devlin, spinster of the parish, deputy head teacher at the four streets convent school and all-round holder-together of the community during a time of crisis. The latter quality had been tested to the limit recently. The four streets had been through more than their fair share of drama and crisis.

'Howard, we are forty minutes early. Let's go outside and walk round the church for a fag. Your bride will kill you if she can't see you from the door for blue smoke.'

Howard, a local detective inspector, had first met Alison during the investigation into the deaths of the priest, Father James, and Molly Barrett. Howard still felt guilty about Molly. Molly had given him information about who had murdered the priest. But no sooner had she confided in them than she had been murdered herself. The confusing thing was that Molly must have been wrong. She had told them that the priest's murderer was Tommy Doherty. But that couldn't have been the case. They knew Tommy Doherty hadn't murdered Molly. As he was under suspicion, they had watched his every move that night. It wasn't him and it was impossible to believe that there were two random murderers on the rampage in the four streets.

It had all been one extended nightmare. The very worst of it had been the tragic drowning of little Kitty Doherty during her visit to Ireland, and the fact that Daisy Quinn, the Priory housekeeper, had gone missing since the day she had left Alison's care to catch the ferry, down at the Pier Head.

It had all been too much for everyone to take in.

'Will the day ever come when you can see us getting married?' Howard had asked Alison a number of times. It seemed to him as though the dark cloud that had settled over the community would never pass.

'I would feel better if I could travel to Dublin and look for Daisy myself,' Alison had responded. 'God alone knows

157

where she is. Her poor family, to have been left standing, waiting for her at the port. They must be desperate and I feel so responsible. I put her on the boat. I even asked two old ladies to look after her. She was so excited about being reunited with her family for Christmas. I just need things to become a little more like normal.'

Howard knew she was right. In order to remove all barriers to his nuptials, as well as its accompanying rights and pleasures, he had arranged for them both to visit Dublin so that Alison herself could speak to the police and Daisy's family.

He had hoped as a result that she might be more reasonable regarding his manly needs. It seemed as though everyone, everywhere, spoke about nothing other than women's liberation and free love. Some women were even burning their bras, what for, Howard wasn't sure, but it seemed to him like a great and generous gesture.

But none of it mattered. Alison was a stickler for propriety and was apparently wholly against joining her sisters on any march that would make it easier for Howard to stay the night.

'We will, Howard, when the time is right and things are happy again,' Alison replied, each and every time he asked. This would be followed by four very disappointing words, which achieved their unambiguous purpose.

'When. We. Are. Married.'

The door of illicit sex slammed with finality. Words of steel held it shut.

Bang. Bang. Bang. Bang.

'I would be very happy, if I could go to bed at night and

wake up with a wife,' Howard said over and over, but there was little point in complaining.

The nuns, the school and the entire community had become mired in grief. Although not touched by events in quite the same way as his fiancée, Howard realized that to pursue his aim, under such a veil of sorrow, was fruitless.

Daisy's brother had not blamed Alison in any way for his sister's disappearance and had been grateful for the care she had given to the sister of whom he had known nothing until the death of his parents.

The family were still in shock at the news that, after a difficult birth leading to fears that she would be brain damaged, Daisy had been placed in what was in effect a Dublin orphanage, under the care of nuns. As if that were not enough, they had been dismayed to hear that, whilst still a child, she had then been shipped to Liverpool, where she had been pressed into service as a housekeeper to the murdered priest.

Via his own contacts, Howard had arranged for Alison to speak to the police in Dublin. They had then met with Daisy's brother, who was the state solicitor and much respected by the Dublin Gardai.

''Tis is a mystery, so it is,' said the Dublin detective. 'She was seen standing by the boat rails one minute but then, when it came time to disembark, she was nowhere to be seen.'

Alison asked the question that had been preying on everyone's minds since the moment they heard that Daisy had not met up with her family at the agreed rendezvous.

'Could she have drowned?'

'Not impossible,' replied the detective. 'But, if she had, her body would have washed up somewhere by now. The boat had almost docked the last time she was seen on deck. I would say that her drowning was highly unlikely.'

Reassured that there was a strong likelihood that Daisy was alive and with the knowledge that she would most likely be found at some stage, Alison agree to name the day and to put Howard out of his misery.

Howard and Simon now stood at the back of the church in the graveyard, out of sight, but with a good view of the road so as not to miss Alison's approach. Simon held out his silver cigarette lighter to Howard as they lit up.

The top clicked back into place with a cushioned slickness.

Not for the first time, Howard wondered where Simon got the money from for all his fancy bits. The lighter, the cigarette case packed with Pall Mall cigarettes (which, Howard noticed, Simon bought only on days when he thought he might have to offer a woman a ciggie from his expensive case), his smart suits and the new Ford Capri in which Howard had been grateful to be driven to the church.

'You should be careful smoking those Pall Mall,' said Howard. 'That's the only link to Molly's murder. Just because one was found at the murder scene doesn't make it glamorous to smoke them, you know. What happened to your Woodies? Not good enough now, eh?

Although Simon had the same rank as Howard, his manner was bumptious. He always assumed authority over his colleague, yet both were on the same pay scale. Howard had commented on it to Alison only the previous week following the wedding rehearsal when Simon, much to their surprise, had presented them both with a solid silver rose bowl.

'Even accounting for the fact that he has no wedding to pay for and obviously no intention to start a family and buy a home, he seems to spend his money lavishly,' said Howard.

'I'm not complaining at his foolishness.' Alison had smiled. ''Tis a beauty of a rose bowl all right.'

Howard knew better than to pry or ask Simon for an explanation. No other officer in the force was as close to Simon as he was. Howard never asked personal questions, which Simon obviously appreciated. To Howard's knowledge, Simon had no girlfriend and had never had one, in all the time they had been in the force together. He lived alone in his Aigburth house and visited his mum every other weekend. At lunchtime he enjoyed a roast beef sandwich and a slice of the home-made fruitcake which he brought back from his visits home. That was about as much as Howard knew, or was ever likely to know.

Howard, who was less secretive and more down to earth altogether, was more of a sausage-roll-and-a-custard-slice-from-Sayers man. Simon was a member of a rather posh golf club on the Wirrall where, at the weekend, he sometimes teamed up with the chief super and his friends. One of the officers from over the water had told Howard that a politician often played a round with them. Simon never spoke of it and Howard dared not ask.

Howard knew the closest he would get to the golf club would be if he were ever asked to caddy and the chances of that were very slim indeed. Now he smoked his cigarette down to the tip in less than a minute.

'Let's have another,' he said to Simon, 'and then we will move back inside.'

As Simon offered his cigarette case to Howard, they both peered over the church wall to watch the bridesmaids arrive.

Nellie Deane alighted from the car first, followed by the younger Doherty girls and then the page-boys, Little Paddy and Harry. They had been prepared and made ready for the day at Alison's house by her sister. Everything had to be perfect and Alison had taken no chances.

'Strange that not long ago we had both those girls' fathers in the cells, questioning them over the priest's murder, and now their kids are Alison's bridesmaids,' said Howard.

Simon did not reply. He squinted into the sunlight as the girls fussed about their lilac chiffon dresses and white satin shoes. He could hear the voice of the now oldest Doherty girl wafting up to them on the warm breeze.

'Will you get off my shoes, Niamh. You have put a stain on the white satin. Oh God, would you look at that, now.' Angela bent down and rubbed at the shoe like crazy.

'Stop it,' hissed Nellie. 'You are making your white gloves dirty.'

Neither girl had ever been so dressed up in her life. It was making them nervous to the point of nausea.

Alison Devlin had chosen Nellie Deane and the Dohertys for a reason. Not only were they her favourite pupils at the school, but both families had suffered more than most in their lifetimes. Alison had the softest heart.

That could be the only explanation why Little Paddy had been chosen as page-boy.

'Alison, we would have to disinfect the lad before we could put him in a page-boy outfit,' Howard had remonstrated.

'Aye, we will that and won't that give us just a huge sense of satisfaction now,' Alison replied.

Howard was starting to realize that he had as much influence over what happened at his own wedding as he had over the weather. He would have to accept that this was also the beginning of the rest of his life.

'God, I feel so ashamed,' said Little Paddy, as he tried to pull the ruff down from his throat.

'Don't complain, Paddy,' said Harry. 'Ye have a new pair of shoes for wearing a fancy outfit for the day. Ye won't have to borrow anyone else's for ages now.'

Harry patted his friend on the back. Little Paddy smiled. Sometimes he felt as if Harry was more like what a da should be than his best friend.

Wedding nerves had reached the Priory. This was Father Anthony's first wedding since taking over St Mary's church and he knew the turnout would be huge for the most popular teacher for miles around.

'Harriet! Harriet!'

Father Anthony shouted from the top of the stairs down to his sister, who was carefully decorating the two last trifles with silver sugar balls, fanning out from tinned pears which had been placed in a pattern of flower petals, laid on a bed of Fussell's tinned cream. It was all ready to deliver to the Irish centre for the reception. This would take place straight after the nuptial mass. Harriet had stomped round the kitchen, shaking the cream in the tins to thicken it, and was now running late. The whole process had taken far longer than she had anticipated due to the unexpectedly warm weather.

'Shake them above yer head,' Annie O'Prey had told her the previous day. 'It makes them thicken quicker.'

Harriet couldn't see how this could be true, but she had done it anyway.

Harriet and Alison Devlin had become good friends since Harriet had moved into the Priory. Jointly, they had helped to heal broken families and nursed a community back onto its feet. They had become almost inseparable as a result and it seemed only natural that Harriet would play a main role in the organization of the wedding.

Harriet was a helper and a healer, but, despite the fact that she was the priest's sister, she wasn't terribly holy. Something she took care to keep secret.

The fact that her brother was conducting the nuptial mass of her new best friend made the whole thing very tidy, which was just how Harriet liked things to be.

'You would think no one else had ever been married on this street,' Annie O'Prey had grumpily complained a number of times when Harriet had asked for the sitting room to be given an extra polish and a run over with the Ewbank, ready for yet another wedding-planning tea.

'Wedding planning? I've never heard the like. All she needs to do is make a white frock and turn up at the church. I've never known such a palaver.'

In the Priory there had been talk of nothing but the wedding. The reception, the dress, the food and the endless fittings for the bridesmaids' dresses and the page-boys' outfits. Decisions over colours and flowers and what food to put on the buffet. It had been a huge and never-ending frenzy of activity.

Harriet held onto another secret throughout. Never once did anyone see the pain that sometimes squeezed her heart or the odd tear that sprang to her eye at the sad thought that she, so truly now the spinster of the parish, would possibly always remain so.

Most women were married by the age of twenty-one. Any older was seen as being highly unusual. Alison, who was now thirty, had thought she had been well and truly left on the shelf. But no one, not even Alison Devlin, entertained the thought that, at the grand old age of thirty-five, Harriet Lamb would ever be married herself.

'Anthony, stop shouting.' Harriet ran up the wooden stairs from the basement kitchen, closely followed by Scamp, who had quietly inserted himself into the daily running of Priory life and, subsequently, Harriet's affections.

One advantage of the wedding planning taking place at the Priory was the legitimate reason it gave Little Paddy and Scamp to be useful. There were always errands Harriet needed to be run. Little Paddy also got to eat up the leftovers from Annie O'Prey's baking, despite Anthony's constant complaints about the boy and his dog hanging around the kitchen. Anthony might have been the priest but there was no way he was the boss, not even in his own Priory. Alison and Harriet had a lot in common.

'I cannot find the list of family names I have to read out in the service. Have you put it somewhere when you were tidying? Why do you have to polish my office so often?'

'Because I am your housekeeper, Anthony, that is my job. I look after my holy brother. I have told Annie O'Prey to polish in here on Mondays and Fridays. A twice-weekly damp dust and a polish in a big old priory like this is not too often.'

Harriet removed an envelope from his desk drawer on which Alison Devlin had written a long list of names to be mentioned during prayers. At the top of it was Sister Evangelista's, while the bishop's was nowhere to be found. Father Anthony had discovered the bishop had seriously upset Sister Evangelista before his tenure and no matter how many ways he had tried to extract the reason for this, her lips remained sealed.

'Don't ever mention the bishop if you want the cream to stay fresh,' Harriet had told him a few days after their arrival. 'But don't ask me why. I will find out in good time, but it is a tricky one all right. I have never known a bishop to be so disliked. All I know is that after Father James Cameron's death, the bishop was no help whatsoever. In fact, from what I can gather, he was nowhere to be seen. He ignored Sister Evangelista's phone calls, he was unreasonable with her when she did get through to him, he made poor decisions and he was bad-tempered altogether.'

'Blimey!' said Father Anthony. 'Well, here's hoping I'm never on the wrong side of Sister Evangelista.'

'You?' said Harriet. 'Anthony, you have everyone you ever meet eating out of your hand. You are goodness itself, so how could that ever happen?'

'Now,' said Harriet, 'we had better hurry or we will be late and that will not do for the priest. Let me just place a damp tea towel over the last trifles. It seems to me as if half of

Liverpool is attending this wedding and that trifle is their favourite dish.'

They both stopped short in the hallway, hearing the sound of organ music as if carried on the rays of sunshine that fell in shimmering pillars, through the open Priory door.

'Look at them all,' said Harriet, smiling up at her brother. 'I have never seen so many people stand outside a church to watch the bride arrive.'

'Aye, well, it's no different from home. We may be in Liverpool, but everyone here is Irish and the ways have just travelled across the sea.'

Father Anthony waited while Harriet pulled on her lemon gloves. She picked up a lemon-and-white hat from the hall table and said, with a flourish and a spin, 'There, holy brother, will I do?'

'You are a vision of primroses, sister. Mammy and Daddy would have been very proud.'

'Come along then, Father Anthony,' she said briskly, gently pushing her brother in the small of his back as they stepped outdoors.

They walked down the path together but could barely make their way through the throng of people assembled outside the Priory walls, lining all the way down to the church gates.

The crowd parted to allow the priest and Harriet through. The words, 'Morning, Father,' rang out from everyone they passed.

For everyone in return, Father Anthony had a smile and a greeting. 'Morning to you, 'tis a wonderful day,' he called to the happy well-wishers.

*

No one saw Alison Devlin's car, as it passed the top of Nelson Street and then swung away again.

'Go round once more,' Alison urged the driver with an uncharacteristic impatience. 'I don't think they are ready for me. I can see Father Anthony and Harriet walking to the church. I want to make a big entrance. Turn round quickly.'

'Why not, queen,' laughed her father, as he sat in the back of the car and lit up a cigarette. 'You only get married once. Let's make the most of it.'

'Da, watch my veil with the match,' shouted Alison as a profusion of gauze, trimmed with appliquéd white cherry blossom, almost went up in flames.

Alison was aware that not one resident in the four streets had ever before seen a bride arrive at the church in a car. It was a first. The distance from most people's houses to the church was so short that every bride walked and, besides, cars were a luxury that just could not be afforded. Miss Devlin taught at the school, but she lived in Maghull and her true home was Cork. Her life was so deeply rooted in the four streets and St Mary's church, convent and school that there was never a question she would marry anywhere else.

Alison turned and looked out of the back window as the car moved away. She saw her friend Harriet and Father Anthony, winding their way through the crowd towards the church entrance. Just behind them, Tommy and Maura Doherty, the parents of her bridesmaids, were strolling up to the church with Kathleen and Jerry, Nellie's nana and da. They walked with heads bent, linking arms as if holding each other up. Even though it was her wedding day, Alison's heart turned over in sadness.

Harriet noticed that everyone who could do so had squeezed into the church itself, respectfully leaving four pews empty for the nuns. She grinned at the sight of the sisters pouring out of the convent and making their way towards the church, bustling and giggling like nervous, happy schoolgirls.

She thought to herself how different the nuns in Liverpool were. At her own convent school in Dublin, she had never seen a nun bustle or giggle.

The bells were ringing out in happiness, the sun was shining. Harriet looked about her, amazed at the love and support the community openly displayed for their favourite teacher, Miss Devlin.

Children from the school, both past and present, and residents from the four streets sat scrubbed and clean, in their Sunday best, chattering to each other over the organ music. Rays of sunshine, passing through the stained-glass windows, were reflected by one head of red hair after another, infusing the chancel with an amber glow.

The familiar smell, found in all churches everywhere, of old dark wood, once lovingly carved into pews and altar by hands long forgotten, mingled now with that of fresh flowers and damp moss.

Harriet had attended so many weddings in her lifetime, too many to count and now, here she was, too old even to be a bridesmaid.

'Morning, Harriet, you look lovely, you do. Love your hat.' One of the mothers, Deirdre, edged past her to take her seat next to her neighbour.

'Morning, Deirdre, thank you. You look lovely too. That's a pretty dress.'

'I know,' Deirdre replied with no false modesty. 'I got it in a jumble sale. Isn't it great? And it's got a label that says St Michael, so I did well there. Not just a lovely dress but it's got the name of the Irish centre and a saint on it. Can't be bad, eh? I've got me back covered, me. I'm going to wear it for the bingo, so I am. Reckon it'll bring me luck, Harriet?'

Both women laughed as Deirdre edged her way down the pew.

As she had promised to help Alison with her veil once she arrived, Harriet hovered by the church door and peeped out to see if she could spot the bridal car. The street seemed to be lined with every available officer from the Lancashire Constabulary.

Harriet was amused as she pondered another guilty secret. She had always liked a man in uniform.

Maura was having one of her bad days. Some were merely bad, others were dreadful. Today was just bad. She was coping better than she thought she would as a result of having Kathleen at her side.

'Maybe it's because the girls have been picked as Miss Devlin's bridesmaids, and Harry and Little Paddy as pageboys, that I don't feel so bad today,' Maura had said to Tommy early that morning.

She had packed her excited daughters into the taxi Miss Devlin had sent to take them to Maghull for the bridal preparation rituals, which apparently included lying on the spare bed for thirty minutes with slices of cucumber on their eyes.

Tommy joined Maura on the front step just as she raised her arm to wave goodbye to her daughters.

The daughters left behind. Those who hadn't died. The ones she had been allowed to keep.

'Aye, they will look grand when we see them later,' Tommy whispered into her wire curlers as he hugged her.

'They will and, sure, isn't that something to look forward to?' said Maura, hugging her Tommy back. Today, for the first time in a long while, Maura vaguely remembered what it was like to feel proud. She moved up the brow with her arm linked through Kathleen's and the two men following behind.

Maura still found it difficult to pass through a crowd. She could feel the silent sympathy that flowed towards her from the other mothers and, although she knew it was kind and well meant, she just couldn't handle it, not even now after so much time had passed. Sorry for your troubles. Sorry for your troubles. Sorry for your troubles.

They were the only words anyone had spoken to her for weeks and they still rang in her ears.

Maura and Kathleen stopped for a moment on the way up the hill to exchange words with some of their friends and for Kathleen to have a last cigarette.

'It lasts too long, a nuptial mass, too long to go without a ciggie and it looks rude, stepping out in the hymns for a quick one. And besides, I don't want to get on the wrong side of Father Anthony and Harriet,' Kathleen said, taking her ciggies out of her coat pocket.

'Look at this lot,' she said as she lit up, blinking through a haze of stinging blue smoke that brought tears to her eyes, 'not a curler to be seen anywhere. Doesn't everyone look nice, eh, Maura?'

Maura looked around. She had taken out her own curlers and put a comb through her hair that morning. She had to admit the women of the four streets had scrubbed up well.

'Peggy, how do ye manage to sleep with that beehive?' Kathleen asked, putting up her hand to feel Peggy's hair. The solid tower wobbled to one side as Kathleen pushed at it.

'There's a whole tin of lacquer on it, that's how,' said Peggy, bending her head to take a light from the end of Tommy's cigarette for her own. 'It's like sleeping on a fecking brick some nights.'

'You want to watch that when you light up,' said Kathleen. 'Lacquer is flammable, you know.'

'Flammable, what's that?' said Peggy. 'I use Get Set from Woolworth's. It's the best and costs nearly a shilling a tin. Does the job, though. My hair won't be going anywhere now and it lasts a whole two weeks each time it's done. Jesus, it's fecking itchy, though. Thanks be to God for knitting needles.'

Tommy took another half-ciggie from behind his ear and lit up to join Kathleen. He put his arm across his Maura's shoulders and hugged her to him.

In the past few weeks, they had a newfound closeness, brought about by the realization of how near they had come to the edge of disaster.

Neither would speak of the days when they had almost torn each other apart with blame and hatred. They did not acknowledge that Maura had entered her own temporary

172

world of madness. Tommy, struggling with his own grief, had had to hide the tablets the doctor had given her, as he feared she would wake in the night and swallow the whole bottle. A shiver ran down his spine when he thought of how close they had come to falling apart. Looking at his neighbours all around him today, he knew, without doubt, how they had been saved. If it hadn't been for Harry needing the hospital that night, God alone knows where they would be by now.

Extinguishing cigarettes on the pavement under their heels, they walked into the church where Nellie and the Doherty girls stood at the back, near to the font, in all their lilac fluff and finery, waiting for the bride.

'Not so comfortable with all these bizzies about, are you, Jer,' Tommy whispered to Jerry.

''Tis a great day for robbers today,' said Jerry, 'the lucky bastards.'

Jerry had said as much to Nellie that morning over breakfast.

'They will all be here in the four streets today, every copper in Liverpool. There will be great pickings over at Seaforth on the docks when they know the coast is clear.'

'Eh, pack it in, walls have ears,' said Nana Kathleen, smacking Jerry across his cap with the tea towel and nodding furiously towards Nellie.

'Eat that breakfast. Ye can go nowhere on an empty stomach,' Kathleen had said to Nellie early that morning. Nellie had spent the entire night in yellow sponge curlers and had hardly slept a wink.

'I'm putting those curlers in a parcel to Maeve,' Kathleen had said as she removed them that morning.

Kathleen sent a parcel from Liverpool back to the farm in Ballymara about once a month, as did anyone in Liverpool who could afford the postage home. In County Mayo, the shops carried very little of interest, their stocks being related directly to the need to survive rather than to entertain or amuse.

Nellie had spent more hours than she could count in the post office queue, holding oddly shaped brown-paper packages tied up with string, ready to be weighed and posted by sea mail to Mayo.

'They are no use here. Curlers to sleep in, my backside. What's wrong with just leaving them in all day for decoration? Who would want to sleep in curlers? Curlers are meant to be worn, not slept in.'

The parcel to be sent home lived in a drawer in the press and its contents grew each week.

Only yesterday Nellie had taken a peep at this month's parcel: Ladybird baby vests for someone in the village back home, Vitapointe hair conditioner and a bottle of Coty L'Aimant perfume for Auntie Maeve's birthday, all these lay on the brown-paper sheets, waiting to be posted.

Now, as Kathleen had scooped up the curlers and thrown them into the press drawer, Nellie found she was not sad to see the back of them.

'Howard has no fecking idea that the fruit in his wedding cake came from a sack off the back of the *Cotopaxi* when it berthed six weeks ago. Sandra Dever doesn't get her fruit or sugar from anywhere else. It's always knock-off.'

Both men sniggered and then Tommy stopped. He always

felt guilty when he laughed, feeling he shouldn't. After what had happened to Kitty, laughing must be wrong. He had never, ever wanted to laugh again. It had only been in the past few months that he had wanted to live.

'Howard is all right,' said Jerry. 'It's that Simon who gets to me. When they were questioning us, I always got the impression that he knew exactly what had happened and that, for some reason, he wasn't letting on.'

'That was just yer imagination, Jer. He couldn't have known. How could he? No one saw us.'

Tommy's heart lightened as soon as he saw his girls in church, a cluster of lilac-dipped angels, smiling at him – even Angela. Before Kitty had died, she could rarely raise a smile and she certainly hadn't done so since. Now she stood at the font in her white-satin, T-bar shoes, hopping from foot to foot, beaming.

'Da, hurry up,' she said impatiently. 'The bride is arriving soon. Move, move, Da.'

'I'm not budging until I get a kiss first,' said Tommy, placing his hands on his hips.

The girls laughed and clamoured, more eager to be rid of their embarrassing father than in need of a kiss. He placed a kiss on each of his girls' foreheads as Jerry did the same to his Nellie.

'You all right, Nellie?' asked Jerry, thinking his heart would burst with pride. His little girl was growing through her own personal heartache with dignity, and growing more like her mammy every day with her red ringlets tumbling down over her shoulders.

Nellie grinned up at him. 'I am, Da, but get lost.'

She playfully punched her da in the stomach. Jerry, pretending to be winded, laughed and followed Tommy into the nave.

As he moved down the aisle, a thought struck Tommy.

'Angela gets more like Kitty every day,' he said to Jerry.

'I was just thinking the same thing myself,' said Jerry, patting his mate on the back as they dipped on one knee, blessed themselves and slipped along the pew, taking their seats next to Maura and Kathleen.

Jerry didn't like being in church. It made him uncomfortable and, already, his collar was beginning to make his neck itch. Since the death of his first wife, Bernadette, he had attended only the christenings and communions he could not avoid. Today he had no choice, as Nellie was a bridesmaid. He would be forced to sit and witness another couple take their vows at exactly the same altar where he and Bernadette had knelt all those years ago. Her coffin had lain in front of that same altar a few short years later.

He now struggled to recall those years with the clarity he would like. This often made him panic, feeling that she was fading, which would mean that she was leaving them for good.

It was the same church, the same time of day, the same sunshine. The same people bearing witness. The people of the four streets.

The same shimmering silver ribbon of river flowed past only yards away. Every heart was filled with gladness, just as each had been for Jerry and his beautiful bride, Bernadette.

Jerry and Tommy both knelt in prayer: Tommy, because Maura had prodded him; Jerry, because, for the first time he could remember, he felt compelled to give thanks for Nellie and his mother, Kathleen.

He had lost his Bernadette in childbirth. His wife Alice had run away to America and left him for another docker on the four streets, a man who was supposed to have been his mucker. But he had his mam and his Nellie, both loyal and faithful, and he wanted God to leave them with him forever. For that, he knew, he should pray and ask him for his forgiveness, because sitting next to him was his best mate, Tommy, who had lost his daughter, Kitty. And there was Jerry, with his Nellie, alive and laughing at the back of the church. There, but for the grace of God, thought Jerry as he prayed.

A frisson of excitement swept through the congregation and, without anyone having to turn round or guess, they were all aware that the bride had arrived.

The organ struck up the bridal march and, as everyone stood, the procession began.

Kathleen linked Maura's arm with hers as they left the church, blinking in the bright sunlight. During those first awful weeks Kathleen had felt as though it was her job to prop Maura up. Now, it had become a habit. A physical reaction to Maura's weakness. She had become a human crutch.

The churchyard filled with the sound of cheers and children squealing as they pushed past each other.

'Well, isn't that just a grand sight,' said Kathleen, smiling at Nellie and Maura's daughters. The three girls, holding Alison's bridal train high off the cobbled path, were giggling and ducking as their school friends showered them with confetti.

As they walked on to the Irish centre, Kathleen shouted out to Maura and Tommy's twin boys, 'Run on ahead, lads, and keep our table. Run now, fast.'

Peggy had caught up with them whilst her silent husband, Paddy, fell into step alongside Tommy and Jerry.

'Aye, keep ours too,' said Peggy to her son, Little Paddy, giving him a cuff across the shoulder. He ran off to join Harry. 'There's nothing going to stand between me and that buffet today,' she said, 'and I want a good seat now 'cause I'm in for the night.'

'Will ye be taking to the dance floor tonight, Peggy?' asked Kathleen, squeezing Maura's arm gently.

Maura smiled. Making Maura smile was something Kathleen knew she could sometimes still make happen and it gave her enormous pleasure. There had been times when Kathleen had wondered whether she would ever see her friend smile again.

'I'll be dancing, all right, so I will,' replied Peggy. 'Michael Kenny is putting soap flakes on the floor tonight so we can dance a little faster. I can't wait! Jer, I'll be coming after ye for a spin as Paddy here, he's feckin' useless.'

Tommy and Jerry exchanged glances of dismay. Jerry couldn't think of anything worse than being forced to jitter-bug with the neighbour named by the local kids as 'Smelly Peggy'.

'I have a spare pair of bloomers in me handbag just in case,' said Peggy to Maura without a hint of embarrassment. 'Don't want the same thing happening as last time.'

As they all walked on up the hill engrossed in the midst of comfortable chatter, no one dared ask what that was. All of them were talking, except for Big Paddy, who chain-smoked but never spoke a word. It was impossible to walk and talk at the same time when your lungs provided only enough oxygen for one function or the other.

The bridal retinue stood on the path, posing for the photographer. The tall arched church door provided the backdrop for the former Miss Devlin and her new husband, Howard.

As Nellie watched the departing backs of her da and Nana Kathleen walking up the brow, she felt both alone and very grown up to have been left behind with the wedding party. The girls were bouncing up and down with excitement.

'Would ye look at them flowers,' said Angela yet again, plunging her bouquet straight into her face and inhaling the fragrance. 'Have ye ever smelt anything as wonderful as that?'

Angela spun round and stuck her posy straight into Nellie's face. Nellie's posy was exactly the same and smelt just the same. Nellie fell about laughing as Angela began sneezing repeatedly.

'Girls, girls,' said Miss Devlin. 'Stand still for the photographer now.'

Nellie thought she had never seen anyone look as beautiful as her favourite teacher did today.

'I'm sorry, Miss Devlin,' she said, running up to the bride and grabbing her hand. With her face infused with pride and happiness, she grinned up at Miss Devlin, who slipped her arm across Nellie's shoulder.

Click, click, snapped the camera shutters.

'Smile, girls,' said the photographer.

Click, click. A black-and-white moment, captured forever.

'Look towards me, ladies. Kiss the bride, Howard. Go on, yer allowed, she's yer missus now.'

Nellie and the bridesmaids blushed and giggled at the photographer's friendly taunts. They could hardly believe that Howard was actually going to kiss Miss Devlin, their teacher, right there in front of them, in broad daylight, yet he did just that.

While Howard kissed his blushing bride, Nellie noticed a police car pull up alongside the bridal car that was parked at the church gates.

'Where's Harriet?' said Alison, scanning the churchyard, then spotting Harriet modestly standing back from the main party. 'Harriet, come here. I'm not having my photographs without you in them, so I'm not.'

Harriet walked up to Nellie and, standing alongside her, placed her hand lightly on her shoulder, whispering in a confidential, girls-together way that made Nellie feel as though she wanted to burst with a sense of belonging and pride.

'There are police cars everywhere, Nellie. I've never been to a wedding like this before and that's for sure.'

Nellie smiled up at her. It was not so long ago there were police cars everywhere on the four streets, every day.

'We are used to that around here,' said Nellie in a very matter-of-fact, grown-up kind of way. 'It's how Miss Devlin and Howard met.' Nellie was displaying her life-before-Harriet credentials, her subtext being, not in an unkind way, *we have known her longer than you.*

Harriet smiled down. She knew exactly what Nellie was doing.

'Well, 'tis just a delight that everything has gone so well

now. Don't you think, Nellie? A wedding without a hitch, I think we could safely say.'

Nellie laughed with pleasure. Harriet, a woman of indeterminate age, who was beautiful, travelled, clever and was the sister of the priest, was talking to Nellie as though she were her equal.

'Yes, who would have dreamt that,' Nellie said.

She raised her gloved hand and returned her da's wave as he turned on his heel and, for a moment, walked up the brow backwards to check up on his not-so-little-any-more girl.

'But Miss Devlin is special, so she is. She can do anything. There not being a hitch was how it was always going to be. God, she would have let out a roar if anything had gone wrong, so she would.'

As Nellie spoke, she noticed there was something unusual about the police car which had drawn up by the church gate. Rather than the usual blue-and-white panda, it was black and the officer who stepped out of it wore a flat-peaked cap with a very impressive wide black-and-white chequered band around the middle, not a domed helmet like most of the policemen around.

He began talking to people in the street and casually walked over to some of the officers.

Others, who obviously should have been elsewhere, such as on Seaforth docks, and not at the wedding, slunk back to their cars and began to slowly melt away.

'Ooh, who is this?' asked Harriet, following Nellie's gaze.

'I've no idea at all,' said Nellie. 'I've never seen a police car like that on the streets since the night Molly was murdered.'

She whispered the last few words. It felt inappropriate to

talk out loud about a murder whilst smiling for the camera at a wedding.

'Howard, have you got a minute, lad?'

One of the officers called out this most ridiculous-sounding question to Howard, beckoning him away from Alison, his bride of only minutes. Her smile slipped from her face as fast as her new husband's hand slid out of hers.

'Howard, what is it?' Alison asked. Her feminine antennae were up.

'Can't be anything to do with me, love. I'm off for a fortnight now,' Howard called over his shoulder. 'Back in a second. I will just see what it is. Smile for the camera, girls.'

His size twelve feet crunched on the gravel of the church path. Nellie realized that you could hear it very clearly because, suddenly, everyone else was quiet. The wedding scene stood in freeze frame. Only Howard was moving and the air filled with an intense expectation.

Alison was the first to break the silence in an attempt to mask the sudden absence of her husband.

'Harriet, what can it be?' she said, putting out her hand to her friend, who moved from Nellie's side to Alison's. Nellie stepped closer in and tucked herself under Alison's arm.

Alison called to Sister Evangelista, who stood at the end of the drive, close to the important-looking policeman.

'Who are they?' she asked.

Since Sister Evangelista had been talking to Annie O'Prey at the gate when Alison had called her, it was a fair assumption that she would have heard every word that had been spoken.

'I have no idea, Alison. They asked Mrs Keating if they

could speak to Howard. Annie O'Prey butted in and told them he was getting wed today, but apparently the man said it couldn't wait, and he had to speak to him now.'

As Sister Evangelista finished speaking, Howard was seen talking to the man with the black-and-white chequered band on his hat and frowning.

Howard began to walk back down the path with the important-looking officer, both heading towards Simon, who had moved over to the gravestones without anyone noticing. Simon looked even more concerned than Howard.

'What is it, Howard?' said Alison as they both walked past her towards Simon. Alison sounded agitated. This was not part of her carefully orchestrated wedding-day plan.

'Who are they?' asked Harriet.

She had never seen so many men in uniform in one place before in her life. She felt her face flush; she had never known such excitement occur in one day.

The man in the peaked cap put his hand on Simon's elbow and led him to the back door of the large Black Maria police car, its windows blacked out. Nellie could see that there was someone sitting in the back, but she couldn't see who.

'Alison,' said Howard, shouting back down the path, 'love, they have some news and they are going to need to talk to you.'

'Me?' said Alison, sounding both disbelieving and disappointed all at the same time. 'Why me?'

Suddenly the back door of the car opened and Alison gasped.

'Daisy?' Alison almost screamed her name.

Click, click, snapped the shutters. Click, click.

Wearing the pillbox hat they had presented to her at the Christmas play, and which Maggie had found on a hook in Sister Theresa's section of the linen cupboard, Daisy half raised her hand in a nervous wave to Miss Devlin.

'Oh, thank God.' Alison put her hand to her mouth as tears filled her eyes. 'I thought she was dead.'

Sister Evangelista, Alison and Harriet reached for one another's hands. All three women exchanged glances of relief and happiness that they could not express in words. Harriet knew who Daisy was. How could she not? Alison used to speak of her every day.

'Here, Nellie, hold my flowers,' said Alison, thrusting her bouquet at Nellie. She began to run down the drive towards Daisy, tottering on her high heels while holding up her white satin explosion of a dress.

'Alison, it isn't all good news, love,' said Howard as he put out his hand to help her over the cobbles.

'What do you mean? Daisy being found is the best news I could have on my wedding day. Howard, this is the best present I could have had, ever.'

By now, she was hugging Daisy.

'Alison, love.' Howard was struggling to get through to his new bride, but, in her euphoria at Daisy being found, she was beyond hearing.

It was only Nellie and Harriet who spotted the handcuffs being placed on Simon before he was discreetly slipped into the back of the car Daisy had vacated. The man in the black-and-white cap with the chequered band took the seat next to him and, within seconds, the car had quietly whisked them both away.

Chapter Eight

'I'm coming, Mother,' Ben shouted down the stairs, in response to her repeated calls summoning him to her traditional morning fry-up. His mother's hearing had been damaged by a bomb blast during the war and, despite the fact he had now replied three times, she hadn't heard him once.

Ben couldn't move down the stairs as quickly as he used to.

During the war he had served as an officer in North Africa and Italy. When in France, he had taken a German bullet that had shattered his right tibia and fibula into many pieces, at the same time that a flying piece of shrapnel took up residence in his cheekbone, leaving a four-inch scar running parallel with his right eye. Ben never complained. How could he? He was one of the lucky ones. His brother had returned home in a flag-draped box and his mother had yet to recover.

Immediately following his injury, Ben had been taken by stretcher to a field hospital to be stabilized and made well enough to travel to a military hospital in Belgium. On the long journey back to his home on Queens Drive, he had spent three months in a convalescence home across the water in

West Kirby, where his mother had come to visit once a week. He had managed to see his father just before he passed away of a broken heart. No words had been said but Ben and his mother both knew that the dead son had been his badly disguised favourite.

All the doctors in the world could not have prevented Ben from being left with a right leg three inches shorter than his left. He was awarded a clutch of medals for his endeavour and bravery, which did nothing to ease his pain nor mend his anguish at returning from the war disabled and an only child.

There were some medals he wore on his chest, pinned to his suit when he attended formal regimental dinners. There was also a much larger memorial trinket in the form of an iron leg caliper, which he would wear every day for the remainder of his life. At forty-two years of age, he required a stick to help him walk, very slowly.

A more serious effect of his injuries had been their impact on his self-esteem. Before his facial injury Ben could have been described as handsome, albeit quietly so. He now felt that no woman worth her salt would ever want to look twice at a man as broken and unattractive as he. Since the day he had returned home, he had never once looked a woman directly in the eye. If he didn't see her eyes, she might not see the deeper, hidden scars beneath his own.

This saddened his mother who knew that, at sixty-six years of age, she could not be far from the end of her life. Whenever she felt she could do so, without making him cross, she would raise the subject of marriage with Ben. Her son never became really angry, but his scar would turn a tell-tale red when she had upset him and touched that ever-raw nerve.

The scar spoke for him. It burnt and flamed the message back to his mother: 'Who would take this trophy of war?'

Olive Manning had lost her first son, Matthew, at the outbreak of hostilities and Ben, her second, had been injured close to the end of them. Her husband had died two weeks after Ben's honourable discharge. His last words to his wife were that now Ben was home, injured but alive, and he would look after her. Her husband was quite right. Benjamin did look after her. He was the most dutiful of sons.

Ben often wandered into his brother's bedroom. The telegram, which his mother had received from the War Office, lay folded on the top of the dresser she polished every Friday morning, ready for the weekend, during which nothing of any significance ever took place.

Ben often picked up the envelope, faded to a tea-coloured brown by the bright sunlight that still on occasion slipped into the room, and he read the black ticker-tape words over and over again. It had lain there, in the same place, propped up against the dark mahogany-framed mirror. It was as though his mother had placed the telegram on the dresser to inform any ghostly relative who might pop into Matthew's room that he was dead, that he had joined them already and that he would not be returning to lay his earthly head on his feather pillow with its crisp linen cover. No point hovering here. Matthew has gone. We know this. Read the telegram.

Ben hobbled into the kitchen, ducking his head under the narrow doorway at the bottom of the stairs, and winced, as always, as he managed the last two steps. His mother pretended not to notice.

'What important meetings do you have this morning then?' she asked.

Benjamin worked at the City Corporation offices and was responsible for managing the fund the government had poured into Liverpool. It had taken them almost twenty years after the war, but at last they were building new houses, roads, libraries, nurseries and schools.

Liverpool was about to benefit from a growth spurt and, as the new estates sprang up, private landlords would lose their grip on the poor with their extortionate rents for squalid houses.

'It's a meeting at the Priory of St Mary's, down at the docks, about the new nursery and library we are building. The church want to have a say in running both.'

'And is that possible?' asked his mother. 'St Mary's? Isn't that the church where the priest was murdered? I'm sure it was. Dear me, Ben, you had better take care down there. I would quite like you home in one piece.'

'You're right, Mother. It was that church. Well remembered. If I'm honest, I had forgotten. It was my secretary who pointed that out to me. There is a new priest now, apparently. He is very new school, very nineteen-sixties. He wants the Church to reach out and become more involved in the community. That is why they have asked me to attend the meeting. It is something I am happy to discuss. The more the Church helps, the less it costs the council, but I'm very nervous about the library. We want more than bibles for people to read and that will be a stumbling block.'

'Quite right,' replied his mother with a hint of relief in her voice. 'Don't let the papists take over everything, because they would if given half the chance, Benjamin. That's how they work. It is all about power and control. The more pies they have their fingers stuck in, the more influence they can wield. I'm not saying they are all bad. The Pope seems quite nice as a matter of fact, but they just have too much say in what happens everywhere in this city, if you ask me. This isn't Dublin. It's Liverpool, a different country entirely.'

'Have you finished?' asked Ben with a grin, buttering himself a slice of toast . 'You say exactly the same thing about the Jews. You didn't stop to draw breath there. Anyone would think you ran up the frocks for the Orange Order on march day.'

'Don't be cheeky, Ben. I don't like any religion. They are all trouble, as far as I am concerned. I go to my Church of England service on Easter Sunday and Christmas morning, and that is all that is required from any respectable Christian. All that God bothering. I can't be doing with it. If God existed, he would make sure there were no wars and I would still have my son and ...'

Her voice trailed away. She wanted to say that Ben wouldn't have been injured and he would have a wife and she would have grandchildren and her husband would still be alive and she would make a Sunday lunch for them all and present it on the ten-place dinner service she and Ben's father had bought with love and care for just that day. It had been wished for and spoken about, even longed for. This was not the life they had foreseen in the heady first years of their marriage.

But she didn't say a word. She knew Ben didn't like it when she raised the subject of marriage, even though that didn't always stop her.

She placed in front of Ben his breakfast of black pudding, sausages and fried eggs.

'They've taken over Everton, you know, the Irish,' she said and poured them both tea before sitting down at the table herself, as she did so sliding towards Ben the Royal Albert marmalade pot with its dinky silver spoon popping out from under the lid. 'You can't move for the Irish and Catholics anywhere on the brow now. They even have their own things in the shops.'

'Oh, really,' said Ben, already sounding exasperated. 'Like what?'

'Well, in the butcher's, he has changed the sign from "bacon" to "rashers". It's just the start, Ben. They were all supposed to go back after the famine. It's about time you stopped worrying about all those Irish and concentrated on finding yourself a wife. I will be in a wheelchair by the time I have grandchildren.'

Suddenly, it was as though an icy blast had shot through their little kitchen on Queens Drive. She had uttered the words guaranteed to ruin Ben's day.

For the first five years following his discharge, Ben's mother ceaselessly harped on about his finding a wife until suddenly, without any warning, one day when his leg was particularly painful, Ben had exploded. It was the one and only time he had ever shouted at his mother and now, here she was, poking at his wound once more. Not the one she could see, the visible wound that made her heart ache for the physical discomfort etched on his face when he returned home from a long day at work, but the invisible wound. The raw, lonely, aching wound Ben carried inside.

'Please don't, Mother.' His voice was calm but cold as steel. 'You know the terrible row we had last time you brought this up. Nothing has altered. I don't want a wife.'

Mrs Manning put both of her elbows on the table and leant forward earnestly, nursing her teacup in both hands and speaking across the rim.

'Ben, I will soon have had my threescore year and ten. How can I die a happy woman, knowing you will be all alone?'

Ben carefully returned the marmalade spoon to the pot, replaced the lid and kept his eyes focused on his toast.

'No woman wants to marry a cripple, Mother. It would be a hugely unfair thing to ask anyone and, besides, no self-respecting woman would look twice at this contraption.' He glanced down at his leg.

He no longer felt like eating his breakfast and slowly, with the aid of his stick, rose from the table.

'I have to leave. The meeting at St Mary's Priory begins at nine-thirty. I had better start out now as I need to change buses at the Pier Head and make my way down to Nelson Street.'

'Nelson Street? Heavens above, you are right in the middle of them all down there at the docks. You can't move for bog jumpers.'

'Mother.' Ben's voice rose sharply in condemnation, even though he had heard the expression so many times. It was commonly used amongst those who were not of Irish descent.

Ben took down his coat from the hook on the hall dresser that stood adjacent to the front door. His mother scooped up his plate from the table with annoyance and banged it down on the draining board next to the kitchen sink.

'We need to be a bit less welcoming, if you ask me, and then maybe a few more of them would go back home,' she shouted from the kitchen.

'No wonder the Irish stick together if they have to face comments like that. What would you do in their shoes? I feel obliged now to let the church have whatever they want with the nursery and the library.'

Once outside, Ben let out a long breath. He had closed the front door with unaccustomed force. He hadn't realized how much his mother irritated him when she was mean about others and harped on about their taboo subject, his finding a wife.

'That is never going to happen,' he whispered to himself, leaning on his stick as he began his walk to the bus stop.

Chapter Nine

'WATCH THE ROAD now, Mr Curtis, 'tis a good stretch from here to Dublin. A few hours and you will be safe, back home with your good wife. I am delighted, so I am, that all was in order and you will come again, will you? We will be looking forward to it, won't we, Sister Celia? And be sure to give us plenty of notice now as we wouldn't want you to travel all this way and be hungry, not even for a second, would we, Sister Celia?'

Sister Assumpta was bidding farewell to the visiting councillors and do-gooders who had called to inspect the laundry and the mother and baby home.

'Watch the vans on that road, will you. The boys driving the delivery vans from the village are just demons, the way they speed along that road. They can drive at forty miles an hour, some of them, so the man who delivers the laundry from the hotel in Galway told me, and he is a good Catholic, he never misses mass and would never tell a lie, isn't that so, Sister Celia?'

And the car doors slammed. One. After. The. Other.

At the sound of the car engine starting up, she waved to the retreating boot of a Ford Cortina.

Sister Assumpta and Sister Celia were both rather too enthusiastically waving goodbye to the councillors who were visiting from the county offices.

They had asked far too many questions for the Reverend Mother's liking.

She stomped back down the corridor to her office, Sister Celia bustling behind in her wake, struggling to keep up.

'The nerve of them,' she ranted, once she had closed the big double wooden doors behind them. 'Fancy asking me to make sure all *my* tracks are covered. Can you believe they used those words? You would not believe the nerve of them, would you now?'

'No, Reverend Mother,' Sister Celia gasped. Unused to moving so quickly, she was already puffing and red in the face. It had been a hard day, what with visitors probing around her ovens and making her nerves jangle. 'I've felt like a mad woman all day, trying to keep the surliest of those ungrateful girls out of the way. God alone knows, the moon would crack itself if one of them smiled. They were no sight for visitors, so they weren't, and ye just never know when one of them might try something on, like turning on the waterworks.'

'You were right, Sister Celia. This visit must have something to do with the cut of that interfering woman, Rosie O'Grady, that busybody of a matron. She has never stopped asking questions and probing into our business since her family brought that girl here from Liverpool.'

'Well, they did say that their next visit was St Vincent's, so she must have reported them too. Did they say what we have to do?' asked Sister Celia, aware that after such an important visit, there must at least be something required of them in terms of how they functioned. The officials had taken lots of notes.

'We have to make sure that our own records don't reflect the bank transactions, nor identify which payments come from which government departments, nor for which girls the payments are made. We have to keep everything confidential. As if we didn't already. They must think we came down with the last shower. Why do they think we change everyone's names the minute they arrive?'

'Are we still claiming for the two girls who escaped? Aideen and Agnes?' asked Sister Celia.

'We are that,' Sister Assumpta threw Sister Celia a sharp look, 'but we have to be careful. If you ask me, 'tis no coincidence at all that they became very friendly with the midwife and it was they who delivered the baby of the midwife's girl, Cissy. As sure as God is true, I know she has had something to do with their escape. Not for one minute would she admit it, though. Someone outside the Abbey helped those girls get away. They could not have done it without help. There must have been a car at the very least.'

'Maybe someone on the road gave them a lift if they got through the gates?'

'You know, that could be true. Maybe we need to employ a gate man as St Vincent's have done. We can do without runaways and that's the truth.'

Sister Assumpta flopped into her office chair with little grace and began opening her mail. The official visit had put her a day behind and had thrown the Abbey routine into disarray. In preparation, the areas shown to the visitors had been scrubbed spick and span. Many of the girls with children in the nursery would not see their babies for a week, as a result of the extra work made necessary by the visit.

'It will soon be time for lunch, Sister Celia. I shall have mine whilst I see to the bills in the post. 'I will eat in the office today, but first, to prayers.'

Both women bustled off towards the chapel as the sound of bells called them to prayer.

Sister Assumpta, although disturbed and made bad-tempered by the visit, breathed a sigh of relief. They had survived. The officials hadn't asked to see any further than the first few sinks in the laundry.

They had, however, undertaken a very detailed examination of the kitchens. Sister Assumpta was well aware that the councillors had assumed the food being prepared for the nuns was also for the girls. It wasn't for her to disabuse them of that notion.

'Sure, do they think girls eat beef stew when they are steeped in sin?' asked Sister Celia, running along beside her as they walked to mass. 'Do they not understand the job we have here, to keep these girls under control? If we fed them what we ate, they would think they were forgiven and become impossible to manage. For the sake of heaven, why would they think they know better than we?'

The visitors had, in fact, been extremely impressed with Sister Assumpta's facilities and soul-saving discipline. It served them no purpose to agree with the complaints made by Dublin's most senior midwife. Who did she think would look after such wayward girls if the holy nuns didn't, and at what cost?

'Sure, God alone knows the money these nuns save us and the good they do,' one councillor had whispered to another as they surveyed the spotless kitchens where a rich beef stew was being stirred by a smiling nun.

The officials had understood the need for cleanliness and obedience.

They had needed no convincing that redemption from sin was to be achieved via hard work. There was even talk that they would send them more girls, because they felt the Abbey could easily handle an increase in numbers.

More girls meant more money.

'That high and mighty, overeducated Rosie O'Grady will not be happy if she discovers that her interfering has brought us more penitents,' Sister Assumpta had grumbled. 'I wonder if she knows her complaining has made things better for us. I have no notion what it is that woman was trying to achieve by reporting us to the authorities, as she has half a dozen times. Will she not stop?'

As she prayed, Sister Assumpta gave thanks that the councillors hadn't asked to look at her paperwork, nor enquired what happened to the girls or the babies who died. There were no death certificates to show them, only plots of earth in the garden. Underneath the weeping willows.

Disgraced girls who had arrived at the convent from the country were not even given the grace of a requiem mass, nor a name – their own name – to mark their graves. Only the penitents who came directly from the industrial schools run by the brothers or other convents were issued with a death certificate, but, even then, not always. Money came into the Abbey for living penitents, not dead ones. On occasion, Sister Assumpta would delay as long as a year before informing the authorities that a girl had died.

The dead babies and children were laid together, deep in the earth. She had lost count of how many there were or even what their names had been. There must have been hundreds by now. The nuns had begun digging the plot over fifty years ago at the turn of the century. The previous Reverend Mother had kept a ledger in which she entered in ink the name of each child and the date they were buried. Sister Assumpta had thought for a long time now that the ledger needed to be destroyed.

Babies were lost in childbirth. For those who survived, many fell victim to disease and infection.

Their pitiful bodies had been preserved in the gently receiving, peat-rich earth, condemned to purgatory for eternity.

When mass was over, Sister Celia took the Reverend Mother her lunch on a tray: boiled beef left over from the previous evening's supper, with salad leaves that the nuns grew in their own garden, and an apple pie, made by Sister Celia from the apples stored in the straw-layered wicker baskets, down in the dark cellar.

'Put the tray by the fireplace,' said Sister Assumpta as Sister Celia wobbled precariously through the door, 'and stay for your own. I'd like you to join me as I don't feel like eating alone today.'

Sister Celia flushed with pride. She was the only nun the Reverend Mother ever invited to eat with her.

'I'll be right back then,' she gabbled and rushed from the room with the empty tray.

Sister Assumpta took over to the fire the few letters she hadn't yet tackled and, after pouring the tea, she picked up the last remaining airmail letter.

She noticed it was from America, but this was not unusual by any means. Sister Assumpta received such letters every day. Sometimes they were from priests, writing on behalf of families in need of a baby or a child to adopt easily and quickly. Sometimes the families wrote themselves.

Some might be letters containing begging pleas and offers of money from barren parents willing to pay any price to adopt a child of their own.

Shovelling into her mouth a huge bite of salted beef and lettuce, sandwiched between freshly buttered white bread, the Reverend Mother leant back in the chair, flicked open the letter with the ornate silver-and-bone-handled knife and began to read.

'I'm back,' Sister Celia trilled as she waddled through the office door, laden with an ample lunch for her own consumption.

Reverend Mother didn't answer.

'What is wrong?' Sister Cecilia enquired. 'You look a little pale. Is it the beef? Is it all right now? We saved the best cut for you, Reverend Mother.' Sister Assumpta still did not reply.

She turned the letter over in her hand and looked at the sender's address on the back of the envelope. And then she turned it round and read it again.

'It concerns the child who was adopted by the Moynihans in Chicago, the builders who paid us three thousand dollars for the baby if they could take it quickly. The baby is sick and they need to know who the mother is. They are on their way here on an aeroplane to talk to us. As if we need more visitors. We may as well open as an hotel and start charging an entry fee.'

'Ye can't tell them that anyway.' Sister Celia looked shocked. 'It is against the rules, and the authorities wouldn't allow it. Besides, who is the mother? Is she a penitent?'

'No, it was the girl Rosie O'Grady sent and delivered.'

'Oh, Heavenly Father, no.'

The flush faded from Sister Celia's own cheeks. Rosie O'Grady was trouble. Nothing had been the same since the day she had taken that girl. They had even had a reporter knocking at the door last week because Rosie O'Grady had written a letter to the newspaper, calling for an explanation of the role of the laundries and the mother and baby homes.

'What will ye tell them?' Sister Celia asked.

'I will tell them the truth, which is all I do know: that the girl's name was Cissy, and that she came from Liverpool. She kept her own name because of that Rosie O'Grady's involvement. I shall send them straight on to see Mrs O'Grady in Dublin. Let her deal with it. We upheld our part of the bargain; the girl has nothing to do with us. She was neither a penitent in the laundry nor a country girl from the mother and baby home. She was a favour we did for the matron. I hope they aren't after getting their money back just because the child is sick.'

Sister Assumpta gazed into the fire deep in contemplation while Sister Celia ate. The airmail letter hung loosely in her hand and rested on her knee.

She startled Sister Celia when without warning she said, 'There is no moon tonight, Sister Celia. I want all the ledgers from the locked cupboard to be carried out to the midden. Everything, all the papers dating right back from when the first girl arrived here sixty years ago, except for the contracts each girl signed, agreeing to surrender her baby. Set the lot on fire. We can't be blamed for what can't be proven.'

'Sure, well, we will do that, Reverend Mother. I've plenty of girls to get that done, but then what?'

'No, don't use the girls. Don't even use the novices. Let this be done by the nuns. I don't want the girls' prying eyes seeing this, not that any of them can read. We will burn the lot and, tomorrow, we will pay a visit to the sisters up the road at St Vincent's and suggest they do the same. They have been here only a few years but, sure, they will be keeping good records, I have no doubt.

'That Sister Theresa was always a stickler. I don't want people assuming that what they practise there, we follow suit here. More secrecy is what is needed and, if I know Sister Theresa, that won't even have crossed her mind. Oh, yes, come along in now, she would say to anyone who asked. She always was a foolish woman who could never see what was right under her very nose. They would have her tied up in knots. We will drive over first thing in the morning.'

'SHALL I WAIT, nurse? Will he be long or would you rather I came back in half an hour?'

Stanley was instructed to wait. It was a Monday morning in the X-ray department of the children's hospital. The nurse was obviously keen to finish and empty the department so that she could rush to the canteen and meet the other nurses for their post-weekend, lunchtime gossip.

Stanley sat on one of the hard wooden benches as he waited for the young boy he had brought in a wheelchair to be pushed back out to him. In the meantime, he took the opportunity to roll up two cigarettes for both himself and Austin, then carefully laid them on a bed of tobacco in his tin, which he slipped back into the large pocket of his brown overall.

Stanley always experienced the same frisson of excitement when he took a call at the porter's lodge to collect a little lad from the children's ward. This one had been a disappointment. He was far too young.

Stanley had standards. He regarded himself as above the others in the ring, especially Austin.

Just at that moment, Austin breezed into the X-ray

department in his long brown porter's coat and sat next to Stanley, having himself wheeled into the department another child from the same ward.

Austin seemed agitated.

'She's back,' he whispered to Stanley.

'Who's back?' Stanley asked. A puzzled frown sat on his face.

'The housekeeper, Daisy, she escaped and she's back.'

'Jesus, are you fucking joking?'

'Do I look like I'm fucking joking?'

Indeed, Austin was as white as a sheet.

'How? How did that fucking happen? I thought the bishop had sorted it and that she was put away?'

'He did and she was, but she is back and she has fingered the policeman, Simon, the one who took her to the home. I knew it was fucking crazy, sending someone she could finger if she was asked.'

'Jesus, let's hope she doesn't remember you, Austin. She was one of your favourites. You and the bishop had more than your fair share there when she was a kid. Anyway, she's simple, isn't she? No one will believe anything she says. She's mental, isn't she? That's what you always said.'

'You cheeky bastard,' said Austin, 'don't blame any of this on me.'

'I'm not blaming you, but what do we do now?'

'We do nothing, Stanley. We aren't the main players in this, for fuck's sake. Why do you think everyone's identity is kept secret? You and I only know each other because I took you. We only know Arthur because he took me. The only other people we know are the bishop and that policeman, but I know this,

Stanley: there are people way, way more important than you or me in that ring. Jesus, who do you think I sell all my photos to?'

'I don't fucking care,' said Stanley, his voice rising.

Austin lightly placed his hand on his sleeve.

Stanley dropped his voice and continued, 'Who is that Daisy going to finger next if she's named the policeman? This is a disaster, Austin. She knew all about what went on at the Priory, for fuck's sake. She even opened the door and let some of the kids in. The priest was so up his own arse he thought he was too important to do it himself.'

'It isn't people like me and you at the bottom of the pile that they will be looking for. It's the posh nobs, the politician from London with the chauffeur-driven car, the ones who speak like they've got a finger stuck up their arse – those are the ones they will be after. And anyway, like you say, she was fucking simple. She won't even remember our names. It's much easier for her to say, the policeman, the bishop or the politician. That's why the policeman has been fingered. She said a policeman and then probably identified him. She didn't know where we work or what we do for a job. Relax, mate, haven't I always been right, eh? Eh? Haven't I? Every time you've had a wobbly, didn't I always know what was what and that it would all be all right?'

Stanley nodded. It was true, Stanley was always the nervous one and Austin had always been right.

'It's all right for you, Austin, you live alone. I have me mam to worry about. I can't even think how it would affect her, if she ever knew what I did.'

'Relax, mate,' said Austin. 'There's nothing to worry about with your mam, it will all be good.'

Austin's words weren't having their usual calming effect as, Stanley had noticed, his voice shook slightly.

The nurse called out for Austin as she wheeled her child out of X-ray.

'Let's meet up for a fag in ten in the lodge when you are done here,' he whispered to Stanley as he rose from the bench.

It was Austin who had kept Stanley on the straight and narrow when he had the collywobbles, on the days when he was tormented by guilt, fear and worry about his being caught and his mam being disappointed in him. It was Austin who pulled him up sharp and made him see right again.

Not today, though. Never before had Austin failed to reassure Stanley. His guts had turned to water.

Since he and Austin had become involved in the group to which Arthur had introduced them, they often talked about the legalizing of their own inclination. Stanley had even gone by coach with Austin and Arthur to a meeting in London about that very thing. Times were changing. Arthur never stopped saying, 'Homos will be legal soon, we will be next.'

Soon, paedophiles like themselves would be protected by the law just as homosexuals would soon be. This, they firmly believed.

Stanley knew that someone in the ring was involved in all of this progress. He just didn't know who it was, which was how it would always remain. They were each protected by their own anonymity.

Stanley could tell Austin was spooked. The cool, untouchable swagger was gone, replaced by rounded, almost slumped shoulders.

The pretty little girl in the wheelchair was about six years old, Austin's favourite age, but even this hadn't put the usual grin on his face. He carried his Kodak Brownie in his big overall pocket everywhere he went. In normal circumstances, in the lift, he would have slid the little girl's blanket and nightdress up over her knee and photographed her, before she was returned to the ward, laughing and joking as he did so.

It was so easy. The poorer and more impoverished the children were, the more they loved the attention of the camera. Not today, though.

Stanley stood and, through the circular porthole windows, high in the wooden doors leading to the X-ray department, he followed Austin's retreating back. Agitated at the news that Daisy was in Liverpool once more, he then sat down and turned to look through the large window to the courtyard. He could watch Austin cross, wheeling the chair to the ward doors on the opposite side.

It took a few moments for Stanley to register what was happening as, with an action as slick as an uncoiling snake, a policeman stepped out through the ward doors and snapped a pair of handcuffs onto Austin's wrists.

Stanley immediately knew what he had to do. They had been through the drill so many times at their monthly meetings. Slowly, he rose from the bench and, so as not to draw attention to himself, he walked calmly out of the back door.

'Porter, porter, your patient's ready,' shouted the radiographer from within the lead-lined cubicle. 'Would you believe it,' he heard her say to her workmate on reception, 'the porter has only gone and buggered off for a ciggie.'

By the time he reached the hospital gates, Stanley was running. He turned out on to Queens Drive and kept on running. He knew that he had to reach Arthur, the ringleader as quickly as possible. Arthur would know what to do.

The plan had been in place for over ten years and it was always the last thing discussed each time the group met. Secrecy was their modus operandi. People like them were never, ever, caught. Never. They were methodical and careful. They had strict rules. Should those fail, they would resort to long-established and well-rehearsed procedures. Arthur had people who could protect them, contacts who could offer places to hide. Once the others found out what had happened to Austin, Stanley would need just such a place himself.

Chapter Eleven

'FANCY DELAYING YOUR honeymoon, Miss Devlin. I can't believe it, I just can't. You should be in the Isle of Man by now. I feel so bad that I have upset everything. Do I still call you Miss Devlin, or is it your married name now?'

It was Monday morning. Daisy was ladling as much marmalade as she possibly could onto her last piece of toast before popping it into her mouth. This meant that, for a brief second, she ceased talking and drew breath.

She had almost finished her breakfast in the convent where she had spent the previous two nights. She talked so much and so fast, it was hard for anyone to slide a word in edgeways. Not only was Daisy talking fifty to the dozen, she was surrounded by nuns and children. Annie O'Prey, Sheila from Nelson Street with her children, and a constant relay of neighbours were tripping up and down the convent steps to visit her.

Alison laughed. 'You do love your food, don't you, Daisy? I want to be here because I want to see your brother again and make sure that, this time, I hand you over personally. Besides, they have asked Howard to return to work and to delay our honeymoon. We don't mind at all. In any case, I will have a much nicer time, knowing that everything is properly sorted here. It would have been difficult, Daisy, trying to enjoy myself, having no idea where you were or what had happened to you.'

Sister Evangelista walked into the refectory and sat down at the table with them both. No longer a stranger to a crisis, she was absolutely certain this time about what to do.

'Will you be ringing the bishop to let him know Daisy is back?' Alison asked.

'Sure, I will not. What use would he be if I did tell him? He was as much use as a chocolate fireguard last time we needed him and with half the backbone. No, thank you. We have Father Anthony and Harriet with us now, sent directly to us by the Lord, I have no doubt. They will be a grand help. I have no use for a weak bishop. Father Anthony will know what to do and, if the bishop needs to know what is happening, Father Anthony can tell him. I am washing my hands altogether of that responsibility.'

The new Mrs Davies was almost sure she heard Sister Evangelista mutter, 'Stupid man,' under her breath, following on from the 'chocolate fireguard'.

'The bishop doesn't need to know Daisy has returned or that the police have already been to the Priory to see Father Anthony, who, I will have you know, Alison, has handled everything in an exemplary manner. The man is magnificent in his ability to project authority and calm. That's what a spell in Rome can do for a priest. We have a different quality in the parish altogether now and, sure, we are very lucky here, we are. Is he not the most fabulous priest? We could do no better at all. No, leave it all to Father Anthony, he will know what to do, not the bishop.' She began to mutter as she poured her tea and from behind a plume of steam, Alison was sure she heard what she said.

There it was again, now Alison was certain: she definitely heard Sister Evangelista say, 'Useless man,' when she had finished speaking.

Alison had not wanted to pass comment, but she was quite sure that at one time, she had heard Sister Evangelista heap exactly the same praise she had for Father Anthony on the dead priest, Father James. She would now no longer discuss him, no matter how much Alison tried to persuade her to do so.

Without knowing it, Father Anthony had shamed the bishop over his obscure and evasive behaviour during the previous investigation.

Sister Evangelista looked lighter and happier than she had in months. 'I noticed Harriet leaving the Priory earlier and I wouldn't be surprised to find she is on her way over here. Everyone else appears to be. I've never known the convent so busy, Daisy. You are quite the attraction.'

'Well, I'm here because I cannot go anywhere else and I don't want to leave Daisy,' said Alison. 'Howard has been called back to work to assist the new commander from today onwards. At least we had the weekend, eh? Anyway, thank goodness it is the summer holidays and the school is closed. I don't want to miss having a few days with Daisy. I think it would be nice for her to get to know Harriet and Father Anthony.

'Ah, speak of an angel and hear the rustle of her wings,' Alison trilled as Harriet swept in through the door.

'Morning, everyone.' Harriet's voice rang out from the hallway. 'Are you up already? Have you recovered from the wedding and all that dancing on Saturday night?'

'You will often hear Harriet coming long before you see her,' Alison said to Daisy with an indulgent smile.

'Aye, she seems to forget she's in a convent and silence is a virtue,' Sister Evangelista said drily.

Daisy smiled. To all who had asked her, she had explained about her having been in a convent in Ireland. From the moment she had arrived back in the four streets she had been besieged with questions. Once the wedding festivities had begun, Daisy knew she was safe and so she had the time of her life.

It was hard for Daisy to find words to express the difference between Sister Theresa's convent in Galway and the one in Liverpool. She could not understand why it was that the nuns at St Mary's were kindness itself compared with those at St Vincent's. It was a mystery to everyone other than Daisy as to why Simon had taken her to the convent.

Maggie had told Daisy to be very careful what she told and to whom she told it.

'Keep your powder dry. Tell no one anything they don't need to know, not even the sisters at St Mary's. The only people you should tell almost everything to are the police. But you don't mention another word about that little girl's da, Tommy. It sounds as if that family have been through enough.'

Daisy had listened very carefully to Maggie. She felt mean not telling everything to Miss Devlin, who she must try and remember to now call Mrs Davies, but she knew Maggie was right and had worked everything out meticulously.

'I loved the dancing,' said Daisy. ''Twas fantastic to see all the girls dancing like that, it was just grand. I know I shouldn't laugh but the funniest thing was watching Big Paddy trying to throw Peggy over his shoulder. She wouldn't give the man a rest.'

They all laughed at the memory of Little Paddy hiding his head in his hands in shame.

'Mam, Da, will ye stop!' Little Paddy had shouted, bouncing up and down with the ruff of his shirt collar muffling his words.

When Peggy and Paddy had ignored him, he had tried to cut in between them both, but to no avail. His mother had then taken his hands and, twirling him round on the dance floor, danced with him instead. An experience which had left Little Paddy traumatized with embarrassment at the memory. That morning, it had been the first thing he thought of when he woke and it made him blush with shame when the boys on the green had shouted, 'Give us a dance then, Paddy,' when he ran to the shop for his da's ciggies. Boys didn't dance but if ever one was so misguided as to try, the last person he would dance with in public, and in front of all his school friends, would be his mother.

'Would ye stop,' said Alison, catching her breath. 'I enjoyed my own reception more than I should have. I thought I would be on pins and nervous, but, Daisy, you made it the best.'

'I would like to visit a few of the women if that is all right with you, Sister Evangelista,' said Daisy. 'I told Annie I would call over this morning. Would ye mind if I leave now?'

'Not at all, Daisy, you go ahead. I am here all day and your room is your own until the police say your brother can collect you. Harriet and I are both off this morning to a meeting about the new nursery, but we will be at the Priory if you need us.'

Maura was surprised when she heard a knock on her front door. It was only just audible, more of a gentle, nervous tap than a knock. As it was the school holidays, everyone was still in bed, catching up on their sleep following a weekend of excitement that included a late night after the wedding. None of the children had made it to bed until the early hours on Sunday, and they were still recovering by Monday.

When Maura saw Daisy on the doorstep, she smiled.

'Well, what a commotion you caused on Saturday, miss,' she said as she opened the door wider for Daisy to step into the hallway.

'You were laughing and talking away on Saturday night with everyone, so you were. I never had the chance to catch a word meself.'

Maura hadn't set eyes on her for six months and she noticed a difference in the girl. She was more grown up, with a worldly-wise look about her. As both women moved into the kitchen, Maura gestured for Daisy to take a seat.

'Sit down, love,' she said, 'and I'll make us a cuppa.'

'Thanks, Mrs Doherty,' said Daisy, sitting on a week's worth of Tommy's *Liverpool Echos*, which lived under the seat cushion and crinkled in objection as she gently lowered herself onto the sofa.

'Miss Devlin told me about Kitty. I'm sorry for your troubles. I really am, I'm sorry for your troubles.'

Maura didn't reply. She couldn't. There were no words to be said.

'You haven't been in my kitchen before, have you, Daisy? You were always too busy in the Priory,' said Maura brightly, wanting to change the subject. 'Although I know Molly used to visit you sometimes, and Annie O'Prey. Did ye talk to Annie last night?'

'I did, Mrs Doherty, I am off to see her in a minute, but first I wanted to talk to ye. I have to tell ye summat.'

Maura stood the pot of tea and the cups on the range shelf and poured milk from the bottle into the two cups.

'Will you drop the Mrs Doherty, Daisy. My name is Maura and you aren't working at the Priory now.'

'I saw him, Maura. I saw him every time he left the Priory and walked down the entry towards your door. I watched him from the window and I was glad he was over here and not bothering me. I'm sorry, Maura. I'm sorry I never told you.'

Maura gasped and lowered herself onto the sofa next to Daisy.

Maura couldn't speak. She could make no response other than to wring her hands in her lap and stare at Daisy as though she had grown an extra nose whilst sitting in her kitchen.

'God in heaven, he was doing it to you too? It never crossed my mind.'

Hot tears sprang to Maura's eyes. God knew, she had cried enough to fill the Mersey but they were always there, just beneath the surface, looking for a reason to flow. She reached out and held Daisy's hands in her own.

'It is me who is sorry, Daisy. Me. That man was evil itself and I don't feel sorry when I say that, as God is my judge, I am glad he is dead.'

Now it was Daisy's turn to well up. There, she had finally

said the words she always knew she should share with Maura, so that Maura would know, she hadn't failed Kitty and that there was nothing she could have done. Father James's behaviour had been beyond the comprehension of any decent human being.

The two women looked at each other for a long moment. One was considered simple and vulnerable. The other had thought she was an expert at keeping her children safe and out of harm's way. Maura reached out and took Daisy's hand in her own. They were now keepers of the same secret.

Daisy said, 'You are right, Maura. He was an evil man, a son of the devil, Maggie says, and me and Kitty and the others, there was nothing we could do.'

Daisy didn't tell Maura that he had done the same thing to lots of girls and that she and Sister Evangelista knew this because they had found the photographs in his desk drawer. Daisy didn't say this to Maura, but she was going to say it herself to Sister Evangelista. Maggie had told her she had to. She had written down all the things Maggie had told her she had to do, one by one, and telling Sister Evangelista that she had to tell the police what she had found in the father's desk drawer was number four.

Talking to Maura was number two. Stepping into the police station and giving them the letter from Maggie and Frank, that was number one.

When she had written the list with Maggie, Daisy had thought that she would never be able to do any of it. But now that she was here, seeing Maura had been so easy, and to think she had thought it would be the worst.

'Get the hardest things out of the way first,' Maggie had

said. 'The rest will be straightforward then and nothing to be frightened of.'

Maggie had been right.

Now, Maura and Daisy were both crying.

'But, Maura, there's more, there's more I have to say.'

Maura sat back slightly. She realized this was big for Daisy. She could see a battle raging somewhere inside her and that what she had said had not been easy for her.

Maura picked up Daisy's cup and handed it to her.

'Here, drink some tea,' she said. 'It will help calm your nerves. Shall I get us a couple of Anadin?'

Daisy shook her head and sipped the tea. Maura was right. She felt calmer now. Tea cured all ills.

Maura stood and dropped the catch on the back door. It was a thing she had never done before in all the time she had lived on the four streets, but intuition told her that the last thing she needed today was Peggy barging in.

Maura sat down again, closer to Daisy who, in preparation for her most crucial words, placed her cup and saucer on the floor near her feet. She leant back and took a deep breath. For a second, she heard Maggie's voice.

'Just say it out loud, Daisy, you only have to say it once and then it's done.'

Daisy looked Maura straight in the eye. 'Maura, I also saw what happened on the night the father was murdered. I saw how it happened, from the upstairs window in the Priory.'

Maura felt the room spin. Her foundations were moving, as if a chasm were about to open. She had been clinging onto the edge of a precipice for so long, waiting for something unknown to tip her off, and now here it was. It was Daisy.

She grasped the wooden arm of the chair tightly. She was teetering on the edge of her own sanity and she needed to hold on. She had to brace herself for whatever it was Daisy was about to say. Maura couldn't look. She couldn't see Daisy when she spoke the words that would condemn her husband to death.

'Oh God,' she gasped, putting her free hand to her mouth.

'No, don't worry,' said Daisy, placing her hand on Maura's. 'That is why I am here. I am sorry, I told the police once, but they didn't believe me. They thought I was simple and do you know, I was. I was so upset at what was happening to me. The awful secret I had to keep, it made me simple. That's what Maggie says anyway and I think she is right, because I can see everything so much clearer now. Thank God they didn't believe me. I only did it, I told them, because Molly said I had to. Molly is dead now and I am not simple, but I am the only one who saw it happen. I am the only one who knows and it is the thing Maggie said I had to keep a secret and never speak of it again, except to you, to put your mind at ease. That's what Maggie said.'

'Maggie?' said Maura. 'Who the hell is Maggie?' Maura almost screamed the question.

'She is the lady who looked after me and helped me back to Liverpool. She taught me to speak properly. And she helped me to escape and get to the police and told me everything I had to do and say.'

'What did you see, Daisy?' Maura asked, almost in a whisper. 'Did you see Tommy and Jerry and what they did?'

'Me, I didn't see nothing, Maura. Maggie said that, once I told you, I was never to speak about it again and that I had to forget what I had seen. She said you had suffered enough, that we all have, and that the priest got everything he deserved, and that she would have done the very same.' Maura laughed and cried at the same time as she hugged Daisy. The two of them wiped their eyes. Maura poured more tea and, sitting next to Daisy and placing her hand back in hers, she asked, 'Did you know what happened to Kitty, Daisy?'

For the following hour, Maura sat with her arm round Daisy's shoulders as she told her Kitty's story. Simple Daisy, the first woman apart from Kathleen that Maura had talked to about Kitty. It felt good to talk to Daisy. She had shared Kitty's nightmare. She would understand. Maura cried as she spoke and, at times, her words battled with her sobs to be heard. But nothing could stop the outpouring of emotion Maura felt as she sat, side by side in front of the range fire, with Daisy.

Daisy knew at first hand the evil which Kitty had known. They were now sisters. Blood sisters.

Maura had been so engrossed in talking to Daisy about Kitty that she hadn't heard Harry and Little Paddy on the stairs, nor noticed that they had halted their descent. Having heard voices in the kitchen, they were sitting on the bottom step behind the door.

She usually did hear the children. Since Kitty had died, Little Paddy often stopped over for the night, as he and Scamp were great at dispelling the gloom and lightening the atmosphere. Like all Maura's children, Little Paddy was convinced she could see through wooden doors.

Neither of the boys moved a muscle while they listened to every word. Harry's own tears fell softly as he heard his mother speak about his beloved Kitty, something Tommy had told him he was not allowed to do in front of Maura, for fear of upsetting her. He cried for Daisy too. But boys weren't allowed to cry.

Just as Little Paddy put his arm round Harry's shoulders, they heard Malachi dive out of bed, yelling, 'Mam, I'm starving.'

Harry quickly dried his eyes. Little Paddy held out his little finger. Harry held out his and hooked it through Paddy's and their hands shook.

'Secret forever,' whispered Little Paddy. Harry nodded in response. Both boys jumped up and, stamping on the stairs to announce their arrival, they noisily entered the kitchen just as Scamp began to bark at the back door.

Chapter Twelve

WHEN BEN MANNING arrived at the Priory, it was a hive of activity. He took the letter from the inside pocket of his jacket and reread it carefully, checking the name of the person he was supposed to be meeting.

'Here is a very charming letter,' his secretary had said. 'Well written too. Miss Harriet Lamb, she's obviously had a proper education. Look at that punctuation. I bet she's about ninety. This is a woman who knows how to get her way. Little old ladies can be very disarming, Mr Manning. Be on your guard when you meet her on Monday morning.'

Ben had smiled. It would take more than a little old lady with beautiful diction to make him agree to the library being run by the local church.

As Ben stood at the Priory gates and glanced over at the churchyard where, he knew, the murdered priest had been found, he once again checked the address at the top of the letter. He was at the correct Priory, and the name on the bottom was Miss Harriet Lamb. He scanned the people arriving who were also attending the meeting, searching for a woman with a kindly face. He had already imagined Miss Harriet Lamb.

He half expected her to look like every Irish matron in Liverpool: rotund, wearing a headscarf and a black skirt.

When the door was opened by a young woman in a floral dress, with long dark curls, smiling the broadest smile, he fully expected her to direct him to a room in the Priory where Miss Lamb and her committee would be waiting for him.

'Hello,' the young woman said in a beautiful voice. 'I'm Harriet Lamb. Are you Mr Manning from the City Corporation?'

For a moment, Ben couldn't speak.

'I am sorry to be so presumptuous,' she almost sang. 'It is just that, obviously, it is a very tight community around here and, if you don't mind me saying so, a man who knocks on the Priory door in such a smart overcoat sticks out like a sore thumb. And besides, we are expecting you.' She laughed.

He had no idea what she had just said. He was only aware of her lips moving and had no idea what to say in response.

The woman stopped laughing, but her smile remained. Ben noticed that she never once looked down at his leg, unlike almost every other person he had met, since the day he had been discharged from the army.

'Hello in there,' she said, laughing and pretending to look into and behind his eyes.

Ben spluttered and blurted out, 'I am so dreadfully sorry, but I was expecting someone older.'

The young woman laughed again.

'But your accent?' Ben knew he was being incredibly clumsy but seemed unable to stop himself.

'Ah, yes, well, it may surprise you to know, Mr Manning,

I was educated in Dublin and my father was a doctor. We don't all speak the same, you know. And, if you don't mind me saying so, I have met many people in Liverpool who don't speak with a strong accent.'

Ben blushed, profoundly embarrassed.

Harriett smiled. She had already realized that Mr Manning would be a pushover and that she was halfway to achieving every outcome she wanted from the meeting. She'd had no idea that it would be quite that easy or that the man from the Liverpool Corporation would be so gentle.

'I have to apologize for asking you to come to the Priory. It is just that there are so many of us and your secretary thought it might be better if you came here. Also, I thought that if you did so, you could see the committee in action. I know there was a great deal in the press regarding an unfortunate incident that took place here last year, but I wanted you to see that that is all behind us now. The church is a happy church and the people involved are committed to this community.

'Now, come, Mr Manning, come and meet my brother, Father Anthony, and Sister Evangelista, and my friend who is a teacher at the school, Alison, who was only married on Saturday and should be on her honeymoon now, but that's a different story. You will like them all, I promise you.'

Ben fell in line beside Harriet, unaware that she was deliberately walking more slowly than usual. She had seen the caliper without his having been aware.

Ben, who was painfully shy around women at the best of times, had lost his tongue completely.

'And here is everyone,' she said, leading him to the study where her brother sat behind the desk.

Amid the clatter of chinking china and teaspoons in sugar bowls, Harriet introduced Ben to the people sitting around, beginning with Father Anthony and finishing with Nana Kathleen.

Ben knew nothing whatsoever about the church or its ways. He felt uncomfortable, as though, whatever he said, he would surely put his foot straight in his mouth and show his ignorance.

'Now then,' Harriet said, having introduced everyone, 'I have written to Mr Manning to explain to him that we are delighted that a children's nursery is to be built on the bombed-out wasteland, and the library too. I have explained that we also understand that it is for the benefit of the people living in the tin houses, which, Mr Manning, I know are the prefabs, but everyone around here refers to them as the tin houses. However, as the convent plays such a huge role in the community, including running the school, I am sure Mr Manning agrees with me that there must be ways we can work together to a mutual benefit.'

An hour and a half later, Benjamin Manning made his way back to the bus stop. He had never before spent such a happy time in the company of others.

They were such joyful people. And Harriet Lamb, surely such a beautiful woman could not be single? He smiled ruefully to himself. Miss Lamb. He had granted her every concession she had asked for. He had nothing in his briefcase that could defend him against those bright blue eyes and her lovely smile. All the way home on the bus, he relived every moment, every gesture. He closed his eyes and summoned the sound of her voice.

Benjamin felt sad that his injuries would prevent him from asking Miss Lamb to have tea with him at the Lyons Corner House one afternoon. From living a normal life as most men did. From having a wife. He knew he had to banish her from his mind. A woman as lovely as she was would be ashamed to be seen walking down the road with a man wearing a caliper. Harriet Lamb did not need a cripple on her arm when she could do so much better.

As he looked out of the window on the journey home, he did not see the river, the sprawling warehouses or the ships, waiting patiently at the bar. As the bus turned up the hill into Edge Lane, the familiar terraced houses and the children playing in the streets were just a blur. He was somewhere else, in an imagined life. One he had never dared to visit since the day he was wounded. He could hear the voice of another, one that did not belong to his mother, calling him to breakfast. A voice he had heard for the first time just a few short hours ago.

He did not notice the solitary tear of loneliness that ran down his cheek.

When everyone had left the Priory and only Father Anthony and Harriet remained, she was unusually quiet.

'Has the cat got your tongue?' asked Anthony.

'Don't talk about cats and body parts,' said Harriet and tapped him on the arm.

'Heavens, I forgot,' said Anthony, shuddering.

The murdered priest's body had been discovered, just as Molly Barrett's cat had walked into the street, carrying his langer in its mouth. This was now a source of secret jokes amongst the children on the four streets and the subject of not so secret ribaldry down in the Anchor pub.

'I was just turning over in my mind, who else we should ask to be on the committee for the nursery.'

'May I make a suggestion?' said Anthony. 'Ask Maura Doherty. That woman needs something to occupy her mind. I think that she could benefit from focusing on anything other than the loss of her daughter. It might just be the thing to bring her out of herself and to help her heal. I feel sorry for the twin lads. Little Harry and Malachi always look a bit lost. I know Declan and Kevin are a different pair altogether, but if something doesn't give to restore a bit of happiness into that home, I can see those two going off the rails before long. Declan runs riot at the school and I know Sister Evangelista is loath to say anything to Maura and Tommy because of all their troubles.'

'Would you like me to have a word, Anthony?'

Harriet loved the Dohertys. The hours she had passed helping to heal Nellie Deane had brought her close to the families affected by Kitty's death. She had spent a great deal of time with Maura when she helped the neighbours to look after Maura and Tommy.

Harriet and Anthony had never met Kitty, but they had heard enough from Sister Evangelista to know that there was something they weren't being told. But that didn't matter. They were here to minister and to love their neighbours and that was what they would do. Harriet might not have been holy, but she was good.

'I don't know, Harriet. Maybe you could have a gentle word about the twins at the same time as you ask her to help?'

Harriet smiled. 'I will find a way. Come here and give me a hug.'

Benjamin Manning came unbidden into Harriet's mind again.

'What are you thinking of, Harriet? You surely aren't this pensive about a nursery committee?'

Sometimes Harriet thought Anthony could read her mind. 'Well, I was just thinking what a nice man Mr Manning was.' She blushed.

'And what a pity we hadn't met years ago. Useless thoughts, as no man as handsome as he is would want to date a woman my age, so never fear, they were just idle imaginings.'

'Brought on by Alison's wedding on Saturday, no doubt,' said Anthony, looking at his sister with great care.

They told each other everything. They were the closest of siblings, and had been made even more so by the recent loss of both their parents. They were also bound by the fact that it was silently understood, Harriet as a spinster would remain with Anthony. He felt guilty that his sister had spent the best years of her life nursing first his father and then his mother, whilst he had been away at the seminary.

He felt guilty that she had sacrificed her life. He wanted to do all that he could for her. That was why he was determined to take his sister with him in the role of housekeeper. He could not leave her alone in Dublin in their parents' big house. Anthony was the first priest ever at St Mary's to have a housekeeper as well as a full-time cleaner, but he didn't care. Where he went, his sister would go too.

'I suppose thirty-five is rather late,' Anthony replied. 'But you never know.'

A modern priest in the city of the Beatles, Anthony was trying to be helpful, but he realized it wasn't working.

He sat down at his desk to work, and Harriet went into the kitchen to make their tea. As she filled the kettle, Harriet felt a pain stab her in the chest.

She thought of how happy Alison Devlin had been at her wedding. Alison was also old to be getting married. She had complained about it often enough, even confiding that she thought she might be too old to have children. Was it so impossible for someone Harriet's age to find a husband?

As she stood over the sink, her tears fell and not for the first time. They were hot tears of loss and frustration for the life she knew she could never have, that of a wife and a mother.

Even as she cried, she knew it wasn't just because of the wedding on Saturday. It had something to do with that lovely shy man, with the kind eyes and the caliper, which she could see hurt him as he walked. The gentle man who was softly spoken and nervous, and who had told Sister Evangelista he wasn't married.

She looked down and smiled as Scamp licked her feet. At that moment, they heard Little Paddy and Harry banging on the back door.

'Well, look who's here? The boys to take you on your walk, little fella.'

And within seconds, the kitchen was filled with boys and dogs and the noise that Harriet wished had always been a part of her life.

Chapter Thirteen

S TANLEY WAS TOO afraid to switch on the lights.

The back door had opened, with difficulty and a loud creak, into the kitchen where they had held their crisis meeting after the priest had been murdered. Stanley remembered the men who had sat round the table on that night. Most of them he didn't know, but there were some that he had recognized.

Austin had told Stanley that the key to survival was anonymity. If no one knew who each other was, no one could tell anyone anything.

Austin had now been arrested. Would Austin snitch on Stanley?

Stanley had never touched that Daisy from the Priory, but Austin had and she knew who he was. Austin was fucking mad, always taking risks. He had told Daisy he worked at the children's hospital. He had been showing off, pretending he was a doctor. The priest had Austin's address and details in his diary. Stanley knew that. He had seen it. No one had Stanley's. He had told no one anything. Still, he was taking no risks. If Arthur said this was where he should be, in the safe house, this was where he would stay.

'The bishop will be on his fucking way to Panama now if he's got any fucking sense,' Arthur had said to Stanley.

'Does the bishop know she has come back?'

'He fucking must do, he's the one who had her in hiding. The bishop isn't going to let her fucking escape without doing a runner himself, although how the fuck he let her get away from wherever he had her, I don't know. I would have fucking drowned her myself. All the stupid policeman had to do was push her over the rail. Fucking yeller bastards. Now we are all at risk because the bishop couldn't do his job properly.'

'Bit hard for bishop to get someone topped, I suppose?' Stanley had said.

'What? A bit harder than shagging her when she was only twelve? Yeah, right.'

Remembering there were candles in the hearth of the range, Stanley felt his way across the kitchen. He took the lighter out of his pocket and flicked the flint into life.

The dirty, shoddy room lit up, with images even Stanley didn't want to see.

The floor was covered in newspapers and near the fire a grubby toy doll lay discarded. The flame from the lighter was reflected back to Stanley from the cold, glass eyes.

He lit a candle from the store in the fireplace and began to unpack the bag he had brought with him, placing items one by one on a wooden table that stood at the side of the sink. Corned beef and spam, condensed milk, a packet of tea. He assumed he would be safe to visit the shops. There would be no one looking for him around here. Even if Austin spilt the beans, he wouldn't remember this house, or know that Arthur would send him here and use it as a safe house.

Austin might direct the police to the hospital or Stanley's home, but not here. When he thought of his mam and how distressed she would be, he felt sick.

Maybe he would sneak out in the dark and nip back to see her. He could make up a story, although he knew not what, and tell her he had to lie low for a while. As he sat huddled in the glow of the paltry fire and his solitary candle, he realized he might have to spend many hours doing very little else. He had managed to light the range, using bits of wood he had found in the garden. Some were windfall branches that had fallen way back in wartime, when the house had last been inhabited. The huge tree in the middle of the lawn had shed a pile large enough to keep a fire ticking over in the range for at least a couple of weeks. In the coal store, he had found the best part of a half-hundredweight of coal, which he would use sparingly.

Arthur had sent no message, nor had he called in as promised. This made Stanley feel even more nervous as the day went by.

Days later, he ran short of provisions, and was almost sick with worry about his mother.

'Where the fuck is Arthur?' he said to himself over and over as he paced up and down in the dark back kitchen of the bomb-damaged house. The one trip out that he had made to buy further supplies had alarmed him and he didn't want to have to do it again.

He had slipped out to the shops the day after he had arrived, just before they closed, when shopkeepers were packing up, distracted, thinking of their journey home and putting tea on the table. He had used the big grocery store before the green on Breck Road, just down from Holy Trinity church. The shelves had been piled with good things to eat, but Stanley had no idea how long he would have to make his money last.

His eye was immediately caught by square metal bins with plastic lids, along the front of the long wooden counter, full of every imaginable kind of broken biscuit. He hadn't eaten since the previous day and his stomach growled as the smell of custard creams filled his nostrils. His mouth began to water. He took a brown paper bag and slowly went from one bin to the next, filling the bag. Keeping his head down, he handed it over the counter to the man in a white overcoat to be weighed.

'Anything else I can get for you?' the shopkeeper enquired as Stanley continued to look in the bins, as though fascinated by the contents.

'A quarter-pound of tea, a pint of sterilized milk, a pound of sugar.' Stanley still didn't look up.

Armed in addition with beans, bacon, bread, cheese and twenty Players, he hung around the green until it was dark when he could return to the house, entering through the back door, unseen by neighbours.

Arthur had said he would call on Stanley's mother to tell her that she must not, under any circumstances, contact the police about her son's sudden absence and that she was not to panic. Stanley knew she had never met Arthur and would be out of her mind with suspicion and worry. He was all she had and he meant the world to her. She depended upon him for everything. Without his wages this week, she would be more than a little anxious.

Stanley squatted down on his haunches in front of the range, waiting for the water in the enamel pot to boil. He had found it in a cupboard, covered in dust and cobwebs.

He couldn't stop himself from worrying about his mam. In amongst the mouse droppings and the old newspapers scattered over the terracotta-tiled floor, he made the decision; as soon as it was dark, he would catch the bus back home, just to see if his mam was OK. He would slip in through the back door and stay just a few minutes, long enough to sign his bank-book so that she could take out any money she needed from his savings and to collect a few things.

Then he would take the night sleeper to Edinburgh and, once there, move up to the highlands. He could work as a kitchen porter for a year or so, until everything had died down. When it was safe, he would return home to his mam.

The enamel pot on the range began to bubble softly. Stanley took it off, using discarded newspaper to protect his hands from the heat of the handle. He tipped some of the tea leaves into the pot and stirred them with a stick before adding the sterilized milk. For the first time in days, he felt his panic begin to subside.

He had a plan. He was in control. He would be fine and so would his mam.

Back at Stanley's home, his mother had placed a tea cosy over her best Royal Doulton teapot, after pouring Howard a cup of tea as he charmed her with the tale of his recent wedding.

'Our Stanley never wanted to get married, you know. I tried to persuade him, but he's never been interested. Mind you, I doubt there has been a woman born, who could be as good to him as his mam has.'

The bright blue budgerigar, in the cage inches from Howard's head, had hobbled to the end of its perch and now stared curiously at Howard, with its head on one side.

'He's a good lad, our Stanley. Tips his money out onto the table every Friday night as soon as he walks through that door and no man could be more devoted to his work than our Stan. He makes me knit teddies to take in for them kiddies, you know. There are very few men as good as our Stanley.'

'I've spoken to his employers, who think very highly of him,' said Howard.

'Did they say why they had to send him to another hospital so quickly?' she asked. 'It is all very strange. A man from his work called to tell me what was happening. I gave him Stanley's clean clothes and everything but I can't understand why Stanley didn't come home himself first. The man said Stanley had taken a child in an ambulance to another hospital down south and he would be staying until they returned to Liverpool. Typical of our Stan, that is. I bet no one else would do it. He would have volunteered. That's just what he's like, you know. He loves them kids, he does.'

Howard drank his tea, feeling sorry for the mother of the sick pervert he was determined to catch. Poor woman doesn't have a clue, he thought.

'Well now, the thing is, I am afraid I'm not allowed to tell you anything other than that we need to ask Stanley some questions. He isn't in any trouble, mind. It is all a bit top

233

secret, to do with a case at the hospital. Stanley has been a great help to the police, but we need to speak to him as soon as he gets back. So what I will have to do is leave this police officer here in your house, while you are asleep, to keep you safe until Stanley returns. You must be very nervous on your own with him being away.'

'Well, I am, but what will the neighbours say? They will think our Stan has done something wrong, won't they? Is that really necessary?'

'I am afraid it is. Stanley has been doing some good work for the hospital, but there are a couple of bad lads who work there and we can't catch them without Stanley's help. It won't be for long. I spoke to the doctor at the hospital, and he tells me Stanley should be home any time now.'

'Well, thank God for that. I don't want me neighbours thinking anything is up, here in our house. You had better tell them if they ask when you go out. I feel ashamed having a police car outside me house.'

'There is no police car now. I had it moved down onto Queens Drive. I didn't want you to feel worried about that,' said Howard with all the charm he could muster.

An hour later, Stanley's mother was in bed, having left nothing short of a feast on a tray for the officer whom Howard left behind, with explicit instructions.

'The only thing we have got so far is the name of two of the people who Daisy can confirm visited Father James at the Priory and we know what they were up to. She has given us some shocking details. We also know that Simon worked with them and that it was he who delivered Daisy to the convent. The pieces of the jigsaw are slipping into place.

'Stanley is the next piece. The psychologist at the hospital tells me Stanley will be anxious about his mother and will, at some stage, attempt to return home, if only to reassure himself that she is well. We also know that he is working with someone, because whoever it was called here to spin a story to Stanley's mother. If only the other porter, Austin, or Simon were being as cooperative, eh? Stay hidden and keep your eyes and ears open. If he returns home and you miss him, you will be looking for a new job tomorrow, do you understand?'

The police officer looked terrified. 'Yes, sir.'

'Good, now I'm off to my new home and my new bride. It feels as if I have barely seen my wife since we stood at the altar. Stay out of sight, and make sure the old woman is in bed as soon as possible. If he returns tonight and clocks that the lights are on, he will think she is still up and we don't want her being around when he's nicked.'

'Yes, sir,' said PC Shaw. 'Er, sir, what's that white stuff on your shoulder?'

Howard hadn't heard him. The probationary officer spoke to his retreating back as Howard almost ran towards Queens Drive, where he had left the car parked. The room filled with the squawks of an accomplished budgie.

Stanley's mother lingered before finally taking herself off to bed.

'Are you sure you're gonna be all right now, just sat here in the kitchen on yer own?' she asked PC Shaw at least half a dozen times.

She made one last descent in a hairnet and no teeth, to leave the biscuit barrel on the table and to quiz the officer.

'I don't know what's going on but I've got a funny feeling in me water I have. Is that CID officer all right or what? He kept telling me Stanley was helping the hospital and the police, but with what? He's never said nothin' to me. I don't understand what's going on, like.'

Finally, as soon as PC Shaw heard the bedside light click off, he dived at the food she had left for him, kept fresh between two plates. Corned-beef sandwiches on thickly buttered white bread were piled high, together with a home-made Victoria jam sandwich.

As he munched the first sandwich, he looked round the room.

Who would have thought it, eh? he mused. Normal mam, normal house. So what turns someone into the sick weirdo Stanley obviously was? Shuddering at the thought of a man who desired children, the PC knew what he would do if he ever caught anyone near his own daughter.

'I'd chop his bloody dick off,' he muttered to himself.

His thoughts wandered to the murder of the dead priest and his detached body part. Just as a penny rolled to the edge of his thoughts, about to drop ... he heard a noise. It was a key in the front door.

Begrudgingly, he placed the remaining sandwich on the plate, secreted himself behind the door and waited.

'Mam,' Stanley whispered as he opened the door into the kitchen. Only the glow from a small lamp on the sideboard illuminated the room.

'Mam,' he whispered again, this time with more urgency.

He had opened the kitchen door wide and blinked before he knew what had happened. His arm was up his back and the PC, his handcuffs ready, had snapped them on within seconds.

'Never mind your mam, you dirty perv, you're nicked, mate.'

The budgie squawked his greeting from the cage, 'Hello, Stanley,' just as his mother called down the stairs, 'Stanley, is that you?'

While the PC radioed for a police car, Stanley's mam got up, tied the belt on her dressing gown and ran her false teeth under the tap to wash off the Steradent tablet, quickly popping them back into her mouth. Her bedroom was suddenly filled by the blue flashing light of a police car, parked right outside her front door.

'Oh God, Stanley, what have you done?' she muttered as she walked down the stairs. 'Honest to God, the shame.'

Chapter Fourteen

'I'M BACK,' SHOUTED Harriet as she burst in through the Priory door, causing it to swing on its hinges and crash against the wall. She continued to shout as she threw her hat on the hall table. 'I am so starving hungry, are you?'

Harriet had never in her life entered a room with any degree of caution. There was simply no need. No fearful shock had ever hidden behind any closed door, nor hit her in the face when least expected. Nothing unexpected or out of the ordinary had jumped up and bitten her. Harriet had never known fear.

She had just finished delivering leaflets to the houses on the four streets. She removed the satchel, slung across her shoulders, that held the remaining leaflets and placed it with a thud on the table, next to her hat.

She had spent the early part of morning at the Priory with the plainclothes police officers while they interviewed Daisy, who was excited beyond all notion that her brother would be arriving in Liverpool the following week, to collect her in person. They weren't taking any chances this time. There was no question of Daisy being put on a boat alone, as Alison had argued.

'God alone knows where you would end up this time. We might find ourselves answering a call from America. Only you, Daisy, could board the Liverpool to Dublin ferry and quite possibly end up in New York,' she had joked.

Despite that, they struggled to laugh. Everyone was keeping a very careful eye on Daisy, until she had been handed over to her brother.

The new commanding officer had explained the plan of action in detail to the gathered group – Daisy, Miss Devlin, Sister Evangelista, Harriet and Father Anthony – who had all listened intently over tea and hot toasted muffins, dripping with butter and strawberry jam. Harriet was never happier than when people left the Priory with a full stomach, whatever the time of day.

'We are on our way over to Ireland this afternoon,' Howard had said, 'to determine how the arrangements were made for Daisy to be delivered to the convent and why that particular convent was chosen. The police officer in custody is refusing to tell us anything, so, ladies, we are slightly stuck. However, it will take only a little good old-fashioned footwork to sort things out.'

They were all impressed with the competence of the commander who had taken over the reins of the investigation, immediately drafting Howard in as his number two. This made sense, given that Howard was completely up to date on all that had happened during the previous investigation and was already an invaluable member of the team. The commanding officer had even hinted at promotion, if the case reached a successful conclusion.

The fact that Howard and Alison had cancelled their

honeymoon to the Isle of Man, losing their deposit on the bed and breakfast they had booked months ago, had not gone unnoticed by Howard's senior officers. The uniformed officers down at Whitechapel were hugely disappointed that one of their own was locked in a police cell, and stinking guilty as hell.

'Do you have to shout every single time you walk in through the front door, Harriet?' Father Anthony placed his finger to his lips, which were smiling at his little sister, always so full of life. 'Shh,' he said, 'I have a visitor in the office.'

'Oh, gosh, I'm sorry. Wayward housekeeper here, not doing her job properly.'

Harriett grimaced playfully.

'Not at all. Could you make tea? I have no idea what has happened to Annie O'Prey. Sheila knocked on the Priory door and Annie just disappeared without a by-your-leave. That woman is the end, Harriet. If you didn't like her so much, she would have to go. She makes delicious cakes but she is really a law unto herself. Anyway, fetch the tea, would you, and bring it to the study. I want you to join us as this is very much your project, not mine. Mr Manning is here to talk to us.'

Harriet felt a thrill run down her spine. Oh God, how should I act? Indifferent? Cold? Friendly?

'Mr Manning?' she hissed. 'Were you expecting him?'

'No, although I did tell him to call in if he had any news or if he wanted further information. But I didn't really expect him to just pop in without at least a phone call from his secretary first, unless, of course, he had an ulterior motive for visiting.' Anthony winked at Harriet who blushed from head to toe.

Harriet quickly checked her hair in the hall mirror. Licking her fingertips, she ran one along each eyebrow, pushing them into shape. Having fluffed up her hair and pinched her cheeks, she swept into the office where, without any warning whatsoever, her beauty knocked Benjamin Manning completely off his feet.

'Mr Manning,' Harriet trilled breezily.

Just in the nick of time, she erased from her face the instinctive look of sympathy that threatened to appear as Ben struggled to rise from his chair to greet her.

Harriet was beset by feelings she had never known before, despite her age, and she had no idea how to deal with them.

She blushed again, her palms sweated, her eyes shone and her heart fluttered like a trapped bird.

He noticed.

'Good morning,' he replied, but his mouth was so dry that his response was barely audible. He held out his hand, which trembled like a leaf in the breeze.

She noticed.

It had begun.

Chapter Fifteen

MAGGIE AND ONE of the orphan girls were in the process of removing fifteen loaves of hot bread from the oven when Sister Theresa arrived, unannounced.

As was her way, she issued no greeting.

'Are we managing to bottle enough gooseberries for the winter? Sister Perpetua thinks we have less in hand than last year, despite the good weather.'

'Oh, aye, we are that,' replied Maggie, barely hiding a hint of indignation. 'I have plenty bottled in the cellar and if there's any more late crop come through, Frank thinks we may be able to squeeze out another half-dozen jars or so from the plants in the glasshouse.'

Sister Theresa looked far from mollified.

'Good. Sister Perpetua also tells me some of the apples have been stolen.'

'Ah, well, I think one or two of the windfalls from the other side of the railings may have gone, but, sure, they would have been full of maggots and no good to us now,' Maggie replied.

'That's not the point, Maggie. Any child who steals from us should be up before the magistrate. Thou shalt not steal is an important lesson to be learnt.'

'But, sure, Sister Theresa, these children have walked a mile to steal a rotten apple, because they are hungry. Surely the good Lord wouldn't mind a bit of that in their bellies? It would give them the cramps as it is. Is that not a fair punishment?'

'There is no excuse for stealing, Maggie. It is wrong. If you see any child doing it, I want them caught and reported.'

'Yes, Sister,' said Maggie, with a heavy heart and no intention of doing any such thing.

The children hadn't stolen any apples. She and Frank had picked the windfalls and kept them in a basket behind the lodge. They knew every child from the village and their parents. Frank and Maggie dished out the apples when the children came along, to save them from the sin of stealing or, worse, being caught.

'We are using the salt fish today with tatties,' said Maggie, in a desperate attempt to change the subject.

As Sister Theresa looked round the kitchen, her gaze alighted on the orphan girl helping Maggie.

There was a note of alarm in her voice as she asked, 'Where's the girl?'

Maggie didn't need to ask, which girl? 'She has the vomiting bug and, sure, I don't want it, Sister, so I've confined her to her room. The last thing we need is vomiting to sweep through this place now and I don't want to be laid up or none of us will eat.'

Sister Theresa looked at the door of the storeroom where Daisy was expected to sleep and which opened straight onto the kitchen. It was closed and Maggie had locked it. The key felt as though it were burning a hole through her apron pocket and scalding her thigh.

Her heart beat wildly as the Reverend Mother stared at the door for what seemed like a lifetime. Suddenly she turned back to Maggie.

'Very well, but don't let her shirk, though. Back to work as soon as she is well. The bishop is in Liverpool for a meeting about the new cathedral, but he told me he wants to see her when he returns.'

'Yes, Sister,' said Maggie.

Maggie kept her head bent as she turned the loaves out onto the long wooden table. She daren't look up in case Sister Theresa detected the panic in her eyes.

Later that evening, when her work was done and she was back at the lodge, Maggie recounted the visit to Frank. They had settled in front of the fire, the way they did each night before bed. Rain was falling steadily, as it had done for most of the day. The fire struggled to catch and throw out a decent flame as smoke billowed back into the kitchen. In another of their familiar nightly rituals, each held an enamel mug of poteen, brewed by Frank himself in a still kept hidden, behind a false wall in the potting shed. He and Maggie often laughed at the thought of what the nuns would do, if they knew Frank brewed his own poteen in the convent grounds.

'Jesus, they would choke and die, wouldn't they just,' said Maggie as she took her first sip.

Tonight, they talked about the Reverend Mother's visit to the kitchen and Daisy's whereabouts.

'That's three days she has been gone now. I reckon we have another week. Reverend Mother, she never visits the kitchen more than once a week. What will we say, Frank, when they discover she has disappeared?'

'You will wail and cry, Maggie, about how that girl took advantage of you, letting her rest whilst she was sick, that's what. No finger of suspicion must ever point at us. Let's hope the police are listening to Daisy and her story.'

'Aye, if she is following the instructions I gave her and there is a God, all should be well.'

Maggie looked again at the letter they had received from the foreman, Jack.

'Carry on reading now, before the poteen knocks ye out for the night,' said Frank.

Frank had worked in the fields since he was six years old and had never learnt to read. Maggie had attended the local school religiously and had excelled at English and maths, despite frequently receiving the cane across her palms whenever she made the slightest error.

The nuns had failed to beat an aptitude for learning out of Maggie, as they had with most children. Rather, they beat a resilience and determination into her, to get her own back one day.

Maggie resumed reading.

Because she told me on the way over that one of the men she needed to report was a policeman from Liverpool, I decided to take her to the police station in Holyhead.

They were very good and kept her in overnight. I agreed to keep an eye on her, as promised, and booked into the pub next door to the police station for the

night. When I called back the next morning, they told
me they had got a mighty statement from her and they
were taking her to Liverpool where they were hopefully
going to make an arrest before the day was out. I have
no idea who he was, but a very senior man from the
Welsh police came to the station. They let me go and
told me that what Daisy had told them amounted to a
kidnapping, which is a very serious offence.

I have to say, your comments in the letter about her
brother being the state solicitor of Dublin made them
jump and I know they telephoned him. I didn't
mention your names as promised.

It was a pleasure to get to know you both and,
Frank, I look forward to welcoming you to the
Shamrock pub in Liverpool, for a return Guinness one
day soon, mate.

Your pal from Liverpool,
Jack

'That makes me feel good, so it does, that such a bad man will get his due deserts because we have played our part.'

'Aye, it does. Me too, Frank,' said Maggie thoughtfully. 'Watch out for Sister Perpetua. She wants to see kids from the village locked up for stealing apples. Telling tales to the Reverend Mother so she is. She's a wicked one, that one. Watch yer back.'

'Aye, I've noticed her snooping around the vegetable gardens a few times. I will, Maggie, don't worry about me. I keep my wits about me at all times. No one can catch me out.'

Frank had no idea. Someone already had.

Sister Perpetua sat in her room, making yet another entry in the journal she had been keeping over the last month. She knew that when she approached the Reverend Mother, she would need to present a cast-iron case. Not of a single event that could be explained away, but a whole list, which would demonstrate a pattern of deceit, theft and bad behaviour.

Only a few weeks earlier, Sister Perpetua had caught one of the girls returning to the orphanage from the kitchen with her pockets stuffed full of biscuits. When they were removed from her and she was beaten, she confessed to Sister Perpetua that the cook, Maggie, had given them to her.

This had not been an isolated incident. Only the previous week, Sister Perpetua had seen Frank passing vegetables through the railings to the village children. Last night, she had seen him taking a bottle of clear liquid from the potting shed and slipping it into his jacket pocket. Her suspicions now thoroughly aroused, she kept an eye on Frank from the orphanage, which overlooked the vegetable gardens, and with her own eyes she had seen him sneakily carry a basket of apples round the back of the orchard to the lodge.

Sister Perpetua was sure in her own mind that the Reverend Mother had employed a pair of thieves and it was her duty to point this out. When she did so, maybe then she would be relieved of the job that she hated so much. Dealing day after day with ungrateful children and digging graves.

The Reverend Mother knew she could trust Sister Perpetua. Only two nuns were allowed to dig graves and Sister Perpetua was one of them. She was also the only nun entrusted with the paperwork, when children died. It was she who decided whether or not to obtain a death certificate and at what point to report the death to the authorities.

'We have no idea who will come asking questions or when,' Sister Theresa had said. 'We must keep everything as obscure as possible and, sure, if no one wanted these children in life, I am quite sure there will be no interest when they are dead, but you never know. Better to be safe than sorry. We must protect ourselves from any charge that could be brought to our door. There are people who indulge children and fail to discipline them. Sentimental, they are, and just the type to think they could do a better job than we have. No traces, Sister Perpetua. Always be vigilant. Nothing recorded that anyone at any time in the future could behold.'

Sister Perpetua had done her work well. There was at least one death a week at the orphanage. She knew this was high.

'We could blame a disease, Reverend Mother,' Sister Perpetua had commented. Sister Theresa was always anxious about the children sent to the orphanage by the authorities.

'Really, Sister Perpetua?' the Reverend Mother snapped. 'Then they would all have died in the same week, not at the rate of four or five a month. Just do as I say.

'There must be nothing that can be traced. No mass at the graveside. Most of those children were born out of wedlock. They are steeped in a sin that no mass could erase. No headstones. We don't ever want to encourage mourners.'

Sister Perpetua had created an environment of obedience and orderliness in which penitents could seek forgiveness, exactly as she had been asked. However, after four years of disciplining children and burying them, she was heartily sick of the orphanage. She knew it was difficult to ask for a transfer to the retreat. That was solely in the gift of the Reverend Mother. A reward for loyalty and discretion.

She bent over the journal in the orphanage office and continued with her record-keeping.

The cook and the gardener deserved to be in prison, and Sister Perpetua knew that she was the only nun in the convent sharp enough to make sure it happened. Her reward would be guaranteed and soon, God willing, she might have thrown the last lice-ridden, sin-soaked child into the pit.

Chapter Sixteen

'T HAT HARRIET HAS ants in her pants, she cannot keep flamin' still,' said Kathleen as she dried her hands on her apron and took the leaflet out of Nellie's hands to read it for herself.

'But, Nana, it sounds so exciting, a Rose Queen of the docks and eight people in her retinue, and we can all enter the competition. There is going to be a big fair with a street party on the green and afternoon tea. I've never known the like. It is too exciting for words. I'm off to tell Angela.'

Nellie jumped up from the kitchen table and already had her hand on the back doorknob when Kathleen stopped her.

'Nellie, stop. Come here a minute while I tell ye something.'

Nellie knew what that meant. It was a summons to sit down and wait for a lecture. She knew from experience that she wouldn't be going anywhere until it was over. With a sigh, she walked back to the table and sat down.

'Now, child, listen to me. The Rose Queen, that's a fantastic idea and I'm not surprised that Harriet has dreamt it up, an' all. She has transformed these streets in the months she has been here. Jesus, she's even trying to make me run

250

the Mothers' Union and the committee for the new nursery because she reckons that, if I do, it will be easier to get Maura to help. And she's right, it will be good for Maura. I won't have to do nothing, so I won't, I will just act stupid. We have to pray to God that Maura's famous spirit for organizing and bossing everyone will return, but that's not what's worrying me.'

Nellie could tell this was going to be a long one so she helped herself to a biscuit from the tin on the press. Nana Kathleen had made syrup oaties that morning, using a nice deposit from a load en route from the docks to the Lyons factory.

'I'm listening, Nana Kathleen,' she said, munching. 'Go on, don't stop, keep talking.'

'Cheeky madam,' said Kathleen, whacking Nellie's bottom with the tea towel. 'Look, Nellie, I'm just saying, have ye seen the date on that leaflet, the date of the Rose Queen competition?'

Nellie looked down at the leaflet. She hadn't noticed the date at all, so caught up had she been with the long list of events Harriet planned: a fancy-dress competition, a tombola, a beat-the-rat stall, a best-cake competition, a cake stall and a jumble sale too. There was so much, how did Harriet think they could fit it all in on one day?

Nellie picked up the leaflet and read it again.

'Oh God,' she said, placing her hand over her mouth. 'I feel terrible. Oh God, I am so stupid and she was like my sister too.'

Nellie began to cry. The shock of Kitty's death had numbed her, crushing her free spirit for what had seemed like a very long time. Not until recently had she started to seem like her old self. Kathleen and Jerry were only just beginning to notice the true signs of their old Nellie returning.

'Hush now, ye were so caught up with the news, I'm sure ye didn't even notice that the date was Kitty's birthday. I just wanted to point it out because when ye go over to Maura and Tommy's, they will notice it straight away, and Angela too, I've no doubt, so just be a little bit careful, eh?'

'Shall I not go over then?' said Nellie.

'Tell ye what, give me five minutes to finish these dishes and we will go together, shall we?'

Nellie dried her eyes and took the tea towel from Nana Kathleen. As she did so, Kathleen drew Nellie to her, burying the child's head in her chest for a brief moment, and then kissed the top of it, noting that in no time at all she would have to reach up, not bend down, to give their Nellie a kiss.

Meanwhile, Declan Doherty had taken the leaflet into the kitchen and read out the list of events with a similar degree of enthusiasm. Harry lay on the mat in front of the fire, reading his book.

He looked up on hearing the events that interested him the most: races for the children on the green, a street party and a kestrel-flying display.

'Well,' said Maura, in the subdued voice that had become the norm of late, 'that all sounds fantastic now. Angela, I think we should enter the cake competition and start practising with some recipes. What do you think?'

'When is it?' asked Harry after Declan finished.

As Declan read out the date, only Harry and Maura exchanged glances. Harry had realized immediately what day it was. None of the others had. Harry knew he couldn't say anything. Kitty's name had barely been mentioned since the day of the funeral. It was as if by pretending she had never existed, it would become easier for everyone to bear her absence.

It didn't work like that for Harry. Right now he wanted to yell out loud, 'That's our Kitty's birthday!' But he knew that if he did, his mother would cry and the others would cast their eyes downwards and behave as if he had never spoken.

Through the kitchen window Maura spotted Nellie and Kathleen, walking up the back path towards her door.

'Well now, there's a bit of news we have,' said Kathleen as she let herself into the kitchen.

'Cuppa tea, Kathleen?' said Maura.

Kathleen didn't stop to draw breath or to answer, saying, 'Would ye credit that Harriet and Miss Alison?' So Maura poured her one anyway, on the basis that never once had she known her to refuse. Kathleen even had her own cup and saucer in the Doherty kitchen.

'She's Mrs Davies now,' said Maura. 'Seems funny calling her Alison, as if it's disrespectful for someone in her position, her being a teacher.'

'Well, I'll never get used to that in a month of Sundays,' said Kathleen. 'It's not even an Irish name, so it's not. Maura, those women are on a mission to exhaust us, what with the nursery an' all. I hope Mrs Davies gets caught quick now that she's married and has her hands too full with a baby to be finding things for the rest of us to do.'

Kathleen sat herself down on the chair beside the fire and ruffled Harry's hair by way of a greeting. He looked up at Kathleen and smiled.

'You all right, lad?' she asked him with a wink. Her words went unnoticed by anyone else, below the noise of Nellie and Angela re-reading aloud to Maura from Harriet's proposed list of events.

'Yeah, ta, Nana Kathleen,' said Harry. He turned to look at Nellie and Angela and then back to Kathleen. 'It's on our Kitty's birthday,' he whispered earnestly, so that no one would hear him mention Kitty's name.

'I know, lad,' said Kathleen quietly, smoothing down errant wisps on the crown of his head. 'No one will forget such an important day, Harry. We will all go to the church and put our mass cards in and light a penny candle for her. She won't be forgotten, Harry. Kitty was like you, lad, very special. No one will ever forget her.' Whilst she spoke she continued to stroke Harry's hair, licking her fingertips and then pushing his fringe to the side, over and over. Harry pulled his head away.

'Get away with ye,' she laughed. 'Ye love it when I mess yer hair up now. Where's yer mate then? Little Paddy?'

'He's coming over now. His mammy has sent him with the pram to fetch a bag of coke. He will be back in a minute.'

Sometimes Kathleen wondered if Maura and Tommy were handling things the best way. Since Kitty's death, Harry always seemed to be hiding in a book.

When the girls had finished babbling, Maura sat next to Kathleen with her own cup of tea.

'Well, sure, that's got them two going and our Angela

laughing and, God knows, that isn't easy. She works miracles, that Harriet.'

'Tell ye what, Maura.' Kathleen's face lit up as she carefully placed her cup back on the saucer. 'Why don't ye take the mop out and let's get the others in. This Rose Queen is big news. We had better start planning. Where are we going to find the frocks for this lot for a start? It's time for a pow wow.'

For a moment, Maura didn't respond. Over the past six months she hadn't banged on the wall once for her neighbours to meet in her kitchen for a natter. She wasn't sure if she was ready for rapid chatter and street gossip.

What did any of it matter? Their Kitty was dead, drowned. Who cared a fig about gossip? She looked sideways at Kathleen.

'Go on, love,' Kathleen urged her gently. 'Knock on for Peggy. They have all been patiently waiting and, sure, aren't the best days any of us have ever had been spent in this kitchen? We have solved more problems and had more laughs than most people do in their whole lives, sitting round your table. Everyone has been worried sick about you, Maura. Knocking on would be a sign to them and I think they deserve that.'

'Go on, Maura.' Kathleen put her hand on Maura's arm. 'Time to take the next step and this Rose Queen, 'tis a God-sent opportunity now.'

Maura sighed, knowing Kathleen was right. She walked over to the back door, picked up the mop and, as had always been the tradition, banged the handle against the wall that adjoined Peggy's kitchen, with three loud thumps.

The children fell silent. After a moment that seemed to last forever, they all heard it, Peggy knocking on her wall three times for Sheila. Moments later, Maura's neighbours began trotting down her path, chatting to each other, their heads full of bobbing curlers, balancing babies on hips, with cigarettes half smoked in one hand and their babies' bottles in the other. Each one walked over to Maura and hugged her.

They had been waiting patiently for Maura to let them know when she was ready. Now, they couldn't keep the smiles off their faces. Maura had turned a corner and they were turning it with her. Every single one of them breathed a sigh of relief when the Nelson Street mops once more began knocking.

'Enough of that,' shouted Nana Kathleen from the sink where she was in the process of filling the kettle. 'There's tea to be drunk and who has brought the biscuits?'

'I have, Kathleen,' said Deirdre above the chatter. 'I have a bag of broken which I got from the tin, in Keenan's.'

'And I've brought a brack, I made one extra today,' said Sheila, taking her plate to the press. 'Shall I run and fetch Annie?'

'Do you know, that's not a bad idea, Sheila. Aye, 'tis is a grand idea. The more the merrier.'

And with that, Sheila was back out of the door and across the entry to fetch Annie, back to where the beating heart of the four streets traditionally rested. In Maura's kitchen.

As they settled round the table, the chatter was so loud, Kathleen would have to shout to be heard. She breathed a deep sigh of relief. It felt as though she had been holding her breath for months and, for the first time, she could relax.

Suddenly there was an unfamiliar, tinkling sound. Little Harry looked up from his book and, catching Nana Kathleen's eye, he smiled. It was the sound of Maura laughing. A sound they had all forgotten.

Chapter Seventeen

AFTER HER MEETING with Sister Evangelista, Daisy walked down the convent steps with a confidence and self-assurance that had been wholly absent during the time she had worked as the dead priest's housekeeper. Sister Evangelista had insisted that Daisy stay with them in the convent guest room, until her brother arrived to collect her. As she reached the bottom step, Daisy spotted Harriet rushing down the Priory driveway.

'Morning, Daisy, love, isn't it a glorious day?' Harriet shouted across to her as she turned and almost ran down Nelson Street in the direction of Maura Doherty's house.

Daisy waved across the road and smiled. Although it was early, the river already shimmered in the bright sunlight. From years of observing how the river responded to the weather, Daisy could tell that today would be a scorcher. She liked Harriet. It was a very strange feeling seeing her run out of the house that had been Daisy's prison. She had arrived at the Priory as a young girl not knowing that it was the place where her childhood would be stolen.

Daisy had been nervous about her meeting with Sister Evangelista. Once she had finished her breakfast with Alison and the nuns, she had taken out Maggie's note and read it again. It told her exactly what she had to say and to whom she had to say it. This morning, it had been Sister Evangelista's turn.

Although the school was empty, with the children at home for the holidays, Sister Evangelista had been working in the school office.

'Morning, Daisy, come on in,' she said as she pulled out a chair next to her desk. 'I'm just preparing the lessons for next term as I want to visit Ireland myself. It is time I had a little break.'

Sister Evangelista had been alarmed to discover that whilst they had thought she was lost, Daisy had been held like a prisoner at the new convent near Galway. Sister Evangelista knew the Reverend Mother well, as Sister Theresa was related by blood to the bishop. Like the police, Sister Evangelista had plans to pay a visit to the convent personally and discover just what had been occurring.

She wanted to find out for herself who had told the police officer to take Daisy to St Vincent's and why. There were many hidden secrets still to be uncovered and she should know; she was probably hiding the very worst.

'Sister, I have something to say.' Daisy sounded very serious.

Sister Evangelista looked at Daisy, slightly amazed. This was the girl who would never say boo to a goose. Who would ever have thought it? Such a transformation.

Daisy continued, 'Sister, you and I, we found photographs in the priest's desk that were very bad.'

'Aye, we did, Daisy, but they are burnt now and that is all over.'

'Well, they weren't all burnt, Sister. There are some in the safe in the cellar and I don't think it is all over. If it was, I wouldn't have been taken to the convent, would I? There was a reason I was taken there—'

'What safe?' Sister Evangelista interrupted Daisy.

Sister Evangelista felt the return of a familiar feeling of panic that she was sure she would never shake off. Every night before she went to sleep, she often wondered: was this the effect of shock? Would she spend her remaining years looking over her shoulder, jumping each time a telephone rang or a door slammed? Her life until recently had been one of serenity and devotion. The most serious problem she ever had to tackle was a severe outbreak of nits at the school.

Since she had opened the desk drawer of the dead Father James and found it stuffed full of those disgusting photographs, nothing had been the same. As she closed her eyes at night, the images of schoolchildren once entrusted to her care swam before her eyes. It took prayers and tears to wash them away.

'The safe in the wall in the cellar,' Daisy said. 'Father James asked me to put a cardboard box of photographs in it. He kept them in there for a man called Arthur. He didn't like the dark, did Father James. At night he always liked the landing light to be left on. Down in the cellar, it is very dark, so he always sent me instead. I had the notion he was scared.

'There were some big flat round tins as well, with films in. Sometimes Arthur used to come to the Priory to collect them and sometimes he brought them to the father. Quite often, the two men who worked at the hospital came. You remember them, Sister, they came to the convent one night when the bishop sent them to collect me. 'But you know, Sister, it wasn't only Father James who was a bad man, it was the bishop too. I have to tell the police about that now. But I also have to tell them about the photographs in the desk drawer, the ones which you burnt.'

Sister Evangelista felt as though she were falling.

'No, Daisy,' she whispered. 'Do you realize what that would do? I am not fond of the bishop any more than you are, now, but he would be arrested and I might be as well. God only knows what would happen to the church and the school. Haven't I always taken care of you, Daisy? I think the best thing is if we keep all this to ourselves and make sure those two hospital porters get their come-uppance. But, please, keep it just between us about the bishop and Father James. Let us keep as our secret the photographs we found in the desk.'

'I can't, Sister.' Daisy's voice sounded stronger than she felt. 'I can't, because although you have been good to me since the father died and you are a good and kind Reverend Mother, you haven't always done the right thing. For years I was stuck in that Priory with Father James doing to me the same things you saw in the photographs, and the bishop too. And you want me to keep that just between us? I can't do that, Sister. I can't. I have to tell the police everything. That's what Maggie told me I had to do.'

Shocked, Sister Evangelista was unable to speak. Her life had been sent out of control with her future spinning away from her.

'I will also give the police the key to the cellar safe. I took it with me, because Father James told me to never let anyone have it and to always keep it hidden when he wasn't around.

Maggie told me, that now that he is dead, I don't have to do that any more.'

'Who is this Maggie?' Sister Evangelista almost screamed the words.

'She is the person who looked after me and smuggled me out of the St Vincent's convent and got me back home. She told me I was no more simple than she was, Sister. Maggie said I only couldn't speak very well because no one ever spoke to me and I thought I was simple because everyone told me I was. Maggie said, if people didn't use their brains and keep their wits about them, everyone would be simple. Maggie told me, no one should keep secrets with the devil himself. If we don't tell the police, Reverend Mother, that is what we would be doing. That's not the right thing, is it? You should meet Maggie. You would really, really like her.'

With that, Daisy stood up and, with her head held high, she walked out of Sister Evangelista's office.

Chapter Eighteen

'IS HE STILL sleeping?' Mrs McGuire leant across and whispered to Mary.

She was sitting next to her daughter in the back seat of a taxi, travelling from the airport to Galway. The bags piled between them were now full of wet terry-towelling nappies and everything a baby could possibly need on a journey from Chicago to Galway.

Alice travelled in a cab following on with the remainder of the bags.

A large carrycot was wedged into the front seat and was also full of baby accessories. As she spoke, Mrs McGuire craned over the pile of bags to take a peep at the baby lying on her daughter's lap. He had slept for almost the entire journey.

Having had a blood transfusion before they left for Ireland, the sickly boy had transformed into a jolly pink bundle of joy.

'Aye, he is, but not for long, I reckon. He will have me awake all night now,' an exhausted Mary replied.

With a sigh, she gently ran her thumb across the latest dark bruise to appear on his leg. The gesture alone spoke volumes.

'Look, Mammy, he's dying in my lap. This bruise, it tells me so.'

Mrs McGuire pushed a bag aside and slipped her arm round her daughter's shoulders, her own gesture of concern encompassing both her daughter and her baby.

Mrs Mcguire was delighted they were returning home, even though, given the circumstances, that feeling had to be wrong. This made her feel guilty, which was the default position for every self-respecting Roman Catholic.

If the child had not been as sick they would never have attempted the journey whilst he was so young and it would have been a very long time before she set foot once again in her village on the outskirts of Galway.

However, Mary had insisted Mrs McGuire came too. She would find it hard to travel to Ireland alone with Dillon. If she had to travel to find his birth mother, they would do it together.

Mrs McGuire still knew her way around every back kitchen in every house in her village and, despite the many years she had spent in Liverpool and Chicago, Galway was the only place that truly felt like home.

'That's the thing about home,' Mary had explained to her. 'No one is anonymous. The chances are, someone we know will know someone who knows the people we are looking for and that's why I need you, Mammy, because, sure, don't you know half of the people in Ireland anyway.'

Every sensible person they knew in Chicago had tried to persuade Mary to leave the baby behind. She had refused to budge.

'He has been ours for only a few months and I have waited

my whole life for him. I will not be parted from him for a day. God in heaven, he will have forgotten who his mother is if I leave him.'

Henry gave up trying to stop Mary from doing what she wanted to do. 'Jesus, she's like a woman possessed,' he had said to Sean as they stood in the garden, watching the new gardeners prune Henry's conifers. Henry didn't trust anyone to do anything he couldn't do himself. He might be a rich man now, but if he had had the time to do his own garden, he would have done.

'Ever since the baby has been sick, there has been no talking to her. She's driven, so she is. She will do whatever it takes to make him better and I for one am not standing in her way.'

'I wouldn't try, Henry,' Sean had replied. 'She is her mother's daughter. Nothing you can say will make a ha'p'orth of difference. Da would vouch for that if the poor man were still alive.'

Henry nodded in agreement as he lit two cigarettes and handed one to Sean.

'I'm glad Alice is travelling with Mary and Mammy to Ireland. I think it will take the three of them to manage the baby and all the luggage. I would feel better if she were with them.'

Sean agreed. Maybe Alice herself needed a break. They had been arguing a great deal of late. Sean was finding it impossible to say or do anything to please Alice. It felt as if everything had become an effort. Every single day at some point they would have the same argument and the last time had been just hours ago.

'Get your hands away from me,' Alice had said as she stormed out of bed. 'I am not falling for that. I know what your plan is. I have an appointment at the doctor's office today and I'm asking him for the new birth control pill. It takes a month to work and then I am safe. Until then you can keep your hands to yourself.'

As the bathroom door banged shut, Sean lay on his back and remembered Brigid, who had done everything in her power to make him happy. The images of his daughters' faces swam before his eyes as tears prickled. He wished it was he who could have travelled home and kept Mary company because, if it had been possible, wild horses wouldn't have kept him from visiting his children. For the first time, Sean realized he was a wealthy man. He had all he had ever dreamt about and yearned for, but without a loving wife and children to share it with, what did any of it mean?

He turned his head towards the bathroom door.

An en suite bathroom. Who had ever heard the like? He imagined the expressions on his children's faces if he could show them around Mary's house, how beyond excited they would be. He could see Emelda and Patricia bouncing up and down on his king-sized bed, jostling each other as usual to be picked up first. Then he saw the deep blue eyes of his baby, looking up at him trustingly from the pram as he had bent down to place a kiss on her cheek the morning he had left her, for the last time.

He allowed his tears to flow, because he knew that to see them all again was a dream that would never materialize.

*

As the taxi bumped along the uneven road, Mrs McGuire looked out of the window at the familiar countryside. She had already sent a letter on ahead to her daughter-in-law, Brigid, and her grandchildren, to let them know she would be visiting as soon as she arrived in Ireland. Neither her son, Sean, nor his mistress, Alice, were aware of this but, as far as Mrs McGuire was concerned, no one would keep her away from her own granddaughters, certainly not her son's fancy bit on the side.

'Are you sure you don't want to come with Alice and me to the convent tomorrow, Mammy?' asked Mary in a whisper, careful not to wake the sleeping baby.

'No, Mary, ye and Alice go. I have friends I want to catch up with and I have the taxi booked to take me. No point me coming all this way back home now and not saying hello to my friends, is there? That would just be a waste of a visit now. Ye and Alice, sure, that's enough to be dropping in on the nuns unannounced.'

'Well, if you are sure, Mammy. I don't want ye to think I don't want ye with me.'

'Sure, child, why would I think that? Just because my blockhead of a son thought I shouldn't visit my grandchildren? I know what's going on in his head all right. He doesn't want me carrying tales to Brigid and the girls about him and Alice. He should have stopped the boxing years ago. I swear to God it sent him mad.'

Mary looked out of the back window of the taxi. Alice was now following closely behind them in the second taxi.

'Are you off to see Brigid, Mammy?' Mary had seen right through her mother's story of visiting her friends and knew exactly what she was up to.

'I am, Mary, and nothing ye or anyone else can say is going to stop me. I almost brought those girls up. Your brother broke my heart, leaving them all like he did and landing us with that harlot back there.' This with a backwards nod towards Alice.

Seeing the taxi driver's eyes light up in the rear-view mirror as he heard the word 'harlot', Mary gently pressed her mother's arm and nodded towards the driver.

'Sure, I'm not bothered by Porick,' her mother replied. 'I knew his daddy when he was just a child and I've changed his nappies often enough. D'ye not remember him? Ye was at the convent together with his big sister. They live on the Knock Road. Porick, repeat a word ye hear in this car and I'll slap yer legs raw. D'ye understand?'

Porick, who was at least twenty years of age, winked at Mary in the rear-view mirror and replied with a grin, 'Aye, Mrs McGuire. Yer secrets are all safe with me, so they are. I'll not say a word to the harlot, so I won't.'

Mary smiled. She thought that there was possibly not a single person in all of Ireland that her mother didn't know. She also knew that by tonight every detail of their conversation would be the main topic of discussion in the pub.

'Can ye put me out at the main street, Porick,' Mrs McGuire said.

'What for? We are staying at the hotel, Mammy. You don't need to go to your house and we don't need anything until tomorrow.' Mary looked at her mother and frowned, knowing exactly what Mrs McGuire was doing. 'You can't wait, can you?' she whispered to her. 'You want to show off to your mates, don't you?'

Mary smiled indulgently, holding the baby tight to her chest so as not to wake him. If Mrs McGuire had a fault, it was that she could never resist the chance to brag.

'I don't know what you mean,' her mother replied, her voice loaded with indignation. 'Ye have Alice to help with the baby and Porick here will carry the bags into the hotel. Sure, Mary, ye have come a long way in the world. Ye don't need me to show ye how it works any more. I just want to have a bit of a wander round the shops now. To see what's changed an' all.'

Mrs McGuire had made sure that she was known by her friends and neighbours in Ireland as a bit of a jet-setter. It wasn't difficult, given that she was the only woman in the village to have ever set foot on a jet. Now she tried to change the subject.

'Let's go to the chippy for our tea tonight, Mary. God knows, I can't remember the last time I went to one.'

Mrs McGuire loved to regale her friends back home in Ireland with stories of the exotic delicacies to be found in Mr Chan's chippy on Liverpool's Dock Road.

Saveloys. Oh my, how she loved the way that word rolled off the tongue.

Was there ever a more exotic word?

'In Liverpool, I often pop to the chippy for saveloys,' she would say to her friends. Slowly.

'God in heaven, s-a-v-e-l-o-y-s? What would they be?' her friends would demand to know.

She loved the way their mouths fell open when she described sodas, burgers, corn dogs, barbecues, air-conditioning and ice-making machines.

And, as everyone knew, the person she most liked to impress with her stories was the butcher, Mr O'Hara, who also owned the village shop. Mr O'Hara was a man of business. He wore a brown overall and carried himself with the air of a man of the world.

Mr O'Hara often travelled as far as Dublin, which gave him some standing in the local community, Dublin being such a dangerous place by all accounts.

There was a time when Mrs McGuire could easily have become Mrs O'Hara, that's if Maisie O'Toole hadn't pushed herself in first.

Maisie had died ten years back and, a month later, so had Mr McGuire, leaving behind a pair of once-upon-a-time, almost-young lovers with stars uncrossed.

Mrs McGuire liked to pop into Mr O'Hara's shop and brag about her international travels, to which he would listen patiently before he responded with his own prepared tales of daring and bravery, as he sliced rashers and laid out pig's trotters.

It was a ritual they both engaged in, each and every time she returned home.

Tales at dawn.

And even though it was she who had travelled oceans and had shared experiences, she had yet to win their battle of words.

Mrs McGuire leant against the car window and peered at the low, white-stone cottages they passed. Closing her eyes for a moment, she remembered the last time she had come home and their parting conversation.

'Sure, now, I have to travel to Dublin most weeks. If ye were contemplating such a visit these days, Mrs McGuire, ye would need to carry a gun around in your handbag before ye set foot out of the bus.'

'Surely, Liverpool and Chicago are far safer places altogether, I think,' she had replied, never missing a chance to casually drop her jet-setting credentials into the conversation.

Mr O'Hara nodded sagely as he wrapped up her two pounds of bacon rashers in waxed paper, handing them over with a very solemn expression.

'I would think that would be so, Mrs McGuire, safer altogether I would be saying now,' he replied, in a tone as serious as if he were telling her the Pope had visited his shop and dropped dead, then and there, on the sawdust-covered floor, right on the spot where she was standing.

She had left that day feeling strangely empty. She had failed to impress.

It was a task unfinished, awaiting her return.

On a jet plane.

Porick pulled over in the main street for Mrs McGuire to alight.

The taxi with Alice pulled up behind. Mrs McGuire noticed that Alice's head was on the seat. She was fast asleep, so she had no need to explain herself. Mrs McGuire walked round to the front of the taxi and spoke through the driver's window. 'Porick, will ye meet me back here now in an hour to take me to the hotel?'

'Aye, Mrs McGuire. Should I meet ye here, or go straight to the butcher's?' Porick grinned from ear to ear, feeling very smug and pleased with himself.

Sure, apparently everyone knew there had been a thing between Mrs McGuire and Mr O'Hara.

His daddy had told him only that morning.

'If there have ever been two mismatches in marriage, it was them two not seeing the obvious right under their noses. But then, Maisie O'Toole, she was far from stupid, that one. She knew what she was up to and Mr O'Hara, he was just an eejit of a man who was knocked off his feet with a roll in the hay and a story of a babby on the way. God knows, that was the longest pregnancy in history. Two years until after the wedding, it lasted.'

'Ye cheeky beggar, Porick, I will meet ye here, as I said.'

She turned to Mary. 'I will be an hour now. I'll just say a few hellos.'

'Aye, take as long as ye want, Mammy,' Mary said. 'I'm going to have a nap and take the little fella with me.'

Mary was true to her word. The twenty-four hours she had spent in the company of Alice and her mother had been enough. She was in need of some peace and quiet of her own. Exhausted by the journey, she took herself off to bed within half an hour of checking into the hotel.

Mrs McGuire had walked for only a few minutes before regretting her hasty decision to leave the taxi, wishing she had popped into the hotel for a quick bath and a change of clothes before venturing out. She felt nervous, probably because this was her longest absence from home ever. Now she felt uncomfortable, like a stranger in her own village.

As she was continually halted on her way down the main street by people she had known all of her life, she made slow progress.

'Howarye?'

She answered this greeting a dozen times before finding herself at the kerbside, facing the butcher's shop belonging to the man who had passed her over all those years ago.

A young boy ran out of the school gates towards the tobacconist's shop, splattering her legs with dirt from the gutter. She recognized him from her own childhood. She knew his look. He was a Power, all right, and if she had to ask him, she would put money on him belonging to the eldest lad, who was the son of Colm, who was the son of PJ.

She knew them all. Grandfather, father and son.

The familiarity of his face, in his run, in his shouts to his friends, made her realize just how many of the years she had spent away.

From the opposite side of the road, she saw Mr O'Hara, standing in the same place, in the same brown coat, as he had done for almost forty years. Man and boy.

'Hello, howarye?' he shouted across to her, moving swiftly to fill the shop doorway with his bulky frame.

Mrs McGuire stepped off the kerb, ready to cross the mud-and-dirt road, towards the shop and the life that might once have been hers, if Maisie O'Toole hadn't slipped in first.

As she checked for traffic and looked towards the school gates, there they all were, their ghosts of the past: Maisie O'Toole and herself, running home, pigtails flying in the air. Maisie, her once best friend. Maisie, in whom she had confided her heart's deepest secrets and desires. Maisie. The thief. Dead but not forgiven.

'Howaryerself? I'm grand and glad to be back home,' she called back as she reached the front of the shop.

Now that she stood in front of him, feeling more like sixteen than sixty, she had forgotten all the boastful anecdotes she had dreamt up on the plane.

'Well, ye are a sight for sore eyes and that's for sure. I was wondering only the other day how long it would be before we saw ye back here. Mrs Kennedy, she said now, no, ye won't be seeing her back in these parts. Gone for good she is, to Chicago, and I thought, well now, isn't that a great shame.'

He had thought about her?

She was speechless. He had thought of her and spoken to others in the shop about her.

'Well now, I will always come back. 'Tis my home after all.'

'Aye, but many don't. Time passes and they forget. We have houses now standing empty for years and no one to sell them on or to claim them. Families in America, long gone. Old Catherine, over a hundred she was, now, when she died. Her house has stood empty these two years or so. Solicitors, they have tried but, sure, they cannot find the son. He emigrated to America sixty years back, and could be long dead himself now. It will stand empty forever, I would say.'

He smiled. 'I'm about to lock up. How d'ye fancy a glass in the pub and a catch-up over old times?'

Mrs McGuire nodded, but said nothing. She couldn't have spoken even if she had wanted to. He had asked her to the pub as though he were commenting on the weather. And yet her heart was beating as fast as it had when they had been teenagers, and he had kissed her, one burning hot day, when they had both helped out at the Finnegan's harvest for a penny each.

On that day, just as they were about to leave together,

Maisie had interrupted and spirited Mrs McGuire away on a spurious excuse, saying she was needed urgently by her mother. Mrs McGuire found her an hour later, sitting in a bar drinking Guinness with no notion at all as to why anyone should be looking for her.

Leaving her mother, she had gone in search of Maisie and Mr O'Hara. It was Colm Power who had given her the news that had shattered her world.

'Would ye be looking for Maisie? Ah, well, ask yer man. They was sneaking off looking very sweet with one another, I would say now. Kissing the two prettiest colleens in the village in one day. Isn't he just the lucky bastard?'

Mr O'Hara turned the closed sign to face the window and put the key in the door ready to lock up.

She hesitated, thinking about Mary and Alice, back at the hotel.

Mary could manage. Alice could manage. They could all manage. Bugger them.

She was about to do something she had wanted to do for a very long time and a thrill shot down her spine. She would spend time alone with the man she had first fallen in love with, over forty-four years ago.

No one could ever say Mrs McGuire wasn't a patient woman.

The following morning, Porick drove Mary and Alice to the convent. Long before he reached its gravel drive he began to slow down.

'Shall I wait at the bottom of the drive for ye, Mary?' he said without turning round.

Porick didn't like the nuns and the closer he got to the convent steps, the more anxious he became. Given a choice, he would have preferred to have dropped both women and the baby at the bottom of the drive and agree to pick them up there later, or even at the gates of hell, anywhere they wanted. He just did not want to hang around outside the convent, waiting.

'I would prefer it if you waited outside the main building,' Mary replied. 'But, if you don't want to, park up outside the gates and we will walk down the drive to you when we have finished. Just keep an eye out for us now.'

'Why didn't Mrs McGuire want to come with us?' Alice asked Mary.

Alice was holding the baby while Mary used her compact mirror to reapply her lipstick and check her hair before they stepped out of the taxi. Mary had her own stories of being educated by the nuns. Lipstick was her warpaint. Her armour of defence.

Mary carefully outlined her lips. Her intense focus on keeping a straight line provided her with an excuse to act distracted, delaying the moment she might have to lie. She did not want to be the one to inform Alice that Mrs McGuire had taken herself off to see Brigid. Mary had wanted to join her herself to visit the woman who was legally married to her brother and see her lovely nieces. She had packed presents for them all in her suitcase. Alice didn't know that either. Unperturbed by Mary's silence, she continued, 'Do you think they will be able to tell I'm not a Catholic, Mary? Am I actually allowed to step inside?'

'Oh, for goodness' sake, Alice, we don't look any different.'

Mary sounded impatient, which was unusual for her. Alice didn't take offence; she understood that Mary was nervous about meeting the nuns.

'Mammy didn't come because she had a hangover, I reckon,' Mary now said to Alice. 'When I popped into her room this morning she said she felt as if a rocket had landed on her head and, my God, she did look ghastly. I thought it was best to leave her. I think she ended up in the pub with one of her friends last night.'

Mary was quite sure that, as soon as they had left the hotel, Mrs McGuire would recover and be on her way to visit Brigid.

Mary felt a moment of panic as she looked at Porick. She hoped he would keep his mouth shut and not mention Mrs McGuire this morning. It was his father who would be driving her mammy, she imagined, as soon as she and Alice were down the road and out of sight.

It was Sister Celia herself who answered the door of the Abbey.

She recognized Mary instantly. It was not often a parent offered three thousand dollars for a baby. Sister Celia's face instantly transformed from its normal grumpy setting to a smiling mask of compassion and care. A carefully crafted pretence, masking abject indifference.

'Ah, come on in now,' she said as she gently took hold of Mary's arm. 'Come in.'

Mary gratefully stepped into the hallway. 'This is Alice, my sister-in-law, Sister. We are so sorry to call in on you unannounced, but I did write ahead to Sister Assumpta. It's just that we didn't know what flights we would be able to catch and everything was so rushed as we left. I am so sorry.'

'Stop, would ye, stop, not at all, not at all,' said Sister Celia as she ushered Mary down the corridor. 'Reverend Mother has a visitor with her, Sister Theresa from St Vincent's, but, sure, she was on her way when the bell rang, which is why I was in the hall. Come along now, I will make sure ye go straight in.'

Alice hung back a little. Surrounded by statues of the sacred heart and paintings depicting scenes from the bible, she was uneasy, and felt as though the initials C of E burnt brightly on her forehead.

Alice and Mary stepped into the Reverend Mother's huge office with its vast expanse of Persian rug.

'Beautiful carpets,' Alice whispered to Mary. 'Just like the make we had in the foyer of the Grand in Liverpool. That was called Axminster, the best.' The opulence of the carpet made Alice feel at home. This was more like it.

'Come along in, ladies,' Sister Assumpta called out from behind the desk.

Alice felt she had better do something to make herself useful, as well as to divert the nuns' attention away from her, just in case they could spot a soul in limbo. While Sister Celia prattled on and pulled out chairs, Alice whispered to Mary, 'Give me the baby to hold so that you can concentrate.' As she held out her arms to take the sick baby, she noticed Sister Assumpta looking at her with more than a hint of curiosity. Alice smiled back, tentatively, as she rewrapped the shawl around Dillon. The smile was unreturned. God, she can tell, Alice thought. She began to tremble and all thought of defiance in the face of intimidation fled.

Nervously, but calmly, Mary began to explain her situation. She had practised her words over and over the evening before, but now, sitting in front of the Reverend Mother, she was unable to prevent the tears from filling her eyes and thickening her throat, making it difficult to speak without almost breaking down.

'I'm so sorry,' she sniffled as she opened the clasp on her handbag and took out a hankie.

Mary felt overwhelmed. Neither nun spoke or offered a gesture of comfort.

On the plane over, she had rehearsed this scene in her mind. In her imagined scenario, the nuns had been kindly. In reality, they were unyielding, devoid of compassion.

'We are in a desperate situation, Sister. We have no choice other than to come here and ask for your help. The baby is very poorly and we need to find his mother urgently, or he will die. There is almost no chance of finding a stranger with a good enough match. We must find the woman or the girl who gave birth to him.'

As Mary spoke, Sister Assumpta occasionally altered the position of something or other on her desk.

She moved her pen slightly further up. Straightened the blotter. Stroked the silver and ivory letter opener. Raised her eyebrows. Tipped her head to one side.

Mary felt she wasn't really listening and, worse, that the Reverend Mother had known what her answer would be and was waiting impatiently to deliver it.

'We desperately need a member of his family to donate a sample of bone marrow. 'Tis a simple operation and we would pay for the family member to be flown to America. Everything would be covered. There would be no problem with that. We would make sure the family were very comfortable.'

When Mary had finished talking, Sister Assumpta ceased the constant rearrangement of her desk. She remained quiet for an unnaturally long time, as though in prayer, and then, slowly looking up, she gazed first at the baby and then at Mary. For a moment, far too long for comfort as far as Alice was concerned, she fixed her eyes upon Alice. The clock chimed, the fire hissed and an air of expectation built in the room.

Mary felt as though something was wrong. Things were not quite as they should be. She had expected much greater concern. Sister Assumpta and Sister Celia appeared very different from how they had been when the baby was first offered for adoption.

At the time, they had been kindness itself. Had they really altered so much in those few short months? Had her recollection been warped by her own emotional state when she had collected her son? Mary felt sick to her stomach as every nerve in her body told her, this is not right, and yet what could she say? There could be few circumstances in life more serious than the one she was trying to explain and this was the one place she had expected to find help and compassion. She had even expected Sister Celia to be overfussy, just as she had on the day they had collected her baby boy.

The atmosphere in the room now was tainted and surreal. She wondered to herself, do they not understand? This is life and death.

Mary was about to speak again, fearing that maybe she had not explained the gravity of the situation clearly enough, when Sister Assumpta broke the silence.

'Well now, 'tis a dreadful problem you have there.' Sister Assumpta broke her silence at last.

She emphasized the word 'you'. This was not her problem, nor that of the convent. There would be no return of a faulty baby.

'We do, however, have the greatest sympathy for your situation, don't we, Sister Celia.'

Sister Celia had not taken a seat, but hovered near the door, waiting for the tea to arrive. 'Oh yes, Reverend Mother, sure, 'tis a shocking state of affairs.' She was saved from having to say anything more by a novice arriving with a tray of tea, which she gratefully took and placed on the table between the chairs occupied by Alice and Mary. Saved by the tray.

'Tea, ladies?'

Two words, which gave everyone a moment to think and Sister Assumpta, time to nuance her message.

She knew very well what her answer had to be. There must be no room for ambiguity when she delivered her response. This was the last time she would ever want this mother and baby in her office.

The ceremony of tea and cake commenced. Alice began to relax. No one had asked her a question and it didn't look as if anyone was about to. She breathed a sigh of relief, as she adjusted the baby in her arms and reached for her teacup. She really wanted to look occupied, too busy to speak.

Two doves had landed on a branch on the tree outside the window behind Sister Assumpta's chair. Alice tried not to look but became fixated by them. She wanted to be anywhere other than in this room. Mentally joining the two noisy birds on the branch in their mating ritual, she thought it as good a distraction as any.

'You see, the thing is, Mrs Moynihan, would ye believe, we have no idea at all who the mother is, do we, Sister Celia.'

Sister Celia, not expecting to be involved in the conversation until she was required to show Mary and Alice out of the office, looked up and, with her mouth full of cake, answered, 'Well now, no, Reverend Mother, I don't believe we do.'

Crumbs flew out and landed on her lap as she spoke. Sister Celia hurriedly stood and, waddling to the fireplace, held out the skirt of her habit to shake the contents into the hearth.

Mary began to feel angry. This was a farce. She sensed acutely that the nuns were not telling the truth and that, in the midst of this roomful of women, the only person fighting for her baby's life was herself.

The pitch of her voice rose. 'I'm sorry, Sister, but I cannot believe that to be the case and I'm afraid I cannot leave here, without some information. My son will die without help and I have to make contact with his mother and his family. I simply have to. This is not what I want to do. I do not want to meet his mother. I did not want to make the journey from America. But if this baby is to live, I have no choice.'

Tears ran silently down her cheeks.

'Please, please, I'm begging you, check your records for any information you may have. Anything will help.'

'Mrs Moynihan, we would love to do that, now, wouldn't we, Sister Celia, but I'm afraid it just isn't possible. You see, a few weeks ago we had the most desperate fire and all our records were destroyed, weren't they, Sister Celia. We have nothing, can ye imagine, nothing left. But let me check now as some of the paperwork survived. We may have the contract the girl signed when she handed the baby over for adoption.'

Sister Assumpta walked over to the long, tall press at the end of her study and opened one of the lower drawers. A few moments later, she returned to her desk.

Alice was confused. The words 'fire' and 'where?' ran through her brain as she looked round the spotless room.

The convent smelt of incense, not smoke, and there was no sign of the desperate fire Sister Assumpta had spoken of.

'Ah, here we have it now,' the Reverend Mother said with a flourish. Then her voice altered dramatically and took on a tone of disbelief. 'Sure, now, I think the girl may have signed the contract with a false name. Don't they often do that, Sister Celia?'

Sister Celia had just taken a bite of cake the size of a baby's head whilst Sister Assumpta had been distracted, searching through the drawer. She was not about to be caught out again and nodded furiously in agreement.

'Now, I know for a fact that the girl's name was Cissy. She

was brought here by her family, but she was sent here by the matron midwife from the hospital, Rosie O'Grady and she wouldn't get a name wrong. But see here, on the contract the girl has signed her name Kitty Doherty, and yet her name was very definitely Cissy. The girl must have been deluded when she signed this. All we know is that she was from Liverpool. My best suggestion to you would be to travel to Dublin and visit the midwife because the girl obviously lied when she signed this.'

Sister Assumpta felt foolish. This was the first time she had bothered to check the signature.

The room grew dark as storm clouds gathered in the sky, resulting from the heat of the previous week.

As the light faded, the first drops of rain spattered the glass. The doves huddled together on the branch and Alice looked down at the baby on her lap.

Had she heard right?

The baby spat his dummy out onto the floor. He looked up and smiled seraphically at Alice. She stared back at him, dumbfounded.

She leant down to retrieve his brown rubber dummy from the rug and placed it in her hot tea to clean it, a trick she had learnt on the four streets. Her movements were studied and unhurried, concealing the pace of her thoughts, which were racing.

She spoke for the first time, slowly and deliberately.

'I'm sorry, what did you say the name was on the contract?'

Sister Assumpta held the document out towards Mary as though ignoring Alice.

'Here, see for yourself. Kitty Doherty.'

Maura had taken Kitty to Ireland to have the baby. Alice had read the letter that Kathleen had sent Maura.

Alice felt dizzy as her two worlds collided and became one.

Just at that second, the door to the office swung open and closed again. A novice re-entered with a jug of hot water for the teapot.

Bang. Bang. The door slammed shut.

Alice flinched. This could not be possible. She held out her hand to take the contract Sister Assumpta waved in front of Mary.

'Please, please, let me see,' she whispered.

A thousand reasons flew through her mind as to why it could not be Maura and Tommy's Kitty, but only one thought made any sense, drowning out all else and pounding in her brain.

The sickly baby sitting on her lap was Kitty's child and Maura's grandson. Alice struggled to breathe. This could not be. The reason for the night that no one would ever speak of was right here, on her knee. That awful night, when Alice had become an accomplice to murder. She looked back at the doves taking shelter from the rain, which now battered the windows, and felt the floor shift beneath her chair.

She looked round at the faces in the room, which were fixed upon her and the baby.

Oh good Lord, can the nuns see what I have done? Alice thought. Surely, this was a nightmare. This could not be really happening. The ghosts of her past life filled the room, laughing and taunting her.

Somewhere outside, in the rain, she heard Maura and Tommy crying. Alice rose slowly from her chair. She looked down at the baby in her arms and, as she did so, the eyes of a dead priest stared back at her.

Chapter Nineteen

'ARE YOU SURE you witnessed this with your own eyes? 'Tis a grave accusation. God knows how we will manage without them if this is true. The kitchens run like clockwork and the garden is one of the most productive I have ever known.'

Sister Theresa peered over her glasses at Sister Perpetua who sat in front of her desk, still and calm, with her hands clasped loosely in her lap. A statue of poise, marbled with malice. Sister Theresa had read through the journal of evidence Sister Perpetua had placed before her and the facts were there, in black and white. The trouble was, she would so much rather they weren't.

'Yes, Reverend Mother. I have been keeping a watch for a month now and I have seen everything.' Sister Perpetua didn't even blink.

From the opposite side of the desk, she glanced across at her own handiwork, perched lightly in Sister Theresa's hands.

The list of accusations against Maggie and Frank was damning.

Feeding village children through the railings. Taking garden vegetables to their own kitchen. Giving food to the orphans and slipping bread up to the orphanage in the pockets of the kitchen helpers. The poteen still behind the secret wall in the potting shed.

'I will have to phone the Gardai, you realize that, don't you? This amounts to theft. We prefer to be private here, Sister Perpetua, and I have no notion of calling the Gardai every five minutes. Are you absolutely sure you have seen all this with your own eyes and there is no mistake?'

'Aye, Sister, I saw it all from the orphanage windows.'

'Holy Mother, I have two bishops arriving in an hour. We will leave this until our visitors have left. I cannot have visitors here and nothing to feed them and, besides, only Maggie knows how the kitchen runs, apart from, possibly, Maggie's kitchen helper.

'She was with us in the Dublin orphanage. We heard good reports about her from the bishop in Liverpool. When he arrives today, I shall ask him if he thinks she would be up to taking over the kitchen. She worked as a housekeeper for a priest in Liverpool and she will have had enough experience downstairs by now, I should think, wouldn't you?'

Sister Perpetua looked puzzled and frowned.

'What is it, Sister Perpetua? For goodness' sake, what is the problem now?'

Sister Theresa had never really liked Sister Perpetua. Putting her to work in the orphanage had been the ideal way to keep her out of sight. Or so she had thought. Sister Perpetua was methodical, pedantic and downright humourless. Not that Sister Theresa was in need of a laughing nun, but she did like to see them smiling every now and then. God knew, with the nature of the work they had to undertake and the amount of death they had to deal with, the odd smile was like a tonic to them all. But not Sister Perpetua. It was three years since she had taken her vows and, with each year, she had soured a little bit more than the last. Sister Theresa had never witnessed Sister Perpetua smile. She had also never known her to be wrong, which was why all of this was so depressing.

'Nothing, Sister, it just occurred to me that I haven't seen the new kitchen girl at mass for a little while now.'

Sister Theresa frowned. 'She has been sick, but she surely must be improved. I'm about to check on the meal for tonight, so I shall see her for myself. I have known her since she was a baby. We reared her. She was never a shirker, just a bit simple.'

Changing the subject quickly, she asked, 'Did you burn all the papers from the orphanage as I ordered?'

Sister Theresa closed the pages of the journal as she spoke and handed it across the desk to Sister Perpetua, who took it with her outstretched hand. Sister Theresa rose from her chair.

This was Sister Perpetua's cue to follow likewise.

'I did. Sister Clare helped me. We kept only the contracts the girls have signed at the mother and baby home, agreeing to never make contact with their babies, and we burnt all the death certificates from the orphanage. We lit a bonfire by the compost heap at the end of the potato patch and the furthest away from the house.'

Sister Theresa was now feeling better disposed towards Sister Perpetua. Her manner was tedious but her efficiency very useful.

'Very good. Sister Assumpta has done likewise at the Abbey. There is a midwife in Dublin who will not stop giving out to the authorities, which is making life very difficult indeed for us all. If we have nothing for them to see, if we don't keep any records, they can't look for anything, can they? If we are asked, it will be no sin if we do not have to lie. A simple explanation that the papers were lost in a fire will be all that is needed. That will be no word of a lie. Well done, Sister Perpetua. We should have a little talk when the bishops have left tomorrow about whether it is time you moved back down into the convent. But not yet. Now we have to prepare for our visitors.'

Maggie well knew the determined footsteps of Sister Theresa as they thumped down the stairs into the kitchen. Her inbuilt antennae were programmed to pick up the first step as soon as the top door was opened. By the sound of their tread alone, Maggie could tell even before she had reached the second step which sister was paying the kitchen a visit.

'As dainty as a bleeding elephant,' she muttered under her breath as the familiar black shoes and skirt came into view. She quickly slipped her smouldering pipe back into her apron pocket.

'Maggie.' Sister Theresa was already speaking while still on the stairs. 'Is all in order for our visitors tonight? Did we have a good side of beef delivered from the village? The bishop's teeth aren't that good, so we don't want tough meat now.'

'Have I ever served ye tough meat, Reverend Mother, visitors or not?' Maggie asked her question without impertinence, but her meaning was implicit.

She could feel the heat of her pipe burning in her pocket. It was rare for Sister Theresa to visit the kitchen in the middle of the morning, which was when Maggie always had a cuppa and a 'pull of me pipe'. It was also when she gave the girls from the orphanage or the mother and baby home a cuppa and a slice of bread and butter, telling them to rest their legs for a minute or two.

Maggie had learnt how to make the flour stretch by making slightly smaller loaves for the nuns, so that she could keep an extra one back for the helpers.

The girls had shoved their mugs and bread under the bench and were scrubbing the pots, just as they had been moments before.

Sister Theresa studied them. Maggie sweated.

'Where's the girl? Is she still sick?'

Daisy had supposedly been sick for the best part of a week. Maggie had known this moment would arrive.

Maggie was many things – kind, hurt, wise and damaged – but she was not stupid.

'She is off to the village to collect me baccy, Reverend Mother. She is the only one I can trust. Frank is busy digging up cabbage and I have run out. Did ye want me to send her to ye when she gets back?'

'Maggie, you don't send the girls to the village on your errands. For goodness' sake, not today of all days, and not on any day.'

'No, Sister, well, I can only say that with me baccy, you will likely have a better-tasting dinner and more tender beef, as it is a fact that if I am in a bad mood when I cook, the food never tastes as good and the milk often curdles.'

Sister Theresa stared at Maggie. She played an important role in the convent. Supplying three meals a day to the sisters and any visitors. This left the nuns free to run the mother and baby home, the nursery, the laundry, the orphanage and the retreat. Making money was the order of the day.

Using nuns to run the gardens and the kitchen would have been a waste of resources. The sisters had to be self-sufficient and, in the last few years, they had been successful in that. They were almost as successful as the Abbey, Sister Theresa guessed.

The bishops were visiting tonight and had asked to look over the bank books.

'They can do that gladly,' Sister Theresa had said to Sister Celia. 'We can hand them the books with pleasure. What we do not do is tell them about the biscuit tins with the money in the press. We have upwards of nineteen thousand pounds in there now, so we have, and it will be gone in a flash if the bishop knew we had it. If we ran into trouble, sure, we would have to beg on our knees for a handout. The money in the tins is ours and it stays that way.'

Her nuns were working long hours, for the benefit of the community, and she dreaded the disruption that losing Maggie and Frank would bring. As she stood in the kitchen, she knew she would have to be reconciled to that loss if Sister Perpetua's record-keeping was correct.

Right now, she was too busy to tackle the problem of Maggie or, for that matter, the errand-running kitchen girl. She needed to visit the orphanage to let them know the bishops were arriving and to ensure the sick children were in the isolation rooms. Every one of them would need a bath today and that would be a massive effort in itself.

Frank returned to the lodge, knowing that Maggie would be late back.

The nuns had been all of a flutter all day, preparing for the simultaneous visit of two bishops. Nothing but wailing and crying had been heard through the orphanage windows and, as Frank well knew, the rumpus was being caused by much more than the mere fact that all the children were being bathed in cold water. Tempers were flying.

It made his heart crunch when he saw a nun dragging a child by her hair from the washroom back to the orphanage and it was all he could manage not to say or do something.

'Heavenly Father, my blood boils, so it does, I have to calm me temper. Jaysus, I want to grab the nun by her fecking habit and drag *her* into a cold bath and then across the yard.'

It broke his heart to see the cruelty inflicted upon the children and every day he brought Maggie a different story.

Frank was often quiet when he arrived back at the lodge after work, and Maggie knew it was because he had seen things that upset him. Frank wasn't a great talker. Maggie would have to leave him be to eat his food, smoke his pipe and drink his poteen. Only then would he occasionally make a comment and, when he did, it was frequently shocking.

'Ye know the little one, the lad I told ye about who was only just walking, and so thin I could see the bones of his arse through his fecking trousers? Well, today I saw them putting him in the ground, so I did. They didn't even lay him down with a prayer or a blessing. They just rolled him off the edge, into that pit. Not a coffin in sight.'

Frank would finish speaking with a long drink from his mug of poteen and Maggie would not comment, merely sit in silence, knowing that Frank and she were both doing exactly the same thing: thinking of their own little lad. Frank threw a stick onto the range and then blew on the peat to make it glow red. The oven was still hot from earlier in the afternoon, when Maggie had run back to the lodge from the kitchen to set his dinner over a pan of hot water, with a lid on top to keep it warm.

Today he sat on the rocking chair by the fire with his dinner on his lap, his pot and pipe lying by his side, and he began to eat.

The food was delicious but the sights of the day made it stick in his gullet. He scraped most of it into the grate so that she wouldn't see. It was not to be. Maggie opened the door to the smell of burning beef.

'For feck's sake, ye eat as good as a nun and then throw it on the fire. Are ye crazy, Frank?'

Frank noticed that she looked exhausted.

Throwing her shawl over the back of one of the pair of chairs at the kitchen table, she made her tea, chatting away to Frank who remained sitting by the fire, still, staring into the flames.

'I suppose ye let the bishops and the band of followers in through the gates, did ye? Holy Mary, what a commotion today has been, but I tell ye what, Frank, Sister Theresa came into the kitchen, looking for Daisy, she did. She made a pretence at first, but I know that is what she was after. I know that woman like the back of my hand, I can see right though her, I can. Wanting to know if the beef was tough, my fecking arse. She was checking up. If I didn't know better, I would say someone was on to us.

'Daisy has been gone nearly a week now and do you know what else, Frank? I was shocked to see that bishop tonight. He's the same one, ye know, the one Daisy was on about, the dirty fecking bastard. That has worried me because if Daisy did what we told her, surely to God he would not be a free man by now.'

'Don't believe it, Maggie, the bishops are as powerful as the Lord God himself. No man would dare arrest a bishop. They look after one another and poor girls like Daisy, they are just left to suffer.'

Maggie looked at Frank with disbelieving eyes. 'I cannot believe that. Not everyone in Liverpool is a Catholic. She would have no luck here in Ireland and, God knows, she would be put in the asylum for the rest of her days if she ever claimed such a thing. But in Liverpool, surely to God, they are more civilized altogether? Surely someone there will believe her?'

'What do you think about this then?' said Frank, as he removed what appeared to be bits of charred paper from his pocket. Smoothing the larger pieces out carefully, he said, 'Well, go on then, you are the reader, what do they say?'

'What are they?' asked Maggie, peering at the blackened, burnt papers.

'I don't know, but Sister Perpetua and Sister Clare spent three hours burning them at the back of the tatties. 'Tis something they was desperate to be rid of. They ran up and down from the orphanage and the mother and baby home with boxes flying everywhere, so they was, and Sister Perpetua, she was shouting to Sister Clare to get a move on before the rain came and, sure, I have never seen Sister Perpetua so much as speak above a whisper, never mind shout. 'Twas all very odd indeed.'

Maggie sat down in the chair, pulling towards her the largest and most complete document.

'It's a letter signed by a priest,' she said. 'Her family can no longer manage to contain the girl's nature for flirtation. No man is safe from her advances. She must seek penance and be punished for forcing her neighbour to commit a shameful sin. She is pregnant. Her father never wants to see her face again and they have committed her to your care.

'Here ye go, some of the letters have gone, but there's enough to make it out.'

'Jesus, who would that be?' asked Frank.

'It says here,' Maggie replied, 'her name was Julie, Julie Dempsey.'

Frank rubbed his bearded chin thoughtfully. 'Aye, Julie, that one died in childbirth, as did the child. She is one of the few to have a wooden cross with her name on. She was one of the first. The nun who asked me for a mallet to put the cross in told me. Not one of them has a cross now.'

As Maggie studied the remaining burnt pieces of document, the dog began barking; someone was ringing at the gate. They both moved to the window to see a Gardai car, waiting to be admitted.

'Well, what do you know?' said Frank, when he was back indoors. 'They asked, was the bishop here and I told him we have two tonight, and which one did he want? He has told me to leave the gate open as he won't be staying long.'

A smile leapt across Maggie's face. 'Do you think it could be to do with Daisy?'

'I have no idea, but ye may be right.'

Minutes later, as they stood at the door with their pipes, Frank waiting to lock the gate, the Gardai car drove past with a very white-faced bishop sitting in the back.

'Right,' said Maggie. 'We have two things to do. I want a drink with me pipe and I want to read through all those bits of paper and then keep them somewhere safe. They could be our insurance for the future, Frank. Things are happening but I tell ye what: those nuns, they need to run a little faster to keep up.'

Chapter Twenty

H ARRIET TAPPED POLITELY on Maura's back door. She had yet to become comfortable with the habit of walking uninvited into the houses on the four streets.

She spotted Maura's face at her back kitchen window, in the midst of a steam cloud, and waved as Maura beckoned her inside.

Harriet put her head round the back door, still feeling the need to ask. 'Hello, do you mind me popping in?'

'Not at all. Ye don't have to stand on ceremony with us, Harriet,' said Maura, who stood at the sink, drying her hands on her apron.

Harriet noticed an enamel bucket on the floor next to Maura. The smell of hot Napisan and ammonia filled the kitchen, stinging her nostrils and making her eyes water.

'Come on away in. I've just finished now, that was the last nappy. Come on, come on. Have ye time just to sit down and have some tea? God alone knows, I've washed out ten dirty nappies this morning and I need a cuppa. Or are ye here to give me a message or a list of instructions maybe?'

Harriet grimaced. She was aware that she moved at a pace slightly faster than that of the four streets.

It seemed to everyone as though Harriet never sat still and that she spent her every day organizing something or someone.

Tommy had formed a very firm opinion about Harriet.

'Miss Bossy Knickers, that Harriet one. I had to walk round the back of the Anchor last night, when I spotted her turning the corner at the top of Nelson Street. I daren't bump into her without she asks me to do something or help her with a committee. I'm not a committee man, Maura, tell her, will ye? It's not safe any more to walk down me own street, so it's not. She has Jerry on a mission to clean the untended graves in St Mary's. That was a wicked play on his conscience.' Then he whispered with a guilty glance at the back door, 'The last place we want to be is in the fecking graveyard, for feck's sake.'

Maura soothed his worried brow with a kiss and, sitting on the arm of his chair in front of the fire, she let him talk without interruption. That was a novelty in itself in their passionate and noisy marriage. She let Tommy speak for as long as it took. I can't remember when we were last like this, Maura thought. We used to do this all the time.

The thin wooden arm of the chair dug painfully into her backside, numbing it, but she didn't stir or break the spell. She shuffled slightly and re-crossed her legs, worried that even her slightest fidget would stem his flow, but he carried on, jumping from Harriet to Kathleen and Jerry without pausing for breath.

'Kathleen and Jer, they have been good to us. Better than our own family even. As God is true, no one ever had better neighbours than we do, thank God. What can we ever do to repay them? It is beyond me. I have nothing to repay a man

299

who has burdened himself with the debt Jerry has on my behalf. He could be in prison, Maura, and, surely to God, without Kathleen these kids would have starved. I have no notion or recollection of the first few weeks. Do ye, Maura?'

Maura shook her head.

'Has the cat got yer tongue? Are ye fecking dumb all of a sudden?' said Tommy with a hint of surprise. It wasn't often that he was allowed to talk for so long without being interrupted. He looked up at Maura with suspicion.

'I'd rather he had my tongue than your langer,' Maura replied.

Tommy put his arm round Maura's waist and pulled her down onto his lap. The springs underneath the thin cushion groaned with their dual weight and they both rocked with laughter. They could now laugh about the dead priest and without guilt too. It felt strange and, at the same time, right. They hadn't laughed together for months. In the midst of their merriment the thought came to Maura: we are healing.

Tommy had complained about Harriet, but with affection. No one could do anything other than agree to whatever it was she asked.

It was impossible to refuse. Her manner was always so charming, and she implored in a way that made grown men melt and women feel sorry for her.

'Oh, I would love a cup of tea, thank you, Maura,' Harriet now replied.

''Tis a cuppa round here, Harriet, and ye don't have to thank me or stand on ceremony in my kitchen. Take the weight off your feet and sit down. The kettle is always on and we can spare a bit of tea. I'll even put fresh leaves in the pot as we have a guest.' Maura lifted the lid on the large tin teapot and peered inside. 'These leaves have been used three times today already, weak as a maiden's piss they will be by now.'

Maura set the kettle back on the range, where it simmered away all day and took only seconds to boil. Harriet, a maiden, was already blushing.

'Mary and Joseph, would ye look who is coming down the path,' said Maura. 'I swear to God she hears the clatter of the kettle on the range, that one, and pops in here to save the job of making herself a cuppa. Or, more like, she heard the back gate when ye arrived and has come for a nose to see who it is.'

Maura stopped talking just as Peggy opened the back door. As soon as Peggy saw Harriet by the fire, a look of disappointment crossed her face and she cried out, 'Oh, Jesus, no. I only came in for a cuppa tea and now I'm going to walk out with work to do. Fecking hell, how did that happen?'

'No, no,' Harriet said, as both her hands flew to her mouth in horror. 'I must have a terrible reputation for bothering people. I am here for something entirely different altogether, although I will admit there is a reason.'

Peggy didn't have time to respond, before Nana Kathleen joined them.

'Well now, a pow wow and no one invited me?' she said as she bustled in and placed a bulky white paper bag on Maura's press.

'Goodness me, it's like Lime Street station in here, it's so busy,' said Harriet.

'Aye, this kitchen was very rarely empty at one time,' said Maura. 'Some of the kids on the four streets used to be confused about where they lived, because their mothers spent so much time nattering round my kitchen table. My house has always been full of kids and friends and I don't have a problem with that now. My neighbours have been good to me, so they have.'

Harriet felt mildly embarrassed. She hadn't met or known Kitty, although she wished she had, as Maura might then have felt a closer connection to her. Harriet was always on the lookout for a lost soul to heal. She was as close as she could be to Kathleen's granddaughter, Nellie, and she knew they were aware of the role she had played in helping Nellie recover. It was that which made it possible for her to pluck up the courage to knock on Maura's door, seeking an answer to a question that was burning away in her mind.

'It wasn't a pow wow five minutes ago, Kathleen,' said Maura, 'but sure, 'tis about to become one. Peggy, go and knock on for Sheila and Deirdre with the mop, and tell them we have a guest. I feel guilty, them not being here.'

Peggy looked grumpy, but she stood up from the kitchen chair where she had made herself comfortable, preparing to waddle back into her own kitchen to bang the mop on her wall and send out the call.

'How do ye reckon I let them know there's a guest? D'ye think I bang on the wall in fecking Morse code now?' Unused to such raw language, Harriet blushed again.

They sat and listened to her footsteps shuffle down the yard, until they heard the back gate latch snap. Then Kathleen and Maura both began to laugh.

'Gosh, she was cross,' said Harriet.

'Not at all, no, she wasn't. Don't you be taking no notice of Peggy now,' said Maura. 'Peggy never stops grumbling.

She's all right. Right as rain she will be in five minutes when she comes back in. There are a few things ye need to know about Peggy. She hates to move her backside and she loves her tea and cake. Apart from that, there's not a lot to her.'

'Apart from the smell,' Kathleen whispered and winked at Harriet.

'That's the reason I'm here, to be honest,' said Harriet.

'What, because of the way Peggy smells?' exclaimed Nana Kathleen.

'No, no. I wanted your advice, Maura. I'd like to get to know a bit more about the neighbours. Alison and I are good friends, but I want to know everyone else too.'

'Well, ye have come to the right place to be sure,' said Maura. 'We can do that. We can provide all the advice ye need and tell ye everything you need to know about everyone around here. There's nothing we don't know about on these four streets, isn't that a fact, Kathleen?'

Kathleen smiled. ''Tis true. Now, tell me, Harriet, ye haven't taken the veil and yet there's no husband in yer life. Why is that now?'

Harriet gasped. She had known people in Liverpool were direct and to the point, but she had at least expected them to be onto their second cuppa before being asked such deeply personal questions.

'Well, I have never taken to anyone, I suppose, and no one has ever taken to me. I had to look after Mammy and Daddy until they died. I don't know really. I was so busy and time just flew and then there I was, on my way to Liverpool with Anthony and no husband to speak of. I would love to be married and have children, but I expect it is too late now, though.'

Kathleen or Maura were saved from having to answer by the sound of the back gate opening and familiar chatter flooding the yard. The kitchen was crowded within minutes. Neighbours, old and new, sat round the yellow Formica table that had once belonged to Bernadette. The precious Formica table with which Maura refused to part, no matter how large her family grew.

Sheila had spotted Daisy, leaving the school office, and had called her over to join them.

Kathleen helped Maura pour the tea at the range.

'I bought the kids some custard slices in Sayers, your Harry loves them. They are in that bag on the press for when they get home from school.'

'Kathleen, ye spoil them kids but they do love it,' said Maura, smiling.

'Aye, well, they deserve a bit of spoiling with what they have been through,' replied Kathleen, pouring from the sterilized-milk bottle into the cups.

Kathleen nodded her head in the direction of the table.

'I will have ye a penny, that Harriet is here with troubles of the heart. I can hear it in her voice. Hope these is fresh tea leaves as we might have to give her a little reading.'

Maura wanted to say, 'Harriet, no,' but she knew better. Nana Kathleen was never wrong.

Life on the four streets was mundane. It was about survival and making ends meet. Harriet had lived in a large house in Dublin and had been brought up in a professional household. Her brother was a priest. She was a cut above. She wore stockings every day, never ever went outside her front door with curlers in her hair, and she carried a handbag with a fresh handkerchief in it at all times.

Harriet was a source of fascination to the women of the four streets, especially to Peggy.

'So, is there anyone takes ye fancy now?' she asked.

Harriet spluttered, 'Well, that was why I came to see Maura, er, there is and I have no idea what to do. And Alison, she told me Maura and Kathleen know the answer to everything, including things that haven't even happened yet. She was very mysterious, though, and wouldn't say why.'

Kathleen now spoke.

'Put three spoons of sugar in your tea, queen, drink it up as quick as yer can and then, with the last dregs, rinse them round your teacup three times, making a wish. Tip the cup up on the saucer, quick now, and then pass it to me. I will read your fortune and then we can decide what you should do.'

Harriet looked horrified. 'Read my tea leaves? Isn't that a sin?'

'Well, if it is, Harriet, we are all going to hell together. Tell me now, how do ye think your friend Alison got her man down the aisle? Do ye think she has never sat round this table and passed me her teacup?'

Harriet's hand shook as she spooned the sugar into her tea. If Alison had done it, she would too.

'No one must tell Anthony, though,' she added quickly before drinking her scalding tea as fast as she could. Then she told them all about Mr Manning. His caliper, his war wounds and his sad eyes.

'I'm sorry to burden you all but I don't know what to do. It is the first time I've been stuck. I usually know how to solve a problem and now it is just about me and I have no idea.'

Maura reached out and placed her hand over Harriet's. 'Don't worry, Harriet. If there is a way, we will find it here round this table, as we have done so many times with so many problems. I'm sure Alison won't mind me saying, but she was heartbroken when she called here to see me and Nana Kathleen. And do you know what?'

There was a sharp intake of breath as everyone leant forward and gasped, 'What?' at exactly the same time.

'Alison met Howard two weeks after she walked out of this back door, having had her reading. You don't know about Bernadette, Harriet, but she was my best friend, Nellie's mother and Jerry's wife. This is her table we are sitting at.'

'We know it's our Bernadette, and she works through Nana Kathleen. She will get ye sorted, have no worry about that,' said Maura.

Harriet felt scared and exhilarated at the same time. It was true, Alison had urged her to visit Maura, but hadn't said why. If she had, Harriet would probably never have come.

Nana Kathleen picked up Harriet's cup. 'Now then,' she said. 'I see him here, right in the middle of your cup.'

Harriet gasped and put her hand to her throat.

'He's not really in there,' said Peggy, looking sideways at Harriet, slightly alarmed at how frightened she looked. 'It's just the shape Bernadette makes in the tea leaves for Nana Kathleen that makes it look like him.'

'He works in a tall government building,' Nana Kathleen continued. 'He can't work today, as his mind is distracted

306

and he keeps thinking about a woman he met recently who has turned his head. He hasn't eaten his lunch either. It is there on his desk in front of him, still wrapped in greaseproof paper, unopened. He feels sick and doesn't know what to do. He is daydreaming about her, about the things they could do together if he was brave enough to ask if he could court her, but he is too afraid in case she should say no. He thinks his caliper and walking stick would turn a woman off.'

A tear ran down Harriet's cheek. Maura jumped up to comfort her. 'Shush, don't cry,' she said. 'I know, it really gets to you, doesn't it? Alison was just the same.'

Everyone watched as Harriet undid the clasp of her handbag and took out her white linen handkerchief edged in lace. No one had ever seen such a pretty hankie.

'Well, 'tis as clear as the nose on yer face if ye ask me,' said Nana Kathleen. 'Ye organize everyone else, Harriet, and ye boss us all about with yer fêtes and committees and the Rose Queen. There's a man out there waiting to be organized by ye, I would say, and so ye had better get cracking. Ask him to join ye for a cuppa down by the docks. There's a nice café where Jerry proposed to Bernadette, not fancy, mind, but if Bernadette is helping us, I reckon she will make sure there's a bit of magic around on the day.'

'Well,' said Peggy, leaning back on her chair and folding her arms across her ample bosom. 'I'll say this, Kathleen, that is good advice, an' all. The only advice anyone ever gave me, before I met my Paddy, was to never trust a man who doesn't like potatoes, and, surely to God, what a ridiculous piece of advice that was. There was never a man in all of Ireland who didn't like his tatties now, was there?'

'Aye, and yer still chose Paddy,' said Kathleen.

The clock chimes could barely be heard over their laughter. Maura stood to refill the teacups as Deirdre asked Kathleen, 'Will ye do mine? Will I need to put more money in the club for Christmas or will I have enough?'

'Oh, my goodness me,' Harriet squealed. 'I have a meeting in town about an organizing committee for the cathedral they are planning to build.'

And with that, her chair was scraped back, her hat scooped up from the chair where she had placed it earlier, and she was heading for the back door, but not before running back to give Maura and Kathleen a hug.

They sat and waited silently until they heard the back gate slam.

Deirdre lit up a cigarette and narrowed her eyes against the haze of blue smoke. 'Reckon she'll be having her leg over within six months, that one.' Then she frowned, crossing her eyes to look down her nose. Picking a stray shred of tobacco from the tip of her extended tongue with her fingertip and thumb and flicking it into the ashtray, she added, 'Not before he takes his caliper off first, mind.'

And with that, the laughter continued, just as it always had, year after year.

Nana Kathleen joined in. She had no intention of telling anyone she'd had a nice little chat with Mr Manning after the meeting about the nursery. As for the rest of it, she had no idea where her words had come from. She didn't have a clue whether or not he took his sandwiches to work in grease-proof paper and normally she shied away from providing such detail.

But she felt in her heart what had really happened. There was no other explanation. Bernadette was back.

Nana Kathleen had been wondering where she had gone to. She seemed to have left them all for some time now. The catastrophic sequence of events that had hit them with the force of a tank had broken the spell.

First Alice had left, then Kitty had died and finally Brigid had moved away. All within days. It felt as though Bernadette had vanished too. No ghostly sightings, no feeling that she had joined them. Nothing.

Maura began collecting up the dirty cups for a quick rinse.

'No doubt we shall all have another round now,' she said as she carried them over to the sink.

And for the second time in twenty-four hours, Maura thought once again, I am healing.

Daisy had sat silent throughout the chatter but had joined in the laughter. She wondered what her life would have been if her parents had never placed her in the convent, believing her to be simple, for no other reason than following a difficult birth, she struggled as a baby. Maggie had told her it was a common practice, but Daisy still asked herself, why?

'I won't have any tea, thank you, Maura,' she said when asked. 'I have to go and meet the police at the Priory at half past.'

'The police, why?' asked Nana Kathleen, more than a little interested.

Maura had returned to the table, carrying the dripping cups by their handles, three in each hand. 'Harriet didn't mention that. Does she know?'

'I don't know,' Daisy replied. 'The police said they would

telephone the Priory to let them know. I have to take them down into the cellar and give them the key to the safe.'

'What key?' said Nana Kathleen. 'If ye have the key, doesn't Father Anthony have one too?'

'I don't think so. I'm sure I have the only one and, besides, I don't think he would find the safe. Only me and Molly Barrett knew where it was and Molly only knew because I showed her. It's behind the bricks in the cellar. The police say 'tis very important they have everything that is in it.'

It was a full minute after Daisy had left the kitchen before Peggy said, 'Fecking hell, she's a dark horse, that one.'

Maura sipped her tea and, taking out the cigarette packet from her apron pocket, she removed the last one.

Maura held her hand out to Peggy and, without the need for words, Peggy gave Maura the lit cigarette from her lips for Maura to light her own.

'She's that, all right,' Maura said as she exhaled. 'Daisy and her Maggie.'

Astonished, everyone looked at Maura, awaiting an explanation.

Maura milked the moment. She liked this feeling, being first with the news. Walking to the hearth, she screwed up the empty cigarette packet and threw it onto the fire. Her face took on a warm glow from the sudden rush of flame.

Resting her forehead on the mantelshelf, with one hand in her front apron pocket and the other still holding her cigarette, she stared intently at the blaze. A small piece of foil from inside the packet had curled up on itself, refusing to catch alight, and now it dropped down into the ashes, where Maura would brush it away in the morning.

'Who the hell is Maggie?' six women asked in unison.

Maura walked back to the table and, as she sat, she smiled. 'Well, then.'

It was going to be a long pow wow today.

Chapter Twenty-one

FATHER ANTHONY WAS far from happy at having to leave the new cathedral community meeting. Archbishops and bishops were attending from all over Europe and he was excited about meeting his friend from Rome.

As he left the Grand hotel to retrieve his car, he saw Harriet, running up the street for a meeting of the Mothers' Union. All this activity had one purpose: to ensure that the new cathedral, known by everyone as Paddy's wigwam, became a vibrant Christian community.

'I hope 'tis the last time the police want to spend time at the Priory,' Anthony grumbled at Harriet as he passed her in the street. 'I'm beginning to feel as though my office is a police cell.'

'Well, who's the grumpy one today then?' said Harriet, rushing past him, through the hotel's revolving doors.

She had deliberately not dallied. She did not want to lie to Anthony about where she had been and what she had been doing. She was on fire with excitement after having had her tea leaves read by Kathleen.

Harriet felt a thrill as she replayed Nana Kathleen's words in her mind. She had been told, with the help of a ghost, that she had to be bold and ask Mr Manning to meet her for a cup of tea in the café at the docks.

During the journey to Lime Street, her mind had raced ahead. It didn't matter what she, or anyone else, thought of Kathleen's fortune-telling. The fact was that her feelings, which were swamping her, were beyond explanation. How could she account for them?

It was as if someone had wrapped an invisible shawl of love around her shoulders. She knew, she just knew, it had come straight from Bernadette, the woman they all loved and spoke of with such fondness. She was sure that it was she who had sat down next to her, but no one else had appeared to notice. Did it happen all the time? What was Bernadette like? Why on earth would Bernadette possibly want to help Harriet? All Harriet knew was that Bernadette was Nellie's mammy. As she ran up the wide carpeted staircase to the meeting room, Harriet resolved to visit the churchyard to place some flowers on Bernadette's grave. She would thank Bernadette and tell her, I love your little girl. I will always do whatever I can for Nellie.

If Bernadette had already talked to her through three sugars and a cup full of tea leaves, she might work a miracle, if Harriet took her some flowers, sat next to her plot of earth and said a prayer.

The police commander was waiting in the hallway of the priory when Daisy stepped through the open front door. Having spent years using a key, she now felt at a loss as to the correct etiquette. Should she knock?

Hearing the sound of tyres on gravel, she saw Father

Anthony's car turn into the drive. Father James had never owned a car.

'My, how quickly times are changing,' said Daisy out loud.

'Hello, Daisy,' Father Anthony called as he joined them. 'Go along into my office. You know the way. I will be just one minute. Oh, for goodness' sake, what are the boys doing now?'

Father Anthony looked over the wall into the churchyard and saw Harry and Little Paddy, charging between the headstones, shouting.

'Scamp, Scamp, come here!'

But Scamp was faster than they were.

'Sorry, Father,' the boys shrieked as they flew past.

'Harriet wasn't in, so we were playing truth or dare in the graveyard,' Harry explained breathlessly, as he struggled to keep up with the errant Scamp.

'Priests in cars and little boys tearing through the graveyard, chasing a dog. I have never known the like.' Daisy laughed.

'Don't let them see me laughing, Daisy,' Father Anthony whispered. ''Twould be the end of me for sure.'

Daisy realized that, after all the years she had spent in the Priory as housekeeper, this was the first time she had laughed out loud.

The commander had been pacing up and down the Priory hallway, pondering aloud his dilemma to the officer who had accompanied him. It was the tall and tubby PC Shaw, who had successfully nicked Stanley.

'It is all becoming very complicated and we need to ensure we keep each crime isolated. We have a priest's murder, Mrs

Barrett's murder, a kidnapping and what appears to be an organized paedophile ring. It is unlikely the kidnapping and the child abuse had anything to do with the poor priest. I am very sure that whoever killed Molly Barrett killed him too, eh, boyo? But it's unlikely we are ever going to find out who that was. Apart from the butt of a Pall Mall ciggie found on the outhouse floor next to the dead woman, Molly Barrett, we have not a single clue and that's the truth.'

'What about the fact that they all happened at around the same time?' said PC Shaw. 'Surely that links them all in some way.'

'I'm not sure it does, boyo. That may just be a coincidence. On the other hand the case is turning out to be something far bigger and deeper than we thought, with new developments unfolding by the day. In the cells we have the two hospital porters and a policeman. None of them is saying a word. You would think they were all bloody nuns who had taken a vow of silence and they all look as guilty as hell. What with a kidnapping, child abuse and a double murder. We should have clues coming out of our ears, and yet hardly a sausage. You wouldn't believe it, would you?

'Let's hope Daisy comes up trumps again, eh? God knows why she thought she needed to keep the safe a secret all this time. The priest must have been worried about robbers stealing the collection money and who could blame him? The O'Prey boys came from around here somewhere, didn't they? Bad lads, they were. The most notorious thieves on the docks. Let's hope they throw away the key on the oldest. They say Callum, the youngest, has turned over a new leaf, but I'll believe it when I see it.'

Annie O'Prey, standing at the bottom of the kitchen stairs, heard every word.

Her elderly eyes pricked with tears. She bent her weary back to rest the tea tray she was carrying for the officers on the stair in front of her and, taking her grey and tattered hankie from the sleeve of her cardigan, she wiped her eyes.

So alone, she missed her boys desperately. She was very proud of her Callum, who had been taken on by Fred Kennedy down at the docks, and she suspected and hoped that he had his eye on lovely young Fionnuala down the street. She was the first to admit that they were naughty lads, but they never nicked anything without sharing it with everyone else. She knew that many a house had gone without, now that her eldest lad was in the nick and Callum was doing his best to behave.

Everyone missed the antics of the O'Prey boys.

Annie took out her rosaries from her cardigan pocket, said her Hail Mary and asked for forgiveness for having wallowed in her own despair. Drying her eyes, she picked up the tray and carried on up the stairs as though she hadn't heard a thing.

PC Shaw was about to offer up an idea of his own regarding the murders. Anger boiled in his belly when he thought of the men involved and he knew what he would want to do to anyone who went near his own daughter.

He thought the commander was wrong to think the murders had nothing to do with the kidnapping, nor with the way Daisy had been abused, and she had described others being abused too.

When Daisy walked into the hall, his moment for speaking out was gone.

'Ah, Daisy, I don't know if you remember my name? I'm Commander Lloyd. I'm from Wales, across the border.'

Daisy nodded. 'I remember,' she replied. 'I'm not simple, you know.'

There, she had said exactly what Maggie told her she must say.

'No, quite, Daisy. I apologize if I caused any offence. Mrs Davies is also on her way. She thought you might need a bit of female company. Do you have the key to the safe? Where is this safe, anyway?'

Daisy reached into her blouse and pulled out a chain from around her neck. Her gold crucifix hung from it – the only possession to have accompanied her to the orphanage when she was a baby.

'It's down in the cellar,' said Daisy, 'and so we need to go through the kitchen first.'

'Well, that explains why the safe wasn't in the office,' said the commander.

Annie O'Prey heard them coming down the stairs. 'Daisy, are ye after your job back, queen? 'Cause I'm done in, I am. I'm too old for this malarkey now.'

Daisy gave Annie a hug. 'I have to go down to the cellar, Annie,' she said. 'I have the key for the safe.'

'The cellar?' said Annie, amazed. 'Well now, I haven't put one foot in that place since the new father arrived and, do you know, I don't think anyone else has. A creepy hole altogether, that is.'

Ten minutes later, the commander was on his way back up the stairs, loaded with round tin cans the size of dinner plates, a projector, a screen and a pile of envelopes. He laid them all out on the hall floor and sent his officer down to collect the rest.

Alison was turning into the drive to the Priory when she saw her page-boys, Little Paddy and Harry, walking through the gate from the graveyard. Paddy was carrying Scamp and Harry, something large and wooden.

'Paddy, Harry,' she shouted. 'Is Scamp misbehaving himself?'

Alison could see that something was up. 'Is something wrong, boys?'

'I don't know,' Harry replied. 'Scamp found this on the other side of the wall, on one of the graves. It was covered with ferns but it looks a bit weird.'

Harry struggled to hold what looked like a lump of wood while Scamp wriggled in Little Paddy's arms.

'Here, let me take Scamp,' Alison said, extracting the rather sheepish-looking dog from under Little Paddy's arm. But she gasped with shock as Harry held up the wooden mallet he was carrying.

The end was soaked in what was obviously old, stale blood.

Commander Lloyd sat in the temporary office he had been allocated in Whitechapel where he and his officer had set up the screen and projector. It was eight in the evening. They had been waiting for days for clearance to view the films, as well as for a lab-test result on the mallet. It was being examined for fingerprints, and, more importantly, to check whether the blood on it belonged to the murdered priest.

'Have you eaten, boyo?' he asked Howard.

'Yes, sir, but I'm half wishing I hadn't now, if these films are too bad.'

The commander looked at the brown paper bag on his desk.

'Now then, before we begin, nip down to the canteen and bring up a few empty cups.'

Howard looked confused. 'Empty?'

'Because, boyo, we need something inside us, to line our stomachs and give us a bit of Dutch courage.' He slipped a large bottle of whiskey out of the bag on his desk.

'Now then, let's see how this thing works,' said the commander, as he wound one of the films around the wheel and PC Shaw switched on the projector.

He took a large swig from the bottle and then turned out the lights.

Images appeared on the screen in black and white. Although the filming was obviously amateur, they were clear enough.

'Oh God, fucking hell,' he said. He took another swig of whiskey, just as Howard walked back into the room with three mugs.

'Come here, boyo,' said the commander. 'Do you recognize him?'

Howard joined PC Shaw, who was staring at the screen, transfixed. Howard wanted what he was watching not to be true. But it was. It was there in front of him in black and white.

'I do, sir, he's that politician fella, he's always on the news. Drives round here in a big black Rolls with a chauffeur, and eats a lot of pies by the look of him.'

Peter, from the main desk, had come into the room unnoticed. 'Eh, that's that politician, isn't it?' he said.

'Aye, boyo, it is that,' said the commander. 'But keep it under your hat, mate, we have a bigger problem here. Did you want something?'

'Yes, sir, your lab and fingerprint tests are through. One of our lads has just run back from the labs with them. If you thought you had a problem before, wait until you hear this. They managed to get a fingerprint from the mallet. It belongs to Simon, the copper. Thank God he's already in the cells, eh? And the blood, well, that isn't the priest's blood group, but we know whose it is, all right – it belongs to the old lady who was murdered, Molly Barrett. I reckon it will be only half an hour before the *Echo* are on to it.'

'Jesus, fucking Christ! So if he murdered the old woman, he murdered the priest too. Unless we have two crazed murderers running around the docks, who both happened to strike within weeks of each other.'

Howard slowly lowered himself onto a chair. Simon – the man he had worked with for years, who had driven him to his wedding and bought him and Alison a silver rose bowl as a wedding gift – was a murderer.

All of them stared at the screen for a second longer. Then the commander leant forward and flicked up the off button. The room became dark. He turned to Howard and PC Shaw.

'You guys look through the photographs, quickly, before we have the press breathing down our necks. Let's try to keep this to ourselves and make sure the *Echo* only get to hear about that dirty, stinking creep Simon being charged with the double murder. I need to speak to my boss, as this will go way above my pay grade. Number Ten will be involved in this.'

And with that, he left the room.

'I don't know what he's worried about,' said PC Shaw. 'No one is going to let anything like this concerning a politician get out to the public. It will definitely all be covered up. It will all be pinned on the policeman now. He's a goner with those lab results, and that's for sure.'

But when PC Shaw opened an envelope of photographs, he blanched in horror.

'And here we have it,' he said. 'Yet another link. Jesus, someone is shaking that tree pretty hard. They are falling like leaves.'

'Let me see,' said Howard. 'Well, what do you know? Here they are, both together, very cosy, the priest and Simon. So now we have it, the link that binds them together, that and a bloody mallet.' Howard sounded sorrowful when he added, 'Simon can only be hanged once, but hanged he will be, for both.'

There was something painfully sad and disappointing about the fact that Simon was one of their own. PC Shaw drained the last of the whiskey bottle into two mugs and handed one to Howard.

'Here, drink this,' he said. 'Makes it all much easier to stomach.'

Chapter Twenty-two

M RS MCGUIRE SAT in the window seat of the hotel foyer, looking out onto the main road, drinking her tea and pondering. What a strange situation it was indeed that, because of Mary's new affluence, she could now afford to do this.

Some of the local children were walking past, on their way home. They stared in at the three-tiered plate, piled high with fancies and millionaire's shortbread, just as she and Maisie had done when they were girls.

A scruffy-looking young boy, who looked as though he hadn't seen soap and water for a month and wearing a jumper with more holes than stitches, his face full of envy and resentment, put out his tongue at Mrs McGuire.

She was far from shocked. Sure, didn't me and Maisie do the same, she thought, as she leant forward and put out her own tongue back at him. The other boys laughed and pushed the cheeky boy to move him along.

'Sorry, Mrs McGuire,' shouted a boy she recognized, but for the life of her, could not name.

She smiled back, to let him know, she took no offence.

I've been away for too long and missed too much, she

thought, as she sipped her tea and waited for Mary and Alice to return.

Mary had been delighted that Sister Assumpta was happy to hand over the contract signed by Kitty.

'All we have to do now is get ourselves to Dublin. We will talk to this Rosie O'Grady and then we can find the girl who gave birth to my baby. I know that, no matter what, she will want to help. Who wouldn't, Alice? No one would deny a child the gift of life, now, would they? I will make it worth her while. I bet she is just a poor girl from the country.'

'Of course she will help. Anyone would,' Alice replied. 'When do you think we should leave for Dublin?'

'Tonight, if Mammy agrees. We don't have hours to waste, never mind days.'

Alice was distracted. She wished she could speak to Sean. She knew who the mother of the baby was and, what's more, she knew where she lived. There was no need for any visit to Rosie O'Grady.

The baby was dying and only his parents could save him. Alice knew for sure that one was already dead. Alice was part of the conspiracy, an accomplice in that parent's murder, a murder that would never be spoken about.

And the other parent was Kitty. She could get them to Kitty Doherty within a couple of days.

'Oh God, this is awful,' Alice groaned.

'What is?' asked Mary, unwrapping the shawl from around the baby and laying him on his back on her knee. Holding his little feet in her hands, she smiled at him and blew him kisses. Her heart felt lighter than it had since the day she had first received his diagnosis.

'Oh, it's nothing, I'm just tired,' said Alice, pressing her forehead on the cold glass and looking out of the window.

How could Alice explain that Kitty lived on the four streets, doors away from Alice's own son, Joseph?

'No woman who leaves her son has the right to call herself a mother,' Mrs McGuire had said to Alice when she had first arrived in America. She was right. Alice had no business thinking of herself as a mother, but that didn't stop her heart from breaking every day for the baby boy she had never wanted, had finally learnt to love and then had left behind in running away with Sean. And now Sean wanted her to have another child, as though Joseph had never existed. Alice had never wanted children but she knew in her heart that Joseph had taught her to love. She might have left him, but she would not desert him. He would remain her only child.

If she told Mary where Kitty lived, she would have to return to Liverpool and face her demons. If she didn't tell Mary, this Rosie O'Grady would lead them straight there anyway.

A baby was dying. Alice would be obliged to tell Mary that she knew who Kitty Doherty was. It was going to happen. Alice would have to return to the four streets. The thought made her stomach clench and her heart scream, for a sight of Joseph. Sean no longer occupied all her thoughts. She was smart enough to realize that things were not as she had expected them to be. She loved America, the freedom and the way of life, but she was also beginning to acknowledge, if only to herself, that she no longer loved Sean.

Mrs McGuire watched the taxi pull up outside the window and asked the waiter to bring another tray of tea for Mary and Alice.

'Well, hello there, and how is the little man?'

Mrs McGuire stood up, to take the baby from Mary.

'He is grand, so he is, and so are we,' said Mary, grinning.

'Well, that's the first time I have seen a smile on your face for some weeks. So the visit must have been worthwhile then?'

'It was, Mammy. We have the name of the girl and the name of a midwife in Dublin who sent her with her family to the Abbey. All we need to do is travel to Dublin, find the midwife and then we will have the address of where the girl lives. It has all been much easier than I thought. I'm famished. Are those cakes for us?'

Mrs McGuire smiled. Tea and cake. Always her daughter's favourite. There wasn't a problem in the world that she and her Mary couldn't solve, over a cuppa and an almond tart.

'They are delicious fancies, so they are. Tuck in, Mary. And you, Alice. Sit down now while ye tell me, what was the Abbey like? Was it nice to see the Reverend Mother again? I bet she and Sister Celia made a great fuss of this little fella, didn't they just?'

Mary and Alice exchanged a glance that Mrs McGuire missed as she lifted the baby into the air and bounced him up and down in her arms, making cooing and gurgling baby noises at him.

'I will speak to Porick. He and his da will take us to Dublin to see the midwife. What hospital's she at, then? What is her name?'

Two waiters began to offload the contents of a trolley onto the low table, placing teacups and saucers in front of them. Alice felt as though they were taking forever, deliberately hovering, to eavesdrop on their conversation. The clinking of the china and the babbling of Mrs McGuire's chatter grated. She willed the waiters to hurry and felt her heart beating faster in panic. Her mouth became dry. The sooner she did it, the better.

'Mrs McGuire,' said Alice.

She hadn't realized that it would come out as a dry croak. Mrs McGuire didn't hear.

Alice tried again. 'Mrs McGuire, Mary.' She reached out and touched Mary's arm, to attract her attention. 'I know who the girl is. I know the name on the contract and, Mrs McGuire, so do you.'

Mary and Mrs McGuire stared at Alice, waiting for her to continue.

'Is this why you have been acting strange since we left the convent?' asked Mary. 'Who is she then?'

Alice stared Mrs McGuire straight in the face.

'It's Kitty Doherty, Mrs McGuire, Maura and Tommy's daughter.'

'My God, no,' Mrs McGuire replied.

'Well, Mammy, is that not good? It saves us the visit to the midwife. We can go straight to wherever the girl lives,' said Mary, sounding encouraged. But now, for reasons beyond her understanding, the atmosphere tightened as hope took flight.

Mrs McGuire looked pale. 'Kitty's mammy, Maura, was one of Brigid's best friends. They live on the four streets. But

I am afraid I have bad news for you both. Kitty Doherty is dead.'

'What do you mean, dead? She can't be.'

Alice felt as though she had been hit. Tears sprang to her eyes and, for no apparent reason, an image of Bernadette, Maura's closest friend, leapt into her mind. Bernadette, whom Alice had usurped before her body was even cold in her grave, was here, in her mind's eye.

Alice spoke again. 'How do you know she is dead, anyway? I'm sure you must be wrong. Kitty is only, what, fifteen at the most? She can't be dead.'

'She is. She drowned in the river near Kathleen's farm on the Ballymara Road, about six months ago. By my reckoning, if she is his mother, it must have happened only days after she gave birth to this little fella, although no one knows about him and that's for sure.'

Mrs McGuire blessed herself as she laid the baby over her shoulder, hugging him tight.

Quietly, her voice loaded with sorrow, Alice asked, 'How do you know all this, Mrs McGuire?'

'Because today I visited the woman who is truly married to my son, the woman who carries my family name and who is the mother of my Sean's children. I didn't visit my friends. I travelled to see my daughter-in-law, Brigid, and she told me. She was at the wake in Liverpool. She rushed to the side of her friend as soon as she heard the news.'

Mary picked up the teapot and stared at her mother. The consequences of what she had just said sank in. The baby's mother was dead and no one knew who the father was.

Mrs McGuire took control.

'We will set off for Liverpool in the morning, Mary. The doctor said we needed a family member for a match, did he not? Well, Maura is this little fella's grandmother and Tommy is his grandad, and their children, Kitty's brothers and sisters, are his family too, and nicer people you could not meet. Maura is from Killhooney Bay and Tommy, well now, he is from Cork. And you, Alice, can come with us. Maybe ye would like to see your own little lad, while we are there.'

Now it was Alice's turn to cry.

Mrs McGuire slid the cup of tea that Mary had poured across the low table towards Alice, and handed the baby to Mary.

'Here, drink this,' she said, passing a cup to Mary and lighting herself a cigarette.

She felt compelled, always, to make Alice suffer for what she had done to her family, but, being a kind woman at heart, she felt bad afterwards.

Leaning back in the chair and taking a deep pull on her cigarette, she thought through what tomorrow would now hold. We will have to leave early, she thought. I have tonight. I have this one night finally to get even with Maisie.

While she pondered, she looked across the road and watched Mr O'Hara as he locked up the butcher's shop. It was why she had chosen this table. She and Maisie used to stare at this very table and imagine which cakes they would order, when they were ladies, taking afternoon tea in the hotel.

She was meeting him again, tonight, at O'Connolly's pub. The lives, and the demands, of the younger generation were exhausting her. She was too involved. They were far too dependent upon her. Most of the time, she didn't mind at all. But the arrival of Sean, with Alice, in America had altered things. He had let her down, broken her heart. Mary's willingness to be complicit in their deceit had surprised her. The disappointment she felt in her son, for leaving his wife and daughters, never faded.

She had spent too long being a hands-on grandmother and, in the process, had lost much of her own life. Tonight, she would take some of that back. She would be daring, do something that no respectable woman, at sixty years of age, would even consider. If her friends in the village knew what she was planning, they would disown her.

To hell with them, she thought. Just one night, that's all I want. Just one. I want to remember the last time I ever slept with a man. I want to grow old, thinking: that was it. It was him. It was there and it was then and I loved it.

She looked at her daughter and at her fake daughter-in-law. Mary was tucking the blanket around the baby in the carrycot.

'Right, Mammy. I'm off to pack. Alice, are you OK?'

Alice looked anything but OK.

Mrs McGuire answered for her.

'She has to face her own healthy little boy, Mary, and the women she deserted and the families she destroyed and the stepdaughter she left distraught and stunned into silence by her own grief when Kitty died. Where was Alice then? Why shouldn't she be all right? I hear Alice has always been good at getting her own way, so she shouldn't worry. Liverpool will be a breeze, won't it, Alice?'

'Mammy, enough, stop. You are only acting like this because Sean isn't here.'

Mary was shocked at the way her mother was behaving. Mary didn't like what Sean and Alice had done any more than her mother did. Every time she attended mass she prayed for their forgiveness, and she saw her job as acting as referee, to keep the peace as far as that was possible. It had been Mary's idea to bring Alice along. It was an act designed to involve her and make her feel part of the family.

'I for one am very glad you are here with us, Alice.' Mary threw a look to Mrs McGuire that said, stop, now.

Alice didn't bother to say anything. She thought of the fifty thousand dollars she had drawn from her bank account and had used to line her suitcase. Sean had entrusted her with the money that Henry had paid them for the house. She didn't have to return to America at all, nor put up with the likes of Mrs McGuire, nor Sean's demands for another baby. Fifty thousand dollars was a huge sum of money. With that amount she could be set for life in England. Even as she had placed the bundles in her suitcase, she had failed to acknowledge to herself that this was her intention all along.

As the lift door closed on Mrs McGuire, Alice whispered, 'Go to hell, you witch.'

That night, as Alice lay in bed, she hatched her plan. There was no court that would refuse a mother custody of her child. She would return to England with Mary and then claim back her son. Mrs McGuire might be no Kathleen and Sean no Jerry, but Alice had burnt her boats. She knew that neither Kathleen nor Jerry would ever want to know her again. She was alone now. She would take Joseph away and the two of them would find a little house, over the water in Birkenhead, or one of those nice suburbs, and they would live a quiet, gentle life, just Alice and her boy.

He already had her drink waiting when she arrived at O'Connolly's.

He was sitting at the corner table, as far away as possible from the toilets and the jukebox. For the first time since they were kids, she thought he looked nervous.

'I got ye a gin and orange squash, the same as before. Is that all right, now?'

He had stood up to greet her and removed his cap as she approached the table. Waiting for her reply, he stubbed his cigarette out in the ashtray, rolled up his cap and stuffed it deep down into his pocket. His black waistcoat strained against buttons that threatened to pop. The thought crossed her mind that it had been many a year since he had last worn it.

'Aye, that's grand, thanks. If you don't mind me saying, I need that right now and another to follow, after the day I have had.'

He picked up his Guinness. 'Aye, well, for a long time now mine has been much the same as every other day. There are never any surprises for me. It does always come as a great shock, I suppose, when a customer dies and hasn't paid their bill, but that is as bad as it gets.'

They both burst out laughing. She realized it wasn't something she did very often any more. Laugh. She was often concerned, busy, useful, needed, but not for herself, always for someone else. As their laughter abated, she looked into his eyes.

She didn't see a sixty-year-old face, laughing back at her. She saw the face of over forty years ago, just the same. Unaltered. Hidden by extra weight and some wrinkles, it might have been, but she looked through that to the boy she had known before.

Be bold. Be bold. The words raced through her mind as they weighed each other up.

He still has nice eyes, she thought.

She has the figure of a woman half her age, he thought.

She knew he would be shy. He would have no idea of her wild thoughts or crazy intentions. If she weren't bold, she would lose her nerve and change her mind.

Be bold.

She leant across the table to say the most daringly outrageous words she had ever uttered, but, even as she began to speak, she had no idea what those words would be.

He surprised her and spoke first.

'Ye are a sight for sore eyes and one that hasn't left my mind for these forty years gone, now, do ye know that?'

'But you married Maisie,' she replied, very matter-of-fact.

'Aye, 'tis true and, sure, I was the father of a child that grew in the womb for two years. I was a stupid fool, easily led, and what lad isn't? But I will tell ye this: there was only one woman I wanted to marry and, God knows, I paid the price for my mistake every day for years. God rest her soul. She couldn't help it but, sure, nothing good comes from trickery, now does it, and so I feel no guilt.'

Mrs McGuire's heart was beating like the wings of a captive bird. 'No, I suppose not. I couldn't forgive ye for years.'

'Sure, didn't I know that. Ye bought yer meat in Castlefeale. Now that's a woman with a grudge, I'd say.'

Mrs McGuire turned round to look towards the bar and saw that, as she had guessed, they were under close scrutiny from Mrs O'Connolly, who repeatedly wiped the same section of the counter.

She turned back to face him. Be bold. She took a deep breath. This would be it. Her chance.

'Do ye have any gin at home? Because if ye do, why don't we pop back there for a drink, without Mrs O'Connolly watching? We can catch up on some of the fun we missed out on, forty years ago.'

It took him what felt like forever to respond. 'Jesus Christ, I missed out altogether all these years, didn't I just?'

Less than five minutes later, they sneaked in through his back door, giggling like a pair of errant teenagers. Thirty minutes later, they were in his bed.

At four in the morning as he lay next to her, gently snoring, she thought to herself, so this was it. It was here.

She gazed out of the window and listened to the rain gently fall, as it so often did. The window was open wide. She grinned to herself and thought, Holy Mother, I hope next door didn't hear me. But instead of feeling washed in shame, she felt exhilarated and half hoped that the neighbours, the miserable, God-fearing, mass-four-times-a-day O'Byrnes, had heard her after all.

She looked at the outline of his body, older and heavier but still fit and healthy, and thought to herself, I want a life of no surprises. I'm not going back to America. From now on, I'm going to squeeze two days into each one, to make up for lost time.

He opened his eyes and saw her leaning over him.

'Bloody hell,' he said. 'It was real, then. I thought maybe I had been dreaming.'

She smiled. Be bold.

'How about I don't go back to America, but stay here in the village? Would ye like that? Would ye like more nights like this?'

He reached up and pulled her down to him. 'No, I'm not dreaming, that's for sure I'm in fecking heaven.'

She laughed, as she hadn't done in a very long time. She felt like a girl. It was as though her wrinkles and her age were nothing to him. As she spoke she stroked the base of his neck and traced around the outline of his lips.

'It'll be a shock for them all, but, God, who helped me when I had my kids? No one. 'Tis time they learnt to manage without me. God knows, for sure, I'll be dead in ten years or so. I haven't much time left.'

And they made love again. Not as they would have done as teenagers, but gently and slowly, with a passion so intense that she knew she could never handle the sadness of knowing when it was to be the last time.

Chapter Twenty-three

HARRIET KNELT AT the foot of the headstone with a bunch of floppy-headed, deep-burgundy roses, which she had cut from the Priory garden just that morning. Annie O'Prey had wrapped wet newspaper round the base of the stems to keep them fresh but now that Harriet was at the graveside, she felt silly. Despite that, she was glad of the five minutes to sit down. The following day was the Rose Queen competition and parade, the first of what Harriet hoped would become a regular grand day of festivities, for everyone who lived on the four streets.

'Do you know, Anthony, no one who lives here has ever had a holiday. The Rose Queen fête is something for everyone to look forward to and to plan for. And it is great fun for the kids.'

'You are right, Harriet, and you always are.' Anthony had smiled. 'Just don't overwhelm yourself. It is a massive under-taking, if you don't have enough help.'

Even Harriet had been amazed at how many women had stepped forward to volunteer their services. Lots had their own ideas and Harriet had relished every minute of taking on the role of event co-ordinator.

This was the last quiet moment she would have until it was all over, so it seemed as good a time as any to pay her visit to Bernadette.

Annie had told her, 'There's an old pickling jar on Bernadette's grave. Brigid put it there. She was always leaving flowers. She thought none of us knew it was her but we knew, all right. I don't think it has cracked. You can put some water in from the fountain.'

'Do Jerry and Nellie visit the grave, Annie?'

'Oh Jesus, now, Jerry is there all the time. He always was, even when he was married to Alice. I shouldn't think she knew but, God only knows, I cannot even tell you the number of times I have seen that man standing there.'

'He must have loved her very much,' said Harriet.

'Loved her? Well now, listen while I tell ye. If I lived to be a hundred, never in all my life will I have known two people who loved each other as much as they did. It was as if the sky had fallen down, the day she died. Oh God, now you've set me off.'

And here Harriet was, at the grave of a woman people still spoke of as if she had died just yesterday and who appeared to have been one of the nicest women ever to have lived.

'These are for you, Bernadette,' Harriet whispered, as she placed the roses in the jar and looked carefully around to see if anyone was listening.

Kneeling back on her heels, she sat still for a moment and gradually became aware of the noise around her. Traffic passed by on the road, the cranes were lifting their loads down on the docks, tugs were tooting angry horns, and yet she felt as though she were in an oasis of peace and tranquillity.

Tentatively, she began. 'I just wanted you to know that I think the world of Nellie and I know she is hurting. Nana Kathleen is just the greatest woman, Bernadette, and everyone does their best, but I think you know that Nellie and I have a special bond. We are a similar age, you and I, Bernadette, and I think Nellie knows that. Anyway, I just wanted you to know that I will do my utmost for your little girl. My eye will always be on your Nellie and my heart will always be full of care for her.'

Harriet felt guilty for what she was about to say, but she knew, in her heart, that there was another reason she had visited the grave.

'Bernadette, Nana Kathleen and the women, they say you are like a guardian angel to everyone on the four streets. I think that's true, because I felt it. I know you and Jerry were very much in love too. I would so love to have someone special of my own. I always have. Just someone I can love and who would love me back. My mammy told me to find myself a nice Irish boy, but I don't care about things like that. I would just love someone kind. Bernadette, I think I have found someone I would like to get closer to, if you can be my guardian angel too.'

As Harriet spoke, it was as though a feeling of utter serenity and optimism swept over her. Without understanding why, she knew, without any doubt whatsoever, that the wish she had made to Bernadette would come true.

He will be mine and I will be happy, she thought.

Over at number forty-two, Maura Doherty felt that if she never saw another scone or jam tart again, it would not be too soon.

'Where did the flour and sugar come from, Tommy?' she asked as her husband brought a sack of each into the kitchen.

'Don't ask, queen,' Tommy replied. 'But if the captain of the *Cotopaxi* comes knocking on the door, you've never heard of me.'

'Thank the Lord for the *Cotopaxi* and all who sail in her,' said Maura. 'What in God's name would we have done without her all these years? I bet Harriet doesn't know where they have come from, does she?'

'Good God, no, are ye mad? That woman has me run ragged. I have to go now, to set out the road with marking chalk for the kids' races tomorrow, and then I have to help Jerry carry the weight for the strongest-man machine she has borrowed from God knows where.'

'Oh, stop complaining,' Maura laughed. 'The kids are beside themselves with excitement. The girls are trying on their retinue dresses upstairs and then they will be both off down to Mrs Green, who made the headdresses. I have enough to do, getting the cake stall ready without your moaning mouth. Nana Kathleen and Nellie are making coffee cake with Camp coffee and coconut golf balls, but they have run out of Camp, so Harry has run a message to buy another bottle. Deirdre is making giggle cake and fudge squares, and I am making the bannock cake.'

'Can I have one of those?' said Tommy, putting his arms round her. 'Ye are doing grand, queen, but don't let all the extra work or this Rose Queen fair get to you, d'ye hear me?'

Maura lifted her head. 'Tommy, I am loving all this activity, so I am. It's grand for the kids, to have something to be excited about. I just can't help thinking that our Kitty would have been in the Rose Queen competition and might well have won it. Can ye imagine the picture she would have made in that frock? Beside herself she would have been. Oh, and how big that head of hers would have quietly swollen. She never needed to brag, our Kitty, Angela would have given out forever more and without meaning to, done it all for her. There would have been no telling her now, no, there wouldn't. She would never have shut up and our Kitty, not a word would she have said back. But God, I'd put up with all that, if we could just have her back. She would have been the Rose Queen, Tommy. She was so beautiful.'

Tommy hugged Maura closer into him. He didn't want her to see the tears that sprang to his eyes as he imagined Kitty in the white Rose Queen dress. He didn't want to tell Maura that, on the day Alison Devlin got married, it was all he could do to hide the pain in his heart as he realized he would never walk his Kitty down the aisle, nor see her in her wedding gown.

He had never revealed to Maura that, when he closed his eyes, he could still see Kitty's face. It was the last time he ever saw her. She was looking out of the window of the wooden hut on the Pier Head, on the night when he had taken her to meet Nana Kathleen and Nellie. The night she left for Ireland and exile.

Maura felt his tears soaking through her hair and she held him tight, as they both stood there, in the same place, on that well-trodden, rocky road together.

Annie O'Prey was also baking, in her own kitchen. She had inherited Molly's handwritten cookbook and was in the middle of one of Molly's most famous recipes. Examining

Molly's precise writing, she rested for a moment and took her rosary out of her cardigan pocket.

'Ah, Molly, I wish I knew what happened to you and why I didn't hear a thing that night. I have yer cat and I'm looking after him for yer. He's a good cat. Brings me a mouse every morning. Never a langer now, he saved that for ye, Molly, and I know in my heart that was why ye was killed. It was summat to do with the priest's murder, wasn't it, Molly?'

Annie peered out of the window to see the flatbed coal lorry easing its way down the entry, piled high with chairs and beds. She wiped her hands on her apron and, Molly and cakes forgotten, ran out of the back gate.

'What's going on?' she asked the coalman.

'New family moving in next door, into Molly's old house, Annie, to keep ye company.'

'Well, what a day to be moving. 'Tis the fair tomorrow – do they know?'

'I have no idea. Why don't ye tell them yourself? They will be along in a minute.

'Have ye heard the news? They have arrested the policeman for the murder of the priest and Molly. 'Twas the policeman himself that did it.'

'God, no, I didn't. How did ye know that?'

'The paper boy is shouting it outside Lime Street station. They found a mallet with his fingerprints and Molly's blood on it.'

'Does anyone else know yet? God, does anyone else on the four streets know?' Annie almost screamed the question.

'I shouldn't imagine so, not until the *Echo* is delivered here and that's not until six o'clock.'

He had barely finished speaking before Annie was away and over the road to be the first to break the biggest news to hit the street in months. The first kitchen she ran into was Tommy and Maura's.

'All right, you young lovers, break it up. Come here while I tell ye. Ye will never have a notion of what I'm about to say.'

The baby woke and began to scream at the sound of Annie's voice.

Maura shouted, 'Oh God, no, not again.'

The commotion brought the girls thundering down the stairs, as fast as they could, in their long dresses.

'What's going on?' said Angela. 'What is all the noise about?'

'I'm sure I have no idea,' Maura replied, picking the baby up. 'She's teething real bad,' she said to Annie, by way of an apology for having snapped.

Annie grinned at the girls. She was going to relish every minute of this.

'Would ye like some tea, Annie?' Even Tommy was intrigued by the high colour on Annie's cheeks and the twinkle in her eye. He wanted to stay and hear the latest news.

'Aye, I will, thanks, but, Maura, I reckon ye need to knock on because I have big news, so I do.'

Just as Annie finished speaking, Angela ran to the corner of the kitchen, picked up the mop and said, 'I'll do it, I have to learn soon enough.'

Tommy smiled at Angela as he put the kettle on the range. Suddenly the back door burst open and in ran Little Paddy, with Scamp hot on his heels. Little Paddy yelled at the top of his voice, 'Maura, Maura, the policeman is going to hang for murdering Molly and the priest, so he is.'

Behind him, Peggy puffed and panted up the path, shouting, 'Paddy, ye fecking little bastard, get out, 'tis my news.'

'No, it isn't!' yelled Little Paddy. 'I was the one who told you. The paper boy is shouting it on the Dock Road.'

Ducking the slap from his mother, which was meant for his head, he and Scamp legged it up Maura's stairs to find the boys.

The kitchen fell silent. Even the baby stopped grizzling. Maura wasn't even sure whether she had spoken the words, or whether someone else had, when she said, 'How do they know?'

'Because,' said Annie forcefully, peeved at Little Paddy's interruption and determined to deliver the last shred of the news, 'they found a mallet in the graveyard with the policeman's fingerprints on it and Molly's blood all over. He must have carried it from the outhouse and dropped it when he ran.'

'Will he hang?' said Maura, her face ashen.

'Aye, he will, but he can only be hanged once for one murder. They can't hang you twice, can they?'

Maura spoke quickly. 'How do they know 'twas him who murdered the priest as well, then, Annie?'

Annie was not happy. She had been expecting stardom, at the very least, not an inquisition.

'How would I know?'

'I do.' Tommy spoke. 'They think there can't be two murders so close together by two different people so it must be the same man who committed both.'

'Aye, that makes sense,' said Maura slowly, as she wondered why in God's name Molly would have been killed.

'I'm popping down to the shops, to buy the *Echo*.'

With that, Tommy slipped out of the front door, unnoticed by the women who began to arrive through the back gate as a result of Angela banging on the kitchen wall with the mop like a madwoman.

Running down the street, he met Jerry.

They fell into step, each not having to ask where the other was heading.

'Have ye heard then?' asked Jerry.

'Aye, I have and I have only one question: what the fecking hell is going on? Why would the policeman have murdered Molly? Why didn't we know? 'Twas us what did for the priest, so how can he be taking the rap for us?'

'That was more than one question, Tommy. Shall we call in to the Anchor on the way to the shop? Someone will have an *Echo* in there.'

'Grand idea, but only for a quick one. Then ye have to help me mark out the streets with this block of chalk Harriet has given me for the races tomorrow, 'cause I couldn't stand the thought of that one breathing down my neck, now, if it wasn't done.'

With that, both men turned up the Anchor steps and into their place of refuge, where even someone as determined as Harriet wouldn't dare try to reach them.

Chapter Twenty-four

A S SOON AS it was light Harriet woke and reached for the list on her bedside table. She read down the long line of additions that she had written, either before she went to sleep or when she had twice woken during the night.

'You couldn't function without that list, could you?' said Anthony, as they ate breakfast in his study.

'Do you know, Anthony, if I lost this list, I would surely die. I could not think of anything worse, so please stop hiding it, even as a joke. It is no longer funny.'

'Will your Mr Manning be coming to the Rose Queen competition today?' Anthony teased.

'I have no idea,' she replied.

'I only ask,' he said, 'because I know Alison is in charge of judging the Rose Queen and I saw his name, on her list of judges.'

Harriet looked at him, aghast.

'Stop,' she said. 'For goodness' sake, she hasn't done that, without telling me, has she? The judges are due here for tea and sandwiches, at one o'clock, before they begin judging, at two. Why would she do that? Not that it makes any difference. He's a judge, like any other.'

'Really?' said Anthony. 'I think your friend may be trying to play Cupid.'

Now that it was finally the morning of the Rose Queen fair, Harriet realized she had yet to sort out an outfit for herself. And if Mr Manning was to be a judge, she wanted to make an effort to look special. Alone in her room, her stomach filled with butterflies, she became giddy as she tore through her wardrobe, looking for a suitable dress, while downstairs Anthony was reaching for his bible and a reason to believe. Not just for Harriet, the doubt of true faith.

Outside, the women were already marching their young boys down the four streets, to carry kitchen tables outdoors and cover them with cloths for the afternoon street party. The dockers, who were taking a day off, were building a platform and erecting side poles, just as Harriet had asked them, for the judging of the Rose Queen.

The coalman had scrubbed his float almost clean and covered it with sacking, a skirt of hessian sackcloth hiding the wheels.

Mothers who had stood at St John's market at closing time the previous day, to buy leftover flowers and greenery, were laying them on the ground next to the float.

Two chairs, covered with white sheets and tied with pink-and-white ribbons, were being carried out of Mrs Green's front door, ready to be lifted onto the lorry, as thrones for the Rose Queen and her maid of honour. The attendants would sit in a circle on the floor around their feet.

Harriet pulled up the sash window in her bedroom and shouted out to Maura, who was walking past with a cardboard box full of cakes. She thought that Maura looked sadder than usual and on a morning like this, too.

'Morning, Maura. Are the girls excited?'

Maura looked up. 'Everyone is excited, Harriet. Ye have done a grand job. It is going to be a special day today. Look, the sun is out, too.'

Harriet laughed as she ducked back inside. Now all she had to do, on top of everything else on her list, was try to make herself look halfway decent. At the thought of Mr Manning, her stomach turned a somersault. Little did she know that, at that very moment, his was doing the same.

'Nellie, would ye get out of that bed. Everyone else is already out on the streets, doing their jobs. Come down and let me get those curlers out.'

Nellie stared at her Nana Kathleen. How could she tell her that she felt almost too sad to leave her bed? Her heart felt heavy and her legs even more so. Today was Kitty's birthday, but she wasn't here for the best party the four streets had ever known. It hurt too much. She didn't want to move an inch, unless it was to slip further under the bedclothes.

Nana Kathleen sat down on the edge of the bed.

'I know what's up, queen,' she said, 'but do you know who is outside already, setting up the cake stall and being as bright as she can for everyone else? 'Tis Maura, Kitty's own mother, and how do ye imagine she is feeling inside?'

Nellie felt embarrassed.

'And Angela and Niamh, well, a pair of troupers they are, already downstairs in the kitchen, with their hair done, waiting for ye to go with them, to have their headdresses clipped in. Kitty was their sister. How do ye think they feel?'

Nellie's eyes were full of tears as she threw her arms round Nana Kathleen and buried her head in her hair, breathing in the distinctive musty smell that was her nana: of tobacco and chips, mingling with her new, sticky, Get Set hairspray.

'I know, queen, I know. We all feel it,' said Nana Kathleen, as she stroked Nellie's back. 'Today is a first. A first birthday without her and for that we should be thankful for the Rose Queen. It will help it pass more quickly.'

By mid-afternoon the noise from the docks had been drowned out by the sound of music and laughter ricocheting around the four streets.

When Malachi and Little Paddy won the three-legged race, the cheers could be heard for miles.

To no one's surprise, Angela was crowned Rose Queen. Her twelve attendants were dressed in peach-coloured dresses, all handmade in the Priory by Harriet's sewing circle. They behaved regally, as though used to such grandeur and with no notion of the tattered clothes they would be dressed in the following morning. Maura and Kathleen did a roaring trade on the cake and jumble stalls, and with the bric-a-brac.

Little Harry had sidled up to Maura, holding out the purchase he had made with the sixpenny piece Tommy had given him for the morning.

'Look, Mammy, I got this for you.'

Harry held out a square glass ashtray, washed and sparkling. It was one Maura had used herself when visiting

347

another house on the four streets and it had been donated as a contribution to the bric-a-brac stall.

'There's a glass sugar bowl, on three legs, as well. Shall I get that, with another penny? We don't have a sugar bowl.'

Maura looked at her son, whose pain was, she knew, as great as her own, yet his only thought was of how he could ease hers. She pulled him into her side.

'The money is for you to buy sweets and things with, Harry. It's for you to have a nice day with, not to buy things for me.'

As she ruffled his hair, Harry squeezed his mother's waist and said, 'I'm going to buy the sugar bowl.'

'I don't know what I did to deserve a lad as good as that,' said Maura to Nana Kathleen who was serving next to her.

But Kathleen was preoccupied with something else. She had noticed a woman with a baby, who had been looking hard at Maura and was now walking up to the stall. There wasn't a woman at the Rose Queen fair not known to either Maura or Kathleen. This woman wasn't from the four streets, Kathleen could tell that much straightaway. But she did look familiar.

Kathleen nudged Maura, who was wrapping a slice of giggle cake in greaseproof paper for the youngest McGinty girl.

'That'll be a ha'penny, queen,' she said.

The crestfallen look told Maura in a flash that the child had no money.

It was a look Maura knew well. She could smell shame a mile away.

Maura thrust the cake into the little girl's hand. 'Well, there you go, then, you have it anyway. I need to be rid of it now.'

The child's look of despair instantly vanished, to be replaced by one of gratitude. As she walked away, Maura watched her break the cake and hand half to her little brother, whom she was holding tightly by the hand.

'That bastard McGinty. He doesn't deserve to have kids as good as that,' said Maura.

'Are you Maura Doherty?'

It was a voice Maura did not recognize. She looked up to see the best-dressed woman she had ever laid eyes on, with an accent she could not identify, but which had a trace of Irish in it somewhere.

Maura looked instantly suspicious. 'Yes, I am. Why?' she replied. 'Do I know you?'

'No, you don't, but you do know my sister-in-law, Brigid.'

'Brigid?' Maura looked incredulous. 'Brigid doesn't live here any more. She moved back to Ireland months back.'

'Yes, I know,' the woman replied. 'My mammy visited her yesterday.'

'Your mammy?' said Kathleen, joining in the conversation. 'Mrs McGuire, would that be now?'

'Yes, that's right. I am Mary, her daughter. I live in America.'

'Jesus, by all the saints, would that be ye, so? That means ye are the sister of Sean, who ran off with my son's wife, Alice.'

'I am that, yes,' she replied wearily. 'And it is their sin, not mine. I am not here to talk about them, Maura.' The woman's voice began to tremble as she looked down at the baby in her arms.

The thought flashed through Maura's mind that it was the sickliest baby she had ever seen.

'This baby, Maura, is your grandson. I adopted him from the Abbey. He is the baby your daughter Kitty gave birth to. He is very ill and needs your help.'

Maura could not speak, but as she looked towards the Green, her eyes searching for Tommy, she saw her once again, on the very spot where Maura had first laid eyes on her on the day of Bernadette's funeral. Alice, standing on the corner of the street, tucking her hair back into her hat.

Jerry had lifted Joseph out of his pushchair. The excitement of the children running around was all too much for him and he wanted to be on his feet, not pushed by his da.

'Come here, little fella,' said Jerry as he bent down to unclip his reins.

Once on his feet, Joseph grasped the handle of the push-chair, which Jerry slowly propelled along, and toddled down the street.

'Let's visit Nana Kathleen on the cake stall, shall we, and see what treats she has for ye?'

'Shall I look after Joseph, Jer?' Little Paddy appeared out of nowhere.

'Aye, go on then, Paddy,' said Jerry, failing to hide the relief in his voice.

He put his hand into his pocket. 'And here's a threepenny bit, Paddy. I'll go and help Tommy now. You keep in my sight so I know where ye go. And buy yerself and Joseph a cake and play one of the games. '

'Aye, I will, Jerry, thanks, Jerry.'

Little Paddy tied to the pushchair handle the piece of string he used as a dog lead for Scamp and lifted Joseph into his arms. He half staggered as he wheeled the pushchair towards the cake stall. Scamp had become a local canine hero. It hadn't taken many minutes before everyone on the four streets knew that Paddy's little friend had found a murder weapon.

'I was thinking of charging people to stroke Scamp,' Little Paddy had confided to Harry, 'but I changed me mind. I don't want Scamp to get above himself. 'Tis magic, Harry, that the *Echo* took our photo with Scamp. Who would have known that us playing in the graveyard would lead Scamp to the mallet, to be sure it was a miracle, it was.'

Little Paddy was delighted to have money in his hand. He had felt slightly detached from the fun, not having had a penny with which to join in, but that was Little Paddy's life, always on the outside. Nothing in his life was quite enough.

He wasn't loved enough, fed enough or respected enough. The kids on the four streets sensed who was the weakest in the pack and it was always Little Paddy everyone made fun of. His only true friend had been Harry, until now. Little Paddy and Scamp were enjoying hero status for having found the murder weapon, which had elevated Little Paddy to a level of contentment he had never known existed before today.

Harriet was aware that some of the children would have been excluded from the fun because they had no money, so she made sure much of the entertainment was free. However, she was also mindful of the fact that the aim of the fair was to raise funds for the new library.

Jerry waved across at Tommy, who was red in the face from blowing his brass whistle, trying to impose some sort of order on the eighty children running around, demanding to know which race was next.

Jerry ran over to help his mate and, as he did so, he noticed Harriet walking into the tea tent with one of the Rose Queen judges.

'Well, if she wasn't the priest's sister, I would say that they was flirting outrageously now, wouldn't you?' he said to Tommy.

'Jesus, I haven't a fecking clue. Would ye stop that fight at the finishing line, Jerry? It was definitely Brian what won, will ye tell them for me.'

Little Paddy, having struggled with Scamp and an objecting toddler, put his foot down and, with it, Joseph back into his pushchair. He was already salivating at the thought of buying one of the huge cheese scones that he had watched Maura pile high on a plate. Little Paddy had had only a slice of bread and dripping for breakfast and his stomach had begun to rumble the second Jerry had placed the money in his hand.

'Let's go and get some grub, eh?' Little Paddy said to Joseph who had voiced no objection to being put back in his pushchair, now that he was being pulled along by Scamp. Little Paddy spun the pushchair round to head towards the cake stall, but his progression was halted suddenly in midflight.

'Oh, Holy Jesus, Joseph, is that yer mammy?'

It took Little Paddy only seconds to recognize the woman walking towards them. Her eyes were fixed on Joseph, and she appeared sadder than Little Paddy had ever seen her when she lived on the four streets.

'Hello, Alice,' said Little Paddy nervously. 'Have ye come back?'

Alice glanced around. She was safe; everyone was busy. With her plain headscarf pulled low over her forehead and tied under her chin, she looked very unlike the Alice who had left the four streets only months before.

'I have, Paddy. I've come to collect Joseph. I'm taking him with me now.'

At the sound of his mother's voice, Joseph sat up in his pushchair and his bottom lip began to tremble. His mother had been absent for a large part of his very short life, but he knew her. He knew her features and her voice, and he put out his arms. He wanted to be close to her and feel her.

But Little Paddy swung the pushchair round, away from Alice. Joseph strained against the reins, beginning to turn red in the face and working himself up into a scream as he attempted to scramble his way out.

'Right, well, ye see, Alice, Jerry has paid me, like, three-pence to look after Joseph, so I can't let him go until I take him back to Jerry first.'

'Don't be silly, Paddy.'

Alice spoke firmly but no louder than was necessary so as not to attract attention. The last thing she wanted was to alarm Little Paddy or her beloved son. The sight of him made her heart crunch in pain. She had been thousands of miles away, and here she now was, only six feet from him, yet the barrier between her and the child was just as if an ocean lay between them.

'Don't be silly, Paddy,' Alice said again, her tone laced with tension. 'I am his mammy and, look, he needs his mammy. He wants me to pick him up.

'Shh, Joseph, Mummy's here,' she whispered, moving forward and bending down to unclip the reins.

Little Paddy broke out in a sweat. He knew this wasn't right; he couldn't run off and leave Joseph but he had no idea how to stop Alice either.

'Oh God, no, please don't get me into trouble, Alice. Shall I shout for Jer to help ye?'

Little Paddy looked around frantically. Jerry was down at the bottom of the green, organizing children to collect their prizes. Tommy had lined up a group of children for the next race. There were adults everywhere, but each was busy and distracted, and not one was looking his way. Music drifted over from the accordion, competing with the sound of children squealing and laughing.

'Oh God, please, please help,' Little Paddy whispered to himself, jumping up and down frantically. He shouted to Harry, standing on the side of the green, watching the games with Declan.

Little Paddy knew Harry couldn't join in the races and so he shouted louder, 'Harry, Harry, over here!'

But the noise drowned him out and Harry didn't so much as turn round.

Little Paddy looked at Alice.

'Please, Alice,' he begged, 'I think Jer will be mad with me and ye know what my da's like. Please, Alice, don't take him until I fetch Jer.'

Alice was struggling with the reins. When Little Paddy

had fastened them and put Joseph back in his harness, he had accidentally crossed the leather straps. Alice paid no attention to Little Paddy. It was as if he weren't there and she was in a world of her own, where only Joseph existed.

'Oh, for goodness' sake.' Her voice was heavy with frustration. 'I will just take the pushchair with me. Sit down, Joseph, Mummy is here now.'

Joseph held out his hands. Alice leant forward and wrapped her arms round the son who had so obviously missed her. It tore her heart apart that he remembered her, that he loved her and wanted to be in her arms, that he did not pull away or condemn her for leaving him. Love was forgiveness and her baby son had needed no words. He had only his open arms. Alice knew she was forgiven. Leaning against the pushchair, she held him tightly, but he didn't object. His crying subsided as hers began and her hot, salty tears ran onto his scalp, darkening his blond curls. Alice was not a woman known to cry, until today.

Joseph, comforted, allowed Alice to stand as she held onto his hand. He grasped her fingers tightly. He was not about to let her go or leave his sight. As she stood, she pressed the pushchair handle down and spun it round, ready to head towards the Dock Road.

Little Paddy had broken out into a sweat. He felt faint with fear and knew that, at any second, he would have to do something.

'Alice.' Little Paddy sounded stronger than he felt. 'Please don't take Joseph. I might have to do something drastic. The dog is tied to the pushchair. I might have to set him on to ye or sumthin'.'

Alice seemed not to hear as she strode quickly away. Suddenly Little Paddy saw Jerry wave towards him and then break into a sprint. He heaved a huge sigh of relief.

'Paddy, hold onto the baby,' Jerry shouted as he ran, but Alice was already on her way down the road.

Scamp now took exception to being separated from Little Paddy and, with one bound, he leapt up, bit Alice on the arm and lodged his teeth in her coat sleeve. Alice screamed. Joseph screamed. Little Paddy screamed. The air was filled with growling, snarling and screaming, and then as Joseph began to cry, Alice found her voice.

'Get this dog off, Paddy, get him away,' she yelled, as the dog's yellow teeth refused to dislodge from the woollen cuff of her Macey's coat.

In a split second, Jerry had reached the pushchair and detached the dog, while Little Paddy untied his well-knotted string dog lead from the handles.

'Thanks, Paddy, ye did a good job there. Take Joseph to Kathleen, please, will yer,' said Jerry.

Little Paddy felt sick with relief. 'Aye, Jerry. D'ye want the threepence back?'

Little Paddy held out the coin and was thankful that Jerry didn't notice. He quickly popped it back into his trouser pocket and ran with the pushchair over to Kathleen, bumping into Harry on the way.

'Jesus, Harry, Alice came back from nowhere. She just appeared like a ghost and scared the feckin' shite outta me she did. She stared at me with her weird eyes and I swear to all that is holy, she was trying to turn me into stone and then when it didn't work, she tried to kidnap Joseph and run away with himself sat in the pushchair. Scamp wasn't having that and attacked her, hung from her arm with his teeth he did and bit her, and then Jerry came and paid me for looking after Joseph and saving him. I'm away to Nana Kathleen with Joseph now, so we can be safe in case she comes after us and tries it again.'

Harry looked at Little Paddy gravely.

'Paddy,' he said, placing both hands on his hips, 'you have to stop telling lies and making stuff up, or, I swear to God, you will get locked up one day.'

Jerry held Alice by her arm and inspected the small puncture wound on her wrist. They could both hear Joseph crying for his mother as Little Paddy wheeled him away, and Jerry could see the pain in her eyes.

'The dog hasn't drawn blood, Alice, so ye will be fine. Have ye come back to steal my son?'

Alice hesitated. Her answer should be yes. But she knew that if she said that out loud, it would be a lie. She had returned for so much more.

She looked first at the man who had loved her without ever being loved back, then turning to the green and Joseph, saw the woman who had been a mother to her and who was now lifting Alice's baby into her own arms to comfort him.

Alice had discovered that it was nowhere near as difficult to leave behind a person as it was to leave behind an entire life. She hadn't just left Jerry; she had unfastened herself from her own existence. It felt now as though each day in America had passed in a haze of unreality.

Alice met Jerry's eyes. She stalled. 'How can you ask me that?'

'Because I can't believe, Alice, that even you would try to steal my own son away from under my very nose without so much as a by-your-leave. You did that when you walked away as my wife, but ye surely cannot think you can do it with my son?'

She could see Maura standing by Kathleen's side. Alice wanted to run over and tell her that she had loved Kitty and cared for her, and that her heart had broken for the first time ever when she had heard the news that Kitty was dead. That was why she had visited the abortionist on Kitty's account. Because she had wanted to help, to find a solution. She had wanted to find a way out for Kitty, because she had cared.

All around her, everything and everyone was familiar and safe and known to her. She was surrounded by the people who had helped her through her transition from that wretched woman she had once been, to a mother. And someone they regarded as one of their own. Although she had traded this life for a new one of opulence and opportunity, even Alice knew that no amount of money could buy the security she had here, with these people. She and they were bound forever by a secret, a deadly secret, one she would find hard to carry alone for the rest of her life, without them.

Jerry knew Alice well enough to read her thoughts and know exactly what was flashing though her mind.

'If you've not come to steal Joseph away, have ye come back to us then?'

'I can't. I've caused too much damage,' she whispered.

'If ye mean Sean and Brigid, he was always going to live in America and she never was. His leaving would have happened anyway.'

'Would ye have me back?' Alice looked at Jerry, but she dared not hope.

The money and the big house, they were as nothing compared to the homely comfort of the two-up, two-downs on the four streets. And what she and Sean McGuire, the man she hadn't really known and never would, had for each other was a sham compared with the love she had for her son, Joseph. It had taken another woman's desperate fight to save the life of a child who wasn't even her own flesh and blood to make her realize that.

She held her breath as she waited for his reply, knowing that, if he said no, the torrent of tears now building up inside her, for the second time in her life, would overwhelm her.

Jerry didn't answer straightaway, despite the words being on the tip of his tongue. He could deal only with how he felt. The imaginary arguments and discussions with Alice that he had had in his head in the minutes before he fell asleep each night appeared to have temporarily deserted him. Even so, the fact that she had left with his own friend, one of his workmates, was surely beyond healing or repair. Would his other workmates and friends understand? Would the four streets forgive her? Amongst them again, would she become a living scandal? Would they all shun her?

He made no reply as he let go of her arm.

'Alice.'

Jerry turned as he heard Maura's voice. She was coming towards them with a smart woman whom Jerry had never seen before, carrying a baby.

Alice looked at Maura. With tears rolling down her cheeks, she whispered, 'I'm so sorry, Maura.'

Jerry stared, amazed. It was the first time he had seen Alice cry.

'Are ye home to stay, Alice?' asked Maura.

Alice turned to look at Jerry.

In those few words, Maura had answered all of his doubts.

'Aye, she is,' he replied. 'She is.'

Epilogue

Six months later
The Ballymara Road

Liam had collected Nana Kathleen and Nellie, as he always did, in the old van. He and Kathleen chattered away as they travelled cross-country. They talked about the farm and each and all of the people who now lived, or had ever lived, in Bangornevin and Ballymara, going back as far as Nana Kathleen could remember.

'Do ye remember the Reagans?' Kathleen asked. 'They farmed up on Craighorn, back in my grandmother's day. The youngest son did three jobs to save up to emigrate to America and he kept his money hidden in the cowshed. The oldest, who never lifted a stick, watched him hide the money away for years. Never touched it he didn't and, when there was enough for a passage, he nicked it himself and took a ship from Cobh. Well, Jesus, I hear now that the youngest saved and saved again and when he got to America, he hunted his brother down and shot him. He is now spending his life in an American gaol, for all his troubles.'

Liam laughed. 'I do, 'twas the news here for at least a week, Mammy. His family moved to Galway a good while back now.'

'Things never turn out as you may plan, or think they will, do they, Liam? Holy Mother, we have had a year of it in Liverpool.'

Kathleen looked over her shoulder at Nellie who, exhausted from the night crossing, was fast asleep.

'This one struggled to get over Kitty, now, even more than Kitty's sisters, it would appear, although who knows what goes on inside a girl's head? Nothing cheered her up but, thank the Lord, the fact that she could face coming back here, the place where Kitty died, that is progress, so it is, and 'tis all thanks to the priest's sister, Harriet. She worked wonders with Nellie, so she did. Harriet got married all of a sudden, to a nice Mr Manning from the City Corporation. My tea leaves and prophesizing helped there, Liam. Now, the wedding was a surprise and she only had one bridesmaid and that was Nellie, for no other reason than to make her feel special. Oh, and Jesus, you should have seen the dress she was put in and the cut of her. She looked like a princess. Did you get the pictures I sent ye?'

Liam nodded.

'Did ye hear about the court case?'

'We did, we read about the court case as well, Mammy. That was shocking. Some people over here don't even know what a paedophile is. The kidnapping in the convent, it was all over the papers over here and on the television.'

'Aye, there were bad things going on, all right. Poor Sister Evangelista, she thought she was going to cop it, but the judge was very lenient with her and let her off for concealing information. Thank the Lord he was an Irish Catholic. There are five men in prison, you know, Liam, and one of them is a bishop. We will never see that happen again in my lifetime, as God is my judge. We sat in the public gallery every day we did. We had to take it in turns to keep each other's seat, there was so many nosey buggers trying to get in. You would not believe how awful curious some women can be. 'Tis an affliction, surely?'

Liam smiled to himself and, without drawing breath, she continued.

'Have you seen much of Maura and Tommy since they moved to Killhooney Bay?'

Kathleen galloped so fast from one subject to the next, it was difficult for Liam to keep up.

'Aye, we do. Maeve and Maura visit each other every week and I've kept it a surprise from Nellie,' Liam whispered. 'Angela and Niamh are waiting at the house for Nellie to arrive and they are staying with us for the week. Maura and Tommy are coming over tonight to eat with us. Tommy is driving his own van now, and doing a grand job, with a bit of land on Killhooney. About to open his own pub he is. Tommy reckons that things are so bad in England and America that everyone who ever left will be so homesick and desperate to return, there will be a roaring tourist trade soon enough on the West Coast. Everyone seems to be mad about the salmon from our waters and Tommy reckons he will have a good business there.

'He has a couple from Galway, Maggie and Frank, who have come across to work for him and Maura. Grand people, so they are. They were in the papers, over the convent being closed down. Seems they had a bad time of it locally they did. Because they spoke to the police and gave a statement, they had to leave before they were hounded out of the village. Made the locals very mad, so it did. Meself, I reckon 'twas the priest behind all the bad feeling. He was the maddest of them all. They will be running the pub and helping Maura with the paying guests.'

'Who would ever have thought it, eh?' Nana Kathleen shook her head. 'Little Harry spends a few days in Alder Hey Hospital, saves a baby's life, and Maura and Tommy are handed a fortune.

'Well, I want to meet this Maggie. Daisy has a lot to say about her. She was due to set off to Dublin, was Daisy, to live with her brother, but the Priory was too much for Annie and so, with Harriet getting married, Daisy has stayed put. Her poor brother was distraught, they said, but Daisy visits them for nice holidays. She is attached, like, to the four streets, and to Alison and Harriet, I would say. She won't leave ever, I don't think.

''Tis a strange world, Liam, and getting stranger by the day. There was a lot of money flying around. Alice brought a suitcase-load with her from America and she gave it back to Mary and then, lo and behold, Mary gave her it back and wished her luck. I think she was feeling mighty generous, because she arrived in Liverpool with a sick baby, and left with a healthy one. Fifty thousand pounds it was and, Liam, there is some of it in my case for you. Jerry has sent ten over for you and Maeve to compensate for your trouble and for you to build a milking shed. And with the rest, he is going to buy a little house for Nellie and Joseph. The talk about the four streets being knocked down, 'tis nonstop, and our Jerry, he has said he would rather die than move to Speke with the rest of them. And, as I was saying before, Little Harry has to fly to America soon, to help out a bit, give some more of the jelly from his bones. God, doesn't even flinch he doesn't, but I reckon ye are more ahead on that news than I am, Liam. Ah, here she is, she's waking now.'

Nellie rubbed her eyes and yawned. 'Are we there yet?' she asked.

'Passing through Bellgarett now,' said Liam. 'Not long until we are on the Ballymara Road and, God, Nellie, 'tis a road that has missed yer footsteps.'

Nellie smiled. She put one hand to her other wrist, to check that it was still there: the gold charm bracelet, given to Kitty by Maeve, the last time she saw her, when Kitty had promised to return. Nellie turned the bracelet round and round. She wanted Maeve to notice that she was wearing it. She had missed Maeve so much and she knew that Maeve had sent the bracelet across to Liverpool to let Nellie know, it was time. She was to return to the Ballymara Road.

As the van turned into Bangornevin, Nellie noticed that not a thing had altered. The school looked just the same. The river, the shops and the children playing in the street: all as if it had been only yesterday when she had last been driven through the village. As they turned left and crossed the roaring river on to the Ballymara Road, Nellie felt overcome with emotion and her eyes flooded with tears.

'Nana, Nana Kathleen,' she whispered.

'Oh, God in heaven, would ye look at ye. In just two minutes we will be with Maeve. Now dry your eyes. God, she will be upset, so she will, if ye arrive crying.'

Kathleen looked to Liam for help.

'Come on, Nellie, we aren't that bad. Ye only have two weeks to put up with us now and I promise to behave.' Liam tried his best to raise a smile.

Both he and Nana Kathleen knew what was wrong. In a minute or so, they would reach the place in the river where Kitty had drowned.

Returning Nellie to the farmhouse and taking her back down the Ballymara Road was the last step on the road to her recovery.

The chain of events that had begun with an evil priest had been far-reaching.

The four streets had settled down and life had returned to normal. New concrete towns were being erected to the south of the city, but the people on the four streets had dug in and refused to move. Neighbours had died, new families had moved in and old ones, such as the Dohertys, had moved out. The community had altered in appearance but remained firm in the bonds of poverty, love and the instinct to survive, which kept it strong.

'Look,' whispered Nana Kathleen to Nellie, 'look out of the window.'

Nellie looked and there, on the Ballymara Road, in the same spot where she had last seen her, stood Maeve, with her hand shielding her eyes, squinting into the sunlight. As the van approached, Nellie saw a smile light up Maeve's face, and she began to wave.

'There she is, our Maeve. I imagine she got notice now, when we passed through Castlefeale. Not much changes around here, Nellie,' said Liam.

'Praise the Lord for that,' said Nana Kathleen. 'That's exactly what we need a little of.'

As the van began to slow down, Nellie spotted the others running out of the front door of the house, laughing and waving. There was Rosie, and Auntie Julia, and Aengus, and Mrs and Mrs McMahon. She could hardly believe her eyes when Angela and Niamh appeared, with Maura and Tommy behind them.

'Well, ye couldn't ask for a better welcoming committee than that, now, could you?' said Nana Kathleen, squeezing Nellie's hand.

Nellie's eyes blurred. She could barely focus and yet, through the river of tears which flooded her eyes, she saw her. Her mother, Bernadette, holding Kitty by the hand. They smiled and waved to her. Immediately she knew of the love that they brought to her and it filled her heart, which had ached and felt so empty for so long.

The car door opened and she was aware of Maeve, helping her out and sweeping her into her ample bosom.

'Would ye look at her now, almost as tall as meself,' said Maeve as she pulled Nellie into her arms. Nellie's tears turned to laughter as she heard everyone asking her questions, all at once.

In the midst of excited chatter, people fighting with each other to carry the bags and Angela trying to drag her out of Maeve's arms, she looked back towards the river and she just caught them as, with a last smile, they turned away from her and, walking together, faded into the blinding sunlight, down the Ballymara Road.

Dear reader,

I hope you enjoyed my book.

Soon I'll be launching
nadinedorries.co.uk

Please visit and sign up to my
newsletter to learn more...

Thanks so much,

Nadine x

Totally addictive reading